PRAISE FOR SERAPHINA

A *New York Times* Bestseller

An Indie Bestseller

An Amazon Top 20 Teen Book of the Year

A Chicago Public Library Best of the Best Book

A *Kirkus Reviews* Best Teen Book of the Year

A *School Library Journal* Best Book of the Year

A *Library Journal* Best Young Adult Literature for Adults Selection

A *Booklist* Editors' Choice

An ABA Top 10 Kids' Indie Next List Selection

An ABC New Voices Pick

A Finalist for the William C. Morris Award for a YA Debut

"Just when you thought there was nothing new to say about dragons, it turns out there is, and plenty! Rachel Hartman's rich invention never fails to impress—and to convince. It's smart and funny and original, and has characters I will follow to the ends of the earth."

—Ellen Kushner, World Fantasy Award–winning author

"Seraphina is strong, complex, talented—she makes mistakes and struggles to trust, with good reason, and she fights to survive in a world that would tear her apart."

—Tamora Pierce, *New York Times* bestselling author of the Beka Cooper series

"A wonderful mix of thrilling story, fascinating characters, and unique dragonlore. I loved being in Seraphina's world."

—Alison Goodman,

New York Times bestselling author

of *Eon* and *Eona*

★ "The medieval-esque world, filled with saints and dragons, is as deftly crafted as the characters themselves; Goredd has a distinct history, fraught with struggle and survival, and its residents reflect the conflicting ideologies and traditions that inform their world. Secondary characters are given just as much nuance, and the romance between Seraphina and a bastard prince proceeds with believable hesitation and wariness. Readers will want to plan to return to this richly developed world to see where this intricate fantasy goes next."

—*The Bulletin of the Center for Children's Books*, Starred

★ "[A] complex, intrigue-laden fantasy. As Seraphina navigates the complicated politics of a court where human-dragon relations are growing ever more fragile following a royal murder, she has to come to terms with her true nature and powers."

—*Publishers Weekly*, Starred

★ "To the innovative concept and high action, add Seraphina's tentative romance with Kiggs, rich language lively with humor and sprinkled with an entire psaltery of saints and an orchestra's worth of medieval instruments, and a political conspiracy aimed at breaking the dragon-human truce, and what you have is an outstanding debut from author-to-watch Hartman."

—*The Horn Book Magazine*, Starred

★ "Reading this novel is like falling into Alice's rabbit hole and never wanting to come out. Fans of fantasy will devour this book."

—*Voice of Youth Advocates*, Starred

"[Hartman's] world-building is so detailed and well-integrated, one wonders if they truly exist somewhere. An engaging and innovative fantasy that uses the plights of dragons and humans as an allegory for the real prejudices we all must face."

—*BookPage*

"A beautifully written fantasy debut about a young girl's journey to gain acceptance of herself."

—SheKnows.com

Seraphina

RACHEL HARTMAN

RANDOM HOUSE · NEW YORK

Text copyright © 2012 by Rachel Hartman
"The Audition" copyright © 2012 by Rachel Hartman
"A Q&A with Rachel Hartman" and "Rachel Hartman's Favorite Authors"
copyright © 2013 by Rachel Hartman
Jacket art copyright © 2012 by Andrew Davidson
Title page illustration copyright © 2012 by Juliana Kolesova

"The Audition" originally appeared on EW.com on June 19, 2012.

Visit us on the Web! randomhouse.com/teens

Educators and librarians, for a variety of teaching tools, visit us at
RHTeachersLibrarians.com

Library of Congress Cataloging-in-Publication Data
Hartman, Rachel.
Seraphina : a novel / by Rachel Hartman. — 1st U.S. ed.
p. cm.
Summary: In a world where dragons and humans coexist in an uneasy truce and dragons can assume human form, Seraphina, whose mother died giving birth to her, grapples with her own identity amid magical secrets and royal scandals, while she struggles to accept and develop her extraordinary musical talents.
ISBN 978-0-375-86656-2 (trade) — ISBN 978-0-375-96656-9 (lib. bdg.) —
ISBN 978-0-375-89658-3 (ebook)
[1. Identity—Fiction. 2. Self-actualization (Psychology)—Fiction. 3. Dragons—Fiction.
4. Secrets—Fiction. 5. Music—Fiction. 6. Courts and courtiers—Fiction. 7. Fantasy.] I. Title.
PZ7.H26736Se 2012   [Fic]—dc22   2011003015

Printed in the United States of America

10 9 8 7 6 5 4 3 2

In memoriam: Michael McMechan.

Dragon, teacher, friend.

Prologue

I remember being born.

In fact, I remember a time before that. There was no light, but there was music: joints creaking, blood rushing, the heart's staccato lullaby, a rich symphony of indigestion. Sound enfolded me, and I was safe.

Then my world split open, and I was thrust into a cold and silent brightness. I tried to fill the emptiness with my screams, but the space was too vast. I raged, but there was no going back.

I remember nothing more; I was a baby, however peculiar. Blood and panic meant little to me. I do not recall the horrified midwife, my father weeping, or the priest's benediction for my mother's soul.

My mother left me a complicated and burdensome inheritance. My father hid the dreadful details from everyone, including me. He moved us back to Lavondaville, the capital of Goredd, and picked up his law practice where he had dropped it. He invented a more acceptable grade of dead wife for himself. I believed in her like some people believe in Heaven.

I was a finicky baby; I wouldn't suckle unless the wet nurse sang exactly on pitch. "It has a discriminating ear," observed Orma, a tall, angular acquaintance of my father's who came over often in those days. Orma called me "it" as if I were a dog; I was drawn to his aloofness, the way cats gravitate toward people who'd rather avoid them.

He accompanied us to the cathedral one spring morning, where the young priest anointed my wispy hair with lavender oil and told me that in the eyes of Heaven I was as a queen. I bawled like any self-respecting baby; my shrieks echoed up and down the nave. Without bothering to look up from the work he'd brought with him, my father promised to bring me up piously in the faith of Allsaints. The priest handed me my father's psalter and I dropped it, right on cue. It fell open at the picture of St. Yirtrudis, whose face had been blacked out.

The priest kissed his hand, pinkie raised. "Your psalter still contains the heretic!"

"It's a very old psalter," said Papa, not looking up, "and I hate to maim a book."

"We advise the bibliophilic faithful to paste Yirtrudis's pages together so this mistake can't happen." The priest flipped a page. "Heaven surely meant St. Capiti."

Papa muttered something about superstitious fakery, just loud enough for the priest to hear. There followed a fierce argument between my father and the priest, but I don't remember it. I was gazing, transfixed, at a procession of monks passing through the nave. They padded by in soft shoes, a flurry of dark, whispering robes and clicking beads, and took their places in the cathedral's quire. Seats scraped and creaked; several monks coughed.

They began to sing.

The cathedral, reverberating with masculine song, appeared to expand before my eyes. The sun gleamed through the high windows; gold and crimson bloomed upon the marble floor. The music buoyed my small form, filled and surrounded me, made me larger than myself. It was the answer to a question I had never asked, the way to fill the dread emptiness into which I had been born. I believed—no, I *knew*—I could transcend the vastness and touch the vaulted ceiling with my hand.

I tried to do it.

My nurse squealed as I nearly squirmed out of her arms. She gripped me by the ankle at an awkward angle. I stared dizzily at the floor; it seemed to tilt and spin.

My father took me up, long hands around my fat torso, and held me at arm's length as if he had discovered an oversized and astonishing frog. I met his sea-gray eyes; they crinkled sadly at the corners.

The priest stormed off without blessing me. Orma watched him disappear around the end of the Golden House, then said, "Claude, explain this. Did he leave because you convinced him his religion is a sham? Or was he . . . what's that one called? Offended?"

My father seemed not to hear; something about me had captured his attention. "Look at her eyes. I could swear she understands us."

"It has a lucid gaze for an infant," said Orma, pushing up his spectacles and leveling his own piercing stare at me. His eyes were dark brown, like my own; unlike mine, they were as distant and inscrutable as the night sky.

"I have been unequal to this task, Seraphina," said Papa softly. "I may always be unequal, but I believe I can do better. We must find a way to be family to each other."

He kissed my downy head. He'd never done that before. I gaped at him, awed. The monks' liquid voices surrounded us and held us all three together. For a single, glorious moment I recovered that first feeling, the one I'd lost by being born: everything was as it should be, and I was exactly where I belonged.

And then it was gone. We passed through the bronze-bossed doors of the cathedral; the music faded behind us. Orma stalked off across the square without saying goodbye, his cloak flapping like the wings of an enormous bat. Papa handed me to my nurse, pulled his cloak tightly around himself, and hunched his shoulders against the gusting wind. I cried for him, but he did not turn around. Above us arched the sky, empty and very far away.

Superstitious fakery or not, the psalter's message was clear: *The truth may not be told. Here is an acceptable lie.*

Not that St. Capiti—may she keep me in her heart—made a

poor substitute saint. She was shockingly apropos, in fact. St. Capiti carried her own head on a plate like a roast goose; it glared out from the page, daring me to judge her. She represented the life of the mind, utterly divorced from the sordid goings-on of the body.

I appreciated that division as I grew older and was overtaken by bodily grotesqueries of my own, but even when I was very young, I always felt a visceral sympathy for St. Capiti. Who could love someone with a detached head? How could she accomplish anything meaningful in this world when her hands were occupied with that platter? Did she have people who understood her and would claim her as a friend?

Papa had permitted my nurse to glue St. Yirtrudis's pages together; the poor lady could not rest easy in our house until it was done. I never did get a look at the heretic. If I held the page up to the light I could just discern the shapes of both saints, blended together into one terrible monster saint. St. Yirtrudis's outstretched arms sprang out of St. Capiti's back like a pair of ineffectual wings; her shadow-head loomed where St. Capiti's should have been. She was a double saint for my double life.

My love of music eventually lured me from the safety of my father's house, propelling me into the city and the royal court. I took a terrible risk, but I could not do otherwise. I did not understand that I carried loneliness before me on a plate, and that music would be the light illuminating me from behind.

One

At the center of the cathedral stood a model of Heaven called the Golden House. Its roof unfolded like a flower to reveal a human-sized hollow, in which the body of poor Prince Rufus lay shrouded in gold and white. His feet rested upon the House's blessed threshold; his head lay cradled by a nest of gilded stars.

At least, it should have been. Prince Rufus's killer had decapitated him. The Guard had scoured forest and marshland, looking in vain for the prince's head; he was to be buried without it.

I stood upon the steps of the cathedral quire, facing the funeral. From the high balcony pulpit to my left, the bishop prayed over the Golden House, the royal family, and the noble mourners crowding the heart of the church. Beyond a wooden railing, common mourners filled the cavernous nave. As soon as the bishop finished his prayer, I was to play the Invocation to St. Eustace, who escorted spirits up the Heavenly Stair. I swayed dizzily, terrified, as if I had been asked to play flute upon a windy cliff.

In fact, I had not been asked to play at all. I was not on the program; I had promised Papa when I left that I wouldn't perform in public. I had heard the Invocation once or twice, but never before played it. This wasn't even my flute.

My chosen soloist, however, had sat upon his instrument and bent its reed; my backup soloist had drunk too many libations for Prince Rufus's soul and was out in the cloister garden, sick with regret. There was no second backup. The funeral would be ruined without the Invocation. I was responsible for the music, so it was up to me.

The bishop's prayer wound down; he described the glorious Heavenly Home, dwelling of All Saints, where all of us would rest someday in eternal bliss. He didn't list exceptions; he didn't have to. My eyes flicked involuntarily toward the dragon ambassador and the goodwill contingent from his embassy, seated behind the nobility but ahead of the common rabble. They were in their saarantrai—their human forms—but were immediately distinguishable even at this distance by the silver bells at their shoulders, the empty seats around them, and their disinclination to bow their heads during a prayer.

Dragons have no souls. No one expected piety from them.

"Be it ever so!" intoned the bishop. That was my signal to play, but at that exact moment I noticed my father in the crowded nave, beyond the barrier. His face was pale and drawn. I could hear in my head the words he'd said the day I left for court a mere two weeks ago: *Under no circumstances are you to draw attention to your—*

self. If you won't think of your own safety, at least remember all I have to lose!

The bishop cleared his throat, but my insides were ice and I could barely breathe.

I cast about desperately for some better focus.

My eyes lit upon the royal family, three generations seated together before the Golden House, a tableau of grief. Queen Lavonda had left her gray locks loose around her shoulders; her watery blue eyes were red with weeping for her son. Princess Dionne sat tall and glared fiercely, as if plotting revenge upon her younger brother's killers, or upon Rufus himself for failing to reach his fortieth birthday. Princess Glisselda, Dionne's daughter, laid her golden head upon her grandmother's shoulder to comfort her. Prince Lucian Kiggs, Glisselda's cousin and fiancé, sat a little apart from the family and stared without seeing. He was not Prince Rufus's son, but he looked as shocked and stricken as if he'd lost his own father.

They needed Heaven's peace. I knew little of Saints, but I knew about sorrow and about music as sorrow's surest balm. That was comfort I could give. I raised the flute to my lips and my eyes toward the vaulted ceiling, and began to play.

I began too quietly, unsure of the melody, but the notes seemed to find me and my confidence grew. The music flew from me like a dove released into the vastness of the nave; the cathedral itself lent it new richness and gave something back, as if this glorious edifice, too, were my instrument.

There are melodies that speak as eloquently as words, that flow logically and inevitably from a single, pure emotion. The Invocation is of this kind, as if its composer had sought to distill the purest essence of mourning, to say, *Here is what it is to lose someone.*

I repeated the Invocation twice, reluctant to let it go, anticipating the end of the music as another palpable loss. I set the last note free, strained my ears for the final dying echo, and felt myself crumple inside, exhausted. There would be no applause, as befit the dignity of the occasion, but the silence was itself deafening. I looked across the plain of faces, across the assembled nobility and other guests of quality, to the crushing mob of common folk beyond the barrier. There was no movement but for the dragons shifting uneasily in their seats and Orma, pressed up against the railing, absurdly flapping his hat at me.

I was too drained to find him embarrassing. I bowed my head and retreated from view.

※

I was the new assistant to the court composer and had beaten out twenty-seven other musicians for the job, from itinerant troubadours to acclaimed masters. I was a surprise; no one at the conservatory had paid me any heed as Orma's protégée. Orma was a lowly music theory teacher, not a real musician. He played harpsichord competently, but then the instrument played itself if he hit the right keys. He lacked passion and musicality. Nobody expected a full-time student of his to amount to anything.

My anonymity was by design. Papa had forbidden me to fraternize with the other students and teachers; I saw the sense in that, however lonely I was. He had not explicitly forbidden me to audition for jobs, but I knew perfectly well he wouldn't like it. This was our usual progression: he set narrow limits and I complied until I couldn't anymore. It was always music that pushed me beyond what he considered safe. Still, I hadn't foreseen the depth and breadth of his rage when he learned I was leaving home. I knew his anger was really fear for me, but that didn't make it any easier to bear.

Now I worked for Viridius, the court composer, who was in poor health and desperately needed an assistant. The fortieth anniversary of the treaty between Goredd and dragonkind was rapidly approaching, and Ardmagar Comonot himself, the great dragon general, would be here for the celebrations in just ten days. Concerts, balls, and other musical entertainments were Viridius's responsibility. I was to help audition performers and organize programs, and to give Princess Glisselda her harpsichord lesson, which Viridius found tedious.

That had kept me busy for my first two weeks, but the unexpected interruption of this funeral had piled on additional work. Viridius's gout had put him out of commission, so the entire musical program had been left up to me.

Prince Rufus's body was removed to the crypt, accompanied only by the royal family, the clergy, and the most important guests. The cathedral choir sang the Departure, and the crowd began to dissipate. I staggered back into the apse. I had never performed for an audience of more than one or two; I had not anticipated the anxiety beforehand and the exhaustion afterward.

Saints in Heaven, it was like standing up naked in front of the entire world.

I stumbled about, congratulating my musicians and supervising their removal. Guntard, my self-appointed assistant, trotted up behind me and clapped an unwelcome hand upon my shoulder. "Music Mistress! That was beyond beautiful!"

I nodded weary thanks, twisting out of his reach.

"There's an old man here to see you," Guntard continued. "He showed up during your solo, but we put him off." He gestured up the apse toward a chapel, where an elderly man loitered. His dark complexion meant he'd come from distant Porphyry. His graying hair was done in tidy plaits; his face crinkled in a smile.

"Who is he?" I asked.

Guntard tossed his bowl-cut locks disdainfully. "He's got a mess of pygegyria dancers, and some daft notion that we'd want them dancing at the funeral." Guntard's lips curled into that sneer, both judgmental and envious, that Goreddis get when they speak of decadent foreigners.

I would never have considered pygegyria for the program; we Goreddis don't dance at funerals. However, I couldn't let Guntard's sneering pass. "Pygegyria is an ancient and respected dance form in Porphyry."

Guntard snorted. "*Pygegyria* literally translates as 'bum-waggling'!" He glanced nervously at the Saints in their alcoves, noticed several of them frowning, and kissed his knuckle piously. "Anyway, his troupe's in the cloister, befuddling the monks."

My head was beginning to hurt. I handed Guntard the flute. "Return this to its owner. And send away this dance troupe—politely, please."

"You're going back already?" asked Guntard. "A bunch of us

12

are going to the Sunny Monkey." He laid a hand upon my left forearm.

I froze, fighting the impulse to shove him or run away. I took a deep breath to calm myself. "Thank you, but I can't," I said, peeling his hand off me, hoping he wouldn't be offended.

His expression said he was, a little.

It wasn't his fault; he assumed I was a normal person, whose arm might be touched with impunity. I wanted so much to make friends at this job, but a reminder always followed, like night after day: I could never let my guard down completely.

I turned toward the quire to fetch my cloak; Guntard shuffled off to do my bidding. Behind me, the old man cried, "Lady, wait! Abdo has to coming all this way, just for meeting you!"

I kept my eyes straight ahead, ducking up the steps and out of his line of sight.

The monks had finished singing the Departure and begun it again, but the nave was still half full; no one seemed to want to leave. Prince Rufus had been popular. I had barely known him, but he had spoken kindly, a sparkle in his eyes, when Viridius introduced me. He'd sparkled at half the city, to gauge by the loitering citizens, speaking in hushed voices and shaking their heads in disbelief.

Rufus had been murdered while hunting, and the Queen's Guard had found no clues as to who'd done it. The missing head would suggest dragons, to some. I imagined the saarantrai who attended the funeral were only too aware of this. We had only ten days before the Ardmagar arrived, and fourteen days until the anniversary of the treaty. If a dragon had killed Prince Rufus, that was some spectacularly unfortunate timing. Our citizens were jumpy enough about dragonkind already.

I started down the south aisle, but the southern door was blocked by construction. A jumble of wooden and metal pipes took up half the floor. I continued down the nave toward the great doors, keeping an eye out lest my father ambush me from behind a column.

"Thank you!" cried an elderly lady-in-waiting as I passed. She put her hands to her heart. "I have never been so moved."

I gave half courtesy as I walked past, but her enthusiasm attracted other nearby courtiers. "Transcendent!" I heard, and "Sublime!" I nodded graciously and tried to smile as I dodged the hands that reached for mine. I edged my way out of the crowd, my smile feeling as stiff and hollow as a saarantras's.

I put up the hood of my cloak as I passed a cluster of citizens in homespun white tunics. "I've buried more people than I can count—sit they all at Heaven's table," declaimed a large guildsman with a white felt hat jammed onto his head, "but I *never* seen the Heavenly Stair until today."

"I never heard nobody play like that. It weren't quite womanly, do you think?"

"She's a foreigner, maybe." They laughed.

I wrapped my arms tightly around myself and quickened my pace toward the great doors, kissing my knuckle toward Heaven because that is what one does when exiting the cathedral, even when one is . . . me.

I burst out into the wan afternoon light, filling my lungs with cold, clean air, feeling my tension dissipate. The winter sky was a blinding blue; departing mourners skittered around like leaves in the bitter wind.

Only then did I notice the dragon waiting for me on the cathedral steps, flashing me his best facsimile of a proper human smile. No one in the world could have found Orma's strained expression heartwarming but me.

Two

Orma had a scholar's exemption from the bell, so few people ever realized he was a dragon. He had his quirks, certainly: he never laughed; he had little comprehension of fashion, manners, or art; he had a taste for difficult mathematics and fabrics that didn't itch. Another saarantras would have known him by smell, but few humans had a keen enough nose to detect saar, or the knowledge to recognize what they were smelling. To the rest of Goredd, he was just a man: tall, spare, bearded, and bespectacled.

The beard was false; I pulled it off once when I was a baby. Male saarantrai could not grow beards under their own power, a peculiarity of transformation, like their silver blood. Orma didn't need facial hair to pass; I think he just liked the way it looked.

He waved his hat at me, as if there were any chance I didn't see him. "You still rush your glissandi, but you seem finally to have mastered that uvular flutter," he said, dispensing with any greeting, Dragons never see the point,

"It's nice to see you too," I said, then regretted the sarcasm, even though he wouldn't notice it. "I'm glad you liked it."

He squinted and cocked his head to one side, as he did when he knew he was missing some crucial detail but couldn't work out what. "You think I should have said hello first," he hazarded.

I sighed. "I think I'm too tired to care that I fell short of technical perfection."

"This is precisely what I never comprehend," he said, shaking his felt hat at me. He seemed to have forgotten it was for wearing. "Had you played perfectly—like a saar might have—you would not have affected your listeners so. People wept, and not because you sometimes hum while you play."

"You're joking," I said, mortified.

"It created an interesting effect. Most of the time it was harmonious, fourths and fifths, but every now and then you'd burst into a dissonant seventh. Why?"

"I didn't know I was doing it!"

Orma looked down abruptly. A young urchin, her mourning tunic white in spirit if not in fact, tugged urgently at the hem of Orma's short cloak. "I'm attracting small children," Orma muttered, twisting his hat in his hands. "Shoo it away, will you?"

"Sir?" said the girl. "This is for you." She wormed her small hand into his.

I caught a glint of gold. What lunacy was this, a beggar giving Orma coin?

Orma stared at the object in his hand. "Was there some

message with it?" His voice caught when he spoke, and I felt a chill. That was an emotion, clear as day; I'd never heard the like from him.

"'The token is the message,'" recited the girl.

Orma raised his head and looked all around us, sweeping his eyes from the great doors of the cathedral, down the steps, over the peopled plaza, across to Cathedral Bridge, along the river, and back. I looked too, reflexively, having no notion what we were looking for. The sinking sun blazed above the rooftops; a crowd gathered on the bridge; the garish Comonot Clock across the square pointed to Ten Days; bare trees along the river tossed in the breeze. I saw nothing else.

I looked back at Orma, who now searched the ground as if he'd dropped something. I assumed he'd lost the coin, but no. "Where did she go?" he asked.

The girl was gone.

"What did she give you?" I asked.

He did not reply, carefully tucking the object into the front of his woolen mourning doublet, flashing me a glimpse of the silk shirt beneath.

"Fine," I said. "Don't tell me."

He looked puzzled. "I have no intention of telling you."

I inhaled slowly, trying not to be cross with him. At that very moment a commotion broke out on Cathedral Bridge. I looked toward the shouting, and my stomach dropped: six thugs with black feathers in their caps—Sons of St. Ogdo—had formed a semicircle around some poor fellow to one side of the bridge. People streamed toward the noise from all directions.

"Let's go back inside until this blows over," I said, grabbing for Orma's sleeve a second too late. He'd noticed what was happening and was rapidly descending the steps toward the mob.

The fellow pinned against the bridge railings was a dragon. I'd discerned the silver glint of his bell all the way from the steps of the cathedral. Orma shouldered his way through the crowd. I tried to stay close, but someone shoved me and I stumbled into open space at the front of the throng, where the Sons of St. Ogdo brandished truncheons at the cringing saarantras. They recited from St. Ogdo's Malediction Against the Beast: "Cursed be thine eyes, worm! Cursed be thy hands, thy heart, thy issue unto the end of days! All Saints curse thee, Eye of Heaven curse thee, thine every serpentine thought turn back upon thee as a curse!'"

I pitied the dragon now that I saw his face. He was a raw newskin, scrawny and badly groomed, all awkward angles and unfocused eyes. A goose egg, puffy and gray, swelled along his sallow cheekbone.

The crowd howled at my back, a wolf ready to gnaw whatever bloody bones the Sons might throw. Two of the Sons had drawn knives, and a third had pulled a length of chain out of his leather jerkin. He twitched it menacingly behind him, like a tail; it clattered against the paving stones of the bridge.

Orma maneuvered into the saarantras's line of sight and gestured at his earrings to remind his fellow what to do. The newskin made no move. Orma reached for one of his own and activated it. Dragons' earrings were wondrous devices, capable of seeing, hearing, and speaking across distances. A saarantras could call for help, or could be monitored by his superiors. Orma had once taken his earrings apart to show me; they were machines, but most humans believed them to be something far more diabolical.

"Did you bite Prince Rufus's head off, worm?" cried one of the Sons, a muscled riverman. He grabbed the newskin's twiggy arm as if he might break it.

The saarantras squirmed in his ill-fitting clothes, and the Sons recoiled as if wings, horns, and tail might burst out of his skin at any moment. "The treaty forbids us biting off human heads," said the newskin, his voice like a rusty hinge. "But I won't pretend I've forgotten what they taste like."

The Sons would have been happy with any pretext for beating him up, but the one he'd handed them was so horrifying that they stood paralyzed for a heartbeat.

Then with a feral roar, the mob came alive. The Sons charged the newskin, slamming him back against the railing. I glimpsed a gash across his forehead, a wash of silver blood down the side of his face, before the crowd closed ranks around me, cutting off my view.

I pushed through, chasing Orma's shrubby dark hair and beaky nose. All it would take for the mob to turn on him was a gashed lip and a glimpse of *his* silver blood. I shouted his name, screamed it, but he could not hear me above the commotion.

Shrieks arose from the direction of the cathedral; galloping hooves rang out across the plaza. The Guard had arrived at last, bagpipes brawling. The Sons of St. Ogdo flung their hats into the air and disappeared into the crowd. Two threw themselves over the bridge railing, but I only heard one splash in the river.

Orma was squatting beside the crumpled newskin; I rushed toward him against the current of fleeing townspeople. I dared not embrace him, but my relief was so great that I knelt and took his hand. "Thank Allsaints!"

Orma shook me off. "Help me raise him, Seraphina."

I scrambled to the other side and took the newskin's arm. He gaped at me stupidly; his head lolled onto my shoulder, smearing my cloak with his silver blood. I swallowed my revulsion. We hauled the injured saar to his feet and balanced him upright. He shrugged off our help and stood on his own, teetering in the biting breeze.

The Captain of the Guard, Prince Lucian Kiggs, stalked toward us. People parted before him like the waves before St. Fionnuala. He was still in his funeral weeds, a short white houppelande with long dagged sleeves, but all his sorrow had been replaced by a spectacular annoyance.

I tugged Orma's sleeve. "Let's go."

"I can't. The embassy will fix on my earring. I must stay close to the newskin."

I'd glimpsed the bastard prince across crowded halls at court. He had a reputation as a shrewd and dogged investigator; he worked all the time and was not as outgoing as his uncle Rufus had been. He was also not as handsome—no beard, alas—but seeing him up close, I realized that the intelligence of his gaze more than made up for that.

I looked away. Saints' dogs, there was dragon blood all over my shoulder.

Prince Lucian ignored Orma and me and addressed the newskin, his brows drawn in concern. "You're bleeding!"

The newskin raised his face for inspection. "It looks worse

than it is, Your Grace. These human heads contain a great many blood vessels, easily perforated by—"

"Yes, yes." The prince winced at the newskin's gash and signaled to one of his men, who rushed up with a cloth and a canteen of water. The newskin opened the canteen and began pouring the water straight onto his head. It trickled down his scalp in ineffectual rivulets, soaking his doublet.

Saints in Heaven. He was going to freeze himself, and here were Goredd's finest just letting him do it. I snatched the cloth and canteen from his unresisting hands, wet the cloth, and demonstrated how he was to dab at his face. He took over the dabbing and I backed away. Prince Lucian nodded cordially in thanks.

"You're rather transparently new, saar," said the prince. "What's your name?"

"Basind."

It sounded more like a belch than a name. I caught the inevitable look of pity and disgust in the prince's dark eyes. "How did this begin?" he asked.

"I don't know," said Basind. "I was walking home from the fish market—"

"Someone as new as yourself should not be walking around on your own," snapped the prince. "Surely the embassy has made that abundantly clear to you?"

I looked at Basind, finally taking stock of his clothing: doublet, trunk hose, and the telltale insignia.

"Were you lost?" probed Prince Lucian. Basind shrugged. The prince spoke more gently. "They followed you?"

"I do not know. I was cogitating upon preparations for river plaice." He flapped a soggy parcel in the prince's face. "They surrounded me."

Prince Lucian dodged the fishy packet, undeterred from questioning. "How many were there?"

"Two hundred nineteen, although there may have been some I couldn't see."

The prince's mouth fell open. He was unused to interrogating dragons, evidently. I decided to bail him out. "How many with black feathers in their caps, saar Basind?"

"Six," said Basind, blinking like someone unused to having only two eyelids.

"Did *you* get a look at them, Seraphina?" asked the prince, clearly relieved that I'd stepped in.

I nodded dumbly, a light panic seizing me at the prince's speaking my name. I was a palace nobody; why would he know it?

He continued addressing me: "I'll have my boys bring round whomever they've nabbed. You, the newskin, and your friend there"—he indicated Orma—"should look them over and see if you can describe the ones we've missed."

The prince signaled his men to bring forth their captives, then leaned in and answered the question I hadn't asked. "Cousin Glisselda has been talking about you nonstop. She was ready to give up music. It's fortunate you came to us when you did."

"Viridius was too hard on her," I muttered, embarrassed.

He flicked his dark eyes toward Orma, who had turned away and was scanning the distance for embassy saarantrai. "What's your tall friend's name? He's a dragon, isn't he?"

This prince was too sharp for my comfort. "What makes you think so?"

"Just a hunch. I'm right, then?"

I'd gone sweaty, despite the cold. "His name is Orma. He's my teacher."

Lucian Kiggs scrutinized my face. "Fair enough. I'll want to see his exemption papers. I've only just inherited the list; I don't know all our stealth scholars, as Uncle Rufus used to call them." His dark eyes grew distant, but he recovered himself. "Orma has hailed the embassy, I suppose?"

"Yes."

"Bah. Then we'd best get this over with before I have to go on the defensive."

One of his men paraded the captives in front of us; they'd only caught two. I'd have thought the ones who jumped into the river would have been easily identified when they came out soaking wet and shivering, but maybe the Guard hadn't realized . . .

"Two of them leaped the bridge railing, but I only heard one splash," I began.

Prince Lucian apprehended my meaning immediately. With four swift hand gestures, he directed his soldiers to both sides of the bridge. On a silent count of three, they swung themselves underneath the bridge, and sure enough, one of the Sons was still there, clinging to the beams. They flushed him out like a partridge; unlike a partridge, he couldn't fly even a little. He splashed down in the river, two of the Guard leaping in after him.

The prince cast me an appraising look. "You're observant."

"Sometimes," I said, avoiding his eye.

"Captain Kiggs," intoned a low female voice behind me.

"Here we go," he muttered, stepping around me. I turned to see a saarantras with short black hair leap down from a horse. She rode like a man in trousers and a split caftan, a silver bell as large as an apple fastened ostentatiously to her cloak clasp. The three saarantrai behind her did not dismount, but kept their eager steeds at the ready; their bells jingled a disconcertingly merry cadence on the wind.

"Undersecretary Eskar." The prince approached her with an outstretched hand. She did not deign to take it, but strode purposefully toward Basind.

"Report," she said.

Basind saluted saar fashion, gesturing at the sky. "All in ard. The Guard arrived with tolerable haste, Undersecretary. Captain Kiggs has come directly from his uncle's graveside."

"The cathedral is a two-minute walk from here," said Eskar. "The time differential between your signal and the second one is almost thirteen minutes. If the Guard had been here at that point, the second would not have been necessary at all."

Prince Lucian drew himself up slowly, his face a mask of calm. "So this was some sort of test?"

"It was," she said dispassionately. "We find your security inadequate, Captain Kiggs. This is the third attack in three weeks, and the second where a saar was injured."

"An attack you set up shouldn't count. You know this is atypical. People are on edge. General Comonot arrives in ten days—"

"Precisely why you need to do a better job," she said coolly.

25

"—and Prince Rufus was just murdered in a suspiciously draconian manner."

"There's no evidence that a dragon did it," she said.

"His head is missing!" The prince gestured vehemently toward his own head, his clenched teeth and windblown hair lending a mad ferocity to the pose.

Eskar raised an eyebrow. "No human could have accomplished such a thing?"

Prince Lucian turned sharply away from her and paced in a small circle, rubbing a hand down his face. It's no good getting angry at saarantraí; the hotter your temper, the colder they get. Eskar remained infuriatingly neutral.

His pique under wraps, the prince tried again. "Eskar, please understand: this frightens people. There's still so much deep-seated distrust. The Sons of St. Ogdo take advantage of that, tap into people's fears—"

"Forty years," interrupted Eskar. "We've had forty years of peace. You weren't even born when Comonot's Treaty was signed. Your own mother—"

"Rest she on Heaven's hearthstone," I mumbled, as if it were my job to make up for the social inadequacies of dragons everywhere. The prince flashed me a grateful glance.

"—was but a speck in the queen's womb," continued Eskar placidly, as if I hadn't spoken. "Only your elders remember the war, but it is not the old who join the Sons of St. Ogdo or riot in the streets. How can there be deep-seated distrust in people who've never been through the fires of war? My own father fell to your knights and their insidious dracomachia. All saarantraí re-

26

member those days; all of us lost family. We've let that go, as we had to, for the peace. We hold no grudge."

"Do your people pass emotions through your blood, mother to child, the way we dragons pass memories? Do you inherit your fears? I do not comprehend how this persists in the population—or why you will not crush it," said Eskar.

"We prefer not to crush our own. Call it one of our irrationalities," said Prince Lucian, smiling grimly. "Maybe we can't reason our way out of our feelings the way you can; maybe it takes several generations to calm our fears. Then again, I'm not the one judging an entire species by the actions of a few."

Eskar was unmoved. "Ardmagar Comonot will have my report. It remains to be seen whether he cancels his upcoming visit."

Prince Lucian hoisted his smile, like a flag of surrender. "It would save me a lot of difficulty if he stayed home. How kind of you to consider my well-being."

Eskar cocked her head, birdlike, and then shook off her perplexity. She directed her entourage to collect Basind, who had drifted to the end of the bridge and was rubbing himself against the railing like a cat.

The dull ache behind my eyes had turned into a persistent pounding, as if someone were knocking to be let out. That was bad; my headaches were never just headaches. I didn't want to leave without learning what the urchin had given Orma, but Eskar had taken Orma aside; they had their heads together, talking quietly.

"He must be an excellent teacher," said Prince Lucian, his voice so close and sudden that I startled.

I made half courtesy in silence. I could not discuss Orma in detail with anyone, let alone the Captain of the Queen's Guard.

"He'd have to be," he said. "We were amazed when Viridius chose a woman as his assistant. Not that a woman couldn't do the job, but Viridius is old-fashioned. You'd have to be something astonishing to get his attention."

I made full courtesy this time, but he kept talking. "Your solo was truly moving. I'm sure everyone's telling you this, but there wasn't a dry eye in the cathedral."

Of course. I would never be comfortably anonymous again, it seemed. That's what I got for disregarding Papa's advice. "Thank you," I said. "Excuse me, Highness. I need to see my teacher about my, er, trills. . . ."

I turned my back on him. It was the height of rudeness. He hovered behind me for a moment, then walked away. I glanced back. The last rays of the setting sun turned his mourning clothes almost golden. He commandeered a horse from one of his sergeants, leaped up with balletic grace, and directed the corps back into formation.

I permitted myself one small pang for the inevitability of his disdain, then shoved that feeling aside and moved toward Orma and Eskar.

When I reached them, Orma held out an arm without touching me. "I present: Seraphina," he said.

Undersecretary Eskar looked down her aquiline nose as if checking human features off a list. Two arms: check. Two legs: unconfirmed due to long houppelande. Two eyes, bovine brown: check. Hair the color of strong tea, escaping its plait: check.

Breasts: not obviously. Tall, but within normal parameters. Furious or embarrassed redness upon cheeks: check.

"Hmph," she said. "It's not nearly as hideous as I always pictured it."

Orma, bless his shriveled dragon heart, corrected her. "She."

"Is it not infertile as a mule?"

My face grew so hot I half expected my hair to catch fire.

"She," said Orma firmly, as if he himself had not made the same mistake the first time. "All humans take a gendered pronoun, irrespective of reproductive fitness."

"We take offense otherwise," I said through a brittle smile.

Eskar lost interest abruptly, releasing me from her gaze. Her underlings were returning from the other end of the bridge, leading saar Basind on a skittish horse. Undersecretary Eskar mounted her bay, wheeled it in a tight circle, and spurred it forward without so much as a backward glance at Orma and me. Her retinue followed.

As they passed, Basind's reeling eye lit on me for a long moment; I felt a sharp shock of revulsion. Orma, Eskar, and the others may have learned to pass, but here was a stark reminder of what lay beneath. His was no human gaze.

I turned to Orma, who stared pensively at nothing. "That was thoroughly humiliating," I said.

He startled. "Was it?"

"What were you thinking, telling her about me?" I said. "I may be out from under my father's thumb, but the old rules still apply. We can't just go telling everyone—"

"Ah," he said, raising a slender hand to fend off my argument.

"I didn't tell her. Eskar has always known. She used to be with the Censors."

My stomach turned; the Censors, a dragon agency accountable only to themselves, policed saarantraí for undragonlike behavior and routinely excised the brains of dragons they considered emotionally compromised. "Wonderful. So what have you done to attract the Censors' attention this time?"

"Nothing," he said quickly. "Anyway, she's not with the Censors anymore."

"I thought maybe they were after you for exhibiting undue affection for me," I said, then added mordantly: "You'd think I would have noticed something like that."

"I bear you an appropriate interest, within accepted emotive parameters."

That seemed like overstating it, alas.

To his credit, he knew this subject upset me. Not every saar would have cared. He squirmed, as usual not sure what to do with the information. "You will come for your lesson this week?" he said, making a verbal gesture toward the familiar, as close to comfort as he could contrive to give me.

I sighed. "Of course. And you'll tell me what that child gave you."

"You seem to think there's something to tell," he said, but his hand went involuntarily to his chest, where he'd stashed the bit of gold. I felt a stab of concern, but knew it was no good haranguing him. He would tell me when he decided to tell me.

He declined to tell me goodbye, as was his usual custom; he turned without a word and took off toward the cathedral. Its facade blazed red with the setting sun; Orma's retreating figure made a dark hatch mark against it. I watched until he disappeared around the end of the north transept, and then I watched the space where he had vanished.

I barely noticed loneliness anymore; it was my normal condition, by necessity if not by nature. After today's stresses, though, it weighed on me more than usual. Orma knew everything about me, but he was a dragon. On a good day, he was friend enough. On a bad day, running into his inadequacy was like tripping up the stairs. It hurt, but it felt like my own fault.

Still, he was all I had.

The only sounds were the river below me, the wind in the empty trees, and faint snatches of song, carried all the way downstream from the taverns near the music school. I listened with my arms wrapped around myself and watched the stars blink into being. I wiped my eyes on my sleeve—surely it was the wind making them water—and set off for home thinking of Orma, of everything I felt that must remain unsaid, and of every debt I owed him that could never be repaid.

Three

Orma had saved my life three times.

When I was eight years old, Orma hired me a dragon tutor, a young female called Zeyd. My father had objected strenuously. He despised dragons, despite the fact that he was the Crown's expert on the treaty and had even defended saarantraí in court.

I marveled at Zeyd's peculiarities: her angularity, the unceasing tinkle of her bell, her ability to solve complex equations in her head. Of all my tutors—and I went through a battalion—she was my favorite, right up to the point where she tried to drop me off the bell tower of the cathedral.

She had lured me up the tower on the pretext of giving me a physics lesson, then quick as a thought snatched me up and held me at arm's length over the parapet. The wind screamed in my ears. I looked down at my shoe falling, ricocheting off the gnarled heads of gargoyles, hitting the cobbles of the cathedral square.

"Why do objects fall downward? Do you know?" Zeyd had said, as pleasantly as if she'd been holding this tutorial in the nursery.

I was too terrified to answer. I lost my other shoe and barely kept my breakfast.

"There are unseen forces that act upon all of us, all the time, and they act in predictable ways. If I were to drop you from this tower"—here she shook me, and the city spun, a vortex ready to swallow me up—"your falling form would accelerate at a rate of thirty-two feet per second squared. So would my hat; so did your shoes. We are all pulled toward our doom in exactly the same way, by exactly the same force."

She meant gravity—dragons aren't good at metaphor—but her words resonated with me more personally. Invisible factors in my life would inevitably lead to my downfall. I felt I had known this all along. There was no escape.

Orma had appeared, seemingly out of nowhere, and pulled off the impossible, rescuing me without appearing to rescue me. I didn't understand until years later that this had been a charade put on by the Censors, intended to test Orma's emotional stability and his attachment to me. The experience left me with a deep, un-shakable horror of heights, but not a distrust of dragons, absurdly.

The fact that a dragon had saved me played no part in that latter calculation. No one had ever bothered to tell me Orma was a dragon.

When I was eleven, my father and I came to a crisis. I found my mother's flute hidden in an upstairs room. Papa had forbidden my tutors to teach me music, but he had not explicitly stated that I was not to teach myself. I was half lawyer; I always noticed the loopholes. I played in secret when Papa was at work and my stepmother was at church, working up a small repertoire of competently played folk tunes. When Papa hosted a party on Treaty Eve, the anniversary of peace between Goredd and dragonkind, I hid the flute near the fireplace, intending to burst out in an impromptu performance for all his guests.

Papa found the flute first, guessed what I intended, and marched me up to my room. "What do you think you're doing?" he cried. I had never seen his eyes so wild.

"I'm shaming you into letting me have lessons," I said, my voice calmer than I felt. "When everyone hears how well I play, they'll think you are a fool not to let—"

He cut me short with a violent motion, raising the flute as if he might strike me with it. I cringed, but the blow did not land. When I dared to raise my eyes again, he pulled the flute hard against his knee.

It broke with a sickening crack, like bone, or like my heart. I sank to my knees in shock.

Papa let the fractured instrument drop to the floor and staggered back a step. He looked as sick as I felt, as if the flute had been some piece of himself. "You never understood this, Seraphina," he said. "I have neutralized every trace of your mother, renamed her, reframed her, given her another past—another life. Only two things of hers can still harm us: her insufferable brother—but he won't, with my eye upon him—and her music."

"She had a brother?" I asked, my voice dense with tears. I possessed so little of my mother, and he was taking it all away.

He shook his head. "I am trying to keep us both safe."

The lock clicked when he closed my door behind him. It was unnecessary; I could not have returned to the Treaty Eve party. I felt sick. I lowered my forehead to the floor and wept.

I fell asleep on the floor, my fingers wrapped around the remains of the flute. My first impression upon waking was that I should sweep beneath my bed. My second was that the house was oddly quiet, considering how high the sun had risen. I washed my face at the basin, and the cold water shocked me lucid. Of course everyone was asleep: last night had been Treaty Eve, and they'd all stayed up till dawn, just like Queen Lavonda and Ardmagar Comonot thirty-five years previously, securing the future of both their peoples.

That meant I couldn't leave my room until someone woke up and let me out.

My numb grief had had an entire night to ripen into anger, and that made me reckless, or as close as I'd ever come. I bundled up as warmly as I could, strapped my purse to my forearm, threw open the casement, and climbed down from my window.

I followed my feet through alleys, over bridges, and along the icy quays. To my surprise, I saw people up and about, street traffic, open shops. Sledges glided by, jingling, heaped with firewood or hay. Servants lugged jugs and baskets home from the shops, caring little for the mud on their wooden clogs; young wives gingerly picked their way around puddles of slush. Meat pies competed with roast chestnuts for passersby, and a mulled-wine merchant promised raw warmth in a cup.

I reached St. Loola's Square, where an enormous crowd had gathered along both sides of the empty roadway. People chatted and watched expectantly, huddled together against the cold.

An old man beside me muttered to his neighbor, "I can't believe the Queen lets this happen. After all our sacrifice and struggle!"

"I'm surprised that anything surprises you anymore," said his younger companion, smiling grimly.

"She will rue this treaty, Maurizio."

"Thirty-five years, and she hasn't rued it yet."

"The Queen is mad if she thinks dragons can control their thirst for blood!"

"Excuse me?" I squeaked, shy of strangers. Maurizio looked down at me, eyebrows gently raised. "Are we waiting for dragons?" I said.

He smiled. He was handsome, in a stubbly, unwashed sort of way. "And so we are, little maidy. It's the five-year procession." When I stared at him confusedly, he explained, "Every five years our noble Queen—"

"Our deranged despot!" cried the older man.

"Peace, Karal. Our gracious Queen, as I was saying, permits them to take their natural form within the city walls and march in a procession to commemorate the treaty. She has some notion that it will ease our fears to see them in all their sulfurous monstrosity at regular intervals. The opposite seems more likely true, to me."

Half of Lavondaville had flocked to the square for the pleasure of being terrified, if so. Only the old remembered when dragons were a common sight, when a shadow across the sun was enough to shoot panic down your spine. We all knew the stories—how whole villages had burned to the ground, how you'd turn to stone if you dared look a dragon in the eye, how valiant the knights were in the face of terrifying odds.

The knights had been banished years after Comonot's Treaty took effect. Without dragons to fight, they'd turned to antagonizing Goredd's neighbors, Ninys and Samsam. The three nations engaged in festering, low-grade border wars for two decades, until our Queen put an end to it. All the knightly orders in the Southlands had been disbanded—even those of Ninys and Samsam—but rumor had it that the old fighters lived in secret enclaves in the mountains or the deep countryside.

I found myself glancing sidelong at the old man, Karal; with all his talk of sacrifice, I wondered whether he'd ever fought dragons. He'd be the right age.

The crowd gasped in unison. A horned monster was rounding the block of shops, his arched back as high as the second-story windows, his wings demurely folded so as not to topple nearby chimney pots. His elegant neck curved downward like a submissive dog's, a posture intended to look nonthreatening.

At least, I found him innocuous enough with his head spines

flattened. Other people didn't seem to be catching on to his body language; all around me horrified citizens clutched at each other, made St. Ogdo's sign, and muttered into their hands. A nearby woman began shrieking hysterically—"His terrible teeth!"—until she was hustled away by her husband.

I watched them disappear into the crowd, wishing that I could have reassured her: it was good to see a dragon's teeth. A dragon with his mouth closed was far more likely to be working up a flame. That seemed completely obvious.

And that gave me pause. All around me, the sight of those teeth was making citizens sob with terror. What was obvious to me was apparently opaque to everyone else.

There were twelve dragons altogether; Princess Dionne and her young daughter, Glisselda, brought up the rear of the procession in a sledge. Under the white winter sky the dragons looked rusty, a disappointing color for so fabled a species, but I soon realized their shades were subtle. The right slant of sunlight brought out an iridescent sheen in their scales; they shimmered with rich underhues, from purple to gold.

Karal had brought along a flask of hot tea, which he doled out stingily to Maurizio. "It's got to last till evening," grumped Karal, sniffing up a drip at the end of his nose. "If we must celebrate Comonot's Treaty, you'd think Ard-braggart Comonot could be bothered to show. He scorns to come south, or take human form."

"I heard he fears you, sir," said Maurizio blandly. "I think that shows sense."

I wasn't sure, afterward, how it all turned ugly. The old

38

knight—I felt the "sir" confirmed it—called out insults: "Worms! Gasbags! Hell-beasts!" Several solid citizens around us joined in. Some of them began throwing snowballs.

A dragon near the center got spooked. Maybe the crowd drew too close, or a snowball hit him. He raised his head and body to full height, as tall as the three-story inn across the square. The spectators closest to him panicked and ran.

There was nowhere to run. They were surrounded by hundreds of half-frozen fellow Goreddis. Collisions ensued. Collisions led to screaming. Screaming made more dragons raise their heads in alarm.

The lead dragon screamed, a blood-chilling bestial cry. To my shock, I understood him: "Heads down!"

One of the dragons opened his wings. The crowd reeled and churned like a storm-tossed sea.

Their leader shrieked again: "Fikri, wings folded! If you take off, you will be in violation of section seven, article five, and I will have your tail before a tribunal so fast—"

To the crowd, however, the dragon's exhortation sounded like feral screams, and their hearts were stricken with terror. They stampeded toward the side streets.

The thundering herd swept me away. An elbow banged my jaw; a kick to the knee toppled me. Someone trod on my calf; someone else tripped over my head. I saw stars, and the sound of shouting faded.

Then suddenly there was air again, and space.

And hot breath on my neck. I opened my eyes.

A dragon stood over me, his legs four pillars of sanctuary. I nearly fainted again, but his sulfurous breath jolted me conscious. He nudged me with his nose and gestured toward an alley.

"I'll escort you over there," he cried, in the same horrible scream as the other dragon.

I rose, putting a shaky hand against his leg to steady myself; it was rough and immovable as a tree, and unexpectedly warm. The snow beneath him was melting to slush. "Thank you, saar," I said.

"Did you understand what I said, or are you responding to my perceived intent?"

I froze. I did understand, but how? I'd never studied Mootya; few humans had. It seemed safer not to reply, so I started toward the alley without a word. He walked behind me; people scrambled out of our way.

The alley led nowhere and was full of barrels, so the crowds were not frantically squeezing through it. He planted himself at the entrance nonetheless. The Queen's Guard arrived, trotting in formation across the square, plumes waving and bagpipes brawling. Most of the dragons had organized themselves in a circle around Princess Dionne's carriage, shielding her from the mob; they exchanged this duty with the Guard. The remnants of the crowd cheered, and confidence, if not order, was restored.

I curtsied thanks, expecting the dragon to leave. He lowered his head to my level. "Seraphina," he screamed.

I stared, shocked that he knew my name. He stared back, smoke leaking from his nostrils, his eyes black and alien. And yet not so alien. There was a familiarity that I could not put my finger on. My vision wavered, as if I were staring at him through water.

"Nothing?" cried the saar. "She was so sure she'd be able to leave you at least one memory."

The world grew dark around the edges; the shouting faded to a hiss. I keeled over face-first in the snow.

I lie in bed, hugely pregnant. The sheets are clammy; I shiver and reel with nausea. Orma stands across the room in a patch of sunlight, staring out the window at nothing. He isn't listening. I writhe with impatience; I don't have much time left. "I want this child to know you," I say.

"I am not interested in your spawn," he says, examining his fingernails. "Nor shall I stay in contact with your miserable husband after you die."

I weep, unable to stop myself but ashamed that he will see how my self-control has eroded. He swallows, his mouth puckering as if he tastes bile. I am monstrous in his eyes, I know, but I love him. This may be our last chance to speak. "I'm leaving the baby some memories," I say.

Orma finally looks at me, his dark eyes distant. "Can you do that?"

I don't know for certain, and I don't have the energy to discuss it. I shift beneath the sheets to ease a stabbing pain in my pelvis. I say, "I intend to leave my child a mind-pearl."

Orma scratches his skinny neck. "The pearl will contain memories of me, I presume. That's why you're telling me this. What releases it?"

"The sight of you as you really are," I say, panting a bit because the pain is growing.

He emits a horselike snort. "Under *what possible circumstances* would the child see me in my natural state?"

"You decide, once you're ready to admit that you're an uncle," I inhale sharply as a fierce cramping grips my abdomen. There will barely be time to make the mind-pearl. I'm not even sure I'll have the wherewithal to concentrate sufficiently. I speak to Orma as calmly as I can: "Get Claude. Now. Please."

Forgive me, child, for including all this pain. There is no time to separate it out.

My eyes popped open, pain searing through my head. I lay in Maurizio's arms, cradled like a baby. Old Karal, a few steps away, was dancing an odd jig in the snow. The knight had found a pole-arm, which he brandished at the dragon, driving it away. It retreated across the square to its brethren.

No, not *its*. His. That was Orma, my . . .

I couldn't even think it.

Maurizio's concerned face swam in and out of my vision. I managed to say, "Dombegh house, near St. Fionnuala's," before blacking out again. I revived only when Maurizio transferred me to my father's arms. Papa helped me upstairs, and I collapsed into bed.

As I struggled in and out of consciousness, I heard my father yelling at someone. When I awoke, Orma was at my bedside, talking as if he had believed me awake already: ". . . an encapsulated maternal memory. I don't know what exactly she revealed, only that she intended you to know the truth about me, and about herself."

He was a dragon and my mother's brother. I had not yet dared deduce what that made her, but he forced the conclusion upon me. I leaned over the side of the bed and vomited. He picked his teeth with a fingernail, staring at the mess on the floor as if it could tell him how much I knew. "I did not expect you to attend the procession. I did not intend you to learn this now—or ever. Your father and I were in agreement on that," he said. "But I could not let you be trampled by the crowd. I'm not sure why."

That was all I heard of his explanations, because a vision seized me.

It wasn't another of my mother's memories. I remained myself, though disembodied, looking down upon a lively port city nestled in the gap between coastal mountains. I did not just see it: I smelled fish and market spices, felt the ocean's salty breath upon my incorporeal face. I soared through the pristine blue sky like a lark, circled over white domes and spires, and glided above the bustling dockyards. A lush temple garden, full of chuckling fountains and blossoming lemon trees, drew me in. There was something there I needed to see.

No, some*one*. A little boy, perhaps six years old, hung upside down like a fruit bat in a spindly fig tree. His skin was as brown as a plowed field, his hair like a fluffy dark cloud, his eyes lively and bright. He ate an orange segment by segment, looking thoroughly satisfied with himself. His gaze was intelligent, but he looked right through me as if I were invisible.

I returned to myself just long enough to catch my breath before two more visions hit me in short succession. I saw a muscular Samsamese highlander playing bagpipes on the roof of a church and then a fussy old woman with thick spectacles excoriating her cook for putting too much coriander in the stew. Each fresh vision compounded my headache; my wrung-out stomach had nothing more to give.

For a week I was bedridden; the visions came so thick and fast that if I tried to stand I collapsed under their weight. I saw grotesque and deformed people: men with wattles and claws; women with vestigial wings; and a great sluglike beast churning up mud in a swamp. I screamed myself hoarse at the sight of them, flailing against my sweaty bedclothes and frightening my stepmother.

My left forearm and midriff itched, burned, and erupted in weeping, crusty patches. I tore at them savagely, which only made them worse.

I was feverish; I couldn't keep down food. Orma stayed by me the entire time, and I suffered the illusion that behind his skin—behind everyone's—was a hollow nothingness, an inky black void. He rolled up my sleeve to look at my arm, and I shrieked, believing he would peel back my skin and see the emptiness beneath it.

By the end of the week, the angry mange on my skin had hardened and begun to flake off, revealing a band of pale rounded scales, still soft as a baby snake's, running from the inside of my wrist to the outside of my elbow. A broader band encircled my waist, like a girdle. At the sight of them, I sobbed until I was sick. Orma sat very still beside the bed, his dark eyes unblinking, thinking his inscrutable dragon thoughts.

"What am I to do with you, Seraphina?" asked my father. He sat behind his desk, nervously rifling through documents. I sat across from him on a backless stool; it was the first day I'd been well enough to leave my room. Orma occupied the carven oak chair in front of the window, the gray morning light haloing his uncombed hair. Anne-Marie had brought us tea and fled, but I was the only one who'd taken any. It grew cold in my cup.

"What did you ever intend to do with me?" I said with some bitterness, rubbing the rim of my cup with my thumb.

Papa shrugged his narrow shoulders, a distant look in his sea-gray eyes. "I had some hope of marrying you off until these gruesome manifestations appeared on your arm and your—" He gestured at my body, up and down.

I tried to shrink into myself. I felt disgusting to my very soul—if I even had a soul. My mother was a dragon. Nothing was certain anymore.

"I understand why you didn't want me to know," I muttered into my teacup, my voice rough with shame. "Before this . . . this outbreak, I might not have felt the urgency of secrecy; I might have unburdened myself to one of the maids, or . . ." I'd never had many friends. "Believe me, I see the point now."

"Oh, you do, do you?" said Papa, his gaze grown sharp. "Your knowledge of the treaty and the law would not have kept you si-lent, but being ugly makes it all clear to you?"

"The time to consider the treaty and the law was before you married her," I said.

"I didn't know!" he cried. He shook his head and said in a gentler tone, "She never told me. She died giving birth to you, bleeding silver all over the bed, and I was thrown into the deep end of the sea, without even the woman I loved best to help me."

Papa ran a hand through his thinning hair. "I could be exiled or executed, depending on our Queen's humor, but it may not be up to her, ultimately. Few cases of cohabiting with dragons have ever come all the way to trial; the accused have usually been torn to bits by mobs, been burned alive in their houses, or simply disappeared before it came to that."

My throat was too dry to speak; I swallowed a mouthful of cold tea. It was bitter. "Wh-what happened to their children?"

"There are no records of any of them having children," said Papa. "But do not imagine for one moment that the citizenry wouldn't know what to do with you if they found out. They need only turn to scripture for that."

Orma, who had been staring into space, snapped his focus back to us. "St. Ogdo had some specific recommendations, if memory serves," he said, tugging at his beard. "'If soe'er the worms defile your women, producing misshapen, miscegenated abominations, suffer not such ghastly issue to live. Cleave the infant's skull with a thrice-blessed axe, ere its fontanelles harden like unto steel. Sever its scaly limbs and burn them in separate fires, lest they return in the night, crawling like worms, to kill righteous folk. Tear open the monster child's belly, piss upon its entrails, and set ablaze. Half-breeds are born gravid: if you bury the abdomen intact, twenty more will spring up from the ground—'"

"Enough, saar," said Papa. His eyes, the color of stormy water, scanned my face. I stared back in horror, my mouth clamped shut to keep myself from crying. Did he eschew religion because the

Saints themselves extolled the killing of his child? Did Goreddis still hate dragons after thirty-five years of peace because Heaven demanded it?

Orma had not registered my distress at all. "I wonder whether Ogdo and those who express similar revulsion—St. Vitt, St. Munn, many others—had experience with half-breeds. Not because Seraphina resembles the description, obviously, but because they acknowledge the possibility at all. There is no recorded case of crossbreeding at the great library of the Tanamoot, which is astonishing in itself. You'd think, in almost a millennium, someone would have tried it on purpose."

"No," said Papa, "I wouldn't think it. Only an amoral dragon would think it."

"Exactly," said Orma, unoffended. "An amoral dragon would think it, try it—"

"What, by force?" Papa's mouth puckered as if the idea brought bile to his throat.

The implication didn't bother Orma. "—and record the experiment's results. Perhaps we are not as amoral a species as is commonly supposed in the Southlands."

I could hold back tears no longer. I felt dizzy, empty; a cold draft under the door set me swaying unsteadily. Everything had been stripped away: my human mother, my own humanity, and any hope I had of leaving my father's house.

I saw the void beneath the surface of the world; it threatened to pull me under.

Even Orma couldn't help noticing my distress. He cocked his head, perplexed. "Give her education over to me, Claude," he said, leaning back and gathering condensation off the diamond panes of the little window with a fingertip. He tasted it.

"To you," sneered my father. "And what will you do with her? She can't go two hours without these infernal visions giving her seizures."

"We could work on that, to start. We saar have techniques for taming a rebellious brain." Orma tapped his own forehead, and then tapped it again as if the sensation intrigued him.

Why had it never struck me how deeply peculiar he was?

"You'll teach her music," said my father, his golden voice pitched an octave too high. I could see the struggle beneath his face as clearly as if his skin were glass. He had never been merely protecting me; he had been protecting his broken heart.

"Papa, please." I held out my open hands like a supplicant before the Saints. "I have nothing else left."

My father wilted in his chair, blinking away tears. "Do not let me hear you."

Two days later, a spinet was delivered to our house. My father instructed them to set it up in a storeroom at the very back of the house, far from his study. There was no room for the stool; I ended up sitting on a trunk. Orma had also sent a book of fantasias by a composer called Viridius. I had never seen musical notation before, but it was instantly familiar to me, as the speech of dragons had been. I sat until the light at the window began to fade, reading that music as if it were literature.

I knew nothing of spinets, but I assumed one opened the lid. The inside of mine was painted with a bucolic scene: kittens frolicking upon a patio, peasants making hay in the fields behind them. One of the kittens—the one aggressively assaulting a ball of blue wool—had a peculiar glassy eye. I squinted at it in the semi-darkness and then tapped it with my finger.

"Ah, there you are," crackled a deep voice. It seemed to come, incongruously, from the throat of the painted kitten.

"Orma?" How was he speaking to me? Was this some draco-nian device?

"If you're ready," he said, "let us begin. There is much to be done."

And that was how he saved my life the third time.

Four

For the next five years Orma was my teacher and my only friend. For someone who'd never intended to declare himself my uncle, Orma took his avuncular duties seriously. He taught me not just music but everything he thought I should know about dragonkind: history, philosophy, physiology, higher mathematics (as close as they came to a religion). He answered even my most impudent questions. Yes, dragons could smell colors under the right conditions. Yes, it was a terrible idea to transform into a saarantras right after eating an aurochs. No, he did not understand the exact nature of my visions, but he believed he saw the way to help me.

Dragons found the human condition confusing and often overwhelming, and they had developed strategies over the years for keeping their heads "in ard" while they took human form. Ard was a central concept of draconic philosophy. The word itself meant roughly "order" or "correctness." Goreddis used the word to

50

refer to a dragon battalion—and that was one definition. But for dragons, the idea went much deeper. Ard was the way the world should be, the imposition of order upon chaos, an ethical and physical rightness.

Human emotions, messy and unpredictable, were antithetical to ard. Dragons used meditation and what Orma called cognitive architecture to partition their minds into discrete spaces. They kept their maternal memories in one room, for example, because they were disruptively intense; the one maternal memory I'd experienced had bowled me over. Emotions, which the saar found uncomfortable and overpowering, were locked away securely and never permitted to leak out.

Orma had never heard of visions like mine and did not know what caused them. But he believed a system of cognitive architecture could stop the visions from striking me unconscious. We tried variations on his maternal memory room, locking the visions (that is, an imaginary book representing them) in a chest, a tomb, and finally a prison at the bottom of the sea. It would work for a few days, until I collapsed on my way home from St. Ida's and we had to start again.

My visions showed the same people over and over; they'd become so familiar I'd given them all nicknames. There were seventeen, a nice prime number, which interested Orma inordinately. He finally lit upon the idea of trying to contain the individuals, not the visions as such. "Try creating a representation, a mental avatar, of each person and building a space where they might want to stay," Orma had said. "That boy, Fruit Bat, is always climbing trees, so plant a tree in your mind. See if his avatar will climb it

and stay there. Maybe if you cultivate and maintain your connec-
tions to these individuals, they won't seek your attention at inconvenient times."

From this suggestion, an entire garden had grown. Each avatar had its place within this garden of grotesques; I tended them
every night or suffered headaches and visions when I did not. As
long as I kept these peculiar denizens calm and peaceful, I was not
troubled by visions. Neither Orma nor I understood exactly why it
worked. Orma claimed it was the most unusual mental structure
he had ever heard of; he regretted not being able to write a dis-
sertation on it, but I was a secret, even among dragons.

No unwanted vision had seized me in four years, but I could
not relax my vigilance. The headache I'd developed after Prince
Rufus's funeral meant the grotesques in my garden were agitated;
that was when a vision was most likely to hit me. After Orma left
me on the bridge, I hurried back to Castle Orison as quickly as I
could, anticipating an hour's work attending to my mental hy-
giene, as Orma called it, putting my mind back in ard.

My suite at the palace had two rooms. The first was a parlor
where I practiced. The spinet Orma had given me stood by the far
wall; beside it was a bookcase with my own books, my flutes, my
oud. I staggered into the second room, containing wardrobe, table,
and bed; I'd had only two weeks' acquaintance with the furniture,
but it felt sufficiently mine that I was at home here. Palace servants had turned down the bedclothes and lit the fire.

I stripped to my linen chemise. I had scales to wash and oil,
but every inch of me whimpered for the soft bed and there was
still my head to deal with.

I pulled the bolster off my bed and sat on it cross-legged, as Orma had taught me. I shut my eyes, in so much pain now that it was hard to slow my breaths sufficiently. I repeated the mantra *All in ard* until I had calmed enough to see my sprawling, colorful garden of grotesques stretching all the way to my mind's horizon.

I endured a moment of confusion as I got my bearings; the layout changed each time I visited. Before me squatted the border wall of ancient, flat bricks; ferns grew out of its every cranny like tufts of green hair. Beyond it I saw the Faceless Lady fountain, the poppy bank, and a lawn with bulbous, overgrown topiaries. As Orma had instructed, I always paused with my hands upon the entrance gate—wrought iron, this time—and said, "This is my mind's garden. I tend it; I order it. I have nothing to fear."

Pelican Man lurked among the topiaries, his slack, expansive throat wattle dangling over the front of his tunic like a fleshy bib. It was always harder when I ran into a deformed one first, but I plastered on a smile and stepped onto the lawn. Cold dew between my toes surprised me; I hadn't noticed I was barefoot. Pelican Man took no note of my approach but kept his eyes upon the sky, which was always starry in this part of the garden.

"Are you well, Master P?" Pelican Man rolled his eyes at me balefully; he was agitated. I tried to take his elbow—I didn't touch the hands of a grotesque if I could help it—but he shied away from me. "Yes, it was a stressful day," I said mildly, circling, herding him toward his stone bench. Its hollow seat was filled with soil and planted with oregano, producing a lovely smell when one sat on it. Pelican Man found it soothing. He headed for it at last and curled up among the herbs.

I watched Pelican Man a few moments longer, to make sure he was truly calmed. His dark skin and hair looked Porphyrian; his red baglike throat, expanding and contracting with every breath, looked like nothing of this world. As vivid as my visions were, it was disturbing to imagine him—and others still more deformed—out in the world somewhere. Surely the gods of Porphyry were not so cruel as to allow a Pelican Man to exist? My burden of horribleness was light compared with that.

He remained tranquil. That was one settled, and it hadn't been difficult. The intensity of my headache seemed disproportionate, but maybe I would find others more agitated.

I rose to continue my rounds, but my bare feet encountered something cold and leathery in the grass. Stooping down, I found a large piece of orange peel, and then several more scraps scattered among the towering boxwoods.

I had given the garden permanent features peculiar to each grotesque—Fruit Bat's trees, Pelican Man's starry sky—but my deeper mind, the hidden current Orma called underthought, filled in everything else. New embellishments, peculiar plants or statuary, appeared without warning. Refuse on the lawn seemed wrong, however.

I tossed the peels under the hedge and wiped my hands on my skirt. There was only one orange tree that I knew of in this garden. I would put off worrying until I'd seen it.

I found Miserere pulling out her feathers by the rocking stile; I led her to her nest. Newt thrashed about under the apple trees, crushing the bluebells; I led him to his wallow and rubbed mud onto his tender head. I checked that the lock on the Wee Cottage still held and then picked my way barefoot through an unantici-pated field of thistles. I could see the taller trees of Fruit Bat's grove in the distance. I took the lime walk, ducking into leafy side gardens along the way, clucking, soothing, putting to bed, tending everyone. At the end of the walk, a yawning chasm blocked my way. Loud Lad's ravine had shifted positions and now blocked my path to Fruit Bat's date palms.

Loud Lad represented the Samsamese piper I'd seen. He was a favorite; I am ashamed to say I gravitated toward the more normal-looking denizens. This avatar was unusual in that it made noise (hence the name), built things, and sometimes left its desig-nated area. This had caused me no end of panic at first. There had been one other grotesque, Jannoula, who'd been prone to wander, and she'd frightened me so badly that I'd locked her away in the Wee Cottage.

The visions were like peering into someone else's life with a mystical spyglass. In the case of Jannoula, she had somehow been able to look back at me through her avatar. She had spoken to me, pried, prodded, stolen, and lied; she had drunk my fears like nec-tar, and smelled my wishes on the wind. In the end, she began trying to influence my thoughts and control my actions. In a panic, I'd told Orma and he helped me find a way to banish her to the Wee Cottage. I barely managed to trick her into entering. It was hard to fool someone who could tell what you were thinking.

With the Loud Lad avatar, however, motion just seemed to be characteristic; I had no sense that a real-world Samsamese piper was gazing back at me. Gazebos and pergolas sprouted all over the garden, gifts from His Loudness, and it pleased me to see them.

"Loud Lad!" I cried at the edge of his ravine. "I need a bridge!"

A gray-eyed, round-cheeked head popped up, followed by an oversized body clad in Samsamese black. He sat upon the lip of the cliff, took three fish and a lady's nightdress from his bag—caterwauling all the while—and unfolded them into a bridge for me to cross.

It was very like dreaming, this garden. I tried not to question the logic of things.

"How are you? You're not upset?" I asked, patting his bristly blond head. He hooted and disappeared into his crevasse. That was normal; he was usually calmer than the rest, maybe because he kept so busy.

I hurried toward Fruit Bat's grove, worry beginning to catch up with me now. Fruit Bat was my very favorite grotesque, and the only orange tree in the garden grew in his stand of figs, dates, lemons, and other Porphyrian fruits. I reached the grove and looked up, but he wasn't among the leaves. I looked down; he'd stacked fallen fruit into tidy pyramids, but he was nowhere to be seen.

He had never left his designated space before, not once. I stood a long time, staring at the empty trees, trying to rationalize his absence.

Trying to slow my panicked heart.

If Fruit Bat was loose in the garden, that explained the orange peel on Pelican Man's lawn, and it might very well explain the intensity of my headache. If some little Porphyrian boy had found the way to peer back up the spyglass like Jannoula . . . I went cold all over. It was inconceivable. There must be another explanation.

It would break my heart to have to cut off my connection to one I was so inexplicably fond of.

I pushed on, settling the remaining denizens, but my heart wasn't in it. I found more orange peel in Muttering Creek and upon Three Dunes.

The last piece of the garden tonight was the Rose Garden, prissy domain of Miss Fusspots. She was a short, stout old woman in a gabled cap and thick spectacles, homely but not overtly grotesque. I'd seen her too during that first barrage of visions, fussing about her stew. That was the origin of her name.

It took me a moment to spot her—a moment during which I had panicked palpitations—but she was merely on her hands and knees in the dirt behind an unusually large albiflora. She was pulling up weeds before they had a chance to sprout. It was efficient, if baffling. She did not seem particularly perturbed; she ignored me completely.

I looked across the sundial lawn toward the egression gate; I longed for bed and rest, but right now I didn't dare. I had to locate Fruit Bat.

There upon the sundial's face lay an entire orange rind, peeled off as one piece.

And there was the boy himself, up the ancient yew tree beside the border wall. He looked pleased that I had spotted him; he waved, leaped down, and skipped across the sundial lawn toward me. I gaped, alarmed by his bright eyes and smile, afraid of what they might mean.

He held out a slice of orange. It curled like a prawn on his brown hand.

I stared at it in perplexity. I could deliberately induce a vision by holding a grotesque's hands; I had done so once for each of them, seizing control of the visions and ending their control over me. That was the only time I'd done it. It felt wrong, like I was spying on people.

Was Fruit Bat merely offering me an orange, or did he wish me to take his hand? The latter notion gave me chills. I said, "Thank you, Bat, but I'm not hungry now. Let's go find your trees."

He followed me like a puppy, past Pandowdy's swamp, through the butterfly garden, all the way back to his home grove. I'd expected him to leap right back up into the trees, but he looked at me with wide black eyes and held the orange slice up again. "You need to stay here and not go wandering around," I admonished. "It's bad enough that Loud Lad does it. Do you understand?"

He gave no indication that he understood; he ate the piece of orange, gazing into the distance. I patted his fluffy cloud of hair and waited until he was up a tree before I left.

I made my way to the gate, bowed to the sundial lawn, and said the designated words of parting: "This is my garden, all in ard. I tend it faithfully; let it keep faith with me."

I opened my eyes in my own room and stretched my stiff limbs. I poured myself some water from the ewer on the table and tossed the bolster back onto the bed. My headache had evaporated; apparently I'd solved the problem, even if I hadn't understood it.

Orma would have some idea about this. I determined to ask him tomorrow, and that prospect soothed my worry into sleep.

My morning routine was elaborate and time-consuming, so Orma had given me a timepiece that emitted blasphemy-inducing chirps at whatever early hour I specified. I kept it on top of the bookcase in the parlor, in a basket with a few other trinkets, so that I was forced to trudge all the way in there and dig around to switch it off.

It was a good system, except when I was too exhausted to remember to set the alarm. I awoke in a blaze of panic half an hour before I was due to lead choir practice.

I yanked my arms out of the sleeves of my chemise and shoved them up through the neck hole, lowering the linen garment until it rested around my hips like a skirt. I emptied the ewer into the basin and added the contents of the kettle, which were only slightly warmed from sitting on the hearth all night. I scrubbed the scales on my arm and around my middle with a soft cloth. The scales themselves registered no temperature; the trickle-down was far too cold to be comfortable today.

Everyone else washed once a week, if that, but no one else was susceptible to scale mites or burrowing chibbets. I dried myself and rushed to the bookcase for my pot of salve. Only certain herbs emulsified in goose grease stopped my scales from itching; Orma had found a good supplier in the one dragon-friendly part of town, the neighborhood called Quighole.

I usually practiced smiling while I slathered my scales with goo, figuring that if I could smile through that, I could smile through anything. Today I really didn't have the time.

I pulled up my chemise and wrapped a cord around the left forearm so the sleeve couldn't fall open. I put on a kirtle, gown, and surcoat; I wore three layers at minimum, even in summer. I threw on a respectful white sash for Prince Rufus, hastily brushed my hair, and dashed into the corridor feeling less than ready to face the world.

Viridius, sprawled on his gout couch, had already started conducting the castle choir by the time I arrived, breathless, breakfast rolls in hand. He glared at me; his beetling brows were still mostly red, though the fringe of hair around his head was a shocking white. The bass line stumbled, and he barked, "*Glo-ri-a*, you gaggle of laggards! Why have your mouths stopped? Did my hand stop? Indeed, it did not!"

"Sorry I'm late," I mumbled, but he did not deign to look at me again until the final chord had resolved.

"Better," he told the choir before turning his baleful eye on me. "Well?"

I pretended I thought he wanted to know about yesterday's performances. "The funeral went well, as you've probably already heard. Guntard accidentally broke the reed of his shawm by sit—"

"I did have an extra reed," piped up Guntard, who did double duty with the choir.

"Which you didn't find until later, at the tavern," quipped someone else.

Viridius silenced them all with a scowl. "The choir of idiots will desist from idiocy! Maid Dombegh, I was referring to your excuse for being late. It had better be a good one!"

I swallowed hard, repeating *This is the job I wanted!* to myself. I'd been a fan of Viridius's music from the moment I laid eyes on his *Fantasias*, but it was hard to reconcile the composer of the transcendent *Suite Infanta* with the bullying old man on the couch.

The choristers eyed me with interest. Many had auditioned for my position; whenever Viridius scolded me, they appreciated how narrowly they had escaped this fate.

I curtsied stiffly. "I overslept. It won't happen again."

Viridius shook his head so fiercely his jowls waggled. "Need I underscore to any of you amateur squawkers that our Queen's hospitality—nay, our entire nation's worth—will be judged by the quality of our performances when Ardmagar Comonot is here?"

Several musicians laughed; Viridius quashed all merriment with a scowl. "Think that's funny, you tone-deaf miscreants? Music is one thing dragons can't do better than us. They wish they could; they're fascinated; they've tried and tried again. They achieve technical perfection, perhaps, but there's always some—thing missing. You know why?"

I recited along with the rest of the chorus, though it turned my insides cold: "Dragons have no souls!"

"Exactly!" said Viridius, waving his gout-mangled fist in the air. "They cannot do this one thing—glorious, Heaven-sent, com—ing naturally to us—and it is up to us to rub their faces in it!"

The choristers gave a little "Hurrah!" before disbanding. I let them flow out around me; Viridius would expect me to stay and speak with him. Of course, seven or eight singers had pressing questions. They stood around his gout couch, fondling his ego as if he were the Pashega of Ziziba. Viridius accepted their praise as matter-of-factly as if they were handing back their choir robes.

"Seraphina!" boomed the master, turning his attention to me at last. "I heard complimentary words about your Invocation. I wish I could have been there. This infernal illness makes a prison of my very body."

I fingered the cuff of my left sleeve, understanding him better than he imagined.

"Get the ink, maidy," he said. "I want to cross things off the list."

I fetched writing implements and the roster of tasks he had dictated to me when I first began working for him. There were only nine days left until General Comonot, Ardmagar of All Dragonkind, arrived; there was to be a welcoming concert and ball the first evening, followed a few days later by the Treaty Eve festivities, which had to last all night. I'd been working for two weeks, but there was plenty left to do.

I read the list aloud, item by item; he interrupted me at will. He cried, "The stage is finished! Cross it off!" and then later, "Why haven't you spoken with the wine steward yet? Easiest job on the list! Did I become court composer through masterful procrastination? Hardly!"

We arrived at the item I'd been dreading: auditions. Viridius narrowed his watery eyes and said, "Yes, how are those going, Maid Dombegh?"

He knew perfectly well how they were going; apparently he wanted to watch me sweat. I kept my voice steady: "I had to cancel most of them due to Prince Rufus's inconveniently timed demise—dine he with the Saints at Heaven's table. I've rescheduled several for—"

"Auditions should never have been put off until the last minute!" he shouted. "I wanted the performers confirmed a month ago!"

"With respect, master, I wasn't even hired a month ago."

"Do you think I don't know that?" His mouth worked up and down; he stared at his bandaged hands. "Forgive me," he said at last, his voice rough. "It is a bitter thing not to be able to do everything you are accustomed to. Die while you're young, Seraphina. Tertius had the right idea."

I did not know how to respond to that. I said, "It's not as dire as it seems. Each of your many protégés will attend; the program is half filled already."

He nodded thoughtfully at the mention of his students; the man had more protégés than most people have friends. It was nearly time for Princess Glisselda's lesson, so I corked the ink and began hastily cleaning my pen with a rag. Viridius said, "When can you meet with my megaharmonium fellow?"

"Who?" I said, placing the pen in a box with the others.

He rolled his red-rimmed eyes. "Explain why I write you notes if you don't read them. The designer of the megaharmonium wants to meet you." Apparently I continued to look blank, because he spoke loudly and slowly, as if I were stupid: "The enormous instrument we're building in the south transept of St. Gobnait's? The me-ga-har-mo-ni-um?"

I recalled the construction I'd seen in the cathedral, but not the note, which I must have overlooked. "It's a musical instrument? It looks like a machine."

"It's both!" he cried, his eyes alight with glee. "And it's nearly finished. I funded half of it myself. It's a fitting project for an old man on his way out of this life. A legacy. It will make a sound like nothing this world has ever heard before!"

I gaped at him; I'd glimpsed an excitable young man inside the irascible old one.

"You must meet him, my other protégé, Lars," he proclaimed as if he were the Bishop of Gout Couch, speaking ex cathedra. "He built the Comonot Countdown Clock in the cathedral plaza, too; he's a veritable prodigy. You would get along famously. He only comes by late, but I shall persuade him to visit at some reasonable hour. I'll tell you when I see you this evening at the Blue Salon."

"Not tonight, forgive me," I said, rising and pulling my harpsichord books off one of Viridius's cluttered shelves.

Princess Glisselda held a soiree almost every evening in the Blue Salon. I had a standing invitation to attend but had never gone, despite Viridius's pestering and snarling at me. Being guarded and cautious all day left me exhausted by evening, and I couldn't stay out late because I had a garden to tend and a scalecare regimen I couldn't skip. I could tell Viridius none of that; I had pled shyness repeatedly, but still he pushed.

The old man cocked a bushy eyebrow and scratched his jowls. "You will get nowhere at court by isolating yourself, Seraphina."

"I am exactly where I wish to be," I said, thumbing through parchment sheets.

"You risk offending Princess Glisselda by snubbing her invitation." He squinted at me shrewdly and added: "It's not quite normal to be so antisocial, now is it?"

My insides tensed. I shrugged, determined to give no hint that I was susceptible to the word *normal*.

"You will come tonight," said the old man.

"I already have plans tonight," I said, smiling; this was why I practiced.

"Then you will come tomorrow night!" he cried, bursting with anger at me now. "The Blue Salon, nine o'clock! You will be there, or you will find yourself abruptly out of employment!"

I could not tell whether he was bluffing; I didn't know him well enough yet. I took a shaky breath. It wouldn't kill me to go once, for half an hour. "Forgive me, sir," I said, inclining my head. "Of course I'll come. I had not understood how important it was to you."

Keeping my smile raised like a shield between us, I curtsied and quit the room.

I heard them giggling from out in the corridor, Princess Glisselda and whichever lady in waiting she'd dragged along with her this time. It sounded like an agemate, from the pitch of the giggle. I wondered, briefly, what a giggle concerto might sound like. We would need a chorus of—

"Is she very, very cranky?" asked the lady-in-waiting.

I froze. That question couldn't pertain to me, surely?

"Behave!" cried the princess, her laugh like water. "I said prickly, not cranky!"

I felt my face go hot. Prickly? Was I really?

"She's good-hearted, anyway," added Princess Glisselda, "which makes her Viridius's opposite. And nearly pretty, only she does have such dreadful taste in gowns and I can't work out what she thinks she's doing with her hair."

"That might be easily corrected," said the lady-in-waiting.

I'd heard enough. I stepped through the doorway, fuming but trying not to confirm my reputation. The lady-in-waiting was half Porphyrian, judging by her dark curls and warm brown skin; she put a hand to her mouth, embarrassed at being overheard. Princess Glisselda said, "Phina! We were just talking about you!"

It is a princess's privilege to feel no social awkwardness, ever. She smiled, gloriously unashamed; the sunlight through the windows behind her made a halo of her golden hair. I curtsied and approached the harpsichord.

Princess Glisselda rose from her window seat and flounced after me. She was fifteen, a year younger than me, which made me feel odd about teaching her; she was petite for her age, which made me feel like a gawky giantess. She loved pearl-studded brocade and was possessed of more confidence than I could imagine having. "Phina," she chirped, "meet Lady Miliphrene. She is, like you, encumbered with an unnecessarily long name, so I call her Millie."

I nodded acknowledgment to Millie but held my tongue about the silliness of that comment, coming from someone named Glisselda.

"I have reached a decision," the princess announced. "I shall perform at the Treaty Eve concert, that galliard and pavano. Not Viridius's suite: the one by Tertius."

I had been placing music upon the stand; I paused, book in hand, weighing my next words. "The arpeggios in the Tertius were a challenge to you, if you recall—"

"Do you imply my skill is insufficient?" Glisselda lifted her chin dangerously.

"No. I merely remind you that you called Tertius a 'poxy cankered toad' and threw the music across the room." Here both girls burst out laughing. I added, as gingerly as one stepping onto an unstable bridge, "If you practice and take my advice about the fingerings, you ought to be able to work it up sufficiently well." *Sufficiently well not to embarrass yourself,* I might've added, but it seemed imprudent to do so.

"I want to show Viridius that Tertius played badly is better than his piddling tunes played well," she said, wagging a finger. "Can I attain that level of petty vindictiveness?"

"Undoubtedly," I said, and then wondered whether I should have replied so quickly. Both girls were laughing again, however, so I took it that I was safe.

Glisselda seated herself on the bench, stretched her elegant fingers, and launched into the Tertius. Viridius had once proclaimed her "as musical as a boiled cabbage"—loudly and in front of the entire court—but I'd found her diligent and interested when treated respectfully. We hammered at those arpeggios for more than an hour. Her hands were small—this wouldn't be easy—but she neither complained nor flagged.

My stomach ended the lesson by growling. Trust my very body to be rude!

"We should let your poor teacher go to lunch," said Millie.

"Was that your stomach?" asked the princess brightly. "I'd have sworn there was a dragon in the room. St. Ogdo preserve us, lest she decide to crunch our bones!"

I ran a tongue over my teeth, delaying until I could speak without scolding. "I know deriding dragons is something of a national sport for us Goreddis, but Ardmagar Comonot is coming soon, and I do not think he would be amused by that kind of talk."

Saints' dogs. I *was* prickly, even when I tried not to be. She hadn't been exaggerating.

"Dragons are never amused by anything," said Glisselda, arching an eyebrow.

"But she's right," said Millie. "Rudeness is rudeness, even if unperceived."

Glisselda rolled her eyes. "You know what Lady Corongi would say. We must show them we're superior and put them in their place. Dominate or be dominated. Dragons know no other way."

That sounded to me like an extremely dangerous way to interact with dragons. I hesitated, uncertain whether it would be within bounds for me to correct Lady Corongi, Glisselda's governess, who outranked me in every possible way.

"Why do you think they finally surrendered?" Glisselda said. "It's because they recognized our superiority—militarily, intellectually, morally."

"That's what Lady Corongi says?" I said, alarmed but struggling not to show it.

"That's what everybody says," sniffed Glisselda. "It's obvious. Dragons envy us; that's why they take our shape whenever they can."

I gaped at her, Blue St. Prue, Glisselda was going to be queen someday! She needed to understand the truth of things. "We didn't defeat them, whatever you may have been told. Our dracomachia gave us approximate parity; they couldn't win without taking unacceptable losses. It's not a surrender so much as a truce."

Glisselda wrinkled her nose. "You imply that we haven't dominated them at all."

"We haven't—fortunately!" I said, rising and trying to cover my agitation by rearranging the music on the stand. "They wouldn't stand for it; they'd bide their time until we let our guard down."

Glisselda looked profoundly disturbed. "But if we're weaker than they are . . ."

I leaned against the harpsichord. "It's not about strength or weakness, Princess. Why do you imagine our peoples fought for so long?"

Glisselda put her hands together, as if delivering a little sermon. "Dragons hate us because we are just and favored by the Saints. Evil always seeks to destroy the good that stands against it."

"No." I nearly smacked the harpsichord lid but recalled myself in time, slowing my hand and tapping twice. Nevertheless, the girls stared at me round-eyed in anticipation of my astonishing opinions. I tried to moderate that with a gentle tone. "The dragons wanted these lands back. Goredd, Ninys, and Samsam used to be their hunting ground. Big game ran here—elk, aurochs, felldeer—in herds stretching to the horizon, before our kind moved in and plowed it under."

"That was a very long time ago. Surely they can't still miss it," said Glisselda shrewdly. It would be unwise to make assumptions about her intelligence based on her cherubic face, I noted. Her gaze was as sharp as her cousin Lucian's.

"Our people migrated here two thousand years ago," I said. "That's ten dragon generations. The herds have been extinct for about a thousand, but the dragons do indeed still feel the loss. They are confined to the mountains, where their population dwindles."

"They can't hunt the northern plains?" asked the princess.

"They can and do, but the northern plains are only a third the size of the united Southlands, and they're not empty, either. The dragons compete with barbarian tribes for diminishing herds."

"They can't just eat barbarians?" said Glisselda.

I disliked her supercilious tone but could not say so. I traced the decorative inlay on the instrument lid, channeling my irritation into curlicues, and said: "We humans aren't good eating—too stringy—and we're no fun to hunt because we band together and fight back. My teacher once heard a dragon compare us to cockroaches."

Millie wrinkled her nose, but Glisselda looked at me quizzically. Apparently she'd never even seen a cockroach. I let Millie explain; her description elicited a shriek from the princess, who demanded: "In what manner do we resemble these vermin?"

"Take it from a dragon's perspective: we're everywhere, we can hide easily, we reproduce comparatively quickly, we spoil their hunting, and we smell bad."

The girls scowled. "We do not either smell bad!" said Millie.

"To them we do." This analogy was proving particularly apt, so I took it to its logical conclusion. "Imagine you've got a terrible infestation. What do you do?"

"Kill them!" cried both girls together.

"But what if the roaches were intelligent and worked together, using a roachly dracomachia against us? What if they had a real chance of winning?"

Glisselda squirmed with horror, but Millie said, "Make a truce with them. Let them have certain houses to themselves if they leave the ones we're living in alone."

"We wouldn't mean it, though," said the princess grimly, drumming her fingers on top of the harpsichord. "We'd pretend to make peace, then set their houses on fire."

I laughed; she'd surprised me. "Remind me not to earn your enmity, Princess. But if the cockroaches were dominating us, we wouldn't give in? We'd trick them?"

"Absolutely."

"All right. Can you think of anything—anything at all—that the cockroaches could do to persuade us that we should let them live?"

The girls exchanged a skeptical look. "Cockroaches can only scuttle horridly and spoil your food," said Millie, hugging herself. She'd had experience, I gathered.

Glisselda, however, was thinking hard, the tip of her tongue protruding from her mouth. "What if they held court or built cathedrals or wrote poetry?"

"Would you let them live?"

I grinned. "Too late: you've noticed they're interesting. You understand them when they talk. What if you could become one, for short periods of time?"

They writhed with laughter. I felt they'd understood, but I underscored my point: "Our survival depends not on being superior but on being sufficiently interesting."

"Tell me," said Gisselda, borrowing Millie's embroidered handkerchief to wipe her eyes, "how does a mere assistant music mistress know so much about dragons?"

I met her gaze, clamping down on the tremor in my voice. "My father is the Crown's legal expert on Comonot's Treaty. He used to read it to me as a bedtime story."

That didn't adequately explain my knowledge, I realized, but the girls found the idea so hilarious that they questioned me no further. I smiled along with them, but felt a pang for my poor, sad papa. He'd been so desperate to understand where he stood, legally, for unwittingly marrying a saarantras.

As the saying went, he was neck deep in St. Vitt's spit. We both were. I curtsied and took my leave quickly, lest this Heavenly saliva somehow become apparent to the girls. My own survival required me to counterbalance interesting with invisible.

Five

I t was, as always, a relief to retire to my rooms for the evening. I had practicing to do, a book on Zibou sinus-song I'd been dying to read, and of course a number of questions for my uncle. I seated myself at the spinet first and played a peculiar dissonant chord, my signal to Orma that I needed to talk. "Good evening, Phina," boomed the basso kitten.

"Fruit Bat has started wandering around the garden. I'm concerned that—"

"Stop," said Orma. "Yesterday you were offended when I didn't greet you, but today you leap straight in. I want credit for saying 'Good evening.'"

I laughed. "You're credited. But listen: I'm having a problem."

"I'm sure you are," he said, "but I have a student in five minutes. Is it a five-minute problem?"

"I doubt it." I considered. "Can I come to you at St. Ida's? I'm not comfortable discussing this through the spinet anyway."

"As you wish," he said. "Give me at least an hour, though. This student is particularly incapable."

As I was bundling up, I realized I had done nothing about Basind's blood on my cloak. The dragon's blood had long since dried but was still shiny as ever. I slapped at it, causing a blizzard of little silver flakes. I beat as much of the stain out as I could and swept the gleaming detritus into the fireplace.

I took the Royal Road, which descended in wide, graceful curves. The streets were dark and silent, lit only by a quarter moon, lighted windows, and occasional Speculus lanterns that had been set out early. Down near the river, the air was sweet with woodsmoke and rich with someone's garlicky dinner, then dense with the reek of a backyard cesspit. Or maybe offal—was I near a butcher's?

A figure stepped out of the shadows and into the open street ahead of me. I froze, my heart pounding. It shambled toward me, and the choking odor grew stronger. I coughed at the stench and reached for the little knife I kept sheathed in the hem of my cloak.

The dark figure raised its left hand toward me, palm up as if to beg. It raised a second left hand and said, "Thlu-thlu-thluuu?" A wisp of blue flame played about its beaky mouth as it spoke, illuminating its features for a moment: slick scaly skin, spiky crest like a Zibou iguana, bulging conical eyeholes that swiveled independently of each other.

I exhaled. It was nothing but a panhandling quigutl.

The quigutl were a second species of dragon, much smaller

than the saar. This one was about my height, tall for a quig. The quigutl could not change shape. They lived alongside saar in the mountains, squeezing into the cracks and crevasses of the larger dragons' dens, living on garbage and using their four hands to build intricate, minuscule devices, such as the earrings the saarantrai all wore. Quigs had been included in Comonot's Treaty out of politeness; no one had anticipated that so many would come south, or that they'd find the nooks and crannies—and garbage—of the city so much to their liking.

Quigs couldn't speak Goreddi, having no lips and a tongue like a hollow reed, but most of them understood it. For my part, I understood Quigutl; it was just Mootya with a bad lisp. The creature had said, "Do I thmell cointh, maidy?"

"You should not be begging after dark," I scolded it. "What are you doing out of Quighole? You're not safe on the streets. One of your brother saar was attacked yesterday, in broad daylight."

"Yeth, I thaw the whole thing from the eaveth of a warehouthe," it said, its tubelike tongue flicking out between its teeth and raining sparks down its speckled belly. "You have a friendly thmell, but you're no thaar. I am thurprithed you underthtand me."

"I have a knack for languages," I said. Orma had told me my scales smelled of saar, though not ottrongly. ItU'd said a saarantras would have to put his nose right up to me to smell it. Did the quigutl have more sensitive noses?

It sidled closer and sniffed the dried bloodstain on my shoulder.

The quig's breath was so gut-seizingly foul that I didn't see how it could smell anything subtler. I'd never been able to smell saar, even on Orma. When the quig backed away, I sniffed at the stain myself. I could feel an odor's presence in my nostrils—a sensation more tactile than olfactory—but I could discern nothing else about it.

A sharp pain shot through my head, as if I'd driven spikes up into my sinuses.

"You have two thaar thmells," the creature said. "Altho, a thmall purth containing five thilver and eight copper cointh, and a knife—cheap thteel, rather dull." Even these small dragons were pedantically precise.

"You can smell how sharp my knife is?" I said, pressing the heels of my hands against my temples, as if I might crush the pain. It didn't help.

"I could thmell how many hairs were on your head, if I wished to, which I do not."

"Lovely. Well, I can't just give you coin. I only trade metal for metal," I said, as I'd heard Orma respond to quigutl panhandling. It was not the usual Goreddi response, and nothing I would have attempted with other people watching, but Orma had acquired several odd trinkets for me this way. I kept the eccentric collection out of sight in the little basket. They weren't illegal—they were nothing but toys—but such "demonic devices" might scare the maids.

The quigutl blinked its eyes and licked its lips. The creatures didn't care about money, as such; they wanted metal to work with, and we were all carrying it in convenient, premeasured quantities. Behind the quigutl, half a block up the street, stable doors clattered open. A boy emerged with two lanterns and hung them up on either side in anticipation of riders arriving home. The quig glanced over its shoulder, but the boy was looking the other way.

The quigutl's spiky silhouette stood out against the light, its eye cones extending and retracting as it considered what to trade. It reached into its gullet, down into its extendable throat pouch, and withdrew two objects. "I have only thmall thingth with me: a copper and thilver filigree fish"—the fish dangled between the two thumbs of one right hand—"and thith, which ith mothtly tin, a lizard with a human head."

I squinted in the feeble light from the stable. The man-faced lizard was rather horrible. Suddenly I wanted the thing, as if it were an abandoned grotesque who needed a place to live.

"I would trade two thilver," said the quig, noting where my attention lingered. "That may theem like more than ith worth, but it'th mechanically intricate."

Behind my reptilian companion came the sound of horses. I glanced up, anxious that we would be seen. Quigs had been beaten in this town for harassing human women; I did not care to speculate about what happened to women who treated quigs kindly. The approaching riders stopped at the stable, however, and did not even glance in our direction. Their spurs jingled as their feet hit the paving stones. Each had a dagger tucked into his belt; the steel flashed in the lamplight.

I felt some urgency to send the quig along home and get myself to Orma's. I had assumed the smell of saar blood had caused my sudden headache, but the pain had not yet dissipated. Two headaches on two consecutive days could only be trouble.

I extracted my purse from my sleeve. "I'll trade, but you must assure me that 'mechanically intricate' doesn't mean 'illegal.' " Certain quigutl devices—those that could see, hear, or speak across great distances—could only be carried by saarantraí. Certain others, such as door worms or anything explosive, could be carried by no one.

The creature affected shock. "Nothing illegal! I am a law-abiding—"

"Except for staying put in Quighole after dark," I chided, paying the quig its silver. It tossed the coins into its mouth. I put the lizard figurine in my purse and drew the leather strings tight.

When I looked up again, the quigutl was gone, vanished completely without a sound. The two riders were hurrying toward me, daggers drawn. "St. Daan in a pan!" one cried. "The sticky shite-eater scuttled right up the side of the house!"

"Are you all right, maidy?" asked the other, the shorter of the two, grabbing my upper arm urgently. His breath was tavern-esque.

"Thank you for chasing it off," I said, pulling myself out of his grasp. My head pounded. "It was panhandling. You know how tenacious they can be."

Shorty noticed my purse in my hand. "Aw, cack, you didn't give it any money, did you? That only encourages the vermin."

"Begging worms!" snarled the tall fellow, still scanning the side of the building, dagger held ready. He looked like Shorty's brother, with his identical wide nose. I guessed they were merchants; their well-tailored but sturdy woolen clothing spoke of money mixed with practicality.

Tallfellow spat. "You can't go five blocks without getting hit up."

"You can't go into your own cellar but there's one curled up in a crate of onions," said Shorty, flapping his arms histrionically.

"Our sister Louisa once found one stuck to the underside of her dining room table. It breathed its pestilence all over her Speculus feast and gave her baby the falling sickness. But can her husband defend himself against this invader in his own home? Not without landing in prison!"

I knew of that case. My father had defended the quigutl, but gates went up at the entrances to Quighole, locking its nonhuman denizens in at night—for their own safety, of course. The law-abiding saarantrai scholars at St. Bert's Collegium had objected; my father had represented them too, to no avail. Quighole became more of a hole.

I wished I could have told these brothers that the quigutl meant no harm, that the creatures seemed unable to grasp the difference between *mine* and *yours* when it came to living space, and that pigs smelled just as bad, but no one suspected pigs of harboring malevolent intentions or spreading disease. I could tell the men would not have thanked me for enlightening them.

The brothers glowed, a fierce luminescence just under their skin, as if their innards were molten lead, or if they would burst into flame at any moment.

Oh no. That was the halo, the only warning I got before a vision overtook me. I could do nothing to stop it now. I sat down in the street and curled my head between my knees so that I would not hit it when I fell.

"Are you unwell?" asked Shorty, his voice reaching me in waves, as if he were talking through water.

"Don't let me bite my tongue," I managed to say before I collapsed and all my consciousness whirled down into the vortex of vision.

My invisible vision-eye hovered at the ceiling of a room containing three massive beds and a riot of unpacked luggage. Silk scarves in green, gold, and rose were heaped up in a corner, tangled with iridescent beaded necklaces, feathered fans, and strings of tarnished coins. It was clearly an inn; each of the beds could have held six people.

There was only one person in the room now. I knew him, though he'd grown in the years since my last vision and this time he wasn't up a tree.

A Porphyrian woman stuck her head through the doorway; felted locks as thick as fingers, each tipped with a silver bead, framed her face. She spoke Porphyrian to Fruit Bat, who sat on the center bed with his legs folded and his gaze upon the ceiling. He startled as if she'd broken his concentration. Her eyebrows rose apologetically and she mimed eating something. He shook his head, and she closed the door without a sound.

He stood up, his bare feet sinking into the lumpy straw mattress. He wore Porphyrian trousers and a knee-length tunic, a paedis charm on a cord around his neck, and small gold earrings. He waved his hands slowly through the air as if he were breaking cobwebs overhead. The straw tick didn't have much spring to it, but he leaped as high as he could and touched the ceiling on the third try.

No one in my visions had ever been aware of my presence before. How could they be? I wasn't really there. He could not have touched my face because there was no face for him to touch, but I felt myself trying to recoil from his searching hand.

He frowned and scratched his head carefully. His hair had been arranged into coiled knots all over his scalp, the part lines between sections forming tidy little hexagons. He sat again and stared hard at the ceiling, his brows drawn. If it had not been impossible, I'd have said he was looking right at me.

I awoke with a salty leather glove between my teeth. I opened my eyes to see a woman cradling my head and upper body upon her knees. She held prayer beads in one hand, moving them along rapidly with her thumb, and her mouth moved quickly; my ears were slow to focus, but I heard her say, "St. Fustian and St. Branche, pray for her. St. Ninnian and St. Munn, be at her side. St. Abaster and St. Vitt, defend her—"

I sat bolt upright and yanked the glove out of my mouth, startling the woman. "Excuse me," I croaked before my stomach let loose across the cobblestones.

She held my forehead and handed me a pristine white handkerchief to wipe my mouth with afterward. She called, "Brothers! She's come round!"

Her brothers, Shorty and Tallfellow, emerged from the stable leading a team and a cart with the words *Broadwick Bros. Clothier* painted in black upon the side. The three of them together wrapped me in a fine wool blanket and bundled me into the back. The woman, who I concluded was the sister Shorty had mentioned, hefted her matronly person into the back with me and said, "Where are we taking you, little maid?"

"Castle Orison," I said. I wasn't going to make it to Orma's tonight. Rather belatedly, I remembered to add, "Please?"

She laughed kindly and directed her brothers, who had surely heard me. The cart jostled and swayed. She took my arm and asked whether I was cold. I was not. She spent the rest of the trip instructing me in ways to get stains out of my gown, which I'd soiled by sitting in the filthy street.

It took nearly the whole cart ride for my pulse to slow and my teeth to stop chattering. I could scarcely believe my good fortune, collapsing in front of people who would help me. I could have been lying in an alley, robbed and left for dead.

Louisa was still chattering, but not about stains. ". . . horrid thing! You poor dear. It must have scared you half to death. Silas and Thomas are trying to devise a way to poison the green devils, something you could bury in garbage so's they wouldn't notice. It hasn't been easy. They can eat most anything, can't they, Silas?"

"Milk makes them ill," said the short brother, who had the reins, "but not enough to kill them. Cheese they tolerate well, so it must be the whey. If we concentrate the whey—"

"They won't eat it," I said, my voice creaky from vomiting. "They have such keen noses, they'd be able to avoid it."

"That's why we hide it in garbage," he said, as if I were simple.

I shut my mouth. Anything that could smell how sharp my knife was could smell whey even at the center of a dung heap. But let them try. They would try and fail, and that would be the best possible outcome for everyone.

We reached the barbican, where the palace guard stopped the cart. Louisa helped me climb down. "What do you do here?" she asked, awed. I wasn't noble, clearly, but even a lowly lady's maid carried a certain glamour.

"I'm the assistant music mistress," I said, giving small courtesy. I was still unsteady on my feet.

"Maid Dombegh? You played at the funeral," cried Silas. "Thomas and I were moved to tears!"

I inclined my head graciously, but as I did so I felt a snap in my mind, like a loosed bowstring, and the headache started up again behind my eyes. My evening's excitement was not yet over, apparently. I turned to go inside.

A powerful hand on my arm stopped me. It was Thomas. Behind him, Silas and Louisa chatted at the guards, asking them to mention the Broadwick brothers, purveyors of sturdy woolens, to the Queen. Thomas drew me a little aside and whispered in my ear: "Silas left me to watch you while he fetched Louisa. I saw the quig idol in your purse."

My face burned. I was ashamed against all reason, as if I were the guilty party and not the person who'd been pawing through an unconscious woman's belongings.

His fingers dug into my arm. "I've met women like you. Worm-riding quig lovers. You don't know how close you came to hitting your head during your fit."

He couldn't mean what I thought he meant. I met his eye; his gaze was a shock of cold.

"Women like you disappear in this town," he snarled. "Tied in sacks, thrown in the river. No one calls for justice because they get what they deserve. But my brother-in-law can't kill a filthy quig in his own home without—"

"Thomas! We're going," called Louisa behind us.

"St. Ogdo calls you to repent, Maid Dombegh." He released me roughly. "Pray for virtue, and pray we don't meet again." He stalked off toward his siblings.

I swayed, barely able to keep my feet.

I had thought them kind, despite their prejudices, but Thomas had been tempted to dash my head against the cobblestones, just for carrying a quigutl figurine. That specific statuette didn't carry some deeper meaning, did it? Had I inadvertently chosen the one that indicated I indulged in some particular perversion? Maybe Orma would know.

I staggered through the gatehouse, making for the palace as best I could with my knees trembling so violently. The guards asked whether I needed help—I must have looked terrible—but I waved them off. I thanked every Saint I could think of and prayed that the glow upon the castle's turrets came from torchlight and the moon and not from another imminent collapse.

Six

Sick and exhausted though I was, I could not put off dealing with Fruit Bat. I hauled my bolster onto the floor, threw myself down, and tried to enter the garden. It took several minutes before my teeth unclenched and I relaxed enough to envision the place.

Fruit Bat was up a tree in his grove. I prowled around the trunk, picking my way over gnarled roots. He appeared to be asleep; he also looked about ten or eleven years old and had his hair in knots, just as he had in the vision. My mind had apparently updated his grotesque to conform to new information.

I gazed up at his face and felt a pang of sadness. I didn't want to lock him away, but I saw no alternative. Visions were dangerous; I could hit my head, suffocate, give myself away. I had to defend myself however I could.

One of his eyes opened, then squeezed quickly shut. He wasn't sleeping, the rascal; he wanted me to think he was. "Fruit Bat," I said, trying to sound stern and not afraid. "Come down, please."

He climbed down, his eyes averted sheepishly. He stooped, picked up a handful of dates from one of his tidy piles, and offered me the fruit. I accepted his gift this time, taking care not to touch his hand. "I don't know what you did," I said slowly. "I'm not sure if it was deliberate, but you . . . I think you pulled me into a vision."

He met my gaze then. The keenness of his black eyes frightened me, but there was no malice there. I gathered my courage and said, "Whatever you did, please stop. When a vision comes upon me against my will, I collapse. It puts me in danger. Please don't do it again, or I will have to shut you out."

His eyes widened and he shook his head vigorously. I hoped he was protesting the possibility of being ejected from the garden and not refusing to comply.

He climbed back into the fig tree. "Good night," I said, hoping he knew I wasn't angry. He wrapped his arms around himself and went straight to sleep.

I had an entire garden that needed tending. I stared toward the other end, feeling weary in my very soul and reluctant to get started. Surely I could skip the rest this once? Everything else looked peaceful; the deep green foliage was so pretty with colorful snow falling all around it.

Colorful snow?

I scrutinized the sky. Clouds clustered thickly above me, and from them fluttered thousands of peculiar flakes, rose, green, yellow, more like confetti than snow. I reached out my hands to touch them; they lit upon me, shimmering and ethereal. I twirled in a slow circle, stirring up eddies at my feet.

I caught one on my tongue. It crackled in my mouth like a tiny lightning storm, and for a single heartbeat I was screaming through the sky, diving after an aurochs.

The flake dissolved completely, and I was back to myself in the garden, my heart pounding. In that brief, intense instant I'd been someone else. I had seen the entire world spread below me in unfathomable detail: every blade of grass on the plain and bristle on the aurochs's snout, the temperature of the ground beneath its hooves, the moving currents of the very air.

I tasted another flake, and for the span of a wink I lay upon a mountaintop in full sun. My scales shimmered; my mouth tasted of ash. I raised my serpentine neck.

And then I was back at Fruit Bat's grove, blinking and stammering and shocked. These were memories from my mother, like the one I'd experienced when I first saw Orma in his natural form. I knew from that memory that my mother had tried to leave me others. She had apparently succeeded.

Why was this happening now? Had the stresses of the last two days triggered another round of changes? Could Fruit Bat have dislodged them somehow?

The precipitation slowed. On the ground, individual flakes flowed toward each other and fused together, like scattered droplets of quicksilver. They flattened out into scraps of parchment and blew around.

I could not have my mother's memories scattered all over my head: if I had learned anything from experience, it was that my peculiarities tended to spring out at me unannounced. I gathered up the slips of parchment, stamping on them as they skittered past, chasing them through Pandowdy's swamp and across the Three Dunes.

I needed something to keep them in; a tin box appeared. I opened it, and the parchments—without any prompting on my part—flew up out of my hand, like a trick shuffle of cards, and filed themselves in the box. The lid clanged shut after them.

That had been suspiciously easy. I peeked in the box; the memories stood like note cards, each labeled across the top in an odd, angular hand I took to be my mother's. I leafed through them; they appeared to have ordered themselves chronologically. I pulled one out. It read *Orma gets toasted on his 59th hatch-day* across the top, but the rest of the page was blank. The title intrigued me, but I put it back.

Some cards toward the back were brightly colored. I pulled up a pink one and was dumbfounded to see it wasn't blank; it had one of my mother's songs, in her spidery notation. I knew the song already—I knew all her songs—but it was bittersweet to see it in her own hand.

The title was "My Faith Should Not Come Easily." I could not resist; surely this was her memory of writing that song. The flakes had dissolved upon my tongue; I guessed the same principle applied. The page crackled and sparked in my mouth, like a wool blanket on a winter night. It tasted, absurdly, of strawberries.

My hands dart over the page, a slender brush in each, one for the dots, one for the strokes and arcs, winding in and around each other as if I were making bobbin lace, not writing music. The effect is calligraphic, and highly satisfying. Outside my open window a lark sings, and my left hand—always the more mischievous of the two—takes a moment to jot down the notes in counterpoint to the main melody (with but a little alteration of the rhythm). That is serendipitous. So many things are, when we bother to look.

I know his tread, know it like my own pulse—better, perhaps, because my pulse has been doing unaccountable things recently in response to that footfall. Right now it beats seven against his three. That is too fast. Dr. Caramus was unconcerned when I told him; he did not believe me when I said I did not understand it.

I am on my feet, not knowing how, almost before the knock sounds at my door. My hands are inky, and my voice unreliable as I cry, "Come in!"

Claude lets himself in, his face that shade of sulky that it turns when he is trying not to get his hopes up. I snatch up a rag to wipe my hands and cover my confusion. Is this funny or frightening? I had no idea the two could be so close.

"I heard you wanted to see me," he mumbles.

"Yes. I'm sorry, I . . . I should have answered your letters. I have had to think very carefully on this."

"On whether you would help me write these songs?" he says, and there is something childish in his voice. Petulant. Which is irritating, on the one hand, and endearing on the other. He is transparently simple, this one, and unexpectedly complicated. And radiantly beautiful.

I hand him the page and watch his face soften into wonder. My hands go straight to my chest, as if they could squeeze my heart and slow it. He hands the song back to me and his voice quavers: "Would you sing it?"

I would rather play it for him on flute, but he clearly wishes to hear the words and tune together:

"My faith should not come easily;
There is no Heaven without pain.
My days should never flutter past
Unnoted, nor my past remain
Beyond its span of usefulness;
Let me not hold to grief,
My hope, my light, my Saint is love;
In love my one belief."

He stares at me during the last lines and I fear my voice will falter. As it is, I have barely enough breath left in me for "belief." I inhale, but the air seems to catch on its way in, like the shudder of breath after tears.

This emotion is maddening in its complexity. It's like spotting difficult prey on the ground after a long day of fruitless hunting—there's the exhilaration of an exciting chase mixed with the fear that it may all end in nothing, but there is never any question that you will try, for your very existence hangs on it. I am reminded also of the first time I dove from a sea cliff, keeping my wings folded until the last possible second, then scudding over the cresting waves, just out of reach of their foamy fingers, laughing at the danger, terrified by how close I had come.

"I'm so glad you're here," I say. "I understand now that I made you very sad. That was never my intention."

Claude rubs the back of his neck and wrinkles his nose, about to tell me he was never sad. I believe this is called bravado and is not limited to lawyers, or even men, although that combination makes it almost unavoidable. Normally I would shrug at this, but today I need him to be truthful. Today is the beginning and the end. I reach across and take his hand.

That jolt we both feel—for I see it hit him too—is like electricity, but that is a metaphor I will never be able to give him, a concept that cannot be introduced. One of far too many, alas, but I am hoping—no, gambling, betting my very life—that in the end it will not matter, that this, this thing between us, this mystery, will be enough.

"Linn," he says hoarsely, his jaw quivering just a little. He is frightened, too. Why should this be frightening? What purpose does that serve? "Linn," he begins again, "when I believed you never wanted to see me again, I felt I'd stepped off a ledge and onto empty air: the ground was hurtling toward me at an alarming rate."

Metaphor is awkward, but emotion, by its nature, leaves you no more scalable approach. I have not adequately mastered the art, but his comparisons always move me with their precision. I want to cry Eureka!, but I settle for "I felt that too! That's it exactly!"

My other hand wants to touch his face, and I let it. He leans into it like a cat.

And that is when I know that I will kiss him, and the very thought of it fills me with . . . well, it's as if I have just solved Skivver's predic- tive equations or, even sooner, as if I have treated the One Equation, seen the numbers behind the moon and stars, behind mountains and history, art and death and yearning, as if my comprehension is large enough that it can encompass universes, from the beginning to the end of time.

And I have to laugh a little at this conceit, because I do not even *understand the present, and there is nothing in the world beyond this kiss.*

The memory ended, ejecting me not into the garden but into real life: cold, hard floor; rumpled chemise; bitter taste in my mouth; alone. I was woozy, disoriented, and . . . and ick. That was my father she'd been kissing.

I leaned my head back against the bed, breathing slowly, trying to fend off an emotion so terrible I couldn't bring myself to look at it.

For five years I had suppressed every thought of her. The Amaline Ducanahan of my childhood imaginings had been replaced by emptiness, a chasm, a gap the wind blew through. I couldn't fill that space with Linn. That name meant nothing to me; it was a placeholder, like zero.

With this single memory, I'd increased my knowledge of her a thousandfold. I knew how a pen felt in her hand, how fast her heart beat upon seeing my father, how beautiful sounds moved her. I knew what she'd felt; I'd been her and felt it myself.

That depth of insight should have fostered empathy, surely. I should have felt some connection, some joy at discovering her, some warm, glowy resolution or peace or something. Something good, at least. Surely it didn't matter which flavor of good?

She was my own mother, for Heaven's sake!

But I felt nothing of the kind. I glimpsed the emotion from afar, saw how bad it was going to be, and squelched it so that I felt nothing at all.

I hauled myself to standing and staggered into the other room.

My little timepiece read two hours past midnight, but I didn't care whether I woke Orma up. He'd earned a bad night's sleep. I played our chord and then played it again a bit more peevishly.

Orma's voice crackled forth, unexpectedly loudly: "I wondered whether I'd hear from you. Why didn't you come into town?"

I struggled to keep my voice under control. "You weren't worried, I suppose."

"Worried about what, specifically?"

"One of my grotesques was behaving strangely. I intended to cross town in the dark, but I never made it. It didn't occur to you that something might have happened?"

There was a pause while he considered. "No. I suppose you're going to tell me something did."

I wiped my eyes. I had no energy to argue. I told him all that had happened: Fruit Bat's strange behavior, the vision, the maternal memories. He stayed silent so long after I finished talking that I tapped at the kitten eye. "I'm here," he said. "It is fortunate that nothing worse happened to you when the vision struck."

"Do you have any ideas about Fruit Bat's behavior?" I said.

"He seems to be aware of you," said Orma, "but I don't understand why that would have changed over time. Jannoula saw you right from the beginning."

"And she grew so strong and perceptive that it was hard to get rid of her," I said. "It might be safer to shut Fruit Bat away now, while I still can."

"No, no," said Orma. "If he complies with your requests, he might be a resource rather than a threat. There are so many questions still unanswered. Why are you seeing him? How does he see you? Don't squander this opportunity. You can induce visions: go looking for him."

I ran my fingers over the spinet keys. That last suggestion was a bit much, but cutting Fruit Bat off completely didn't feel right either.

"Maybe he'll find a way to speak to you eventually," Orma was saying.

"Or maybe I'll travel to Porphyry someday, track him down, and shake his hand," I said, smiling slightly. "Not until after Ardmagar Comonot's visit, though. I'll be too busy beforehand. Viridius is a terrible taskmaster."

"That's an excellent idea," said Orma, apparently thinking me serious. "I might come with you. The Porphyrian Bibliagathon is supposed to be well worth seeing."

I grinned at his library obsession and was still grinning when I crawled into bed. I couldn't sleep; in my mind I was already traveling with my uncle, meeting Fruit Bat in the real world, and getting some answers at last.

Seven

Between staying up late and rising early for my morning routine, I got far too little sleep. I stumbled stoically through my duties, but Viridius noticed me struggling. "I'll clean your pens," he said, taking the quill from my unresisting hand. "You are to lie down on my couch and nap for half an hour."

"Master, I assure you I'm—" A gargantuan yawn undermined my argument.

"Of course you are. But we must have you at full capacity for the Blue Salon this evening, and I don't feel convinced that you've been listening quite carefully enough to my dictation." He scanned the parchment where I'd been writing down his compositional ideas as he hummed them. His brows lowered and he turned slightly purple. "You've jotted it down in three. It's a gavotte. Dancers are going to be falling all over each other."

I intended to answer him, but I'd already reached the couch. It pulled me under, and my explanation turned into a dream about St. Polypous dancing a 3/4 gavotte with perfect ease. But then, he had three feet.

That evening I arrived at the Blue Salon early, hoping I might pay my respects, meet Viridius's protégé, and leave before most people had even arrived. I saw my mistake at once: Viridius wasn't there yet. Of course he wasn't; he would likely come late, the old coxcomb. I would get no credit for coming if I ducked out before he arrived. All I'd done was given myself extra time to feel uncomfortable.

I'd always been useless at parties, even before I knew how much I had to hide. Large groups of semi-strangers made me clam right up. I anticipated standing alone in a corner shoving butter tarts in my mouth all evening.

Even Glisselda wasn't there yet; that was how stupidly early I'd come. Servants lit chandeliers and smoothed tablecloths onto sideboards, stealing surreptitious glances at me. I wandered toward the back of the salon, past the upholstered chairs of the formal sitting area, past the gilded columns, into a wide space with a parquet floor intended for dancing. Music stands and stools were piled haphazardly in the corner; I set them up for a quartet, hoping I was doing something useful and not merely eccentric.

Five musicians arrived—Guntard, two viols, uillean pipes, and drum—and I set a fifth place. They seemed pleased to see me, and not altogether surprised that the assistant music mistress should be here, setting up. Maybe I could stand in their corner all evening, turning pages and bringing them ale.

Wine, that is. This was the palace, not the Sunny Monkey.

Courtiers trickled in, resplendent in silks and brocade. I'd worn my best gown, a deep blue calamanco with understated embroidery at all the hemlines, but what passed for finery in town felt shabby here. I pressed myself against a wall and hoped no one would speak to me. I knew some of these courtiers: the palace employed professional musicians such as Guntard and the band, but many young gentlemen liked to dabble in music on the side. They usually joined the choir, but that fair-haired Samsamese across from me played a mean viola da gamba.

His name was Josef, Earl of Apsig. He noticed my eyes upon him and ran a hand through his wheaten hair as if to underscore how handsome he was. I looked away.

The Samsamese were known for austerity, but even they outshone me here. Their merchants dressed in browns in town; their courtiers wore expensive blacks, contriving to be simultaneously sumptuous and severe. In case we Goreddis failed to recognize expensive cloth on sight, the Samsamese also spouted great tufts of lace from their cuffs, and stiff white ruffs at their throats.

The Ninysh courtiers, by contrast, tried to incorporate every possible color in their outfits: embroidery, ribbons, parti-colored hose, bright silk peeking through the slashes in their sleeves. Their country lay deep in the gloomy south; there were few colors to be seen there, beyond what they carried with them.

I glimpsed a Ninysh gabled cap in a vibrant green, worn by an elderly woman. She had thick spectacles, which gave her eyes a peevish, bulgy aspect; the heavy creases beside her wide mouth created the impression of an enormous, disapproving toad.

She looked like Miss Fusspots, poor old darling.

No, that was unquestionably Miss Fusspots. That glare could belong to no one else. My heart caught in my throat. I wouldn't need to travel to Porphyry after all; one of my grotesques was standing right across the room!

Miss Fusspots, who was diminutive, disappeared behind a grove of ladies-in-waiting but reemerged moments later beside a redheaded Ninysh courtier. I began to work my way across the room toward her.

I didn't get far, however, because at that very moment Princess Glisselda and Prince Lucian arrived, arm in arm. The crowd opened a wide corridor to let them pass, and I dared not cross it. The princess gleamed in gold and white, brocade encrusted with seed pearls; she beamed beatifically at the entire room and let a Ninysh courtier lead her to a seat. Prince Lucian, in the scarlet doublet of the Queen's Guard, did not relax until the crowd's adoring gaze had followed his cousin to the other end of the room.

Princess Glisselda took the midnight blue couch, where no one else had dared to sit, and began chatting away to all and sundry. Lucian Kiggs did not sit, but stood a little to the side, his eye upon the room; he never seemed to go off duty. In the adjoining chamber, the musicians finally began with a pleasant sarabande. I looked for Miss Fusspots, but she had disappeared.

"Others may doubt it was a dragon. I do not," said someone behind me in a light Samsamese monotone.

"Ooh, how awful!" said a young woman.

I turned to see Josef, Earl of Apsig, regaling three Goreddi ladies-in-waiting with a tale: "I was part of his final hunting party, *grausleine*. We had just entered the Queenswood when the hounds scattered in all directions, as if there were twenty stags, not just one. We split up, some following north, some west, each group thinking Prince Rufus was with the other, but when we rejoined, he was nowhere to be found.

"We searched for him until evening, then called out the Queen's Guard and searched all through the night. It was his own dog—a lovely brindle snaphound called Una—who found him, lying faceless and facedown in the nearby fens."

The three ladies gasped. I had turned all the way around and was studying the earl's face. He had pale blue eyes; his complexion was without a single blemish or wrinkle by which to gauge his age. He was trying to impress the ladies, certainly, but seemed to be speaking the truth. I disliked jumping in where I hadn't been invited, but I had to know: "Are you so sure a dragon killed him? Were there clear signs in the fen?"

Josef turned the full force of his handsomeness on me. He lifted his chin and smiled like a Saint in a country church, all piety and graciousness; around him the choir of cherubic ladies-in-waiting stared at me and fluttered, silk gowns rustling. "Who else do you imagine could have killed him, Music Mistress?"

I folded my arms, proof against charm. "Brigands, stealing his head for ransom?"

"There's been no ransom request." He smirked; his cherubs smirked with him.

"The Sons of St. Ogdo, stirring up dracophobia before the Ardmagar arrives?"

He threw back his head and laughed; he had very white teeth. "Come, Seraphina, you've omitted the possibility that he spotted a lovely shepherdess and simply lost his head." The heavenly host rewarded this comment with a symphony of titters.

I was about to turn away—he knew nothing, clearly—when a familiar baritone chimed in behind me: "Maid Dombegh is right. It's likely the Sons did it."

I stepped a little aside, letting Prince Lucian face Josef unimpeded.

Josef's smile thinned. Prince Lucian hadn't acknowledged the disrespectful innuendo about his uncle Rufus, but he'd surely heard every word. The earl gave exaggerated courtesy. "Begging your pardon, Prince, but why do you not round up the Sons and lock them away, if you're so sure they did it?"

"We'll arrest no one without proof," said the prince, seeming unconcerned. His left boot gave three rapid taps; I noticed and wondered whether I had such unconscious tics. The prince continued, his tone still light: "Unfounded arrests would give the Sons more fodder and bring new ones out of the woodwork. Besides, it's wrong in principle. 'Let the one who seeks justice be just.'"

I looked over at him then, because I recognized that quote.

"Pontheus?"

"The same." Prince Lucian nodded approvingly.

Josef sneered. "With all due respect, the Regent of Samsam would never permit a mad Porphyrian philosopher to guide his decisions. Nor would he permit dragons to make a state visit to Samsam—no offense to your Queen, of course."

"Perhaps that is why the Regent of Samsam was not the architect of peace," said the prince, voice calm, foot tapping. "Apparently he has no qualms about receiving the benefits of our mad-Porphyrian-inspired treaty without having to shoulder any of the risks himself. He'll be here for this state visit, more's the headache for me—and I mean that with all the love and respect in the world."

As fascinating as this polite, courtly aggression was, suddenly Miss Fusspots arrested my gaze from across the adjoining room. She accepted a glass of tawny port from a page boy. I could not get to her without ducking through the dancing, and they'd just started a volta, so there was a great number of flying limbs. I stayed where I was, but did not take my eye off her.

A trumpet flare brought the exuberant dance to an inelegant halt; the band choked off abruptly, and there were several collisions on the dance floor. I did not take my eyes off Miss Fusspots to see what all the bother was, which resulted in my standing all alone in the wide path that had once again opened up.

Prince Lucian grabbed my arm—my right—and hauled me out of the way.

Queen Lavonda herself stood in the doorway. Her face was creased with age but her back was unbent; she had a spine of steel, they said, and her posture confirmed it. She still wore white for her son, from her silk slippers to her wimple and embroidered cap. Her sumptuous sleeves trailed the floor.

Glisselda sprang up off her couch and curtsied deeply. "Grand-mamma! You honor us!"

"I'm not staying, Selda, and I'm not here for myself," said the Queen. She had the same voice as her granddaughter, but aged and edged with command. "I have brought you some additional guests," she said, ushering in a group of four saarantrai, Eskar among them. They stood stiffly, as if in military formation. They had not bothered to dress up particularly; their bells were not quite shiny enough to be proper jewelry. Eskar was in Porphyrian trousers again. Everyone stared.

"Oh!" squeaked Glisselda. She curtsied again, trying to re-cover her composure; her eyes were still large when she rose. "To what do we owe this, um—"

"To a treaty signed nearly forty years ago," said the Queen, who seemed to grow taller as she addressed the entire room. "I believed, perhaps erroneously, that our peoples would simply grow accustomed to each other, given the cessation of warfare. Are we oil and water, that we cannot mix? Have I been remiss in expect-ing reason and decency to prevail, when I should have rolled up my sleeves and enforced them?"

The humans in the room looked sheepish; the dragons, dis-comfited.

"Glisselda, see to your guests!" the Queen snapped, and quit the room.

Glisselda quailed visibly. Beside me, Prince Lucian fidgeted and muttered, "Come on, Selda." She could not have heard him, but she lifted her chin as if she had, trying to capture her grand-mother's authoritative air. She strode toward Eskar and kissed her on both her cheeks. The little princess had to rise up on her toes to reach. Eskar submitted graciously, inclining her head, and everyone applauded.

Then the soiree resumed, the saarantrai together on one side like a herd of spooked cattle, their bells jingling plaintively, and the other guests milling around them in a wide radius.

I kept my distance, too. Eskar knew me, but I did not care to risk the others smelling me. I wasn't sure what they would do. I might be taken for a scholar with a bell exemption, or Eskar might tactlessly proclaim my parentage aloud, to be overheard by the whole room.

Surely she wouldn't. Orma had told me that interbreeding violated ard so egregiously that no dragon would entertain the idea that I was possible, let alone utter it aloud.

"I dare you to ask her to dance," said a gentleman behind me, snapping me out of my preoccupations. For a moment I thought he meant me.

"Which one?" intoned the omnipresent Earl of Apsig.

"Your choice," laughed his friend.

"No, I mean which one is a 'her'? They're so mannish, these dragon females."

I bristled at that, but why? They weren't talking about me—except that, in some oblique way, they were.

"The real difficulty with these worm-women," said Josef, "is their extremely inconvenient dentition."

"Dentition?" asked his friend, who was apparently slow on the uptake.

I felt my face grow hot.

"Teeth," said Josef, spelling it out. "In all the wrong places, if you follow me."

"Teeth in . . . Oh! Ow!"

"'Ow' is understating it, friend. Their males are no better. Picture a harpoon! And they'd like nothing better than to impale our women and rip out their—"

I could take no more; I rushed away, skirting the dance floor, until I found a window. I unlatched it with trembling hands, desperate for air. Eyes closed, I pictured the tranquility of my garden, until my embarrassment had been replaced by sorrow.

It was just a joke between gentlemen, but I heard in it all the jokes they would tell about me if they knew.

Damn Viridius. I couldn't stay. I would tell him tomorrow that I had been here; there were witnesses. As the patron Saints of comedy would have it, however, I met the old man in the doorway on my way out. He blocked my path with his cane. "You can't be leaving already, Seraphina!" he cried. "It's not even ten!"

"I'm sorry sir, I—" My voice choked up; I gestured hopelessly at the gathering, hoping he would not perceive the tears in my eyes.

"Lars wouldn't come either. He's as shy as you are," said Viridius, his voice uncharacteristically gentle. "Have you paid your respects to the princess and prince? No? Well, you must do that at least." He took my right arm with his bandaged hand, leaning on his cane with the other.

He guided me toward Princess Glisselda's couch. She glittered like a star upon the blue upholstery; courtiers orbited her like planets. We waited our turn, and then Viridius pulled me for-

104

ward. "Infanta," he said, bowing. "This charming young person has a great deal of work to do—for me—but I let her know, in no uncertain terms, how inexcusably rude it would be to leave without paying her respects."

Glisselda beamed at me. "You came! Millie and I had a wager on whether you ever would. I owe her an extra day off now, but I'm glad of it. Have you met cousin Lucian?"

I opened my mouth to assure her I had, but she was already calling the prince to her side. "Lucian! You were wondering how it was that I suddenly held such interesting opinions on dragons—well, here she is, my advisor on dragon affairs!"

The prince looked tense. My first assumption was that he was offended, that I'd been rude without even noticing, but then I saw him glancing over at Eskar and her little group, standing uselessly in a nearby corner. Perhaps he felt uneasy about the princess discussing "dragon affairs" so loudly within earshot of the real, live dragons she pretended not to see.

Princess Glisselda looked puzzled by the awkwardness in the air, as if it were a smell she had never encountered before. I looked to Prince Lucian, but he stared fixedly elsewhere. Did I dare to point out what he did not?

It was fear that permitted the Thomas Broadwicks of the world to flourish, fear of speaking up, fear of the dragons themselves. The latter didn't apply to me, and surely conscience must trump the former.

I could speak for Orma's sake.

I said, "Your Highness, please pardon my forwardness." I gestured toward the saarantrai with my eyes. "It would suit your kindly nature to invite the saarantrai to sit by you, or even if you danced a measure with one."

Glisselda froze. Theoretical discussion about dragonkind was one thing; interacting with them was something else entirely. She cast her cousin a panicked look.

"She's right, Selda," he said. "The court follows our lead."

"I know!" fretted the princess. "But what am I . . . how am I to . . . I can't just—"

"You must," said Prince Lucian firmly. "Ardmagar Comonot arrives in eight days, and what then? We can't shame Grandmother." He tugged the ends of his doublet sleeves, straightening them. "I'll go first, if it's easier."

"Oh yes, thank you, Lucian, of course it's easier," she gushed, relieved. "He's so much better at these kinds of things than I am, Phina. This is why marrying him will be so useful; he understands practical things and common people. He's a bastard, after all."

I was awed, at first, that she could call her own fiancé a bastard so casually without him minding, but then I saw his eyes. He minded. He minded a great deal, but maybe felt he had no right to say so.

I knew what that was like. I permitted myself the smallest of small feelings. Sympathy. Yes. That's what it was.

He gathered his dignity, which was considerable; as a military man, he knew how to carry himself. He approached Eskar as one might sensibly approach a flaming, hissing hell-beast: with a wary calmness and extreme self-possession. All around the room conversations trailed off or were suspended as heads turned toward the prince. I found myself holding my breath; I surely wasn't the only one.

He bowed graciously. "Madam Undersecretary," he said, perfectly audible across the hushed room, "would you join me in a galliard?"

Eskar scanned the crowd as if seeking out the author of this prank but said, "I believe I shall." She took his arm; her Zibou caftan was a riotous fuchsia next to his scarlet. Everyone exhaled.

I stayed a few minutes longer to watch them dance, smiling to myself. It could be done, this peace. It just took a willingness to do it. I silently thanked Prince Lucian for his determination. I caught Viridius's eye across the room; he seemed to understand and waved a dismissal. I turned to quit the salon, happy that I'd helped effect some positive good, but mostly relieved to be leaving the crowd and chatter behind. Anxiety—or the prospect of being free of it—propelled me toward the door like a bubble toward the surface of a lake. The hallway promised me room to breathe.

I rushed into the corridor with such haste that I all but ran into Lady Corongi, Princess Glisselda's governess.

Eight

Lady Corongi was a petite woman, old and old-fashioned. Her wimple was severely starched and her butterfly veil—a decade out of favor among the fashionable—was wired so rigidly that she might have put out someone's eye with it. Her sleeves covered her hands completely, which made eating or writing a challenge, but she was of an antique school that equated fine manners with elaborate rituals. Clothing that impeded basic functioning presumably gave her more opportunities for fastidious fussing.

She stared at me in shock, her eyes goggling behind her veil, her painted lips drawn up into a prim and disapproving rosebud. She said not a word; it was up to me to apologize since I was clearly the one with no manners.

I curtsied so low I nearly lost my balance. She rolled her eyes at my wobbling. "I humbly beg your pardon, milady," I said.

"It astonishes me that a bungling monkey such as yourself is permitted to careen so freely up the corridors," she sniffed. "Have you no keeper? No leash?"

I had hoped to speak with her about the princess's education. Seeing Glisselda so cowed by real, live saarantrai had only increased my impetus to speak, but now I felt cowed myself.

Lady Corongi curled her lip into a sneer and brushed past me, bumping me out of the way with a sharp elbow to the ribs. She only went two steps further before turning abruptly. "What did you say your name was, maidy?"

I dove into a hasty curtsy. "Seraphina, milady. I teach Princess Glisselda—"

"Harpsichord. Yes, she's mentioned you. She said you were smart." She stepped back in front of me, lifted her veil so she could see me more clearly, and scrutinized my face with sharp blue eyes. "Is that why you fill her head with nonsense about dragons? Because you're so very smart?"

Here was the thing I had wanted to discuss, without my having to steer the conversation at all. I tried to reassure her: "It's not a question of being smart, milady. It's a question of exposure. My father, as you may know, is the Crown's expert on Comonot's Treaty. I myself had a dragon tutor for many years. I have some insight—"

"That dragons consider us mere insects? That's an insight?" She stood close enough that I could see her makeup condensing in the creases of her face and smell her cloying Ninysh perfume. "I am trying to give the second her confidence, to make her proud of her people and their victory over dragonkind."

"It's not confidence; it's contempt," I said, warming to my

argument. "You should have seen her alarm earlier at merely speaking with saarantrai. She's disgusted and frightened. She's going to be Queen someday; she can afford to be neither."

Lady Corongi made a ring of her thumb and forefinger and pressed it to her heart: St. Ogdo's sign. "When she is Queen, Heaven willing, we will finish this conflict the way we should have finished it, instead of treating like cowards."

She turned on her heel and stalked into the Blue Salon.

My encounter with Lady Corongi left me agitated in the extreme. I returned to my rooms, practiced spinet and oud to calm myself, and crawled into bed many hours later, still not tired.

I needed to tend my garden, of course, but I could do that lying down. Half the grotesques were already asleep when I reached them. Even Fruit Bat was lolling about dreamily. I tiptoed past and let him be.

When I reached the Rose Garden, I stared a long time at Miss Fusspots shooting aphids off the leaves with a very small crossbow. I had forgotten all about seeing her at the soiree, but some deeper part of my mind had not. Her dress was changed to the green velvet she had worn this evening. In fact, her entire person seemed sharper and more present, stouter and more solid. Was that proof that I'd really seen her, or merely that I believed I had?

If I took her hands right now, what would I see? If she was still at the Blue Salon, I would recognize it instantly. I felt a twinge of guilt about deliberately spying on her, but curiosity overruled it. I had to know.

Miss Fusspots gave me her hands without any fuss. Entering the vision felt like being sucked down a drain and spit out into the world.

The dimly lit room below my vision-eye was not the Blue Salon, which perplexed me only for a moment. It had been hours; she might have gone home. I was peering down into a tidy boudoir: heavy carven furniture in an older style, curtained bed (empty), bookshelves, peculiar bit of statuary, all of it lit only by the hearth. It didn't look like a palace room, but perhaps she had a house in town.

Where was she, though?

"Who's there?" she said abruptly, nearly startling me out of the vision altogether.

The shape I had mistaken for statuary moved, was moving, slowly, one arm raised, feeling around in the empty air as if she were blind, or as if she were looking for something invisible.

"I don't know who you are," snarled the old woman below me, "but you have two choices: identify yourself, or wait for me to find you. You don't want the latter. I don't care if it's the middle of the night. I will come straight to you, and I will make you sorry."

I was still having trouble recognizing her. I blamed the firelight, but it wasn't just the poor illumination. She looked different. She was unclothed and far skinnier than she appeared with her gown on. In fact, she looked almost boyish. Was her portly bosom all made up of padding? I'd caught her in the middle of getting ready for bed, clearly, and while I was utterly embarrassed, I couldn't seem to blink or turn away. One would think such a high lady, even one with fictitious breasts, would have servants to undress her.

Then I saw why not, and the shock of it threw me straight out of the vision and back to myself.

I felt like I'd fallen into my own bed from a considerable height; I was dizzy and disoriented and agog with what I'd seen.

She had a tail, a stubby one, shingled over entirely with silver scales.

Scales just like mine.

I pulled the covers over my head and lay there shivering, horrified by what I had seen, doubly horrified at my own horror, and absurdly excited by the implications.

She was a half-dragon. Surely there was no other way to interpret those scales.

I was not the only one of my kind! If Miss Fusspots was half dragon, could that mean that the rest of my grotesques were as well? Suddenly all the horns and wattles and vestigial wings in my garden made sense. I'd gotten off lightly with nothing but visions, scales, and the occasional blizzard of maternal memory.

I was still awake an hour later when there came a pounding at my door.

"Open this door at once, or I shall fetch the steward to open it for me!"

Miss Fusspot's voice was perfectly recognizable through the door. I rose and crossed through my parlor, preparing an explanation. Fruit Bat had sensed my presence, but no one else in a vision ever had. What had changed? Seeing her in the real world? Being so near? If I had known she would detect me, I never would have looked in on her like that.

There was nothing to do but apologize. I opened the door, prepared to do just that.

She hit me right in the face, with a bloom of stars and a burst of pain.

I staggered back, dimly aware that my nose was gushing. Miss Fusspots stood in the doorway, brandishing an enormous book—her weapon of choice—breathing hard, a maniacal glint in her eye.

She paled when she saw me bleeding, which I mistook for a sign of impending mercy. "How did you do that?" she snarled through clenched teeth, stepping up and kicking me in the shin. She swatted at my head again, but I managed to duck; her arm left an incongruous waft of lilac perfume in its wake. "Why are you spying on me?"

"Nggblaah!" I said, not my most cogent explanation, but I was unaccustomed to speaking with my face covered in blood.

She stopped kicking me and closed the door. For a moment I feared that meant she intended something worse, but she wet a cloth at the basin and handed it to me, gesturing at my nose. She seated herself on the upper bunk while I cleaned up, her tousled mouth worked up and down, from disgust to annoyance to amusement and back. She was dressed now, of course, her figure back to its stout dignity.

How did she contrive to sit on that tail? I dabbed at the blood on my chemise, to keep myself from staring at her.

"Forgive me, lady," I said, pressing the reddened cloth to my nose again. "I don't even know who you are."

Her brows shot up in surprise. "Is that so. Well, I know who you are, Maid Dombegh. I've met your father. He's an excellent lawyer, a humane and gentle man." Her expression grew stern. "I trust you take after him in discretion. Tell no one."

"Tell no one what? That you arrived in the middle of the night to beat me up?"

She ignored that; she was scrutinizing my face. "Maybe you didn't understand what you saw."

"Maybe I saw nothing."

"Liar. I followed my stomach here, and my stomach is never wrong."

The word *liar* rankled; I shifted in my seat. "How did you know you were being watched? Could you see me?"

"No. I felt a presence—eyes upon me? I can't explain—I've never felt such a thing before. Was it sorcery? I don't believe in that, but then, I imagine there are people who don't believe in the likes of me, either." She folded her arms across her artificially portly bosom. "I am out of patience. What did you do, and how did you do it?"

I worried the bloody cloth between my hands and sniffed dismally; the inside of my nose smelled of iron. I owed her an explanation, maybe even the truth. She was a half-breed like me; she must have felt as utterly alone. I could let her know she wasn't just by pulling up my sleeve and showing her my scales.

I had dreamed of this, but now that it came to it my voice didn't work. The sheer weight of my intention hunkered down on my chest. I could not do it. Something would prevent me. The Heavens would cave in. I would roll up my sleeve and burst into flame. My chemise sleeve was unbound. I raised my hand high and let the loose sleeve fall away from my wrist, exposing my arm up to the elbow.

Her face fell, and for a breathless moment it felt like time had stopped.

She stared, bug-eyed, and was silent so long that I began to doubt whether I had really seen what I had seen. Maybe it had been a trick of the light, or I was so desperate for kindred that I had imagined it. I lowered my arm and covered it back up, ashamed.

"I don't believe it," she said at last. "There are no others. This is some sort of trick."

"I promise you, it's not. I am, um, what you are." She had avoided the word *half-dragon*; I found myself absurdly embarrassed to say it.

"You expect me to believe you have a tail?" she said, craning her neck to get a look at my backside.

"No," I said, embarrassed by her gaze. "Just scales on my arm and at my waist."

Her mouth curled into a sneer. "You feel terribly sorry for yourself, I suppose."

My face grew hot. "It may not be as dramatic as a tail, but I "

"Yes, yes, poor you. You must have trouble sitting down, and need your clothing especially made so it looks like you have a proper human body under there. You must have lived an impossibly long time thinking you were alone in the world. Oh no, I'm sorry, that's me."

I felt as if she'd slapped me. Whatever I'd expected, it wasn't hostility.

She glowered. "None of this explains how you spy on people."

"It's unintentional. I have visions. Typically, no one in my visions is aware of my presence." I left it at that. She didn't need to know I could see her at will; let her think she was special, popping into my head unbidden, uniquely able to perceive me.

I would not deliberately look in on her again. I'd learned my lesson.

Some of the bitterness in her expression dissipated; apparently my mental quirks were not as irksome as my scales. "I have something similar," she said. "A very, very short-range predictive skill. It is essentially an uncanny ability to be in the right place at the right time."

"That's what you meant by your stomach?" I hazarded.

She laid a hand on her padded belly. "It's not magic; it's more like indigestion. Typically, its instructions are vague or simple—turn right here, avoid the oysters—but I had quite a keen one that I could find the owner of those invisible eyes." She leaned in toward me, the lines beside her mouth deepening with her scowl.

"Don't do it again."

"You have my word!" I squeaked.

"I can't have you stomping about in my head."

I thought of Fruit Bat and Jannoula and felt some sympathy.

"If it helps, I only see people from above, like a sparrow might. I can't read thoughts—I'd know your name otherwise."

Her expression softened slightly. "Dame Okra Carmine," she said, inclining her head. "I am the Ninysh ambassador to Goredd."

All the ire seemed drained out of her at last. She rose to go but paused with her hand on the door latch. "Forgive me if I was un-diplomatic, Maid Dombegh. I react poorly to surprises."

Poorly hardly covered it, but I said, "Of course," and handed back her book, which she'd left on the spinet bench.

She fingered the leather spine absently, shaking her head. "I must admit, it boggles the mind to learn that your father, whose dearest mistress is the law, should have flouted it so egregiously in carrying on with your mother."

"He didn't know what she was until she died in childbirth."

"Ah." She stared into the middle distance. "Poor fellow."

I closed the door behind her and looked at my quigutl time-piece. I could squeeze in a little sleep before morning if I got right to it. I turned restlessly and threw off my blankets for an hour, excited and unable to turn off my thoughts. How could I ever sleep again?

Fruit Bat, climbing trees in Porphyry, was just like me. My brother Loud Lad piped upon the rooftops of Samsam. Nag and Nagini raced across the sands somewhere; mighty Pandowdy lolled in his swamp. Fierce Miserere fought brigands, malevolent Jannoula plotted, and the rest of the garden denizens walked this world and were mine. Scattered and peculiar—some of us skepti-cal and bitter—we were *people*.

And I was at the hub of this enormous wheel. I could bring us together. In a way, I already had.

Nine

Of course, I couldn't run off in search of my people. I had a job. Viridius was demanding late nights and early mornings. I barely had time to tend my garden properly; taking Fruit Bat's hands and locating him was out of the question. I promised myself I would go looking for him later, once Treaty Eve had come and gone. Fruit Bat kept his part of our agreement and gave me no trouble, although his black eyes scrutinized my face when I visited, and I suspected any rustle in the shrubbery was him, following me around the garden.

A dearth of sleep and a bruised, puffy nose made for a crabby music mistress, which made the days drag by in turn. My musicians weren't bothered; they were used to Viridius, whose crankiness knew no limits. The master himself found me amusing. The more I snarled, the jollier he got, until he was almost giggly. However, he did not insist that I attend any more soirees, or try to pin down a time for me to meet Lars, the mechanical megaharmonium genius. He tiptoed around me; I let him.

I still had to finalize the programs for General Comonot's welcoming concert and the entertainments for Treaty Eve. Comonot was to arrive five days before the anniversary of his treaty. He wanted to experience a bit of what we Goreddis call Golden Week: the cluster of holy days beginning with Speculus, the longest night of the year. It was the season for reconciliation and reunion; for grand acts of charity and grander feasts; for circling the Golden House and praying that St. Eustace keep his hands to himself for another year; for watching the Golden Plays and going mumming door to door; for making grandiose promises for the coming year and asking Heaven for favors. It just so happened that Queen Lavonda had made peace with Comonot during Golden Week, so the treaty was commemorated too with Treaty Eve, where we stayed up all night, and Treaty Day, where we all slept it off. That marked the beginning of the new year.

I had filled half the program with Viridius's students at his recommendation, sight unseen. His darling Lars got a prime spot, though the old man muttered, "Don't let me forget to tell him he's playing!" which was not particularly encouraging. There was a lot of time to fill, especially on Treaty Eve, and I still didn't have enough auditions lined up. I spent several days reading more petitions from prospective performers and auditioning them. Some were excellent; many were dreadful. It would be tough to fill an entire night unless I repeated some acts. I'd been hoping for more variety than that.

One petition kept reappearing at the top of the stack: a troupe of pygegyria dancers. It had to be the same troupe I'd turned away at the funeral, unless there was some pygegyria festival in town. I had no intention of auditioning them; there was no point. Princess Dionne and Lady Corongi had a difficult enough time condoning our native Goreddi dances, which permitted young women to have far more fun than was appropriate. (I had this on the authority of Princess Glisselda, who found herself greatly inconvenienced by the bad attitudes of her mother and governess.) I could only imagine what they would make of a foreign dance with a reputation for being risqué.

I tore up the petition and threw it in the fire. I remembered doing it, quite distinctly, when a pygegyria petition appeared atop the pile again the next day.

Viridius occasionally let me take days off to keep up my studies with Orma; I decided I'd earned a break three days before Comonot and chaos descended upon us. I dressed warmly, slung my oud across my back, packed my flute in my satchel, and set off for St. Ida's Conservatory first thing. I all but skipped down the hill, feeling pleasantly unburdened. Winter had not yet found its teeth; the rooftop frost melted with the first kiss of the sun. I bought breakfast along the river quay, fish custard and a glass of tea. I detoured through St. Willibald's Market, which was covered, crowded, and warm. I let riotous Ninysh ribbons cheer my heart, laughed at the antics of a noodle-stealing dog, and admired enormous salt-crusted hams. It was good to be an anonymous face in the crowd, feasting my eyes upon the glorious mundane.

Alas, I was not as anonymous as I used to be. An apple seller called out laughingly as I passed: "Play us a tune, sweetheart!" I assumed he'd noticed my oud, which hung in plain sight, but he mimed playing flute. The flute was bundled away where he could not have seen it. He recognized me from the funeral.

Then the crowd opened in front of me like a curtain, and there was Broadwick Bros. Clothiers, their stall heaped high with folded felts. Thomas Broadwick himself was just tipping his sugarloaf cap to a wide-hipped matron, the proud new owner of several yards of cloth.

He looked up and our eyes met for a long moment, as if time had stopped.

It occurred to me to approach him, to march boldly up and tell him I'd seen the light and repented my quig-coddling ways. In the same instant, though, I remembered that the lizard figurine was still in my coin purse; I had never bothered taking it out. That consideration made me hesitate too long.

His eyes narrowed, as if guilt were written plainly on my face. My window of opportunity for bluffing him had passed.

I turned and plunged into the densest part of the crowd, pulling my oud in front of me so I could protect it from jostling. The market took up three city blocks, giving me ample scope for vanishing. I ducked around the end of a coppersmith's stall and peered back between the gleaming kettles.

He was there, moving slowly and deliberately through the

crowd, as if he were wading though deep water. Thank Allsaints he was tall, and the sugarloaf hat gave him an additional three inches of bright green. It would surely be easier for me to see him than for him to see me. I started working my way up the arcade again.

I zigged and zagged as best I could, but he was always there when I looked back, a little closer each time. He'd catch up before I found the way out, unless I started running, which would have drawn the entire market's attention. No one but a thief runs in the market.

I began to sweat. Merchants' voices echoed in the vaulted ceilings, but there was another sound, something sharper, shrilling underneath the dull murmur.

It sounded like a good distraction to me.

I turned a corner and saw two Sons of St. Ogdo standing on the edge of the public fountain. One pontificated and the other stood alongside, looking tough and keeping an eye open for the Guard. I skirted the crowd and ducked behind a great fat cobbler—judging by his leather apron and awls—whence I might spy Thomas without his spotting me. As I'd hoped, Thomas stopped short at the sight of the black-plumed Son prancing passionately on the fountain ledge. He listened, openmouthed, with the rest of the crowd.

"Brothers and sisters under Heaven!" cried St. Ogdo's champion, his feather bobbing, fire in his eyes. "Do you imagine that once the chief monster sets foot in Goredd, he intends to leave?"

"No!" cried scattered voices. "Drive the devils out!"

The Son raised his knobby hands for silence. "This so-called treaty—this dishrag!—is but a ruse. They lull us to sleep with peace; they trick our Queen into banishing the knights, who were once the pride of all the Southlands; and they wait until we are utterly helpless. Whither the mighty dracomachia, our art of war? There is no dracomachia now. Why should the worms fight us? They've already sent a stinking quig vanguard, burrowing into the rotten heart of this city. Now they walk in, forty years on, invited by the Queen herself. Forty years is nothing to such long-lived beasts! These are the selfsame monsters our grandfathers died fighting—and we trust them?"

A raucous cry went up. Thomas shouted enthusiastically with the rest; I watched him through a forest of fist shaking. This was my chance to slip out. I shouldered my way through the suffocating crowd and burst out of the labyrinthine market into the feeble sunlight.

The cold air cleared my head but did not slow my racing heart. I had come out only a block from St. Ida's. I set off quickly, fearing he still followed me.

I took the steps of St. Ida's two at a time, reaching the music library within minutes. Orma's office door spanned a gap between two bookcases; it looked like it had merely been propped there, because it had. At my knock, Orma lifted the entire door to let me enter, then set it back in place.

His office wasn't properly a room. It was made of books, or more accurately, the space between books, where three little windows had prevented the placement of bookcases against the wall. I had spent vast tracts of time here, reading, practicing, taking instruction, even sleeping here more than once, when home got too tense.

Orma moved a pile of books off a stool for me but seated himself directly on another stack. This habit of his never ceased to amuse me. Dragons no longer hoarded gold; Comonot's reforms had outlawed it. For Orma and his generation, knowledge was treasure. As dragons through the ages had done, he gathered it, and then he sat on it.

Just being with him in this space made me feel safe again. I unpacked my instruments, my anxiety releasing in the form of chatter: "I was just chased through St. Willibald's, and you know why? Because I was kind to a quig. I scrupulously hide every legitimate reason for people to hate me, and then it turns out they don't need legitimate reasons. Heaven has fashioned a knife of irony to stab me with."

I didn't expect Orma to laugh, but he was even more unresponsive than usual. He stared at motes of dust dancing in the sunbeams from his tiny windows. The reflection upon his spectacles made his expression opaque to me.

"You're not listening," I said.

He did not speak; he removed his glasses and rubbed his eyes with a thumb and forefinger. Was his vision bothering him? He had never gotten used to human eyes, so much weaker than their dragon counterparts. In his natural form he could spy a mouse in a field of wheat. No spectacles, however strong, could possibly bridge that gap.

I looked at him hard. There were things my eyes—and the human mind behind them—could discern that his never could. He looked dreadful: pale and drawn, with circles under his eyes, and . . . I barely dared articulate it, even to myself.

He looked upset. No dragon could have seen that.

"Are you ill?" I sprang to his side, not quite daring to touch him.

He grimaced and stretched pensively, coming to some conclusion. He removed his earrings and deposited them in a drawer of his desk; whatever he was going to tell me, he did not want the Board of Censors hearing. From the folds of his doublet, he drew an object and placed it in my hand. It was heavy and cold, and I knew without being told that this was what the beggar had given him after Prince Rufus's funeral.

It was a gold coin, utterly antique. I recognized the obverse Queen, or her symbols anyway; Pau-Henoa, the trickster hero, pranced on the reverse. "Does this date from the reign of Belondweg?" I said. She was Goredd's first queen, nearly a thousand years ago. "Where would one acquire such a thing? And don't tell me the town beggars were handing them out to everyone, because I didn't get mine." I passed it back to him.

Orma rubbed the coin between his fingers. "The child was a random messenger. Irrelevant. The coin comes from my father."

A chill ran up my spine. In repressing every thought of my mother—and I dared not even think of Orma as uncle very often, lest I slip up and call him that—I had made a habit of squelching all thoughts of my extended dragon family. "How do you know?"

He raised an eyebrow. "I know every coin in my father's hoard."

"I thought hoarding was illegal."

"Even I am older than that law. I remember his hoard from when I was a child, every coin and cup of it." His gaze grew distant again and he licked his lips as if gold were something he missed the taste of. He shook it off and grimaced at me. "My father was forced to give it up, of course, although he resisted for years. The Ardmagar let it pass until your mother's disgrace stained us all."

He rarely spoke about my mother; I found myself holding my breath. He said, "When Linn took up with Claude and refused to come home, the Censors flagged our entire family for mental health scrutiny. My mother killed herself for shame, confirming a second irrefutable case of madness in the family."

"I remember," I said hoarsely.

He continued: "You'll also recall that my father was a prominent general. He didn't always agree with Ardmagar Comonot, but his loyalty and his glorious career were beyond dispute. After Linn ..." He trailed off as if he couldn't say "fell in love"; it was too horrible to contemplate. "Suddenly our father was being watched, every action probed, every utterance dissected. Suddenly they no longer turned a blind eye to his hoard, or to his occasional resistance."

"He fled before his trial, didn't he?" I said.

Orma nodded, his eyes on the coin. "Comonot banished him in absentia; no one has seen him since. He's still wanted for stirring up dissent against the Ardmagar's reforms."

His carefully neutral expression was breaking my heart, but there was nothing human I could do to help him. "So what does the coin signify?" I asked.

Orma looked at me over his spectacles, as if it were the most unnecessary question ever uttered. "He's in Goredd. You may be certain of it."

"Didn't his hoard get reabsorbed into the High Ker's treasury?"

He shrugged. "Who knows what the wily saar contrived to take with him."

"Could no one else have sent it? The Board of Censors, to gauge your reaction?"

Orma pursed his lips and gave a tight shake of his head. "No. This was our signal when I was a child. This very coin. It admonished me to behave at school. 'Don't shame us,' was the sense of it. 'Remember your family.'"

"What can it possibly mean in this context?"

His face looked thinner than before; his false beard fit poorly, or he hadn't bothered to put it on quite straight. He said, "I believe Imlann was at the funeral, and he suspects I may have noticed him, though in fact I did not. He's telling me to stay out of his way, to pretend I don't recognize his saarantras if I see it, and to let him do what honor demands."

I folded my arms; the room seemed suddenly colder. "Do what? And more urgently: to whom? To the man his daughter married? To their child?"

Orma's brown eyes widened behind his spectacles. "That had not occurred to me. No. Do not fear for yourself; he believes Linn died childless."

"And my father?"

"He never permitted your father's name to be spoken in his

presence. Your father's very existence violates ard, and was vigorously denied by everyone."

Orma picked lint off the knee of his woolen hose; he wore a pair of silks underneath, or he'd have been scratching like a flea-bitten hound. "Who knows what Imlann has been stewing upon for the last sixteen years?" he said. "He has no incentive to obey the law or keep his human emotions under wraps. Even for myself, constantly monitored and obeying the law as best I can, this shape takes a toll. The borderlands of madness used to have much sterner signage around them than they do now."

"If you don't think he's after Papa and me, then what? Why would he be here?"

"This close to Comonot's visit?" He stared over the rims of his glasses again.

"An assassination?" He was making great suppositional leaps, or else I was. "You think he's plotting against the Ardmagar?"

"I think it would be foolish to close our eyes and proceed as if he weren't."

"Well then, you've got to tell Prince Lucian and the Guard about this."

"Ah. That's just it." He leaned back and tapped the edge of the coin against his teeth. "I can't. I'm caught—what's your expression?—between a rock and another rock? I'm too involved. I do not trust myself to make an unemotional decision."

I studied his face again, the crease between his brows. He was unquestionably struggling with something. "You don't want to turn him in, because he's your father?"

Orma rolled his eyes toward me, the whites flashing like a

frightened animal's. "Quite the contrary. I want to set the Guard on him, want to see him brought to trial, want to see him hang. And not because he is truly, logically, a danger to the Ardmagar—because you're right, he might not be—but because, in fact, I . . . I hate him."

Absurdly, my first response to this was a knot of jealousy, like a fist to the stomach, that he not only felt something, but felt it intensely about someone who wasn't me. I reminded myself that it was hatred; I could not possibly prefer that to his benevolent indifference, could I? I said, "Hate is serious. You're sure?"

He nodded, finally letting everything show on his face for more than a fraction of a second. He looked terrible.

"How long have you felt this?" I asked.

He shrugged hopelessly. "Linn was not just my sister; she was my teacher."

Orma had often told me that among dragons there was no higher word of esteem than *teacher*; teachers were more revered than parents, spouses, even the Ardmagar himself.

"When she died and the shame fell on our family," he said, "I could not denounce her the way my father could—the way we were all supposed to, for the satisfaction of the Ardmagar. We fought; he bit me—"

"He bit you?"

"We're dragons, Phina. The one time you saw me . . ." He gestured vaguely with his hand, as if he didn't want to say it aloud, as if I'd seen him naked—which I guess technically I had. "I kept my wings folded, so you probably didn't notice the damage to the left, where the bone was once broken."

I shook my head, horrified for him. "Can you still fly?"

"Oh, yes," he said absently. "But you must understand: in the end I denounced her, under duress. My mother killed herself anyway. My father was banished anyway. In the end—" His lips trembled. "I don't know what it was for."

There were tears in my eyes, if not in his. "The Board of Censors would have sent you down for excision if you hadn't."

"Yes, that's highly likely," he mused, his tone back to a studied neutral.

The Censors would have excised my mother, too, reached in and stolen every loving memory of my father. In my head, the tin box of memories gave a painful twitch.

"Denouncing her didn't even free me from the Censors' scrutiny," said Orma. "They don't know my true difficulties, but they assume I have some, given my family history. They suspect, certainly, that I care more for you than is permitted."

"That's what Zeyd was sent to test," I said, trying to keep the bitterness from my voice.

He squirmed, imperceptibly to any eye but mine. He had never shown the tiniest bit of remorse for putting me in mortal danger as a child; this fleeting discomfiture was the best I could expect.

"I don't intend to give them any inkling of my real difficulty," he said, handing me the coin. "Do with it what you think right."

"I'll turn it over to Prince Lucian Kiggs, though I don't know what he can do with your vague premonition. Any advice on recognizing Imlann's saarantras?"

"I'd recognize him, unless he's in disguise. I'd know him if I smelled him," said Orma. "My father's saarantras was lean, but he may have spent the last sixteen years exercising, or forcing custard down his gullet. I can't know. He had blue eyes, unusual in a saar but not in a Southlander. Fair hair is easily dyed."

"Could Imlann pass as easily as Linn?" I asked. "Was he practiced in courtly manners, or musical like his children? Where might he try blending in?"

"He'd do best as a soldier, I should think, or concealed somewhere at court, but he'd know I would expect that. He'll be somewhere no one would expect."

"If he was at the funeral and saw you without your seeing him, it's likely he would have been standing . . ." Saints' dogs. Orma had been at the center of everything. I'd seen him from behind the quire screen; he might have been seen from any angle. Orma stiffened. "Do not go looking for Imlann yourself. He might kill you."

"He doesn't know I exist."

"He doesn't need to know you're *you* to kill you," said Orma. "He needs only believe you're trying to stop him doing whatever he's here to do."

"I see," I said, half laughing. "Better Prince Lucian Kiggs than me, I suppose."

"Yes!"

The vehemence of that *yes* made me stagger back a step. I could not reply; some emotion had seized my throat.

Someone was rapping on the lopsided door. I moved the door to the side, expecting one of the librarian monks.

There slumped Basind, the disjointed newskin, breathing

loudly through his mouth. His eyes pointed two different directions. I recoiled, holding the door before me like a shield. He pushed past, jingling like an Allsaints wreath, gaping at the room, and stumbling over a pile of books.

Orma was on his feet in an instant. "Saar Basind," he said. "What brings you to St. Ida's?"

Basind fished around in his shirt, then in his pants, finally locating a folded letter addressed to Orma. Orma read it quickly and held it out to me. I put the door back in its place, grasped the letter with two fingers, and read:

Orma: You will recall Saar Basind. We find him useless at the embassy. Apparently the Ardmagar owes Basind's mother a favor for turning in her boarding husband. Basind should never have been permitted to come south otherwise. He needs remedial human behavior lessons. Given your family history, and your own ability to pass, it occurs to me that you might be the ideal teacher.

Give whatever time you have to give, recalling that you are in no position to refuse this request. In particular, persuade him to keep his clothes on in public. The situation is that dire. All in ard,

Eskar.

Orma uttered no cry of dismay. I exclaimed for him: "St. Daan in a pan!"

"Evidently they're anxious to get him out from underfoot while they prepare for the Ardmagar's arrival," said Orma evenly. "That's not unreasonable."

"But what are you to do with him?" I lowered my voice, because anyone could be on the other side of the bookcases. "You're trying to pass among the music students; how do you explain being saddled with a newskin?"

"I'll devise something." He gently removed a book from Basind's hands and put it on a high shelf. "I might plausibly be homebound with pneumonia this time of year."

I didn't want to leave until I was sure he was all right, and I particularly didn't want to leave him with the newskin, but Orma was adamant. "You have a lot of other things to do," he said, opening the door for me. "You have a date with Prince Lucian Kiggs, if I recall."

"I had hoped for a music lesson," I griped.

"I can give you homework," he said, infuriatingly oblivious to my dismay. "Stop by St. Gobnait's and observe the new mega-harmonium. They've just finished it, and I understand it puts into practice some intriguing acoustical principles, hitherto untested on so large a scale."

He tried to smile, to show me he was fine. Then he closed the door in my face.

Ten

I strolled to the cathedral, as Orma suggested, having no desire to return to the palace yet. The sky had drawn a thin white veil across the sun, and the wind had picked up. Maybe snow would come soon; it was five days till Speculus, the longest night of the year. As the saying goes: when the days lengthen, the cold strengthens.

The Countdown Clock was visible all the way across the cathedral square. Apparently it changed numbers midmorning, about the time Comonot would be arriving. I appreciated that kind of pedantry, and stopped to watch the mechanical figures emerge from little doors in its face. A bright green dragon and a purple-clad queen stepped forward, bowed, took turns chasing each other, and then hoisted a drapery between them, which I assumed represented the treaty. There was a grinding and clunking sound, and the massive clock hand pointed toward three.

Three days. I wondered whether the Sons of St. Ogdo felt pressed for time. Was it difficult to organize rioting? Did they have enough torches and black feathers? Enough rabid speech-ifiers?

I turned back toward St. Gobnait's cathedral, feeling some curiosity about Viridius's protégé. He had certainly made an interesting clock.

I felt the megaharmonium before I heard it, through the soles of my feet, through the very street, experiencing it not as sound but as vibration and a peculiar oppressive weight of air. Closer to the cathedral, I understood a sound was present but would have been hard-pressed to identify it. I stood in the north transept porch, my hand upon a pillar, and I felt the megaharmonium to the center of my bones.

It was loud. I did not yet feel qualified to offer a more nuanced opinion.

I opened the door into the north transept; the music nearly blasted me back out again. The entire cathedral was packed with sound, every cranny, as if sound were some solid mass, leaving no air, no medium to move through. I could not enter until my ears adjusted, which they did surprisingly quickly.

Once I had ceased to be terrified, I was awed. My paltry flute had made the building ring, but that thin sound had risen like candle smoke; this was a conflagration.

I worked my way toward the Golden House at the great cross-ing, wading through sound, then pressed on into the south tran-sept. I saw now that the instrument had four manual keyboards, gleaming like rows of teeth, and a larger one for the feet. Above, around, and behind it, pipes had been fitted in neat rows, making a palisade fortress of chanters; it looked like the unnatural off-spring of a bagpipe and a . . . a dragon.

A large man in black dominated the bench, his feet dancing a ground-bass jig, his broad shoulders affording him a reach like a Zibou rock ape. I wasn't short but I could not have reached in so many directions at once without straining something.

There was no music on the stand; surely no music had yet been written for this monstrosity. Was this cacophony his own composition? I suspected it was. It was brilliant, the way a thunderstorm across the moors or a raging torrent is brilliant, insofar as a force of nature may be said to have genius.

I was judging too hastily. I began to hear structure in the piece, the longer I listened. The volume and intensity had distracted me from the melody itself, a fragile thing, almost shy. The surrounding bombast was all a bluff.

He released the last chord like a boulder off a trebuchet. A bevy of monks who'd been hiding in nearby chapels like timid mice scurried out and accosted the performer in whispers: "Very nice. Glad it works. That's enough testing; we're about to have service."

"I couldt play durink service, yes?" said the big man in a dense Samsamese accent. His head, close-cropped and blond, bobbed submissively.

"No. No. No." The negative echoed all over the transept. The big man's shoulders slumped; even from the back, he looked heart-broken. A pang of pity surprised me.

Surely this was Viridius's golden boy, Lars. He had designed an impressive machine, taking up an entire chapel with its pipes and tubes and bellows. I wondered which Saint had been evicted to make room for it.

I should greet him. I felt I'd glimpsed his humanity, a piece of his heart in his playing. We were friends; he just didn't know it yet. I stepped up and gently cleared my throat. He turned to look at me.

His middling chin, round cheeks, and gray eyes shocked me speechless. It was Loud Lad, who piped and yodeled and built pergolas in the garden of my mind.

"Hello," I said calmly, my pulse racing in excitement and plain terror. Would all my grotesques, the entire freakish diaspora of half-dragons, walk into my life one by one? Would I spot Gargoyella busking on a street corner and Finch in the palace kitchens, turning the spits? Maybe I wouldn't have to go looking for them after all.

Loud Lad gave courtesy with Samsamese simplicity, and said, "We hev not been introduced, *grausleine*."

I shook his enormous hand. "I'm Seraphina, Viridius's new assistant."

He nodded eagerly. "I know. I am calledt Lurse."

Lars. He spoke Goreddi like his mouth was full of pebbles.

He rose from his bench; he was taller than Orma, and as massive as two and a half Ormas, at least. He seemed simultaneously strong and soft, as if he had ended up with a lot of muscles rather by accident and didn't care about keeping them. He had a nose like a compass needle; it pointed with purpose. He pointed it toward the quire, where the monks had begun cheerful hymns to St. Gobnait and her blessed bees. "They are havink service. Perhaps we can . . ." He gestured past the Golden House, toward the north transept. I followed him out, into the hazy glare of afternoon.

We walked to the Wolfstoot Bridge, a shy silence hanging over us. "Would you like lunch?" I said, gesturing toward the clustered food carts. He said nothing, but stepped up eagerly. I bought us pies and ale; we carried them to the bridge's balustrade.

Lars hefted himself up with unexpected grace and sat on the balustrade with his long legs dangling over the river. Like all proper Samsamese, he dressed gloomily: black doublet, jerkin, and joined hose. No ruffs or lace, no slashing or puffy trunk hose here. His boots looked like he'd owned them a long time and could not bear to give them up.

He swallowed a bite of pie and sighed. "I hev needt to speak with you, *grausleine*. I heardt you at the funeral and knew you were my . . ."

He trailed off; I waited, filled with curiosity and dread.

River gulls circled, waiting for us to drop the smallest crumb. Lars threw bits of pie crust over the river; the gulls swooped and caught them in midair. "I start over," he said. "Hev you noticedt, perheps, thet an instrument can be like a voice? Thet you can tell who plays it just from listenink, without lookink?"

"If I am very familiar with the performer, yes," I said carefully, unsure what he was getting at.

He puffed out his cheeks and looked at the sky. "Do not think me mad, *grausleine*. I hev heardt you play before, in dreamink, in . . ." He gestured toward his blond head.

"I didt not know what I was hearink," he said, "but I believedt in it. It was like crumbs on the forest path: I followedt. They leadt me here where I can buildt my machine, and where I am less the, eh, *vilishparaiab* . . . sorry, my Gorshya not goodt."

His Goreddi was better than my Samsamese, but *vilishparaiab* sounded like a cognate. The "paraiah" part did, anyway. I did not dare ask him about being half dragon; as much as I hoped that was the link between all my grotesques and me, I did not yet have proof. I said, "You followed the music—"

"Your music!"

"—to escape persecution?" I spoke gently, trying to convey sympathy and let him know I understood all about the difficulties of being a half-breed.

He nodded vigorously. "I am a Daanite," he said.

"Oh!" I said. That was unexpected information, and I found myself reevaluating everything Viridius had said about his protégé, the way his eyes had gleamed.

Lars stared intently at the remains of his lunch, a veil of shyness drawn over him again. I hoped he hadn't mistaken my silence for disapproval. I tried to coax him back out: "Viridius is so proud of your megaharmonium."

He smiled but did not look up.

"How did you calculate the acoustics for that contraption?"

He raised his gray eyes sharply. "Acoustics? Is simple. But I needt somethink to write with." I pulled a small charcoal pencil— a draconian innovation, rare in Goredd, but very useful—from the pocket of my surcoat. His lips twitched into a little smile and he started scrawling an equation beside him on the balustrade. He ran out of room to write as the notation approached his bum—he wrote sinister-handed—so he stood up on the railing, balancing like a cat, and wrote leaning over. He diagrammed levers and bellows, illustrated the resonant properties of types of wood, and elucidated his theory of how one might emulate the sounds of other instruments by manipulating wave properties.

Everyone turned to look at the enormous and unexpectedly graceful man balancing on the balustrade, doubled over writing, gabbling about his megaharmonium in intermittent Samsamese.

I grinned at him and marveled that anyone could possess such single-minded passion for a machine.

A cadre of courtiers approached the bridge on horseback but found it difficult to cross with all the merchants and townspeople gaping at Lars's antics. The gentlemen made a ruckus with their horses; people scampered out of their way to avoid being trampled. One courtier, dressed in rich black, smacked dawdling gawpers with his riding crop.

It was Josef, Earl of Apsig. He didn't notice me; his eye was fixed on Lars.

Lars looked up, met the earl's fierce glare, and went white. Goreddis claim that all Samsamese sounds like cursing, but Josef's tone and body language left no doubt. He rode straight for Lars, gesticulating and shouting. I knew the words *mongrel* and *bastard*, and guessed the obscure halves of some compound words. I looked to Lars, horrified for him, but he stoically took the abuse. Josef drove his horse right up against the balustrade, making it difficult for Lars to keep his balance. The earl lowered his voice to a vicious whisper. Lars was strong enough to have pitched scrawny Josef right off his horse, yet he did nothing.

I looked around, hoping someone would come to Lars's aid, but no one on the crowded bridge made any move to help. Lars was my friend, for all that I'd known him two hours; I'd known Loud Lad for five years, and he'd always been a favorite. I sidled up to the horse and tapped at the Earl of Apsig's black-clad knee, gingerly at first and then harder when he ignored me.

"Hey," I said, as if I could talk to an earl that way. "Leave him alone."

"This is not your affair, *grausleine*," Josef sneered over his starched ruff, his pale hair flopping into his eyes. He wheeled his horse, driving me back. Unintentionally—perhaps—his horse's hindquarters swung around and knocked Lars into the freezing river.

Everyone took off running then—some for the river's edge, some to put as much distance between themselves and this fracas as possible. I rushed down the steps to the quayside. Rivermen were already shoving off in rowboats and coracles, extending poles over the choppy water, shouting directions to the flailing figure. Lars could swim, it seemed, but was hindered by his clothing and the cold. His lips were tinged blue; he had trouble getting his hands to close around the proffered poles.

Someone finally hooked him and reeled him in to shore, where old river ladies had hauled piles of blankets off their barges. A riverman brought out a brazier and stoked it high, adding a tang of charcoal to the fishy breeze.

I felt a pricking behind my eyes, moved by the sight of people pulling together to help a stranger. The bitterness I'd carried since morning, since the incident at St. Willibald's Market, melted away. People feared the unfamiliar, certainly, but they still had tremendous capacity for kindness when one of their own—

Except that Lars wasn't one of their own. He looked normal, except for his height and girth, but what lay under his black jerkin? Scales? Something worse? And here were the well-meaning, easily terrified townsfolk about to strip off his soaked clothing. He was shyly evading an old woman's helping hands even now. "Come, lad," she laughed, "ye need not be bashful wi' me. What hain't I seen, in my fifty years?"

Lars shivered—big shivers, to match the rest of him. He needed to get dry. I could think of only one thing to do, and it was slightly mad.

I leaped up on one of the wharf piles, cried, "Who wants a song?" and launched into a stirring a capella rendition of "Peaches and Cheese":

The vagabond sun winks down through the trees,
While lilacs, like memories, waft on the breeze,
My friend, I was born for soft days such as these,
To inhale perfume,
And cut through the gloom,
And feast like a king upon peaches and cheese!
I'll travel this wide world and go where I please,
Can't stop my wand'ring, it's like a disease.

My only regret as I cross the high seas:
What I leave behind,
Though I hope to find,
My own golden city of peaches and cheese!

People laughed and clapped, most of them keeping their eyes on me. It took Lars a minute to grasp that this was all the cover he was going to get. He turned modestly toward the river wall, a blanket draped over his shoulders, and began peeling off his clothes.

He needed to move faster than that; this song only had five verses.

I remembered the oud strapped across my back, pulled it around, and launched into an improvised interlude. People cheered. Lars stared at me again, to my irritation. Had he not believed I could play either? *Thanks for all the faint praise, Viridius.*

Then, however, it was my turn to stare at Lars, because he appeared not to have anything odd about him at all. I spied no trace of silver on his legs, but he quickly covered them up with borrowed trousers. He kept the blanket draped across his shoulders as best he could until it slipped. I ogled his torso. Nothing.

No, wait, there it was, on his right bicep: a slender band of scales running all the way around. From a distance it looked like a bracelet in the Porphyrian style; he'd even found a way to inlay it with colorful glass gems. It might be taken for jewelry, easily, by anyone not expecting to find scales.

Suddenly I understood Dame Okra's irritation with me. How

easy life must be if that slender band was your only physical man-ifestation! And here I'd stood up in front of everybody and risked myself, when he'd barely anything to hide.

I'll ask my true love, and I'll hope she agrees,
How could she not, when I'm down on my knees?
My Jill, say you will, and don't be such a tease.
When it's time to eat,
I say sweets to the sweet,
My love, let your answer be peaches and cheese!

I finished with a flourish. Lars was decent, in mismatched riverman's garb only slightly too small. The crowd called for more, but I was done, my rush of panicked energy spent. All that re-mained was to figure out how to get off my perch; looking down now, I wasn't sure how I'd gotten up. Desperation gives you a lon-ger leap, apparently.

A hand reached up to help me; I looked down to see the dark curls and merry eyes of Prince Lucian Kiggs.

He smiled at the sheer absurdity of me, and I could not stop myself smiling back.

I leaped down, not quite nimbly. "I was heading up to Castle Orison with the evening patrol," said the prince. "Thought we'd stop and see what the commotion was—and the singing. That was nicely done."

Many people had cleared out with the arrival of this small party of Guardsmen; those who remained told our tale with gusto, as if it might replace *Belondweg,* our national epic. The epony mous Brutal Earl of Apsig victimizes an innocent clod on the bridge railing! A fair maidy tries to save him, heroic townsfolk fish him out of the drink, and then—triumphal music!

Prince Lucian seemed to enjoy the tale. I was just glad I didn't have to explain what I'd really been doing; it had seemed perfectly logical to everyone. Lars stood quietly, ignoring an officer who was attempting to question him.

The frustrated officer reported back to the prince: "He has no interest in pursuing justice for this incident, Captain Kiggs."

"Find Earl Josef. I'll speak to him about this. He can't go knocking people into the river and riding off," said Prince Lucian, waving a dismissal. His deputies departed.

The sun was beginning to set and the breeze along the river had picked up. The prince faced my shivering friend. Lars was older and a head taller, but Prince Lucian stood like he was Captain of the Queen's Guard. Lars looked like a little boy who wanted to sink into his boots. I was amazed at how far he succeeded.

The prince spoke, his voice unexpectedly gentle: "You're Viridius's protégé."

"Yes," said Lars, mumbling as a man must who's sunk into his footwear.

"Did you provoke the earl in some way?"

Lars shrugged and said, "I was raised on his estate."

"That's hardly a provocation, is it?" asked Prince Lucian. "Are you his serf?"

Lars hesitated. "I hev spendt more than a year and a day away from his landts. I am legally free."

A question took root in my mind: if Lars had grown up on his estate, might Josef know Lars was half dragon? It seemed plausible, and Josef's hostility made sense in light of his attitudes toward dragonkind. Alas, I could not ask in front of Lucian Kiggs.

Prince Lucian looked disgusted. "Maybe a man can harass his former serfs in Samsam, but that is not how we conduct ourselves here. I will speak with him."

"I'd rather you didn't," said Lars. Prince Lucian opened his mouth to protest, but Lars cut him off: "I can go, yes?"

The prince waved him along; Lars returned my pencil, slightly soggy, and held my gaze for a moment before he turned to go. I wished I could have embraced him, but I felt a peculiar reluctance to do so in front of the prince. We shared a secret, Lars and I, even if Lars didn't know it yet.

He climbed the stone steps up the Wolfstoot Bridge without a word. His broad shoulders sagged, as if under the burden of whole worlds we could not see.

Eleven

"But of course I might say anything, because you are quite far away just now," said Prince Lucian, who had apparently been speaking to me for some time.

"Sorry." I tore my eyes away from Lars and gave the prince full courtesy.

"We can dispense with some formality," he said when I rose, his eyebrows raised in plain amusement. He put a hand to his crimson doublet, right over his heart, and said earnestly, "Right now I'm merely Captain of the Guard. Half courtesy is adequate, and you may call me Captain Kiggs—or simply Kiggs, if you will. Everyone else does."

"Princess Glisselda calls you Lucian," I said breezily, covering my fluster.

He gave a short laugh. "Selda's an exception to everything, as you may have noticed. My own grandmother calls me Kiggs. Would you gainsay the Queen?"

"I wouldn't dare," I said, trying to echo his levity. "Not about something this important."

"I should think not." He gestured grandly toward the steps up the bridge. "If you've no objection, let us walk while we talk; I have to get back to Castle Orison."

I followed, unsure what he wished to speak with me about, but recalling that Orma had given me a task. I put a hand to the purse at my waist, but the little lizard figurine made me anxious, as if it might pop its head out without permission.

How would this prince react if he saw it? Perhaps I could just tell him the story.

A guildsman of the town watch stood on the balustrade as Lars had done, lighting lamps in anticipation of sunset; laughing merchants dismantled their stalls. Prince—*Kiggs* strolled through the thinning market crowd, perfectly at ease among them, as if he were simply another townsman. I started up the gently sloping Royal Road, but he gestured toward a narrow street, the more direct route. The road, not wide to begin with, narrowed even further above us; the upper stories cantilevered over the street, as if the houses were leaning together to gossip. A woman on one side might have borrowed a lump of butter from her neighbor on the other without leaving home. The looming buildings squeezed the sky down to a rapidly darkening ribbon.

When the noise of the marketplace had faded and only the sound of his boots echoed up the street, Lucian Kiggs said, "I wanted to thank you for your intervention with the saarantrai the other evening."

It took me a moment to remember what he was talking about. Dame Okra beating me with a book had rather eclipsed the other events of that day.

He continued: "No one else dared speak so plainly to Selda—not even I. I suffered the same paralysis she did, as if the problem might solve itself if we all refused to acknowledge it. But of course, Selda says you know a great deal about dragons. It seems she was right."

"You're very kind to say so," I said evenly, giving no hint of the anxious knot his words produced in my chest. I did not like him associating me with dragons. He was too sharp.

"It raises questions, of course," he said, as if he'd read my mind. "Selda said your knowledge comes from reading the treaty with your father. Maybe some of it does, but surely not all. Your comfort with saarantrai—your ability to talk to them without breaking out in a cold sweat—that's not something one gains from studying the treaty. I've read the treaty; it makes you wary of them, rather, because it's as full of holes as a Ducanahan cheese."

My anxious knot tightened. I reminded myself that the cheese of Ducana province was famously riddled with holes; he was making a simple analogy, not some veiled reference to Amaline Ducanahan, my fictional human mother.

Kiggs looked up toward the purpling sky, his hands clasped behind his back like one of my pedantic old tutors, and said, "My guess is that it has something to do with your dragon teacher. Orma, was it?"

I relaxed a little. "Indeed, I've known him forever; he's practically family."

"That makes sense. You've grown easy with him."

"He's taught me a lot about dragons," I offered. "I ask him questions all the time; I am curious by nature." It felt nice to be able to tell this prince something true.

The street was so steep here that it had steps; he hopped up ahead of me like a mountain sheep. Speculus lanterns hung along this block; broken mirrors behind the candles cast dazzling flecks of light onto the street and walls. Beside them hung Speculus chimes, which Kiggs set ringing. We murmured the customary words beneath the bright cacophony: "Scatter darkness, scatter silence!"

Now seemed a reasonable moment to bring up Orma's concern, since we had just been talking about him. I opened my mouth but didn't get any further.

"Who's your psalter Saint?" asked the prince with no preamble.

I had been mentally arranging what I should say about Orma, so for a moment I could not answer him.

He looked back at me, his dark eyes shining in the fragmented lantern light. "You called yourself curious. We curious types tend to be children of one of three Saints. Look." He reached into his doublet, extracting a silver medallion on a chain; it glinted in the light. "I belong to St. Clare, patron of perspicacity. You don't appear obsessed with mystery, though, or social enough to be one of St. Willibald's. I'm going to guess St. Capiti—the life of the mind!"

I blinked at him in astonishment. 'Irue, my psalter had fallen open to St. Yirtrudis, the heretic, but St. Capiti had been my substitute Saint. It was close enough. "How did you—"

"It's in my nature to notice things," he said. "Both Selda and I have noticed your intelligence."

I suddenly found myself warm from the exertion of climbing and cold at this reminder that he was so observant. I needed to be careful. His friendliness notwithstanding, the prince and I could not be friends. I had so many things to hide, and it was in his nature to seek.

My right hand had wormed as far as it could under the binding of my left sleeve and was fingering my scaly wrist. That was exactly the sort of unconscious habit he would notice; I forced myself to stop.

Kiggs asked after my father; I said something noncommittal. He solicited my opinion of Lady Corongi's pedagogy; I expressed a small amount of polite concern. He gave his own opinion of the matter, in blunt and unflattering terms; I kept my mouth shut.

The road flattened out, and soon we passed through the barbican of Castle Orison. The guards saluted; Kiggs inclined his head in return. I began to relax; we were almost home and this interview was surely over. We crunched across the gravel yard of Stone Court, not speaking. Kiggs paused at the steps and turned toward me with a smile. "Your mother must have been very musical."

The box of maternal memories gave a sickening twitch in my head, as if it would have liked to answer him. I tried to get away without speaking, with just a curtsy. It came out poorly: my arms were gripped so tightly around my middle that I could barely bend.

"She was called Amaline Ducanahan, right?" he said,

scrutinizing my face. "I looked her up when I was young, intrigued by your father's mysterious first marriage, the one no one had heard of until you popped out like a cuckoo at his second. I was there. I heard you sing."

Every part of me had turned to ice except my hammering heart and the memory box, which bucked like a colt in my mind.

"It was my first mystery: who was that singing girl, and why was Counselor Dombegh so very embarrassed when she appeared?" he said, his eyes distant with memory. His silent laugh manifested as a cloud of vapor in the air, and he shook his head, marveling at his youthful obsession. "I couldn't let it go until I'd uncovered the truth. I may have been hoping you were illegitimate, like me, but no, everything was in order. Congratulations!"

Everything would have been in impeccable order, surely; my father's paranoia had omitted no detail—marriage contract, birth and death certificates, letters, receipts. . . .

"Have you been back to Ducana province?" Kiggs asked out of nowhere.

"Why?" I'd lost the thread of his thought. I felt like a crossbow being drawn: everything he said wound the cranequin a little further.

"To see her stone. Your father had a nice one made. I didn't go myself," he added hastily. "I was nine years old. One of Uncle Rufus's men had family at Trowebridge, so I asked him. He made a rubbing. I might still have it, if you'd like it."

There was no answer I could give. I was so horrified to learn that he'd investigated my family history that I was afraid of what I might say. How close had he come? I was wound to full tension;

I was dangerous now. I waved the last white flag I had: "I don't wish to talk about my mother. Please excuse me."

His brow furrowed in concern; he could tell I was upset, but not why. He guessed exactly wrong: "It's hard that she left you so young. Mine did too. But she did not live in vain. What a wonderful legacy she left you!"

Legacy? Up my arm, around my waist, and scattershot through my head? The hooting memory box, which I feared would burst open at any moment?

"She gave you an ability to touch people's very souls," he said kindly. "What is it like to be so talented?"

"What is it like to be a bastard?" I blurted.

I clapped a hand to my mouth, horrified. I had felt the shot coming; I hadn't realized the bow was loaded with this very quarrel, perfectly calibrated to hit him hardest. What part of me had been studying him, stockpiling knowledge as ammunition?

His open expression slammed shut; suddenly he looked like a stranger, his gaze unfamiliar and cold. He drew himself up in a defensive posture. I staggered back a step as if he'd pushed me.

"What's it like? It's like this," he said, gesturing angrily at the space between us. "Almost all the time."

Then he was gone, as if the wind had whisked him away. I stood in the courtyard alone, realizing that I had failed to speak with him about Orma. My annoyance at forgetting paled before everything else that was clamoring to be felt, so I clung to it tightly, like a stick of driftwood in a tempestuous sea. Somehow, my aching legs carried me indoors.

Twelve

I took comfort in the normalcy and routine of my garden that evening. I lingered a long time at the edge of Loud Lad's ravine, watching him build a tent out of cattails and Pandowdy's shed skin. Loud Lad, like Miss Fusspots, looked sharper and more detailed now that I had seen him in the real world; his fingers were long and nimble, the curve of his shoulders sad.

Fruit Bat was still the only grotesque who looked back at me. Despite my having asked him to stay in his grove, he came and sat beside me at the edge of the gorge, his skinny brown legs dangling over the edge. I found I didn't mind. I considered taking his hands, but just thinking about it was overwhelming. I had enough to worry about right now. He wasn't going anywhere.

"Besides," I told him, as if we'd been having a conversation, "the way things are going, I have only to wait for you to drop in on me."

He did not speak, but his eyes gleamed.

The next morning, I dawdled over washing and oiling my scales. I dreaded facing Princess Glisselda's lesson; surely Kiggs would have spoken to her about me. When I finally arrived at the south solar, however, she wasn't there. I sat at the harpsichord and played to comfort myself, the timbre of that instrument is, to me, the musical equivalent of a warm bath.

Today it was cold.

A messenger arrived with a message from the princess, canceling the lesson without explanation. I stared at the note a long time, as if the handwriting could tell me anything about her mood, but I wasn't even sure she'd written it herself.

Was I being punished for insulting her cousin? It seemed likely, and I deserved it, of course. I spent the rest of the day trying not to think about it. I went about my (sulking) duties to Viridius, drilling the symphonia on the (pouting) songs of state, supervising construction of the (glowering) stage in the great hall, finalizing the lineup for the (self-pitying) welcome ceremony, now just two days away. I threw myself (stewing) into work to stave off the (moping) feeling that descended when I stopped.

Evening fell. I made for the north tower and dinner. The quickest route from Viridius's suite led past the chambers of state: the Queen's study, the throne room, the council chamber. I always passed quickly; it was the sort of place my father would haunt. This evening, almost as if he'd heard me thinking about him, Papa stepped out of the council chamber and into my path, deep in conversation with the Queen herself.

He saw me—Papa and I have a cat's-whisker sensitivity to

each other—but he pretended he didn't. I was in no mood for the humiliation of being pointed out to him by the Queen in the belief he hadn't noticed me, so I ducked down a little side corridor and waited just on the other side of a statue of Queen Belondweg.

I was not hidden, exactly, but out of the way enough that I wouldn't be noticed by anyone who wasn't looking for me. Other dignitaries streamed out of the council chamber; Dame Okra Carmine, Lady Corongi, and Prince Lucian Kiggs all passed my corridor without looking down it.

A merry voice at my back said, "Who are we spying on?"

I jumped. Princess Glisselda beamed at me. "There's a secret door out of the council room. I'm evading that withered courgette, Lady Corongi. Has she passed?"

I nodded, shocked to find Princess Glisselda her usual impervious, friendly self. She was practically dancing with delight, her golden curls bouncing around her face. "I'm sorry I had to miss my lesson today, Phina, but we've been dreadfully busy. We just had the most exciting council ever, and I looked very clever, largely due to you."

"That's . . . that's wonderful. What's happened?"

"Two knights came to the castle today!" She could barely contain herself, her hands fluttered about like two excitable small birds. They lit briefly on my left arm, but I managed not to cringe visibly. "They claim to have spotted a rogue dragon, flying around the countryside in its natural shape! Isn't that awful?"

Awful enough to have her grinning ear to ear. She was a strange little princess.

I found myself fingering my scaly wrist; I hastily crossed my arms. "Prince Rufus's head went missing," I half-whispered, thinking out loud.

"As if it had been bitten off, yes," said Princess Glisselda, nodding vigorously.

"Does the council suspect a connection between this dragon and his death?"

"Grandmamma doesn't like the notion, but it seems unavoidable, does it not?" she said, bouncing on her heels. "We're breaking for dinner now, but we'll take the rest of the evening to figure out what to do next."

I was fingering my wrist again. I clamped my right hand under my armpit. *Stop that, hand. You're banished.*

"But I haven't told you the best part," said Glisselda, putting a hand to her chest as if she were about to make a speech. "I, myself, addressed the council and told them dragons view us as very interesting cockroaches, and that maybe some of them intended the peace as a ruse! Maybe they secretly plan to burn the cockroaches' house down!"

I felt my jaw drop. Maybe this was why her governess didn't tell her anything: give her an inch and she took it all the way to the moon. "H-how did that go over?"

"Everyone was astonished. Lady Corongi stammered something stupid, about the dragons being defeated and demoralized, but that only made her look a dunce. I believe we made the rest of them think!"

"We?" St. Masha's stone. Everyone would think I was giving

157

the princess mad ideas. I'd made the cockroach analogy, yes, but the house of burning bugs—to say nothing of the peace being a ruse!—was her own extrapolation.

"Well, I didn't credit you, if that's what you're hoping," she sniffed.

"No, no, that's fine," I said hastily. "You never need to credit me!"

Princess Glisselda looked suddenly stern. "I wouldn't say never. You're smart. That's useful. There are people who would appreciate that quality. In fact," she said, leaning in, "there are people who *do*, and you do yourself no favors alienating them."

I stared at her. She meant Kiggs, there was no mistaking it.

I gave full courtesy and she smiled again; her elfin face wasn't made for sternness. She skipped off, leaving me to my thoughts and my regrets.

I mulled over her news on the way to supper. A rogue dragon in the countryside was unprecedented. Whose responsibility was it? I knew the treaty well, but that specific question wasn't answered anywhere. On the Goreddi side, we would doubtless try to make the dragons deal with it—and yet how could they, without sending dragons in their natural shape to apprehend the rogue? That was unacceptable. But then what?

We relied heavily upon dragon cooperation in the enforcement of the treaty. If even a few of them refused to accept it anymore, what recourse had we but the help of other dragons? Wouldn't that effectively invite them to battle each other in our skies?

My steps slowed. There wasn't just the one rogue dragon. My own grandfather, banished General Imlann, had attended the funeral and sent Orma that coin. Could there be illegal, unregistered dragons all around, eschewing the bell and blending into crowds?

Or was there just the one after all? Could the knights have seen Imlann?

Could my own grandfather have killed Prince Rufus?

The idea made my stomach knot; I almost turned away from dinner, but I took a deep breath and willed myself forward. Dining hall gossip was a chance to learn more about the rogue, if more was known.

I crossed the long dining room to the musicians' table and squeezed onto a bench. The lads were already deep in conversation; they barely noticed I was there. "Twenty years underground—are the old codgers even sane?" said Guntard around a mouthful of blancmange. "They probably saw a heron against the sun and took it for a dragon!"

"They want to stop Comonot's coming by stirring up trouble, like the Sons," said a drummer, picking raisins out of his olio. "Can't blame 'em. Does it just about make the hairs on your neck stand up, dragons walking among us like they was people?"

Everyone turned in unsubtle unison to peer at the saars' table, where the lowest-ranking members of the dragon embassy took dinner together. There were eight of them tonight, sitting like they had rods up their spines, hardly speaking. Servants shunned that corner; one saarantras returned the serving bowls to the kitchen if they needed a refill. They ate bread and root vegetables and drank only barley water, like abstemious monks or certain austere Samsamese.

A scrawny sackbutist leaned in close. "How do we know they all wear the bell? One could sit among us, at this very table, and we'd have nary an inkling!"

My musicians eyeballed each other suspiciously. I conscientiously followed suit, but curiosity had seized me. I asked, "What happened to the knights in the end? Were they released back into the wild?"

"Banished men, and likely troublemakers?" scoffed Guntard. "They're locked in the eastern basement, the proper donjon being full of wine casks for some significant state visit coming up."

"Sweet St. Siucre, which one might that be?" someone asked with a laugh.

"The one where your mother beds a saar and lays an egg. Omelette for all!"

I laughed mechanically along with everyone else.

The conversation turned to the concert schedule, and suddenly all inquiries were directed at me. I'd had an idea, however, and was too preoccupied with it to focus on their questions. I referred everyone to the schedule posted on the rehearsal room door, handed my trencher to the little dogs under the table, and rose to take my leave.

"Seraphina, wait!" cried Guntard. "Everyone—how were we going to thank Mistress Seraphina for all the work she's doing?"

He blew a pitch whistle while his fellows hastily swallowed their mouthfuls and washed them down with wine.

To the great amusement of the rest of the dining hall, the saarantrai alone excepted, they began to sing:

O Mistress Seraphina,
Why won't you marry me?
From first I ever seen ya,
I knew you were for me!
It's not just that you're sassy,
It's not just that you're wise,
It's that you poke Viridius
In his piggy little eyes!

"Hurrah!" cried all my musicians.

"Boldly taking on Viridius, so we don't have to!" cried a lone smarty-breeches.

Everyone burst out laughing. I smiled as I waved farewell—a real smile—and kept grinning all the way to the east wing. It had occurred to me that these knights might be able to describe the dragon in enough detail that Orma could identify it as Imlann. Then I would have real, concrete evidence for Lucian Kiggs, more than just a coin, a dragon's worry, and the vaguest of vague descriptions.

Then perhaps I might work up enough courage to speak to him again. I owed him an apology, at the very least.

A single guard manned the top of the eastern basement steps. I stood a little straighter and wiped the leftover grin off my face;

I needed all my serious concentration if I was to pull this off. I tried to make my steps ring out confidently as I approached. "Excuse me," I said. "Has Captain Kiggs arrived yet?"

The fellow tugged his mustache. "Can't say I've seen 'im, but I've just come on duty. He might be downstairs."

I hoped not, but I'd deal with that if I had to. "Who's on duty downstairs? John?" John was a good, common name.

His eyes widened a bit. "John Saddlehorn, yes. And Mikey the Fish."

I nodded as if I knew them both. "Well, I don't mind asking them myself. If Captain Kiggs shows up, would you please let him know I'm already below?"

"Hold on," he said. "What's this about? Who are you?"

I gave him a lightly flabbergasted look. "Seraphina Dombegh, daughter of the eminent lawyer Claude Dombegh, the Crown's expert on Comonot's Treaty. Captain Kiggs wanted my insight in questioning the knights. Am I in the wrong place? I had understood they were being held here."

The guard scratched under his helmet, looking conflicted. I suspected he didn't have specific orders against letting anyone down, but he still didn't think he should.

"Come with me, if you like," I offered. "I have a few questions about the dragon they saw. I hope we can identify it."

He hesitated, but agreed to accompany me downstairs. Two guards sat outside a stout wooden door, playing kingfish on an upturned barrel; they lowered their cards confusedly at the sight of us. My guard jerked his thumb toward the stairs. "Mikey, take the top. When the captain arrives, tell him Maid Dombegh is already here."

"What's this, then?" said the one called John as my guard unlocked the door.

"She's to question the prisoners. I'll go in with her; you stay here."

I didn't want him there but saw no immediate way to prevent it. "You're coming in for my protection? Are they very dangerous?"

He laughed. "Maidy, they're old men. You're going to have to speak loudly."

The two knights sat up on their straw pallets, blinking at the light. I gave them half courtesy, keeping close by the door. They weren't as decrepit as reported. They were gray-haired and bony, but had a certain wiry toughness; if the brightness of their eyes was any indication, they were playing "helpless old men" for everything they could.

"What have you brought us, lad?" asked the stouter one, who was bald and mustachioed. "Do you supply your prisoners with women now, or is this some newfangled way of making us talk?"

He was impugning my virtue. I ought to have been offended, but for some reason the idea tickled me. That could be my next career: instrument of torture! Seducing prisoners, and then revealing my scales! They would confess out of sheer horror.

The guard turned red. "Have some respect!" he blustered through his mustache. "She's here on behalf of Captain Kiggs and Counselor Dombegh. You will answer her questions properly, or we will find harder quarters for you, Grandpa."

"It's all right," I said. "Would you mind leaving us?"

"Maid Dombegh, you heard what he just said. It wouldn't be proper!"

"It will be perfectly fine," I assured him in a soothing voice. "Captain Kiggs will be down any minute now."

He set the torch in a sconce and left me, grumbling. The room, which served as storage most of the time, contained some small casks; I pulled one up, sat down, and smiled warmly at the old men. "Which of you is which?" I said, realizing I would already know their names if I were here legitimately. To my embarrassment, I recognized the skinnier of the two, the one who hadn't spoken yet. He had shooed Orma away from me at that disastrous dragon procession five years ago and had helped Maurizio carry me home. I had grown a lot taller since then, and he was old; maybe he didn't remember me.

"Sir Karal Halfholder," he said, sitting up straighter. He was dressed like a peasant, tunic, clogs, grubbiness, and all, but his mien was that of a well-bred man. "My brother-in-arms, Sir Cuthberte Pettybone."

It was Sir Cuthberte who'd taken me for a strumpet. He bowed, saying, "My apologies, Maid Dombegh. I should not have been so boorish."

Sir Karal attempted to preempt my next question: "We'll never tell you where our brothers are hiding!"

"You'd have to seduce us first!" Sir Cuthberte twirled his mustache. Sir Karal glared at him, and Cuthberte cried, "She's smiling! She knows I jest!"

I did know. For some reason, it kept being funny. Old men,

hidden for decades with only other old men for company, found me worth flirting with. That was something.

"The Crown knows where your order is," I said, suspecting that was likely true. "I don't care about that; I want to know where you saw the dragon."

"It came right up to our camp!" said Sir Karal. "We said that!"

Oops. I'd have known that if I weren't lying. I tried to sound impatient: "From which angle? From the north? The village? The wood?" Saints in Heaven, let there be a village and a wood nearby. In Goredd, both were a good bet but not guaranteed.

However, I'd got them thinking, so they didn't notice my ignorance. "It was dark," said Sir Karal, scratching the stubble on his skinny chicken neck. "But you're right, the beast could be staying in the village as a saarantras. That hadn't occurred to us; we'd been looking to the limestone caves, south."

My heart sank. If it was dark, they hadn't seen much. "You're certain it was a dragon?"

They looked at me disdainfully. "Maidy," said Sir Karal, "we fought in the wars. I was left punch in a dracomachia unit. I have soared through the sky, dangling by my harpoon from a dragon's flank while flaming pyria whizzed around me, scanning the ground desperately for a soft place to land when the beast finally caught fire."

"We all have," said Sir Cuthberte quietly, clapping his comrade on the shoulder.

"You don't forget dragons," snarled Sir Karal. "When I am blind and deaf, senile and stroke-addled, I will still know when I'm in the presence of a dragon."

Sir Cuthberte smiled weakly. "They radiate heat, and they smell of brimstone."

"They radiate evil! My soul will know, even if body and mind don't work!"

His hatred hurt me more than it had any right to. I swallowed and tried to keep my voice pleasant: "Did you get a good look at this particular dragon? We suspect we know who he is, but any confirming detail would help. Distinctive horn or wing damage, for example, or coloration—"

"It was dark," said Sir Karal flatly.

"It had a perforation in its right wing," offered Sir Cuthberte. "Closest membrane to its body. Shape of a . . . I don't know. A rat, I want to say. The way they hunch their backs when they eat." He demonstrated, realized how silly he looked, and laughed.

I laughed back, and pulled out my charcoal pencil. "Draw it on the wall, please."

Both knights stared at the pencil, horror writ large on their faces. St. Masha and St. Daan. It was a draconian innovation.

Mercifully, they blamed not me but the peace. "They infiltrate everything, these worms," cried Sir Karal. "They've got our women carrying their blasted devices as casually as smelling oils!"

Sir Cuthberte took it nonetheless and drew a shape upon the wall's graying plaster. Sir Karal corrected the shape. They squabbled a bit but finally settled on something that did, indeed, look like a rodent eating corn.

"That was his only distinguishing mark?" I asked.

"It was dark," said Sir Cuthberte. "We were lucky to make out that much."

"I hope it's enough." Long experience with Orma told me the odds weren't good.

"Whom do you suspect it is?" said Sir Karal, his fists clenched in his lap.

"A dragon called Imlann."

"General Imlann, who was banished?" asked Sir Cuthberte, looking unexpectedly delighted. The knights both whistled, long and low, producing an interval of rather apropos dissonance.

"Did you know him?"

"He led the Fifth Ard, didn't he?" Sir Cuthberte asked his fellow.

Sir Karal nodded gravely. "We fought the Fifth twice, but I never grappled the general. Sir James Peascod, at our camp, specialized in identification. He'd be your best bet. I don't suppose you asked Sir James if he knew this dragon, did you, Cuthberte?"

"Didn't occur to me."

"Pity," sniffed Sir Karal. "Still, how does knowing his name help you catch him?"

I didn't know, now that he mentioned it, but tried to answer logically: "We can't catch him without the embassy's help, and they won't help us if they don't believe us. They might be motivated if we had proof it was Imlann."

Sir Karal turned dangerously red; I could see his pulse at his temple. "That baby-eating worm was in clear violation of the treaty. You'd think that would be enough for them, if they had any honor! Be it known that we upheld our part of that accursed agreement. We didn't attack it, although we could have!"

167

Sir Cuthberte snorted. "Who could have? Pender and Fough-faugh? That would have been over in seconds."

Sir Karal glared venom at Sir Cuthberte. "I tire of this. Where's Captain Kiggs?"

"Good question," I said, rising and dusting off my skirts. "I'll look for him. Thank you for your time, gentle knights."

Sir Karal rose and bowed. Sir Cuthberte said, "What? No kiss?"

I blew him a kiss, laughing, and left.

Outside, the guards seemed surprised to see me. "Captain Kiggs still hasn't arrived, Maid Dombegh," said John, pushing back his helmet.

I smiled, merry with relief that this was over and I'd gotten away with it. I would return to my rooms, contact Orma on the kitten spinet, and see whether he could identify his father from the perforation. "Captain Kiggs must have been detained. No matter—I'm finished here. I'll go see whether I can find him."

"You won't have far to go," said a voice from halfway up the stairs.

Prince Lucian descended the stairs, and my heart descended into my stomach.

Thirteen

I dared not let my eyes widen in horror or the guards would be on to me; to buy myself some time, I curtsied deeply, to a slow count of three.

The prince, when I finally dared to look at him again, seemed amused. He gestured broadly. "You are finished here, one hopes?"

"Yes, thank you," I said, managing to keep any tremor out of my voice. "If you wish to question the knights yourself, perhaps I can meet you tomorrow morning—"

"Oh no," he said lightly, his smile hardening. "I rather think you're meeting with me now. Wait for me upstairs, if you would be so kind."

I had no option but to climb the stairs. Behind me, the prince said, "Who remembers what my token looks like? Right. And did Maid Dombegh bear my token?"

"But, sir, we weren't to start that protocol until Comonot arrives!"

"We're starting it tonight. Only someone with my token speaks in my name."

"Were we wrong to let her down here, Captain?" said John.

Lucian Kiggs paused before answering: "No. You followed your instincts about her, and they did not lead you astray. But it's time to tighten things up, hm? The palace will be full of strangers soon."

He started up the stairs; I hurried to reach the top before he did. The look he gave me when he reached the top was less amused. He acknowledged Mikey the Fish's salute, grabbed me by the right elbow, and marched me up the corridor.

"Who are you working for?" he asked when we were out of earshot.

Was this a trick question? "Viridius."

He stopped and faced me, his brows pulled together darkly. "This is your chance to tell the truth. I dislike games of cat and mouse. You're caught; don't toy with me."

Sweet Heavenly Home, he thought I was some sort of agent for a foreign government, perhaps—or for some individual. A dragon, say. Maybe he wasn't wrong. "Could we talk somewhere besides the hallway, please?"

He glanced up and down the passage, frowning. The east wing was full of servants and storage, kitchens and workshops. He led me up a short hallway and unlocked the heavy door at the end with a key. He lit a lantern at the hall sconce, ushered me through the door, and closed it behind us. We were at the bottom of a spi ral stair leading up into blackness. Instead of climbing the stairs, however, he seated himself about five steps up and set the lantern beside him.

"What is this place?" I said, craning my neck to peer upward.

"My 'beastly tower,' Glisselda calls it." He seemed disinclined to discuss it further. The lantern lit him eerily from below, making it difficult to interpret his expression; he wasn't smiling, in any case. "It would have been easy enough to interview the knights with my blessing. You had only to ask. I dislike your invoking my name under false pretenses."

"I—I shouldn't have. I'm sorry," I stammered. Why had it seemed like a good idea? Why was I more prepared to bluff complete strangers than to speak plainly to this prince? I opened my purse cautiously, blocking any glimpse of the quig figurine, and passed the gold coin to the prince. "My teacher, Orma, also has a concern regarding a possible rogue dragon. I promised him I'd speak to you."

Lucian Kiggs silently examined the coin in the lantern light. He'd been so chatty before; his silence unnerved me. But of course he was doubtful when I claimed to speak on someone else's behalf. How could he not be? Saints' dogs, I'd miscalculated in bluffing his guards.

"A messenger gave him that coin after your uncle's funeral," I pressed on. "Orma claims it belonged to his father."

"Then it probably did," he said, studying the back. "Dragons know their coins."

"His father is General Imlann, disgraced and banished for hoarding."

"Hoarding doesn't usually merit banishment," said the prince, his mouth set in a line. Even his looming shadow seemed skeptical.

"Imlann committed other crimes too, I believe. Orma didn't lay it all out in detail." Here I was, already lying. It never ended. "He believes Imlann is here, in Goredd, and may be planning some harm to the Ardmagar or mischief to the celebrations or . . . he doesn't know what. It's all vague supposition, alas."

Lucian Kiggs glanced from me to the coin and back. "You're uncertain whether he's right to be worried."

"Yes. My hope in speaking to the knights was that they could give me some identifying details, enabling me to confirm with Orma that their rogue dragon is Imlann. I didn't want to waste your time with guesses."

He leaned forward intently. "Might Imlann have wished to harm my uncle?"

He was interested now; that was an immeasurable relief. "I don't know. Did the council conclude that the rogue had something to do with Prince Rufus's death?"

"The council concluded very little. Half the people there suspected the knights of fabricating the whole thing to stir up trouble and prevent Comonot's visit."

"What do you think?" I pressed.

"I think I was on my way to speak with the knights myself when I learned that someone was already speaking to them in my name." He wagged a finger at me, but it was only a mock scolding. "What's your impression? Did they truly see a dragon?"

"Yes."

He raised an eyebrow. "What makes you so sure?"

"I—I suppose it had to do with the kinds of detail they were and weren't able to give me. I wish I could say it was more than just an intuition." I also wished I could say that being a liar myself gave me some insight into these things.

"Don't shrug off intuition so blithely! I advise my men to notice gut reactions. Of course, they were wrong about you." He flashed me an irritated look, then seemed to think better of it. "No, let me amend that. They were wrong to believe I'd given you permission to speak with the prisoners, but they were not wrong about you."

How could he still think well of me after I'd been so awful to him? A warm wash of guilt rolled over me. "I—I'm sorry—"

"No harm done." He waved off my confusion. "In fact, this has turned out very well. You and I appear to be working toward a common purpose. Now that we know, we can help each other."

He thought I was apologizing for the lie; I'd already done that. "I'm, uh, also sorry for what I said to you. Yesterday."

"Ah!" He smiled at long last, and a knot of anxiety in my chest released. "There's the other half of your hesitation. Forget it. I already have."

"I was rude!"

"And I was offended. It was all very by-the-book. But let us set that aside, Seraphina. We're pulling in the same team." I wasn't buying such easy forgiveness; he noticed my doubt and added: "Selda and I had a long talk about you. She spoke quite eloquently in your defense."

"She didn't say I was prickly?"

"Oh, she absolutely did. And you are." He looked vaguely amused by whatever expression sprawled across my face. "Stop glowering. There's nothing wrong with letting people know when they've stepped on your tail. The thing to ask ourselves when you bite is, why?"

Bite. Tail. I crossed my arms over my chest.

"Selda has observed that you dislike personal questions, and certainly I was getting a bit personal. So. My apologies."

I looked at my feet, embarrassed.

He continued: "In this particular case, I think there was more to it than that. You honestly answered my question." He sat back smugly, as if he'd solved a difficult riddle. "I asked what it's like to be so talented, and you gave me a straightforward comparison: like being a bastard! And with a little extra thought, I get it. Everyone gawps at you for something you can't help and did nothing to deserve. Your very presence makes other people feel awkward. You stand out when in fact you'd rather not."

For the merest moment I couldn't breathe. Something inside me quivered, some oud string plucked by his words, and if I breathed it would stop.

He did not know the truth of me, yet he had perceived something true about me that no one else had ever noticed. And in spite of that—or perhaps because of it—he believed me good, believed me worth taking seriously, and his belief, for one vertiginous moment, made me want to be better than I was.

I was a fool to let myself feel that. I was a monster; that could never change.

I almost snapped at him, almost played the monster in earnest as only I could play it, but something stopped me. He wasn't some dragon, coldly observing me. He was offering me something true about himself in return. It shone like a diamond. That wasn't trivial; that was generous. If I knocked this gift out of his hand, I wasn't getting another. I inhaled shakily and said, "Thank you, but . . ." *No, no buts.* "Thank you."

He smiled. "There's more to you than meets the eye. I've observed that more than once. Which of the Porphyrian philosophers do you favor?"

It was such a non sequitur that I nearly laughed, but he kept talking, finally at ease with me again. "You recognized that quote the other evening, and I thought, 'At long last, someone else who's read Pontheus!'"

"I'm afraid I haven't, much. Papa had his *Analects*—"

"But you've read other philosophers. Confess!" He leaned forward eagerly, elbows on his knees. "I'd guess you like . . . Archiboros. He was so keen on the life of the mind that he never bothered to determine whether his theories worked in the real world."

"Archiboros was a pompous ass," I said. "I preferred Necans."

"That morose old twig!" cried Kiggs, slapping his leg. "He takes it too far. If he had his way, we'd all be nothing but disembodied minds, floating and ephemeral, completely disconnected from the matter of this world."

"Would that be so awful?" I said, my voice catching. He'd hit upon something personal again, or else I was so raw I could be hurt by anything, no matter how innocuous.

"I'd have thought you preferred Pontheus, is all," he said,

examining an invisible speck on the sleeve of his doublet, giving me a little space to collect myself.

"A jurisprudence philosopher?"

"Clearly you've only read his early work. All his genius is in his later writings."

*

"Didn't he go mad?" I was aiming for supercilious, but the look on his face told me I'd missed and landed squarely on amusing.

"If it was madness, Phina, it was such a madness as you or I could only dream of! I will find you his last book." He looked at me again and his eyes shone in the lamplight, or with the inner light of delighted anticipation.

His enthusiasm made him beautiful. I was staring; I looked at my hands.

He coughed and rose, tucking the coin into his doublet. "Right. Well. I'll take Orma's coin to Eskar tomorrow morning and see what she says. With my luck, she'll conclude we're harboring criminals; I don't think she's forgiven me for letting that newskin get hurt—or for dancing with her, for that matter. Ask your teacher about the details the knights gave you; I'd appreciate that. If we could identify this rogue, that might impress upon the embassy that we are making a good-faith effort to . . . I was going to say 'maintain order,' but it's a bit late for that, isn't it?"

I said, "Until tomorrow, then." Of course, it was up to him to dismiss me, not the other way around. I cringed at myself.

He seemed not to register the breach in manners. I curtsied to make up for it. He smiled and opened the tower door for me. My mind was racing, scrambling to think up one more thing to say to him before I left, but it came up empty. "Good evening, Seraphina," he said, and closed the door.

I heard his footfall grow faint as he climbed the tower steps. What did he do up there? It was none of my business, to be sure, but I stood for a long moment with my hand upon the oaken door.

I stood so still, for so long, that I nearly jumped out of my skin when a voice said, "Music Mistress? Are you ill?"

I looked behind me; there stood one of my musicians, the scrawny sackbutist whose name I never remembered, who had apparently been passing by and spotted me looking catatonic. He stepped toward me hesitantly. "Is there anything you need?"

"No," I croaked, my voice as rough as if I were breaking a years-long vow of silence. "Thank you," I added. I bent my head, skirted him meekly, and headed back up the hallway toward my rooms.

Fourteen

The next day was the last before Comonot arrived, and Viridius planned to rehearse us within an inch of our lives. I rose extra early; I needed to contact Orma first thing so I could let Kiggs know what he said. I played our chord upon the spinet and waited, scalding my tongue on my tea and wondering where I might find Kiggs this time of day. He had an office near the main guardroom, I knew, but he also spent a lot of time in the city.

When the spinet kitten finally spoke, it startled me so much that I almost lost my teacup. "Can't talk," buzzed Orma's voice. "I'm babysitting Basind."

I'd forgotten all about the newskin. "When can you talk?"

"Dinner? The Mallet and Mullet? Six?"

"Fine, but make it seven. Viridius intends to flog us until we bleed today."

"I'll see you then. Don't eat that!"

I looked to my cup of tea and back. "Don't eat what?"

"Not you. Basind." The kitten crackled, and he was gone.

I sighed, pushed back from the instrument, and heard the great clock above the central courtyard chime. There was more than enough time for my morning routine and breakfast. I was running early, which was just as well. Viridius would find no fault with me today.

I arrived at Castle Orison's vast great hall early and alert. Carpenters were swarming all over the stage, which could not be a good sign, and I saw neither hide nor wispy hair of the gouty old man. Musicians were everywhere, like ants, but no Viridius. Finally his phlegmatic manservant, Marius, crept up with a message for me: "The master's not here."

"What do you mean he's not here? This is dress rehearsal."

Marius cleared his throat nervously. "To quote him precisely: 'Tell Seraphina I leave everything in her more than capable hands. Don't forget to rehearse smooth entrances and exits!'"

I bit back the first word that occurred to me, and the second. "So where is he?"

The man ducked his gray head; apparently my tone had been ungentle. "At the cathedral. His protégé was having some problem—"

"Lars?" I said. Someone with keen hearing stopped in his tracks behind me. I lowered my voice. "What kind of problem, exactly?"

Viridius's man shrugged. "The master wouldn't say."

"The usual, no doubt," sneered Earl Josef, at my back. "Brawling, bringing his filthy *radt-grauser* into the cathedral, getting drunk and smashing up his own machine."

I understood "red-women." "They wear black and yellow stripes here in Goredd," I said, trying to plaster over my agitation with a joke. "But I expect you know that firsthand."

The earl ran his tongue over his perfect teeth and tugged his lace cuffs. "Normally I wouldn't bother, but I like you, *grauseline.* Stay away from Lars. He's a Daanite and a liar and trouble incarnate. He's barely human."

"Viridius trusts him," I said.

"Master Viridius has taken a dangerous fancy to him," the earl said. "Neither of you understands what he is. I pray every day that St. Ogdo destroy him."

I wanted so badly to say I knew exactly what Lars was and did not hold it against him, but the closest I could manage was "I don't care what you say. He is my friend. I will hear no more of this slander."

He snaked an unwelcome arm around my waist; I tried to pull away, but he had a grip like a lobster. "You are the sweetest and most innocent of *grausleiner,*" he murmured. "But there are people in this world who commit horrifying and unnatural acts beyond anything your naïve imagination could conceive. He is your worst nightmare. Heed my warning and stay away from him. I fear for you otherwise."

He leaned in and kissed my ear as if sealing my compliance, but he drew back abruptly. "What is that odd perfume you wear?"

"Let go of me," I said through clenched teeth.

Josef gave a haughty sniff and released me, stalking off without a backward glance.

I beat back a wave of panic. He'd smelled me. Had he recognized the smell as saar?

I gathered what dignity I could muster after being so unpleasantly manhandled, and approached the gathered herd of performers, prepared to go full Viridius on them. They expected nothing better, after all.

The stage was beautiful but turned out to be unsound over the trapdoor in the center, as we learned to our dismay when five bassos disappeared at once. I yelled at the carpenters and drilled the choir on the other side of the hall while they made modifications. Then the curtain mechanism didn't work, the stilt walker's costume fell off mid-jig—funny, under other circumstances—and Josef's viola solo kept drifting flat.

I took no satisfaction in the last; in fact, I suspected it was a ploy to make me look at him. I grimly kept my gaze elsewhere.

That was very little gone wrong for a dress rehearsal, but it was more than my mood would support. I growled bearishly at everyone, deservedly or not. The itinerant performers seemed alarmed, but my palace musicians found me amusing; I made an unconvincing Viridius, even at my crankiest. Snatches of my praise song drifted in my wake as I stormed past, making it difficult to keep scowling.

Evening came at last, and my musicians decided it was high time they refused to work. This, of course, meant they set up a massive session in the great hall playing reels and jigs for fun. Music is only work if someone else makes you do it. I'd have liked to join in—I'd more than earned it, I felt—but Orma was waiting. I bundled up and headed downhill into town.

The warmth of the Mallet and Mullet was welcome, although I never felt quite comfortable in the presence of strangers and smoke, chatter and clatter. The fire and lamps provided too little light. It took me some time scanning the tables to realize Orma had not yet arrived. I claimed a place near the hearth, ordered myself some barley water, to the barmaid's scornful amusement, and sat down to wait.

It wasn't like Orma to be late. I sipped my beverage, keeping my eyes to myself, until a commotion by the door grew too loud to ignore.

"You can't bring his kind in here," snarled the tapmaster, who had come out from behind his bar, dragging a muscular cook with him as backup. I turned around to look; Orma stood in the foyer, unfastening his cloak clasp. Basind lurked behind him, his bell tinkling plaintively. Patrons near the door made St. Ogdo's sign or pressed fragrant sachets to their noses as if warding off disease.

The tapmaster folded his arms over his dingy apron. "This is a respectable establishment. We've served the likes of Baronet Meadowburn and the Countess du Paraday."

"Recently?" said Orma, widening his eyes mildly. The tapmaster took that for disrespect and puffed out his chest; the cook fingered the edge of his cleaver.

I was already on my feet, slapping a coin onto the table. "Go back outside!"

The open night air, when I reached it, came as a relief even if Basind's slouching silhouette did not.

"Why did you bring him along?" I said crossly as we stepped into the empty street. "You should have known they wouldn't serve him."

Orma opened his mouth, but Basind spoke first: "Where my teacher goes, I go."

Orma shrugged. "There are places we can eat."

Places, maybe, but only in one part of town.

Quighole was closed after sunset, technically. Only two streets led into what had once been St. Jobertus's Close; each had been fitted with a tall wrought-iron gate that the Queen's Guard, with great ceremony, padlocked every evening. Of course, the buildings facing the square had back doors, so one had simply to walk through a shop, a tavern, or a house full of quigs to get in and out—and there were always the tunnels below. Disgruntled saarantrai characterized Quighole as a prison; it was a porous prison, if so.

Old St. Jobertus's had once been a church; when the parish outgrew the building, New St. Jobertus's had been built across the river, where there was more room. After Comonot's Treaty, some dragons had aspired to run a little collegium to help fulfill Comonot's proposed interspecies knowledge exchange. Old St. Jobertus's was the largest unused building they could find. While bell-exempt dragon students such as Orma sneaked around studying our mysterious ways, other scholars, fully belled and graduated, came to St. Bert's (as it was now called) to teach their sciences to backward humans.

They got few students, and fewer who would admit to being students. St. Bert's trained the best physicians, but few humans wanted a doctor practicing spooky saar medicine on them. A recent scandal over the dissection of human cadavers hadn't helped matters. Riots all over town had nearly turned into a bloodbath; people demanded vengeance against the saarantraí—and their students—who dared paw through human remains. There had been a trial, with my father right in the middle of things as usual. Dissection was forbidden and several dragons were sent back to the Tanamoot, but physicians continued to train in secret.

I had only been to Quighole once, when Orma took me with him to fetch my itch ointment. It was not a place respectable young girls should be seen, and my father had been adamant that I should avoid the neighborhood. As many of his objections as I had overturned or disregarded, I'd willingly abided by this one.

Orma took us up an alley, reached over top of a gate to unlock it, and led us into someone's muddy kitchen garden. Dead marrow vines squished underfoot. A pig grunted in one enclosure; another was full of rotting vegetables. I feared the house's owner would come after us with a pitchfork at any minute, but Orma walked straight up to the door and knocked three times. No one answered. He knocked three more times and then scratched the flaking paint with his nails.

A little hatch window opened. "Who is it?" asked a scratchy voice.

"It's the polecat," said Orma. "I've come to nix the mink."

An old woman with a wide toothless grin opened the door to us. I followed Orma down the stairs into a fetid semidarkness. We arrived in a humid, stenchy cellar lit by a wide hearth, small lamps, and a hanging light fixture in the shape of a mermaid with antlers, her bosom bared to all the world, brandishing two candles like swords. Her eyes bugged out at me as if she were astonished to see a sister monster.

My eyes adjusted. We were in some sort of underground public house. There were rickety tables and a variety of patrons—human, saarantrai, and quigutl. Humans and saarantrai sat at the same tables here, students engaged in deep discussions with teachers. Here was a saar demonstrating principles of surface tension—just as Zeyd had taught me before her special tutorial in gravitation—by holding a glass of water upside down with only a slip of parchment between his rapt students and a drenching. In another corner I saw an impromptu dissection of a small mammal, or dinner, or both.

No one came to Quighole who didn't have to; I had more personal dealings with saarantrai than most people, and I'd only been the once. I had never seen both my . . . my peoples together like this. I found myself a little overcome.

The human students did not interact much with the quigutl, but it was still remarkable how little fussed they were at the presence of the creatures. Nobody sent back food that had been touched by quigs—there were quig servers! and nobody shrieked upon discovering one under the table. Quigutl had affixed themselves to the rafters and the walls; some clustered around tables with saarantrai. The global stench undoubtedly came from quig breath, but the nose falls asleep quickly. By the time we found a table, I barely smelled anything at all.

Orma went to order us dinner, leaving me with Basind. Our table was covered in chalk equations. I pretended to look at them while studying the newskin sidelong. He gaped vapidly at a nearby table full of quigs.

I couldn't talk to Orma in front of Basind, but I didn't see how to get around it.

I followed Basind's gaze to the next table and gasped. The quigs there had their tongues out and sparks were flying. It was hard to see through the gloom, but they appeared to be altering the shape of a bottle, melting the glass with focused heat from their tongues and pulling it like taffy. The long fingers of their dorsal arms—the twiglike, dexterous limbs they had in place of wings—seemed impervious to heat. They pulled glass as thin as thread, heated it again, and looped it around into lacy structures.

Orma returned and set down our drinks. He followed my gaze to the glass-spinning quigutl. They'd made a hollow, basket-sized egg of green glass threads. "Why don't glassblowers hire them?" I asked.

"Why don't goldsmiths hire them?" said Orma, passing Basind a cup of barley water. "They don't follow instructions willingly, for one thing."

"How is it that you saar don't understand art?" I said, marveling at their gleaming creation. "Quigs make art."

"That's not art," said Orma flatly.

"How would you even know?"

His eyebrows drew together. "They don't value it the way a human would. There's no meaning to it." One of the quigs had climbed onto the table and was attempting to sit on the glass egg. It shattered into a thousand shards. "See?" said Orma.

I thought about the human-faced lizard in my purse; I wasn't sure he was right. That figurine spoke to me somehow.

The tapmaster came rushing toward the quigs, brandishing a broom and shouting. The quigs scattered, some under the table, some up the walls. "Clean this up!" the man cried. "You can't come in here if you're going to jump around like apes!"

The quigs all lisped insults at him, but they crept back and cleaned the table, using the sticky fingers of their ventral hands to pick up splintered glass. They collected it in their mouths, masticated it, and spit molten globs, hissing, into a glass of beer.

There was a glass of beer at our table, too, belonging to Orma. Basind had homed in on it and was leaning over the cup, sniffing. He rose with a drip on the end of his nose. "That's an intoxicant. I should report you."

"Recall clause nine of the exemption papers," said Orma coolly.

"A scholar working incognito may bend Standard Protocols 22 and 27, or such other Protocols as he deems necessary for the successful maintenance of his disguise'?"

"That's the one."

Basind continued. "'Clause 9a. Said scholar will file Form 89XQ for each of his deviations, and may be required to undergo a psychological audit and/or defend the necessity of his actions before the Board of Censors.'"

"Enough, Basind," said Orma. As the patron Saints of comedy

would have it, however, a quigutl brought our dinner at that very moment: lamb olio for me, leek and turnip soup for Basind, and for my uncle, a fat boiled sausage.

"Tell me, must you file a separate form for each item individually, or can you lump together sausage and beer consumed at the same meal?" asked Basind with surprising acuity.

"Separate forms when I'm overdue for an audit," said Orma. He took a drink. "You can help me fill them out later."

"Eskar says rules have reasons," rasped Basind. "I must wear clothing so as not to frighten people. I mustn't spread butter on my itchy skin, because it offends my landlady. Similarly, we may not eat the flesh of animals because it makes us hunger for the abundant flesh around the table." Basind flashed his horrid buggy eyes toward me.

"That's the idea, yes," said Orma. "But I've never found it to be the case—particularly with sausages, where the meat barely resembles meat at all."

Basind looked around the dim basement at the other saarantrai and muttered, "I should report this whole room."

Orma ignored this. He drew a small handful of coins out of the hidden recesses of his doublet, lowered his hand to his lap, and jingled the coins. Suddenly there were quigs on the floor all around us, crawling under the table, winding around our ankles like snakes. This was a bit much, even for me.

Orma broadcast the coins into the tangle on the floor, as if he were feeding chickens; the quigs scrambled for coins, went still a moment, and then swarmed Basind.

"No I don't," said Basind confusedly. "Leave me alone."

I gaped at Basind, not recognizing the opportunity Orma had created until my uncle grabbed my arm, pulled me away from the table, and whispered, "I know quig hand signals; I told them Basind has a hoard at home. If you have news, out with it now."

"I showed Kiggs the coin and told him your concerns."

"And?"

"A rogue dragon has been spotted in the countryside. Two knights came to report it. I interviewed them. They say the dragon had a distinctive perforation in its right wing, in the shape of a rat. Did your father have any such—"

"His wing was once injured by ice, but it was repaired. Sixteen years is ample time to acquire additional perforations, however."

"In other words, it may or may not be Imlann." I sighed, frustrated. "So what can you tell me about his natural shape? How might Kiggs recognize him?"

Orma had described his father's saarantras so vaguely that I did not expect the wealth of detail he gave me now: the sheen of Imlann's skin (different in moonlight), how sharp he habitually kept his talons, the precise shape and color of his eyes (different when he pulled his third eyelid across), the curl of horn and fold of wings (delineated with mathematical precision), the spiciness of his brimstone breath, his tendency to feint left and strike right, the width of the sinews at his heels.

Orma remembered his father's dragon shape as clearly as if it had been treasure. I felt like I was hearing him describe a heap of gold coins, which I would be expected to distinguish from other heaps by description alone. There was no point asking for more. Did dragons find descriptions of humans confusing? Did it take time and experience to tell us apart?

"I can tell you're not going to retain any of this," said Orma. "You have that empty look you used to give your history tutors. You could look for Imlann—"

"You told me not to!"

"Let me finish. You could look for him in your own head, among your maternal memories. Surely Linn left you some image of our father."

I opened my mouth and shut it again. I did not care to go digging around in that box again, not if I could avoid it.

The knights had mentioned a Sir James as their specialist dragon identifier. He was the one I needed to talk to—Kiggs needed to talk to, that is. In the meantime, I hoped Kiggs hadn't put off talking to Eskar in hopes that I might gain good information.

Basind, with the help of the tapmaster and his broom, had cleared off nearly all the quigs. Our time was ending.

"Turn your back toward Basind," Orma whispered. "I don't want him to see me give you this."

It was a bit late to start pretending he was a law-abiding saar. "Give me what?"

Never taking his eyes off the newskin, Orma pretended to scratch his head. His hand came down and pressed cold metal into mine. It was one of his earrings. I gasped and tried to hand it back. Orma said, "The Censors aren't watching. A quig modified them for me."

"Won't the Censors notice they can't check in on you anymore?"

"I'm sure they already have. They'll see to it I get a new pair. It's happened before. Switch it on if you're in trouble, and I'll come as soon as I can."

"I promised I wouldn't go looking for Imlann."

"Trouble may find you," he said. "I have an interest in this particular problem."

I tucked the earring into my bodice and we turned back toward the table. Basind's tunic was covered with grubby handprints; his dinner was gone, but it wasn't clear he'd been the one to eat it. He looked bewildered, or like his face had melted a little. "We must return to St. Ida's," said Orma, extending a hand to me to show Basind how it was done. I shook it, trying to hide my amusement. We never shook hands.

Basind tried it next but he wouldn't let go. When I finally pried him off, he gave me a look I didn't dare identify. "Touch me again!" he rasped, and my stomach turned.

"Home," said Orma. "You have meditation and partitioning to practice."

Basind whined, rubbing his hand fiercely as if he could recover something of my touch, but he followed my uncle up the tavern stairs, docile as a lamb.

I checked with the tapmaster that Orma had paid for our dinner; one could never be certain he'd remember something like that. I took one last look around this peculiar, smelly slice of interspecies coexistence, the treaty's mad dream come to raucous life, then took myself toward the stairs.

"Maidy?" said a hesitant voice at my back. I turned to see a fresh-faced young student with chalk dust in his hair. In one hand he grasped a very short straw; behind him an entire table of young men pretended not to be watching.

"Are you rushing off?" He didn't stammer with his voice but with his waving hands and his nervous blink. "Would you not join us? We're all human over here—well, except for Jim—and we're not bad company. We wouldn't have to talk math. It's just . . . we've seen no human girls in Quighole since dissection was out-lawed!"

Almost the entire table behind him burst out laughing; the saarantras looked baffled by everyone else's reaction, saying, "But he's not wrong, is he?"

I couldn't stop myself from laughing along with them; in fact, I found myself tempted far more by this offer than by Guntard's invitation to the Sunny Monkey. These chalk-dusted fellows, arguing and scribbling trigonometry on the table, felt familiar to me, as if St. Bert's Collegium attracted all the most saar-like humans. I patted his shoulder in a comradely fashion and said, "Honestly, I wish I *could* stay. For future reference: do not underestimate the seductive power of math. If I come again, I shall expect to scrawl on the tables right along with you."

His friends welcomed him back to the table, hooting and toasting his bravery. I smiled to myself. First those aged knights, and now this. I was evidently the sweetheart of all Goredd. That made me laugh, and laughing gave me the courage to plunge out into the night, away from the warmth of this gathering.

Fifteen

It was late enough when I reached Castle Orison that I wasn't sure where I'd find Lucian Kiggs. It occurred to me that I could check the Blue Salon, where Princess Glisselda was almost certainly holding her miniature court, but I feared I smelled of tavern—or worse yet, quigutl—and surely by the time I changed clothes and cleaned up, it would be too late and everyone would have gone to bed.

I knew better than that; I just didn't want to go.

I went to my suite and wrote Kiggs a note:

Your Highness:

I spoke with Orma, but alas, he could not identify the rogue dragon from the knights' description. However, I forgot to mention to you that the knights claimed one of their own, Sir James Peascod, specialized in identifying dragons during the war.

Sir James was there the evening of the rogue's visit and may have recognized him. I think it would be well worth interviewing him about this matter.

I hope you didn't put off speaking with Eskar in hopes that I would return with useful information. My apologies for Orma's vagueness.

I couldn't work out how to sign off; everything seemed too familiar or ridiculously stiff. I decided to err on the side of stiff, given how I'd begun the letter. I found a page boy in the corridor and handed it off to him. I bid all my grotesques good night and went to bed early; tomorrow was going to be the longest of long days.

The sun rose into a dappled sky, pink and gray like the belly of a trout. The maids were pounding on my locked door before I was done washing; the breakfast hall was abuzz with anticipation. The green and purple banner of Belondweg, Goredd's first queen, flew from every turret and hung in long drapes upon the houses in town. A line of carriages ran all the way from Stone Court to the bottom of Castle Hill: dignitaries arriving from all over the Southlands. No one dared miss this rare opportunity to meet with Ardmagar Comonot in human form.

I watched the Ardmagar's slow procession from atop the barbican, along with most of our musicians. Comonot had flown to Southgate before the sun was up so as to minimize alarm at his scaly presence, but everyone in town knew he was coming and a crowd had been gathered there since last night. Representatives of the Crown had been on hand to greet the Ardmagar and to provide him and his entourage with clothing once they transformed. Comonot partook of a leisurely breakfast; it was midmorning before he set out for the palace with his entourage. Comonot refused a horse and insisted on traversing the city on foot, personally greeting the people—cheering and otherwise—who lined the streets.

Apparently he arrived at the cathedral plaza just as the Countdown Clock chimed for the last time. They say it played an eerie, mechanized hurdy-gurdy tune, and that the Queen and the dragon danced a jig together. People who saw it insisted that it was not a machine but a puppet performance. No machine could have put on such a show.

I'd have bet a Lars-built machine could, but alas I didn't get to see it for myself.

Though the Ardmagar was dressed in bright blue, he was hard to spot among the milling throngs and waving flags; his saarantras was not a tall man. Those of us shivering on the barbican did not find ourselves unduly impressed. "He's so tiny!" cooed the scrawny sackbutist. "I could squish him under my boot heel!"

"Who's a cockroach now, Ard Buggert?" crled one of my drum mers, not quietly.

I cringed, hoping no one who mattered had heard. How did word move so quickly at court? I said: "Not one more disrespectful word—any of you!—or you will find yourself playing for your supper on street corners." They flashed me any number of skeptical looks. "Viridius has given me full discretion in this," I assured them. "Push me, if you imagine I don't mean it."

They looked at their shoes. I thanked St. Loola, patroness of children and fools, that no one seemed inclined to call my bluff.

Those of us responsible for the fanfare took off for the reception hall and found it packed to the rafters with the aggregate nobility of the Southlands. From my perch in the gallery, I saw that Count Pesavolta of Ninys and the Regent of Samsam had each colonized a quarter of the room, the former flamboyant and noisy, the latter dour and severe. I spotted Dame Okra among the Ninysh; she was more subdued than most, but then, she had lived a long time in Goredd.

The Ardmagar stepped into the doorway, and the room went instantly silent. He was as stout and as jowly as Viridius. His dark hair looked like it had been wetted and combed severely straight; it was threatening to burst into unruliness as it dried. Nevertheless, his hawkish nose and piercing stare gave him a formidable presence. He radiated intensity, as if compelled by some inner fire he could barely contain; the very air around him seemed to shimmer, like the heat off city streets in summertime. He wore his bell like a medal, on a heavy gold chain around his thick neck. He raised an arm in salutation; the room held its breath. The Queen rose; Princess Dionne rose with her, looking awed. Glisselda and Kiggs, together on the left, were mere shadows playing at the periphery of history.

We gallery rats were supposed to burst forth in fanfare at exactly this point, but we were all struck dumb. My musicians must have found Comonot a bit more impressive up close.

I, on the other hand, had broken into a cold sweat.

I shook all over, filled with a rancorous cacophony of emotions: fear, anger, disgust. The stew of emotions wasn't mine, though.

I closed my eyes and saw the tin box of memories sitting in a puddle, leaking. Fat pearls of condensation rolled down its sides. I couldn't do my job with my mother's feelings about Comonot leaking into my consciousness. I cast around inside my head for a . . . a towel. One appeared at my thought. I mopped up underneath and then wrapped the box in it.

The mess of emotions dissipated, and I opened my eyes. Comonot had proceeded no further up the carpet toward the dais. His arm was still raised; he looked like a plaster statue of himself.

"Wake up, you louts!" I hissed to my musicians. They startled as if they'd been entranced, hoisted their instruments into position, and burst into music on my mark.

At the blare of his tardy fanfare, the general began the long walk toward the dais, leaving a glamour in the air behind him as he passed, waving and smiling. He seemed to wink at every single one of us individually.

He stepped up, kissed the Queen's jeweled hand, and addressed the crowd in a resounding basso: "Queen Lavonda. Princesses. Gathered people of quality. I come to honor forty years of peace between our peoples."

He waited for the clapping to subside, his expression as self-satisfied as a cat's. "Do you know why dragons learned to take human form? We change that we might speak with you. In our natural form, our throats are so rough with smoke that we cannot make your words. You, on your side, fail to recognize our Mootya as speech. It was the dragon sage Golya, or Golymos, as they call him in Porphyry, who discovered how to effect this change almost a millennium ago. He wished to speak with the Porphyrian philosophers and found a mighty university for our people. That was the first incidence of dragons looking to humans for something good and useful, but not the last. Golya has gone down in history as one of our greats—and so shall I."

Applause again shook the hall. Comonot waited it out, wedging his left hand into the gap between buttons at the front of his satin doublet as if he intended to surreptitiously scratch his stomach.

"The idea of peace came to me in a dream when I was a student at Golya's university, the Danlo Mootseye. We dragons do not dream. I took a class on dreaming; we slept in our saarantrai and reported each day on the wonders we had seen.

"One night I saw a hoard, gleaming like the sun. I stepped up to it, to run my fingers through it, but it wasn't gold, it was knowledge! And I realized a wondrous truth: that knowledge could be our treasure, that there were things humankind knew that we did not, that our conquest need not comprise taking and killing, but could consist of our mutual conquest of ignorance and distrust."

He began pacing the dais and gesticulating at oddly precise intervals, as if he'd seen a human do this before and concluded that it was a ritual dance that he could master. He said: "I told my dream in class, and was ridiculed. 'What does knowledge look like? What knowledge could be worth having that we cannot discover on our own?' But I knew the truth of it, I believed it down to my smoldering core, and from that day forward, I acted only for the sake of that vision. I grew mighty for its sake. I wrought a peace of steel. I wrestled with how best to learn your arts, your diplomacy, your ability to band together, while still retaining our essential dragonness. It has not been easy.

"Dragons are slow to change; we each want to fly our own direction. The only way to lead is to drag the rest, flapping and flaming, toward what is right. I treated with Queen Lavonda in secret, knowing it would be better to impose a treaty upon my own people than to endure a century of debating it in the Ker. I was right.

"The treaty has been and continues to be successful, thanks to reforms on our side and continuing good faith on yours. Here's to forty more years, or—if I may extrapolate—a hundred. My co-signer will be long dead by then, and I'll be addressing your grandchildren, but I intend this peace to last until the end of my days, and beyond."

The gathered nobility hesitated, put off perhaps by such a casual reference to our shorter life spans, but in the end they all applauded. The Queen directed Comonot to the chair that had been placed for him between herself and Princess Dionne, and the long, tedious ritual of paying respects began. Everyone in that hall, from the Regent of Samsam to Little Lord Nobody of Pisky-on-the-Pigpond, expected an opportunity to meet Ardmagar Comonot and kiss the rings upon his thick fingers. I noted the Earl of Apsig lining up with everyone else, and felt a certain grim satisfaction.

The endless reception line required musical accompaniment, of course. I was on oud, but I'd forgotten my plectrum; I had blisters on my fingers by lunchtime.

I also had a headache. It had started with the leaking memory box and grown by the hour. "Are you all right, Music Mistress?" asked a voice from . . . I could not pinpoint it. I looked across at my musicians, who seemed bizarrely far away. Their faces wobbled. I blinked. "She's gone so pale!" said a very slow voice indeed, a sound like dark honey through a sieve.

I wondered whether I'd miss lunch, and then my mother's memory ambushed me.

One hundred sixty-one dragons perched atop High Nest. Below us: mountains. Above us: nimbus clouds moving south-southeast at 0.0034 terminus.

The Ardmagar lectures the students and faculty of the Danlo Mootseye as the new term unfurls. His lecture's title: "The Insidious Sickness."

I know what that refers to. I cannot sleep, thinking about it. I am likely infected.

I bring out my note block and turn it on. It was made by one of my father's quigutl. It helps me remember, but nothing helps me forget.

"Humanity can be our teacher," cries the Ardmagar. "The point of peace is the exchange of knowledge. My reforms—the bans on vendetta and on boarding, for two—are buoyed by human philosophies. Where such philosophies are logical, ethical, and quantifiable, we can make them our own.

"But let me warn you, all of you, from the newskin on his first trip south to the venerable teacher who has flown into the macrocloud of unvigilance: there is danger in humanity. Do not lose yourself to the

wet brain. Tempted by the chemical intoxication of emotion, dragons forget what they are."

The Ardmagar is wrong about that. I have never forgotten, to three significant digits, even when I wished to. And here I perch, not forgetting Claude.

"Emotions are addictive!" cries the Ardmagar. "They have no meaning; they are antithetical to reason. They fly toward illogical, non-draconian moralities."

"They fly toward art," I mutter.

He hears the echo of my voice; the acoustics of High Nest have been perfected over a millennium, that everyone may be heard. "Who spoke out of ard?"

I raise my head to an angle of 40 degrees, breaking the submissive stance. Everyone stares. "I said, Ardmagar, that emotions fly humans toward art."

"Art." He fixes me with a hunter's gaze, gauging my speed and defenses. "Art gleams before us all, a board ungathered. I understand that, hatchling. But we study art. We fly over it from every direction, from a sane, safe distance. Someday we will comprehend its power. We will put it in ard. We will learn to hatch it, and why it's worth hatching. But do not be tempted into the human flight path. Is a breath's span of art worth a life span enslaved by the fetid backwash of the meaty brain?"

I lower my head, hiring down on my instinct. This would be anger, for a human; I've felt that. In the dragon brain, it manifests as "flame or flee." Why did I speak? He will measure my words and calculate that I am miasmic. The Censors will come at night; I will be sent down for excision. They will cut the unquantifiable right out of me.

It would put my neurons back in ard. I have wished to forget; it's why I came home. I want it, and don't want it.

One cannot fly in two directions at once. I cannot perch among those who think that I am broken.

I scan the text recorded on my note block. To it I add: Love is not a disease.

I opened my eyes, closing them again immediately when I saw Kiggs leaning over me, looking concerned, his hand on my forehead. Saints' dogs, I'd collapsed under that memory. Why couldn't I have plunged headfirst over the parapet and saved myself the mortification of waking up with everyone staring at me?

"She's coming round," he said. "Phina, do you hear me?"

"It's stuffy up here," said our best trumpeter. "We've been playing for three hours. She's really all right?"

"It's that bastard Viridius's fault. He lets her take everything on herself!" That sounded like Guntard.

The hand on my forehead tensed at the word *bastard*. My eyes opened just in time to catch the irritation on Kiggs's face; it softened upon seeing me awake.

He helped me rise. I swayed dizzily—the ground was so far away!—until I realized I was still up in the gallery, looking down at the almost empty hall. The last few dignitaries were trickling out, trying to pretend they weren't staring up at me.

"What happened?" I croaked, my throat like parchment.

"You fainted," said Guntard. "We thought you'd overheated, but we didn't know how to cool you down decently. We took off your shoes—your pardon, please—and we were just going to roll up your sleeves—"

I looked away, bracing my hands against the railing so they wouldn't shake.

"—but Prince Lucian suggested we fan you. Your oud is undamaged."

"Thank you, Guntard," I said, avoiding his eye and reaching for my shoes.

My musicians hovered solicitously, as if uncertain what I required. I waved a dismissal; they nearly trampled each other rushing off to lunch. Kiggs had claimed a chair and was sitting on it backward, leaning his chin on his hands, watching me. He was wearing a fancier scarlet doublet today, with ropes of gold braid crisscrossing it; his plain white armband looked all the more mournful in contrast.

"Don't you have someplace official to be?" I said lightly as I buckled my shoes, trying to be funny but fearing he'd hear the crankiness beneath it.

He raised his eyebrows. "In fact, I do. But I'm also in charge of security, and there was quite a commotion up here when you keeled over. Selda promised she'd guard my plate. I'll escort you down, if you like."

"I don't feel like eating," I didn't feel like walking either, thank Allsaints. I sat and rubbed my eyes; behind them, my head still ached. "Did you get my note?" I asked.

He sat up straighter. "Yes. Thank you. Sounds like your efforts yesterday were as futile as mine. I didn't manage to speak with

Eskar; she'd left for Dewcomb's Outpost with the rest of the embassy staff to await the Ardmagar's arrival."

I said, "Does the embassy know about the knights' story?"

He puffed out his cheeks as he exhaled. "Grandmother met with Ambassador Fulda before he left, apprising him of the 'rumor.'"

"Rumor?" I said, astonished. "She doesn't believe Sir Karal saw a dragon?"

Kiggs shook his head irritably. "It pains me to say so, but she doesn't want to believe that dragons might violate her treaty. She's staked her entire reign upon the idea that we can trust dragons, and she refuses to consider the possibility of an unauthorized dragon loose in the countryside—to say nothing of killing Uncle Rufus—without an awful lot of unambiguous proof."

"Orma's coin—" I began.

"Convinced her of nothing," he said, drumming his fingers on the back of his chair; his nails were short as if he bit them, an unexpected habit in a Captain of the Guard. His eyes narrowed thoughtfully. "I don't suppose your teacher described Imlann's saarantras at all?"

"Blue eyes, fair hair," I said. "That describes two-thirds of the Ninysh courtiers."

"It describes all the Ninysh, counting the redheads, and half the Highland Samsamese," said the prince. "But there's no reason to think he's at court, surely? Where does Orma think he'd be?"

"Orma has no idea, of course. He only knows Imlann was at the funeral."

Kiggs wagged a finger at me. "Selda and I talked it over. We think your idea about going to see Sir James and the knights—"

A clatter below interrupted him. A cadre of the palace guard had entered the hall; they snapped to attention at the sight of Kiggs up in the gallery. "Captain! The Queen is most displeased that you disregard the dictates of politeness to our—"

"I'll be there directly," Kiggs said, rising. He turned to me apologetically. "We're not finished. Save me the fourth dance at the ball."

I counted off the order of dances. "The pavano?"

"Perfect. We'll talk more then." He raised a hand as if to give me a soldierly slap on the shoulder, but then deftly turned it into a polite bow. He departed for his luncheon with the Ardmagar.

I sat for some moments, my thoughts in a tangle. I'd accepted an invitation to dance. I couldn't dance, by anyone's definition. Beyond that, I had no business dancing with a prince of any kind, even one who appeared to forget the differences in our social standing and who seemed, inexplicably, to find me a plausible person to confide in.

I leaned my forehead upon the cool stone balustrade. He thought I was normal, and that made me feel normal, and that was just cruel. I could have dispelled his illusions in an instant by pulling up my sleeve. Why live in fear that he might find me disgusting someday, when I could make it happen right now? I worked my right hand under the bindings of my left sleeve, feeling the cold plates, the sharp scalloped edges, my bodily horrors, and hating it.

Why had that memory sprung out at me so unexpectedly?

Was it another "mind-pearl," like the one Orma had triggered by revealing his natural form? Were there more? Was my head full of tinder, just waiting for a spark?

I stood up shakily, and my mother's words came back to me: *I cannot perch among those who think that I am broken.* I chafed at her arrogance, and her good fortune. "The thing is, Mother, you weren't broken," I muttered, as if she were standing right next to me. "I am. And it was you who made me this way."

Inside my head, the box twitched like a thing alive.

~Sixteen~

I returned to my room for a nap, making sure to wake in plenty of time to change into my formal houppelande. It was maroon, embroidered with black; I added a respectful white sash for Prince Rufus. I attempted to do my hair nicely, because Glisselda's comments had made me insecure; I redid it multiple times to no satisfactory result. I finally left it loose in sheer frustration and put on nice earrings as an apology to anyone who cared. I didn't own much other jewelry except the earring Orma had given me. I considered hooking it into my hair—it would make an interesting ornament, and no human would recognize it—but a saarantras might discern that it was quigutl-made. I left it in my room.

We'd been preparing this welcoming concert for more than a month, but the sheer scale of the spectacle still astonished me. Maybe everything looks more impressive in the light of hundreds of candles, or an appreciative audience lends a performance a certain glamour, I don't know, but some magic in the air made everything go well. No one was late or out of order; no one fell off the stage; if anyone played a wrong note, they played with such conviction that it sounded right.

That's the secret to performance: conviction. The right note played tentatively still misses its mark, but play boldly and no one will question you. If one believes there is truth in art—and I do—then it's troubling how similar the skill of performing is to lying. Maybe lying is itself a kind of art. I think about that more than I should.

The Ardmagar sat front and center for the stage performances, bright-eyed and keen. I watched him from behind the curtain during Guntard's shawm solo, trying to reconcile the look on Comonot's face with his lecture at High Nest. For someone so convinced of the toxicity of human emotion, he certainly appeared to enjoy himself.

Glisselda sat by Comonot playing the ornament; her mother sat on his other side. I saw the Queen, Dame Okra, and Viridius, but no Kiggs until I looked further afield. He stalked the back of the hall checking in with the guards, one eye on the performance and one on security. It was a stressful job, to gauge by his expression.

I had not put myself on the program. I divided my time between reminding the next performers to ready themselves and listening from the wings of the stage.

During the sackbut quartet, I noticed nobody was waiting to come on. I glanced at my schedule: Lars was up next. He was to play the binou, a smaller, milder type of bagpipe. My heart sank;

I hadn't so much as glimpsed Lars today. I marched up the hallway, poking my nose behind the curtains of the closets we had commandeered for dressing rooms.

Honestly, I had anticipated the rooms being used for warming up and not for the actual changing of clothes. I made one of my lute players scream as if he'd found a quig in his bed.

Further down the hall, I heard tense voices from behind the last curtain. I approached cautiously, not caring to walk in on anyone again, and recognized one voice as Lars's. I raised a hand toward the curtain, but hesitated. Lars sounded angry, and he was speaking Samsamese. I drew closer, listening hard and letting my ear adjust. My Samsamese was rusty, and it had never been completely fluent.

The second voice was, unsurprisingly, the Earl of Apsig's. I understood "You're following me!" but not the rest.

Lars denied it vehemently: "Never!" Then "I am here . . . ," something unintelligible, "for the machine and the flute music." Ah, right. He'd heard me from afar.

Josef swore a lot, followed by "the flute of madness," which struck me as an amusing phrase. Josef's boots clomped as he paced; his voice turned pleading. "No one must learn what you are!"

"And your" said Lars. "What will you do if they learn what you are?"

Josef barked something I didn't understand, and then came a thud and a crash. I whipped the curtain aside. The earl stood with his back to me; Lars was sprawled on the floor among the instrument cases. At the sound of the curtain opening, Earl Josef spun and slammed me into the wall. We stood frozen that way for a moment; Josef pinning me to the wall, breathing hard; me struggling to regain the breath he'd knocked out of me.

He released me abruptly and started tugging his lacy cuffs, making excuses: "I told you not to associate with him! What will it take to make you understand that he is dangerous?"

"You're the one who's dangerous."

His face fell. "Music Mistress, I was just—"

"Punching my piper? Flinging me into the wall?" I shook my head. "You are off the program. Take your viola and go."

He ran a shaking hand through his pale hair. "You can't be serious."

"I will fetch Lucian Kiggs if you'd prefer, and you can explain yourself to him."

Earl Josef brushed past me, jabbing me in the stomach with his elbow and yanking the door curtain violently shut. He'd left his viola behind; I wasn't about to call him back for it.

I turned to Lars, who was just getting to his feet. He avoided looking at me, surely as frightened as Josef that I had heard what I should not. I was ready to tell him everything when I heard Guntard in the hallway. "Mistress Seraphina! Your concert is falling apart!"

I threw back the curtain. "What?"

"Well, not yet," said Guntard defensively, fidgeting with a button on his doublet, "but the sackbuts are almost done, there's no one waiting to take their place, and no sign of you anywhere."

Lars grabbed his instrument and rushed past me, up the stairs, into the wing of the stage.

Guntard was smirking. "That's put you in a better mood, I hope!" he said, batting his eyes at me. He thought we'd been up to something back here, with the curtains drawn. Tuning each other's lutes, as they say. Practicing our polyphony. Playing the crumhorn.

"Do you flirt with Viridius like this?" I said. "Get out of here!"

He took off down the corridor, laughing. He turned back to say one last thing, but at that very moment there was an explosion. The force of it pushed me back a step.

It was Lars. He wasn't playing binou pipes.

For a moment I half fancied he'd somehow brought the mega-harmonium with him, but in fact he was playing the Samsamese war pipes, the largest, fiercest member of the bagpipe family. Samsamese highlanders had invented the instrument as a means of threatening each other's mountain enclaves; it made a sound like a mountain shaking its fist at those bastards across the way. The pipes were not intended for indoor use. Sound filled every cranny of the hall. I glanced up, cringing, expecting to see plaster flake off the ceiling.

It felt like someone was driving a nail into my ear.

I rushed into the wing of the stage, annoyed. Without thinking—without even closing my eyes or entering the garden— I reached inward for Loud Lad's imaginary hand. *You were to play binou pipes! This is too loud!*

Lars stopped abruptly. The silence hit hard, a shock wave of relief, but he wasn't finished playing. He had merely paused to shout: "I like it loud!"

The brawling pipes sprang back to cacophonous life, but there was a smattering of laughter and applause, as if his statement had lent the performance some humor or at least some sense. *The big fellow likes it loud, ha ha! He sure does!* I couldn't stay where I was, however, and not because the nail pierced my eardrum again. I rushed out, down the passage, and back into the dressing room whence I'd come.

Mercifully, there was no one there. I sank to the floor, my hand clapped to my mouth.

Lars had answered me. I had spoken to him just by thinking—no garden, no meditation, no avatar. Meeting my grotesques in person was spooky enough; this was something far spookier.

Or more exciting. I couldn't work out which.

He sounded good from this distance; my appreciation increased with the square of the distance separating us—that is, in proportion to the volume decreasing. I leaned my head against the wall and listened until he'd finished, tapping my fingers along to "The Clumsy Lover" and "The Halfhearted Maidy." The applause was muted, as if his audience was reluctant to spoil the sweet silence by clapping.

The next solo began. There were only three left before the big finale, the castle choir singing Viridius's passionate arrangement of the Mirror Hymn. I was to conduct. I forced myself to my feet. Those ne'er-do-well choristers needed as much advance warning as I could give them. I threw aside the door curtain and ran into a solid wall.

The wall was Lars.

"It is one thing to hear music in my headt," he said, a tremor in his voice. He stepped forward, driving me back into the little room. "But thet . . . thet was your voice!"

"I know," I said. "I didn't mean to."

"Why does this happen?"

His short hair stood up on his head like a boar-bristle brush; his nostrils flared. He folded his arms, as if he had no intention of moving until I had sufficiently explained myself. I said, "I have something to—to show you." The room was not too dark, I hoped, for him to discern the gleam of my grotesquery.

I balked. Showing Dame Okra hadn't turned out like I expected; I had no idea how Lars would react. And this room didn't even have a proper door. Guntard might pop his head through the curtain. Anyone might.

Lars glowered defensively, as if he anticipated a scolding or a profession of love. Yes, that was it: he thought I meant to proposition him. He wore a closed expression, as if rehearsing a speech in his head, a way to let me down gently after I stripped off all my clothes. *Sorry, Seraphina, I dondt like grausleiner thet can put their voices in my headt.*

Or maybe: *I dondt like girls at all. I like Viridius.*

It wasn't that funny, but it gave me enough momentum to untie my sleeve and pull it up.

He froze for three heartbeats and then reached for my forearm gently, almost reverently, cradling it in his large hands, running a finger down the curving band of scales. "Ah." He sighed. "Now thet all makes sense."

I wished I could have shared that sentiment, wished it so hard that tears leaked down my cheeks. His expression closed again. I thought he was angry, but I revised that to "protective" when he wrapped me in a crushing embrace. We stood that way a long time. Thank Heaven no one came in; we'd have fueled palace gossip for months.

A passerby would not have heard the enormous black-clad man whisper in my ear: *"Sesterleine!"*

Little sister.

~Seventeen~

The Mirror Hymn went smoothly. Behind me the audience rose, and some sang along. I managed to keep reasonable time, although I was not as present as I should have been. I kept replaying those moments with Lars: the one where he'd called me sister, and then the conversation after.

"What is Josef to you?" I had asked him. "What's going on, and is there any way I can help?"

"I dondt know what you mean," he'd said, his eyes suddenly cold. "I hev said nothink against Josef."

"Well, no, not to me," I pressed on. "But you can't deny—"

"I ken. And I do. Dondt speak to me of him again, *grausleine*."

With that, he had stormed off.

Music surrounded me as I conducted, lifting my heart and bringing me back to myself. The choir belted out the last two lines: *Undeserving, we are granted grace / We are a mirror raised to*

215

Heaven's face. I smiled warmly at my singers, and they returned the favor fiftyfold from all around me.

The choir cleared the stage and the symphonia moved in. My work was finished now, and I could dance as much as I liked, meaning exactly once. It was kind of Kiggs to choose a pavano, which consisted of walking in a stately circle. I could manage that.

Servants scurried around, pulling chairs and benches toward the walls, redistributing candelabra, bringing people drinks. I was parched myself; being onstage dries you right up. I made for the drinks table in the far corner and found myself behind the Ardmagar. He spoke grandiloquently to a server: "True, our scholars and diplomats drink no intoxicants, but it's less a rule and more of a guideline, a concession to your people, who tend toward paranoia at the idea of a dragon losing control. Dragons, like you, have different tolerances. A bit of wine may be taken by one as conscientious as myself, and no harm done."

His eyes glittered as he took the proffered cup; he looked around at the room as if it were made of gold. Other guests, bright as poppies, paired up in anticipation of the dancing. The symphonia finished tuning and sent a warm chord wafting over the room.

"I haven't taken human form in forty years," said the Ardmagar. With a start, I realized he was addressing me. He turned his cup in his fat fingers, giving me sly, sidelong looks. "I forget what it's like, how your very senses differ from ours. Sight and smell are frustratingly muted, but you compensate with the intensity of the others."

I curtsied, not wanting to engage him in conversation. More

of my mother's memories might be waiting to pounce on me. The tin box was quiet, for now.

He persisted: "Everything tastes of ash to us, and our scales permit little sensitivity to touch. We hear well, but your auditory nerve connects to some emotional center—all your senses link to emotion, absurdly, but that one in particular . . . that's why you make music, isn't it? To tickle that part of your brain?"

I could tolerate this kind of incomprehension from Orma, but this arrogant old saar irritated me. "Our reasons are more complicated than that."

He waved a hand and puffed his lips dismissively. "We have studied art from every conceivable angle. There is nothing rational in it. It is, in the end, just another form of autogratification."

He swallowed his wine and went back to observing the ball. He was like a child gawping at spectacle, dazzled by the vast sensory banquet before him: sweet perfume and spicy wine, the patter of ball slippers, the scrape of bows on strings. He reached out and touched a countess's green silk gown as she rustled past. Mercifully, she did not notice.

Couples took the floor for a cinque pas. Comonot gazed at them tenderly, as if they were cherry blossoms—not an expression one typically sees on a saarantras—and I wondered how many glasses of wine he'd had. It bothered me that he could stand here playing the sensualist while Orma couldn't even talk to me without taking precautions against the Censors.

"Is this dance difficult?" he asked, leaning in close. I stepped away from him; he was unlikely to smell my scales while he was in his cups, but there was no point taking unnecessary risks.

"This one intrigues me," he said. "I want to try everything. It may be another forty years before I take this shape again."

Was he asking me to dance? No, he was asking me to ask him. I could not decide whether this was flattering or irritating. I kept my voice neutral. "I've never danced the cinque pas. If you watch the dancers carefully and analyze the steps, you should uncover repeating patterns, which I suspect parallel the repetitions in the music."

He stared at me; his eyes were slightly bulgy, reminding me unpleasantly of Basind's. He licked his thick lips and said, "That is just how a dragon would approach the problem. You see, our peoples are not so different after all."

Before he could speak again, a regal presence loomed behind us and a woman's stern voice said, "Ardmagar, would you care to try our Goreddi dances?"

It was Glisselda's mother, Princess Dionne, in shining yellow silk; she wore a simple circlet and light veil, her hair tucked up in crispinettes. She gleamed like the golden phoenixes of Ziziba; I, in my maroon houppelande, was a dull little peahen in comparison. I backed away, relieved that she had eclipsed me in the Ardmagar's attention, but Comonot, the old fox, pointed me out to her. "I was just discussing the dances with this peculiar young person."

The princess gazed coolly down her elegant nose. "That is our assistant music mistress. She aided Viridius in organizing tonight's music."

I didn't have a name, apparently; that was fine with me. I curtsied, drifting further away as quickly as I dared.

Something satiny and rose-colored hit me in the side of the

head. I looked up, startled, just in time to get the end of Princess Glisselda's trailing sleeve full in the face again. She laughed, whirling away from me; her partner, the Earl of Apsig, was light on his feet. My heart sank at the sight of him, but he scorned to even look at me. He was an adept dancer, and a handsome fellow when he wasn't threatening anyone. His severe blacks set off her rosy gown; they captivated every eye in the room. He pranced her back toward me. I braced myself for the sleeve again, but she called out to me, "Did Lucian speak with you? I didn't see you dancing!"

Kiggs had said he'd discussed Imlann with her; I hoped she hadn't thoughtlessly babbled everything to the earl. "We're waiting for the pavano," I said as she passed again.

"Cowards! Dancing with you was my idea, you know! You'll be harder to overhe . . ." Josef whisked her away across the floor.

I lost the end of the word, but not the idea.

The second dance ended; the musicians transitioned to a sarabande with almost no pause. I watched the promenading couples; Comonot was not the only one mesmerized by all the pomp. Glisselda still danced with Josef, earning herself a pointed glare from her mother. The Earl of Apsig was not a nobody, presumably, but the second heir could not just dance for fun; serious politics happened on the floor.

Kiggs had danced the cinque pas with Ameera, daughter of Count Pesavolta of Ninys, gavotted with the Regina of Samsam, and now sashayed his way through the sarabande with some duchess I couldn't identify. He danced competently, if not as flashily as Josef, and seemed to enjoy it. He smiled at the duchess, a glorious, unguarded, unself-conscious smile, and for a moment he was transparent to me: I felt I could see all the way to the center of him. I'd glimpsed that at the funeral too, I realized with a start. He didn't wear his heart on his sleeve, exactly, but he did keep it in a place where I could see it.

The sarabande wound down. Half the symphonia got up; after every third dance, half the musicians took a "pie break," and the rest played a repetitive placeholder until everyone came back. It was a nice system in that the dancers got a breather and the elderly—our Queen not least among them—could maintain their stamina.

Beside me stood Princess Dionne and Lady Corongi, eating pie. "Pie break" was, of course, a euphemism; it tickled me that these two highborn ladies should be breaking for pie, in fact. "I confess I'm shocked at the Ardmagar," Lady Corongi said, dabbing the corners of her mouth with a handkerchief carefully, so as not to smear her crimson lips.

"It wasn't his fault," said the princess. "He's short; he tripped. My décolletage was right there."

I tried to picture what must have happened, and regretted it instantly.

"He's a fool," said Lady Corongi, puckering her face as if the Ardmagar were as sour as she was. Her eyes darted slyly, however, and she said, "What must it be like to take one of them to bed?"

"Clarissa!" Princess Dionne's laugh reminded me of Glisselda's. "Now I am shocked, you naughty thing. You hate dragons!"

Lady Corongi smirked nastily. "I didn't say marry one. But one hears—"

I had no intention of sticking around to hear what one hears.

I moved off toward the drinks table, but there was Josef, complaining bitterly. "We Samsanese—those of us who take our faith to heart—don't imbibe the devil's drink," he snapped at the happless serving lad. "St. Abaster never did. Should I spit in the face of his holy example?"

I rolled my eyes; I was not overly fond of wine myself, but there were nicer ways to ask for tea. I dove back into the crowd, shouldering my way through forests of gossamer veils and ermine-edged houppelandes until I was halfway around the hall. The symphonia's holding cycle drew to its conclusion, and they began the opening strains of the pavano. I stepped toward the dance floor but saw no red doublet anywhere.

"You look nice!" Kiggs said in my ear, making me jump.

I blinked stupidly. There was something one said in response to compliments, something normal people instinctively replied, but my heart pounded in my ears and I couldn't come up with it. I said, "No I don't."

He grinned, presumably because I was absurd. He offered me his arm and led me onto the floor into the heart of the pavano. I didn't know where to stand. He pulled me up next to him, our hands palm to palm at shoulder level, the opening stance.

"Your piper was rather remarkable," he said as the promenade began.

"He's not my piper," I said, pricklier than I should have been due to Guntard's earlier innuendo. "He's Viridius's piper."

We did a left-hand pass, and a right. Kiggs said, "I know exactly what he is to Viridius. Tell your guilty conscience to stand down. You obviously love someone else."

I startled. "What do you mean?"

He tapped the side of his head with his free hand. "Worked it out. Don't be alarmed. I'm not judging you."

Not judging me? Whom did he imagine I was in love with? I wanted to know, but not so badly that I would willingly keep the conversation trained on myself. I changed the subject: "How long have you known the Earl of Apsig?"

Kiggs raised his eyebrows as we circled slowly right, the star-hand move. "He's been here about two years." He studied my face. "Why do you ask?"

I gestured toward the other dancers in our circle. Josef's black doublet stood out, only two places away from us in the circle. "He's making life difficult for Viridius's piper. I caught him lambasting the poor fellow back in the dressing rooms."

"I looked into Josef's background when he first came to court," Kiggs said, handing me around in a pas de Segosh as the circle reversed. "He's the first Apsig to crawl out of the highlands in three generations; that house was believed extinct, so of course I was curious."

"You? Curious?" I said. "I find that difficult to believe."

He rewarded my impudence with a grin. "Apparently his grandmother was the last of the line and he revived the name. He's also rumored in Samsam to have an illegitimate half brother. Lars might not be a mere serf after all."

I frowned. If Lars was not some random half-dragon but the familial shame incarnate, that would explain Josef's animosity. Still, I couldn't help feeling it was more complicated than that.

Kiggs was talking; I focused back on him. "They take a harsh stance on illegitimacy in Samsam. Here, it's mostly inconvenient for the poor bastard, there, it taints the entire family. The Samsamese are great devotees of St. Vitt."

"Thy sins burn brightly backward through the ages'?" I hazarded.

"And forward unto all thy sons' horizons'—yes. Well quoted!" He handed me round again; his eyes twinkled, reminding me of Prince Rufus. Kiggs leaned in and added in an earnest voice: "I realize you're conducting a survey on the subject, but I'd recommend against asking Lars what it's like to be a bastard."

Startled, I met his eye. He was laughing silently, and then we were both laughing, and then something changed. It was as if I had been watching the world through oiled parchment or smoked glass, which was yanked abruptly away. Everything grew very clear and bright; the music burst forth in majesty; we stood still and the room turned around us; and there was Kiggs, right in the middle of all of it, laughing.

"I—I shall have to be content with asking you," I stammered, suddenly flustered.

He gestured broadly, encompassing the room. "This is it. The quintessence of bastardy. No rest for the wicked. Dance after dance, until your feet are ready to fall off."

The circle reversed direction for the last time, reminding us both why we were here. "To business," he said. "My grandmother may think there is nothing to be discovered out in the country, but Selda and I think she's wrong." He leaned in closer. "You should carry on as planned. We talked it over, though, and we can't let you go alone."

I drew back in surprise. "You can't let me go where alone?"

"In search of Sir James Peascod. It's not safe," he insisted, his brow creased with worry. "And I'm not convinced you even know where you're going. You were surely bluffing when you told those elderly gentlemen that you knew where they lived?"

My mouth opened, but my torpid brain had not formed any words for it to say. When I'd written that a visit to the knights was warranted, I meant Kiggs should go, not me!

Kiggs put a hand on my waist for the final promenade. His breath warmed my ear. "I'm going with you. That's final. Tomorrow we won't be missed: you've got no musical programs and all the most important people will be shut up in meetings all day—including Selda, to her great disgust. I propose that we ride out at dawn, visit the knights, and then, depending on how late it is . . ."

I heard nothing beyond that. My ears buzzed.

How could anyone think it remotely plausible that I intended to ride off into the countryside—alone, or any other way? It was my own stupid fault for bluffing my way down to the knights. Nothing but trouble had come of that. Everyone had the wrong idea about me now; they thought me brave and reckless.

Looking into Kiggs's dark eyes, though, I felt a little reckless.

No: a little breathless.

"You hesitate," he said. "I suspect I know why." I suspected he didn't. He smiled; the whole room seemed to shimmer around him. "You're worried that it's improper, the pair of us riding off unescorted. I don't see a problem. A larger party would put the knights on the defensive before we even arrived, and as for propriety, well. My fiancée isn't worried, my grandmother won't mind,

Lady Corongi will be off visiting her sick cousin for the next couple days, and I see no one else of consequence likely to judge us."

That was easy for him to say; he was a prince. I imagined I could and would be judged. Lady Corongi would lead the chorus; being away was no impediment to her.

We circled each other in the final pas de Segosh. Kiggs said, "Your beau doesn't seem the jealous type. We have a fair shot at failing to scandalize anyone in any way."

Not the jealous type? Who? Alas, again my mouth failed to launch the requisite questions, and then it was too late. The pavano was finished; people were applauding.

"Dawn," he whispered. "Meet at the Queen's study. We'll take the postern gate."

He let me go. My waist felt cold where the warmth of his arm had been.

Eighteen

I quit the ball very soon thereafter, retreating to the sanctuary of my suite. I needed to tend my garden, and needed sleep if I was to get up early. Those were surely two very good reasons to leave.

Those weren't my reasons. I didn't visit the grotesques, and I didn't sleep.

My limbs buzzed with restlessness. I undressed, folding the houppelande and gown with obsessive neatness, creasing the folds with my fists, as if pleats might calm me. I usually left my chemise on—I hated myself naked—but now I took it off, folded it, re-folded it, flung it fitfully against the privacy screen, picked it up, threw it again.

I paced, rubbing the scales on my stomach, mirror-smooth one way, like a thousand sharp teeth the other. This is what I was. This here. This. I made myself look at the shingle of silver half-

226

moons, the hideous line where they sprouted from my flesh like teeth pushing through gums.

I was monstrous. There were things in this world I could not have.

I climbed into bed, curled up, and wept, my eyes tightly shut. I saw stars behind my lids. I didn't enter my garden; I was nowhere with a name. A door appeared unexpectedly in the undifferentiated fog of my mind. It frightened me that it could just appear, unbidden, but it startled me out of my self-pity, too.

It opened. I held my breath.

Fruit Bat peeked around the edge. I quailed. He had been so well behaved since I'd asked him to that I'd almost forgotten there'd been any trouble. Seeing him outside the garden scared me, though. I could not help but think of Jannoula, with all her peeking and prying, and how she'd practically set up housekeeping in my head.

Fruit Bat's face lit up when he saw me. He seemed incurious about my private mind; he had merely been looking for *me*. To my horror, I was naked in my own head; I changed that with a thought. "You found me," I said, smoothing my imaginary gown, or reassuring myself that it was there. "I know, I haven't been to the garden tonight. I—I couldn't face it. I'm tired of having to tend it. I'm tired of of being ill."

He held out his wiry brown hands.

I considered the offer but could not bring myself to induce a vision. "I'm sorry," I said. "Everything feels so heavy right now, and . . ." I could not continue.

I was going to have to shut him out. I did not see how I could muster the strength to do it.

He hugged me; he was short, not even up to my shoulder. I held him, put my cheek against the soft, dark knots of his hair, and wept. Then somehow, and I'm not sure how, I slept.

Kiggs was woefully cheerful for a man who could not have gotten more than four hours' sleep. I had taken my time with the morning routine, assuming we'd be off to a slow start, but he had arrived at the Queen's study ahead of me, dressed in dull colors like a peasant. No one would have mistaken him for a peasant up close, however; the cut of his jerkin was too fine, his woolens too soft, his smile too bright.

A man hulked beside him; I realized with a start that it was Lars. "He was asking for you last night after you absconded," said Kiggs as I drew near. "I told him he could catch you this morning before we left."

Lars reached inside his black jerkin and pulled out a large, folded parchment. "I hev designedt it lest night, and want you to hev it, Mistress Dombegh, because I hev no other goodt way of . . . to thank you." He handed it to me with a little flourish, and then, surprisingly quickly for such a large man, disappeared up the hallway.

"What is it?" said Kiggs.

The parchment fluttered as I spread it out. It looked like schematics for some sort of machine, although I couldn't make head or tail of it. Kiggs had a more concrete notion: "A ballista?"

He was reading over my shoulder; his breath smelled of anise.

I said, "What's a ballista?"

"Like a catapult, but it flings spears. But this one flings . . . what is that?"

It looked like a harpoon with a bladder full of something unspecified. "I don't think I want to know," I said. It looked like a giant clyster pipe, for delivering a dragon's colonic, but I didn't care to say that aloud before a prince of the realm, bastard or no.

"Stow it in here," he said, handing me a saddle pack, which appeared to contain our lunch. "You're dressed warmly enough to ride?"

I hoped so. I'd never actually ridden a horse, being a city girl, but I'd scrounged up a pair of Porphyrian trousers and wore my usual overabundance of layers.

I had Orma's earring fastened by a cord around my neck. I could feel the cold lump of it if I put my hand to my heart.

We set off through the palace, down corridors, through a door concealed behind a tapestry, and down into a series of passages I'd never seen. Stairs took us below the level of the basements, through a rough tunnel. We passed three locked doors, which Kiggs con scientiously relocked behind us while I held the lantern. We were going roughly west, according to my internal compass. Past a pair of enormous stone doors, the tunnel broadened into a natural cave system; Kiggs avoided the smaller branches, taking the widest, flattest route each time, until we reached the mouth of a cave in the hillside below the western wall of the castle.

The broad valley of the Mews River spread before us, cloaked in morning mist. Thick clouds hid the face of the sky. Kiggs paused, arms akimbo, taking in the vista. "This was a sally port in war times, invisible from below. We saved ourselves a trip through the city, see? There's a stable at the base of the hill; we've horses waiting there."

The dusty cave floor had been recently disturbed. "Who uses these caves now?"

"Uncle Rufus, rest he in the bosom of Allsaints, used this route to go hunting. I thought it couldn't hurt to retrace his steps. No one else uses it that I'm aware of." He looked at me; I gestured toward some discarded clothing behind a rock. "Hm! Shepherds taking shelter from a storm?" He lifted one item, a well-made but simple gown. Every woman in the palace owned a couple like it; I know I did. "Serving girls meeting their lovers? But how would they get through three locked doors, and why would they leave clothing behind?"

"It is peculiar."

He grinned. "If this is the biggest mystery we encounter today, I'll call us lucky." He refolded the gown and placed it back behind the rock. "You're perceptive. You may wish to keep that skill at the ready; the slope is rocky, and it's likely to be wet."

As we picked our way downhill, I found myself breathing easier. The air was clean and empty; the atmosphere of city and court seemed dense by comparison, saturated with troubles and heavy with worries. There were only two of us out here under the weightless, unbounded sky, and I sighed with relief, noticing for the first time how claustrophobic I had been.

Horses were, indeed, waiting for us. Kiggs had apparently sent word that he was riding with a woman, because my horse was fitted with a little sideways basket seat, complete with footrest. This struck me as far more sensible than the usual setup. Kiggs, however, was unhappy with it. "John!" he cried. "This won't do! We need proper tack!"

The old ostler frowned. "Sharpey told me you was riding out with the princess."

"No, Sharpey did not tell you that! You assumed that. Maid Dombegh expects to control her own horse, not be led around on a pony!" He turned to me apologetically, but something in my face stopped him short. "You do intend to ride?"

"Oh yes," I said, resigned to it now. I hoisted the hem of my skirts to show how I was ready with the Porphyrian trousers and all. He blinked at me, and I realized that had been a most unladylike action—but wasn't he setting me up to ride in an unladylike way? I couldn't seem to behave properly, no matter what I did.

Maybe that meant I could stop fretting about it so much.

They brought out my refitted horse; I hitched up my skirts and mounted on the first try, not wanting anyone grabbing me around the waist to help me up. The horse turned in a circle, I'd never done this, but I knew the theory, and it wasn't long before I had her moving in a straight line, in almost the correct direction.

Kiggs caught me up. "Eager to get going? You left without your saddle pack."

I managed to stop my horse and hold her almost still while he secured my bags, and then we were off. My horse had definite ideas about where we should go; she liked the look of the water meadows ahead and thought we couldn't get there fast enough. I tried to hold her back and let Kiggs lead, but she was quite determined. "What's beyond that leat?" I called back to him, as if I had some notion where we were going.

"The fens where Uncle Rufus was found," he said, craning his neck to look. "We can stop there, although I doubt the Guard missed much."

My horse slowed as we approached the little canal; she wanted the water meadow, not the brambly bog. I gestured to the prince to take the lead, as if I were slowing on purpose. My horse tried to turn away from the bridge. "No you don't," I muttered to her. "Why should you play the coward? You outweigh all of us."

Kiggs trotted ahead, his dun cloak flapping behind him. He sat lightly in the saddle, and his horse seemed to respond to his very thoughts; there was none of this unseemly yanking of reins that I was forced to do. He led us off the road almost immediately on the other side of the leat. The fen was relatively dry this time of year; what standing water there was had frozen into a glassy crust that crunched underhoof. I still managed to find a muddy patch where my horse's hooves skidded and sucked. "Steer her toward the grasses," Kiggs advised, but my horse, smarter than me, was already headed that way.

Kiggs paused beside some barren shrubbery and pointed to the hills north of us, black with winter trees. "They were hunting in the Queenswood, there. His courtiers claim the hounds scattered—"

"And the hunters scattered after them?"

"No, no, that's not how it works. The hounds are supposed to investigate all leads; they're bred for independence. They follow a scent to the end, and if it doesn't lead to anything useful, they return to the pack. That's what they're for, so the hunters don't have to follow every dead end in the forest."

"But the Earl of Apsig said Prince Rufus had followed his hounds."

Kiggs stared at me. "You questioned him about that day?"

The earl had required no interrogation; he'd been bragging to the ladies-in-waiting at the Blue Salon. Kiggs had walked in on that conversation, in fact, but apparently he had missed the discussion of hounds. It seemed I had a reputation as a shrewd investigator to uphold, however, so I said, "Of course."

Kiggs shook his head in wonderment, and I felt immediately guilty. "They're supposing that my uncle took off after his prize hound, Una, because he got separated from the group and nobody saw where he went. But he had no reason to do that. She knows what she's doing."

"Then why did he leave the group?"

"We may never know," said Kiggs, spurring his horse a little further along. "Here's where they found him—with Una's help— the next morning, beside this rivulet."

There was little to see, no blood, no sign of struggle. Even the hoofprints of the Guard had been obscured by rain and filled in with seeping fen water. There was a rather deep water-filled crater, and I wondered whether that was where the prince had lain. It was not dramatically Rufus-shaped.

Kiggs dismounted and reached into the pouch at his belt, drawing out a Saint's medallion, tarnished with use and age. Disregarding the mud, he knelt by the water and held the medallion reverently to his lips, muttering as if to fill it with prayers. He squeezed his eyes shut, praying fervently but also trying to stave off tears. I felt for him; I loved my uncle too. What would I do if he were gone? I was a poor excuse for pious, but I cast a prayer up anyway, to any Saint who might catch it: *Hold Rufus in your arms. Watch over all uncles. Bless this prince.*

Kiggs rose, surreptitiously wiping his eyes, and cast the medallion into the pool. The cold wind tossed his hair the wrong way across his head; the medallion's ripples disappeared among choppy little waves.

It suddenly occurred to me to think like a dragon. Could a dragon have sat right here in broad daylight, killing someone without being seen? Absolutely not. I could see the road and the city in the distance. Nothing obscured that view at all.

I turned to Kiggs, who was already looking at me, and said, "If a dragon did it, your uncle must have been killed somewhere else and moved here."

"That's exactly what I think." He glanced up at the sky, which was beginning to spit drizzle at us. "We need to get moving, or we're going to get drenched."

He mounted his horse and led us out of the fen, back to the high, dry road. He took the north fork, toward the rolling hills of the Queenswood; we passed through just the southern corner of that vast forest. It had a reputation for being dark, but we saw daylight the entire time, black branches dividing the gray sky into panes, like the lead cames of a cathedral window. It began to drizzle harder and colder.

Over the third ridge, the forest turned into coppice, the rolling hills into sinkholes and ravines. Kiggs slowed his horse. "This seems a more likely area for a dragon to kill someone. Coppice is thinner than forest, so it could maneuver adequately, if not well. It'd be concealed down one of the hollows, unseen until one was right on top of it."

"You think Prince Rufus stumbled upon the rogue dragon by accident?"

Kiggs shrugged. "If a dragon really killed him, that seems likely. Any dragon intending to assassinate Prince Rufus could find a hundred easier ways to do it without raising suspicions against dragons. If it were me, I'd infiltrate the court, gain the prince's trust, lure him into the forest, and put an arrow through the back of his skull. Call it a hunting accident—or disappear. None of this messy biting off of heads."

Kiggs sighed. "I was convinced it was the Sons of St. Ogdo before the knights came to us. Now I don't know what to think."

A noise had been growing at the edge of my perception, a chittering like locusts in summer. It grew loud enough now that I noticed it. "What's that sound?"

Kiggs paused to listen. "That would be the column of rooks, I assume. There's an immense rookery in a ravine north of here. The birds are so numerous there's always a flight of them above the place, visible from miles away. Here, I'll show you."

He steered his horse off the path, through the coppice, up the ridge; I followed. From the top we saw, half a mile off, a lazy cloud of black birds, hovering, swooping all together. There must have been thousands for us to hear their cries this far away.

"Why do they gather right there?"

"Why do birds do anything? I don't think anyone has ever bothered to find out."

I chewed my lip, knowing something he didn't and trying to work out how best to tell him. "What if the dragon was there? Maybe it left some, uh, carrion," I said, wincing at my own feebleness. Sure, rooks liked carrion; that wasn't the only thing a dragon ever left behind.

"Phina, that rookery has been there for years," he said.

"Imlann has been banished for sixteen."

Kiggs looked skeptical. "You can't believe he would camp out in the exact same spot for sixteen years! It's coppice. Woodcutters tend it. Someone would have noticed."

Bah. I had to try a different tack. "Have you read *Belond-weg*?"

"I couldn't call myself much of a scholar if I hadn't," he said. He was adorable and he made me smile, but I couldn't let him see. "Do you remember how the Mad Bun, Pau-Henoa, tricked the Mordondey into thinking Belondweg's army was mightier than it really was?"

"He made a fake battlefield. The Mordondey believed they'd stumbled across the site of a terrible slaughter."

Why did I have to spell everything out for everyone? Honestly. He was as bad as my uncle. "And how did Pau-Henoa counterfeit that kind of carnage?"

"He scattered dragon dung all over a field, attracting millions of carrion crows, and . . . oh!" He looked back toward the column. "You don't think—"

"That might be a dragon's cesspit over there, yes. They don't leave it scattered about; they're fastidious. In the mountains, there are 'vulture valleys.' Same thing."

I glanced at him, embarrassed to be having this discussion, embarrassed still more that Orma had told me these kinds of things—in response to my inquiries, of course. I tried to gauge how mortified the prince was. He looked at me wide-eyed, not disgusted, not laughing, but genuinely intrigued. "All right," he said. "Let's have a look."

"That's way out of our way, Kiggs. It's just a hunch—"

"And I have a hunch about your hunches," he said, kicking his horse gently in the ribs. "This won't take long."

The raucous cawing grew louder at our approach. When we'd crossed half the distance, Kiggs raised a gloved hand and motioned me to stop. "I don't want to stumble across this fellow by accident. If that's what happened to Uncle Rufus—"

"The dragon isn't here," I said. "Surely the rooks would be alarmed, or silent. These look unconcerned to me."

His face brightened as an idea hit him. "Maybe that drew Uncle Rufus here: the birds were acting strangely."

We rode closer, slowly, through the coppice. Ahead of us yawned a wide sinkhole; we stopped our horses at the edge and looked in. The bottom was rocky where an underground cavern had collapsed. The few existing trees were tall, spindly, and black with quarrelling birds. There was ample room here for a dragon to maneuver, and unambiguous evidence that one had.

237

"Are dragons sulfuric through and through?" muttered Kiggs, pulling the edge of his cloak up over his face. I followed suit. We could handle the stench of sewage—we were city dwellers, after all—but this reek of rotten eggs turned the stomach.

"All right," he said. "Light a fire under that keen brain of yours, please. That looks fairly fresh, there, would you agree?"

"Yes."

"That's the only one I see."

"He wouldn't have to come here more than once a month. Dragons digest slowly, and if he were becoming a saarantras regularly, I understand that makes them . . ." No. No, I was not going into more detail than that. "The rooks would have finished off anything older, perhaps," I offered limply.

Only his eyes were visible above his cloak, but they'd crinkled into a smile at my discomfiture. "Or the rain would have dissolved it, I suppose. Fair enough. But we can't confirm that the rooks live here because a dragon habitually uses this space."

"We don't have to confirm that. A dragon was here recently, without question."

Kiggs narrowed his eyes, thinking. "Say the rooks were acting strangely. My uncle came to see what was happening. He stumbled upon a dragon. It killed him and carried his headless body back to the fen under cover of night."

"Why move the body?" I mused aloud. "Why not eat all the evidence?"

"The Guard would have kept scouring the wood for Uncle Rufus's body. That would lead us here, eventually, to unambiguous proof of a dragon." Kiggs darted his gaze back toward me. "But then, why did it eat his head?"

"It's hard for a dragon to make it look like something else killed you. Biting off the head is fairly ambiguous. And maybe it knew people would blame the Sons of St. Ogdo," I said. "You did, didn't you?"

He shook his head, not exactly conceding the point. "So why did it reveal itself to the knights? Surely it knew we would connect the two?"

"Maybe it didn't expect the knights to risk imprisonment by reporting to the Queen. Or maybe it assumed the Queen would never believe their story—which also happened, didn't it?" I hesitated, because it felt like giving away something personal, but finally added: "Sometimes the truth has difficulty breaching the city walls of our beliefs. A lie, dressed in the correct livery, passes through more easily."

He wasn't listening, however; he stared at a second object of intense rookish interest on the floor of the hollow. "What's that?"

"A dead cow?" I said, wincing.

"Hold my horse." He handed me his reins, dismounted, and was scrambling down into the stony sinkhole before I could express surprise. The rooks swirled, exploding noisily into the air, obscuring my view of him. If he'd been in uniform, I could have made out the scarlet through all that black, but he might have been a mossy rock for all that I could see.

The rooks swirled and dove in unison, screaming, then

scattered into the trees. Kiggs, his arms wrapped protectively around his head, had nearly reached the bottom.

My horse shifted uneasily. Kiggs's horse pulled at the reins and whickered. The rooks had all but disappeared, leaving the coppice and hollow eerily silent. I didn't like this one bit. I considered shouting down to Kiggs, but his horse gave a violent tug, and I had to focus all my attention on not falling off my own mare.

The cold drizzle had continued to fall, and I now saw, to the north of us, a cloud of vapor rising out of the coppice. Maybe it was fog; the mountains further north were nicknamed Mother of Mists. But this seemed too localized to me. This seemed like what you might see if cold drizzle were falling on something warm.

I put a hand to my heart, to Orma's earring, although I did not pull it out just yet. Orma would be in so much trouble for transforming and coming to my rescue that I couldn't afford to call him if I wasn't completely sure.

The mist was spreading, or its source moved. How much surer did I need to be? It would take time for Orma to get here; he would not be able to fly for several minutes after he transformed, and we were miles away. The wisps moved west, then curled toward the sinkhole. There was no sound in the coppice. I listened hard for the telltale rasp of branches on hide, for footsteps, for the hot rush of breath, but heard nothing.

"Let's go," said Kiggs beside me, and I almost fell off my horse.

He swung himself into the saddle; I handed him the reins, noticing a glint of silver in his hand. I couldn't ask about it just then, however. My heart pounded frantically. The mist curled still closer, and now we were making noise. Whether he was consciously aware of the danger or not, Kiggs spurred his horse forward quietly, and we hurried together back toward the road.

He waited until we had cleared the coppice altogether, emerging into rolling farmland on the other side, to show me what he'd found: two horse medals. "This was Uncle Rufus's patron, St. Brandoll: the welcomer, kind to strangers," said Kiggs, trying unsuccessfully to smile. He did not narrate the other medal; he seemed to have run out of words. He held it up, however, and I saw it bore the arms of the royal family: Belondweg and Pau-Henoa, the Goreddi crown, St. Ogdo's sword and ring.

"Her name was Hilde," he said when he recovered his voice, a quarter mile down the road. "She was a good horse."

Nineteen

We pressed on harder after that, ostensibly to make up lost time, an unspoken anxiety hanging over us at how close we might have been. We passed fallow winter fields and brown grazing pastures. Low stone walls crawled up and down the hills. We passed villages—Gorse, Rightturn, Fetter's Mill, Remy, a few too small to have names. Their attendant manor houses squatted sternly nearby. At Sinkpond we opened my saddle pack and ate lunch as we rode: boiled eggs, cheese, a dense sweet loaf shared between us.

"Listen," said Kiggs around his bread. "I know it's none of my business, and I know I said I don't judge you for it, but I can't stay silent, not after what we just saw in that ravine. I know you're of age to decide for yourself—'an autonomous being, unfettered and free, stepping up to the first agon of your heart'—"

Now he was quoting tragedy to me, which couldn't bode well.

"That's 'willful, unfettered, and free'—is it not?" I said, trying to deflect dread with pedantry.

He laughed. "Trust me to omit the most important word! I should know better than to quote Necans to you." His face grew grave again, his gaze painfully earnest. "Forgive me, Phina, but I feel compelled to say, as your friend—"

As my friend? I grabbed my saddle tightly to keep from falling off.

"—that it's a bad idea, falling in love with a dragon."

I was glad I had braced myself. "Blue St. Prue," I cried, "who can you possibly mean?"

He fiddled with his reins. "Your 'teacher,' right? The dragon Orma?"

I said nothing, utterly flabbergasted.

"It didn't add up, to me, that he was merely your teacher," he said, pulling off a glove and slapping it absently against his horse's shoulder. "You know him too well, for one thing. You know too much about dragons in general."

"It wasn't such a liability in the coppice," I said, fighting to keep my voice even.

"No, no! It's never been a liability," he said, his eyes widening. He reached a hand toward me but held off touching my arm. "I didn't mean it that way! We now have concrete evidence linking my uncle and a dragon, and that's all thanks to you. But you're going to an extraordinary amount of trouble for this Orma. You're fond of him, protective of him—"

"Fond and protective equals in love?" I wasn't sure whether to laugh or cry.

"You've put your hand to your heart," he said. He wasn't smiling.

I had unconsciously felt for Orma's earring. I put my hand back down.

"I have agents, you know." He sounded defensive now. "They saw you meeting him the other night. They saw you go to Quighole."

"You're spying on me?"

He turned rather charmingly red. "Not on you! On him. He claims his father is a threat to the Ardmagar. It seemed prudent to find out more about him and his family."

I felt light-headed; the horizon wobbled a bit. "And what have you learned?"

His face brightened; we were back to discussing a mystery. "His entire family seems to exist under a cloud of suspicion, but no one will explicitly say what crime was committed. It seems to have been more than just his father, though. If I had to guess, based on the stony silence at the embassy, I'd say—"

"You asked at the embassy?"

"Where would you have asked? Anyway, my guess is madness. You'd be astonished how many ordinary things dragons consider madness. Perhaps his father started telling jokes or his mother found religion or—"

I couldn't stop myself. "Or his sister fell in love with a human?"

Kiggs smiled grimly. "As grotesque as that sounds, yes. But you see where I'm going with this. Your boy is under scrutiny. If he loved you—I'm not saying he does—he would be taken home and

244

forcibly excised. They would remove all his memories of you and—"

"I know what excision means!" I snapped. "Saints' bones! He feels nothing for me. You needn't concern yourself."

"Ah," he said, gazing off into the middle distance. "Well. He's an idiot."

I stared at him, trying to gauge his meaning. He smiled, and tried to clarify. "Because he's hurt you, clearly."

No, that wasn't clear, but I played along. "Maybe I'm the idiot, for loving him."

He had no answer for that, although I couldn't quite take his silence for agreement, the way he looked off into the distance and frowned.

We turned south onto something more sheep track than road. I began to fret about how long this journey was taking. Today was Speculus, the shortest day of the year; by the time we reached the knights, we'd have to leave almost at once to make it back in daylight. Surely Kiggs did not intend us to ride home in the dark? Maybe that was of no concern to an experienced horseman, but I felt I was barely holding on as it was.

We reached a grim old barn that had caught fire recently; the rear of the roof sagged, the back wall was charred and blistered, and the whole area reeked of smoke. Someone had put it out, or it had been too damp to burn. Kiggs stared at it hard, then abruptly turned off the road toward a thicket. We skirted the thicket, which

Kiggs leaped from his horse, grabbed his pack, and approached the cave on foot. I was not so adept at the dismount. I had substantial difficulty convincing the horse to stand still. Happily, Kiggs wasn't looking at me. He stood near the mouth of the cave, his hands on his head in a gesture of surrender, crying, "By Belondweg and Orison, we come in peace!"

"Don't pretend you're scared of me." An unshorn, bony-wristed, no-longer-exactly-young man emerged from the shadows with a crossbow over his shoulder. He wore a peasant's work smock, incongruously embroidered with fruit, and wooden clogs over his boots.

"Maurizio!" said Kiggs, laughing. "I took you for Sir Henri."

The fellow grinned like a lunatic and said, "Henri would have been ready and willing to menace you a bit. I couldn't have shot you. Bow's not even loaded."

He and Kiggs clasped hands; clearly they knew each other. I stared at my hands, overtaken by a sudden shyness, wondering whether Maurizio would recognize me as the girl he'd carried home five years ago. I had a nagging feeling that I'd vomited at some point during that journey; I really hoped it hadn't been on him.

"What'd you bring me?" asked Maurizio, lifting his pointy

---

turned out to be a small patch of forest; what looked like shrubs from the rise above were revealed to be trees once we'd reached the low end of the hollow. Entering from the far side, we rode up the middle of the shallow creek until we reached its source, the mouth of a cave under the hill.

chin and looking not at the pack but at me, half on, half off my horse.

"Er. Woolies," said Kiggs, following Maurizio's gaze and looking at me in surprise. I waved casually. He picked his way back downstream toward me.

"Have you eaten?" asked Maurizio, joining Kiggs in holding my horse's bridle. He turned lively blue eyes on me. "The oatmeal is fine today. Not even moldy."

My feet landed on solid ground just as an old man in a threadbare tabard emerged from the cave blinking. He had liver spots on his scalp and used a nasty-looking polearm for a walking stick. "Boy! Who's this?"

"I just turned thirty," said Maurizio quietly, so the old knight would not hear, "but I'm still called boy. Time has stopped out here."

"You're free to leave," said Kiggs. "You were just a squire when they were banished; technically, you weren't banished at all."

Maurizio shook his shaggy head sadly and offered me his skinny arm. "Sir James!" he said loudly, as to one hard of hearing. "Look what the dragon dragged in!"

There were sixteen knights in all, plus two squires, holed up in that cave. They'd been there twenty years and had civilized the place, carving out new rooms for themselves that were cleaner and drier than the main body of the cave. They had scavenged and built sturdy furniture; at one end of the main hall stood twenty-five suits of fireproof dracomachia armor, black and quilted. I did not know the proper names of the weapons displayed on the wall—hooks and harpoons and what appeared to be a flat spatula on a pole—but assumed they had some specialized purpose in dracomachia.

They invited us to sit by the fire and gave us warm cider in heavy ceramic mugs. "You oughtn't've come out today," cried Sir James, who was deaf in one ear, at least. "It's like to snow."

"We had no choice," said Kiggs. "We need to identify this dragon you saw. He may be a danger to the Ardmagar. Sir Karal and Sir Cuthberte told us you were the man who knew his generals, back in the day."

Sir James straightened up and raised his grizzled chin. "I could tell General Gann from General Gonn, in my prime."

"All in the midst of general mayhem," chirped Maurizio into his mug.

Sir James flashed him the fish-eye. "Those were terrible times. We had to know who was who, so we'd have some inkling what they'd do. Dragons don't work well together; they prefer an attack of opportunity, like the Zibou crocodile, and they've a devilish fast eye for an opening. If you know who you're dealing with, you know what he's likely to do, and you can lure him in with a false opportunity—not every time, but then, it only has to work once."

"Did you recognize the one that approached your camp?" asked Kiggs, looking around. "And what did it do? Stick its head in the cave entrance?"

"It set the barn on fire. Our third sally port comes out in that barn; there was smoke pouring all the way into the great hall here."

"It's taken two squires a week of dancing around with vinegar-soaked rags to get the smell out of the air," said Maurizio drily.

"Sir Henri went to see what had caught fire. He came back reporting a dragon hunkered beside the barn, and of course we all laughed at him." He grinned at the memory; he was missing a number of molars. "It was getting smokier: the barn burned but poorly, being damp and moldy. We split up. It's been a while since we drilled properly, but you never forget your basic approach."

"You send the squires out first, as bait," said Maurizio.

Sir James didn't hear, or ignored him. "I was upwind, so I was speaker. I said, 'Halt, worm! You are in violation of Comonot's Treaty—unless you have the documents to prove otherwise!'"

"Fierce!" said Kiggs.

Sir James waved a gnarled hand. "They're nothing but feral file clerks, dragons. They used to alphabetize the coins in their hoards. Anyway, this one neither spoke nor moved. He tried to gauge our numbers, but we'd done the standard numbers bluff."

"What's that, then?"

Sir James looked at Kiggs like he was mad. "You conceal your numbers—harder than you'd think. They can distinguish individuals by smell, so you put men downwind and a distracting stench upwind. We brought decoy torches and two sacks of warm cabbages, and made a little extra noise. Don't grin at me, you young rapscallion! You never let a dragon know how many you are, or where you're all concealed."

"That's a prince of the realm you're calling rapscallion," said Maurizio.

"I shall call him what I like! I'm banished already!"

"I'm awestruck that you had warm cabbages sitting around," said Kiggs.

"Always. We are always prepared for anything."

"So what did the dragon do then?" I asked.

Sir James looked at me, a fond spark in his watery eyes. "He spoke. My Mootya's not what it was, and it never was much, but I'd say he was trying to goad us into action. Of course, we took none. We abide by the law, even if the monsters do not."

That was funny, coming from a banished man who hadn't been banished particularly far. Kiggs met my eye; we silently shared the humor of it. He nudged Sir James back toward fact. "Was this dragon anyone you knew?"

Sir James scratched his bald pate. "I was so shocked, I hadn't considered. He reminded me of one I faced, but where? White Creek? Mackingale oast houses? Let me think. We'd lost our pitchman and fork; we staggered back to Fort Trueheart, when we stumbled into the . . . right. Mackingale oast houses, and the Fifth Ard."

A chill coursed down my spine. That was the one.

"A dragon of the Fifth Ard?" Kiggs prompted, leaning forward keenly. "Which dragon?"

"The general. I know they all call themselves General—they're not pack hounds, dragons; don't take orders well—but this fellow really was what we'd call a general. He knew what he was doing and kept the rest 'in ard,' as they say." He rubbed his eyes with a thumb and finger. "His name, though. That will come to me directly after you've gone, I expect."

I wanted so badly to blurt out the name, but Kiggs flashed me a warning glance. I understood; my father was a lawyer. Witnesses can be very suggestible.

"Squire Foughfaugh!" cried the old man, meaning Maurizio, apparently. "Fetch me the old register of ards from my trunk. I don't know why I'm trying to wring water from my stone of a head when I've got it all written down."

Maurizio brought the book. The pages flaked and cracked as Sir James turned them, but the name was still legible: "General Imlann. Yes, that sounds right, now."

I had known it was coming, but I still shivered.

"You're certain it was him?" asked Kiggs.

"No. But that's my best guess, a week later. That's all I can give you."

It was enough, and yet it wasn't. We'd come all the way out here to confirm this, and now that we knew, we were no closer to knowing what to do next.

The knights made tea and chatted at us, asking after their imprisoned comrades and news from town. Maurizio kept joking—that seemed to be his primary function as squire—but Kiggs, lost in thought, did not respond to his banter, and I too sat silently, trying to work out our next step.

No course of action struck me as good. Scour the coppice for him? Search the villages for his saarantras? Kiggs couldn't get enough men out here without diverting them from Comonot's security. Tell Eskar? Why not the Ardmagar himself, and the

Queen? Make the authors of the treaty, the ones most invested in the continuation of the peace, sort this out.

"Are we leaving soon?" I whispered to Kiggs when the conversation died down. Most of our hosts had wandered off for a nap; others stared torpidly at the fire. Maurizio and Pender, the other squire, had disappeared. "I'm not eager to ride after dark."

He ran a hand over his head and looked like he was trying not to laugh. "Had you ever ridden before today?"

"What? Of course I—" His look stopped me short. "Am I that bad?"

"You're allowed to ask for help when you need it."

"I didn't want to slow us down."

"You didn't, until it became clear you didn't know how to dismount." He picked at a fingernail, the silent laugh still in his eyes. "Once again, however, you leave me in awe. Is there nothing you're afraid of?"

I stared dumbly. "Wh-why would you even think that?"

He began counting off on his fingers. "You bluff my guards and determine to come out here on your own. You climb on a horse as if you know what you're doing, assuming it will just come to you." He leaned closer. "You stand up to Viridius and the Earl of Apsig. You ask mad pipers to the palace. You fall in love with dragons. . . ."

I did sound pretty crazy, when he put it that way; only I knew how scared I'd been. Sitting there so close to him was almost the scariest thing of all because the kindness in his face made me feel safe, and I knew it for an illusion. For the merest moment I let myself imagine telling him I feared everything, that the bravery was a cover. Then I would pull up my sleeve and say, *Here's why. Here I am. See me.* And by some miracle he would not be disgusted.

Right. While I was using my outrageous imagination, maybe I should also imagine him not engaged. Maybe he'd kiss me.

I was not allowed to want that.

I stood up. "Esteemed sirs," I said, addressing our hosts, who had dozed off on their benches. "We thank you for your hospitality, but we really must—"

"You were going to stay for the demonstration, I thought?" cried Maurizio, popping out of a side room. His head now had a helmet on it.

Kiggs and I looked at each other. We'd apparently been so preoccupied that we'd agreed to something without it registering. "If it doesn't take too long," said Kiggs. "It's going to be dark soon, and we've a long road ahead of us."

Maurizio and his fellow squire emerged, clad all in dracomachia armor. "We've got to go out to the pasture to show you properly," said the other squire, Pender.

"Putting ourselves out to pasture," said Maurizio with his strange, desperate cheer. "Bring the horses. You can depart from there."

There was a stirring round the cavern as the old men realized the young ones were about to demonstrate the last vestiges of their ancient pride. Dracomachia was once a formidable martial art; Pender and Foughfaugh may have been the last two ablebodied practitioners in Goredd.

We followed the old knights down the creek into a stubbly

field and made a semicircle around a tumbledown hayrick. It had grown considerably colder while we dallied in the cave; the drizzle had turned to light snow, which clung to the stubble, outlining the broken stalks in white, and the wind had picked up. I pulled my cloak closer about me and hoped this wouldn't take long.

Pender and Foughfaugh carried long polearms with a peculiar hook on each end, angled in such a way that it did not hinder them using the pole for vaulting. They flipped and cartwheeled, leaped and spun, exchanged poles in midair, and viciously attacked the hayrick with their hooks.

Sir James undertook to educate us. "These hooks we call the slash. Now we'll show you the punch. Squires! Harpoons!"

The squires exchanged their hooks for a more spearlike weapon, demonstrating its use on the poor, abused hayrick.

"Dragons are flammable," said Sir James. "They developed their flame for use against each other. They don't cook their meat with it, after all. They fear no other beast—or didn't, until we learned to fight. Their hide is tough but it burns, given enough heat for enough time; their insides are volatile, which is how they flame in the first place.

"The key to dracomachia is setting the monster on fire. We've got pyria—St. Ogdo's fire—which clings to them and is not easily extinguished. One good puncture and their blood whistles out like steam. Set that ablaze, and they're done."

"How many knights made up a unit?" asked Kiggs.

"Depended. Two slash, two punch, fork, spider, swift. That's seven knights, but we had pitchmen flinging pyria and squires running weapons . . . Fourteen was full complement, although I've taken out a dragon with as few as three."

Kiggs's eyes gleamed. "Oh, to have seen it in action, just once!"

"Not without armor, lad. The heat was unbearable—and the stench!"

The squires clambered up on each other's shoulders, flipping and leaping over top of the hayrick. I found their precision and strength inspiring. Being banished and having little else to do, they'd clearly spent a lot of time practicing. We should all be as dedicated to our art.

"Sweet St. Siucre!" I exclaimed.

"What's wrong?" asked Kiggs, alarmed by my sudden beeline for the horses.

I fished around in my mare's saddle pack until I found the diagram Lars had given me. Kiggs apprehended my thought at once and helped me unfold the parchment against the side of the horse. We stared at the clyster-pipe ballista, then at each other.

"The bladders would be for pyria," I said.

"But how would you ignite it?" puffed a breathless voice behind us, which turned out to be Squire Foughfaugh.

"It would be self-igniting, Maurizio. Look," said Kiggs, pointing to a matchlock mechanism I hadn't understood.

"Clever," said Maurizio. "The squires could have operated that—anyone could have. Put the knights out of a job, almost."

Sir James came to see what the fuss was about. "Humbug. Machines limit mobility. Hunting dragons is not a question of brute force, or we'd be knocking them out of the sky with trebuchets. It's an art; it takes finesse."

Maurizio shrugged. "Having one of these on our side couldn't have hurt."

Sir James sniffed disdainfully. "We might have used it as bait. Nothing lures a dragon like an odd contraption."

The snow was blowing harder now; it was past time to go. We made our farewells. Maurizio insisted on helping me onto my horse. I cringed, irrationally fearing he'd discern my scales. "It's such a relief after all these years to learn that you recovered from your fright," he said in a low voice, giving my hand a squeeze, "and that you grew up so pretty."

"Were you worried?" I asked, touched.

"Yes. What were you, eleven? Twelve? At that age we're all gawky, and the outcome is always in doubt." He winked, smacked my horse's hindquarters, and waved until we were out of sight.

Kiggs led the way back to the sheep track, and I urged my horse to keep up.

"You appear not to have gloves," said Kiggs as I pulled up beside him.

"I'll be all right. My sleeves almost cover my whole hand, see?"

He said nothing, but pulled off his own gloves and handed them to me with a look that told me I didn't dare refuse. They were prewarmed; I hadn't realized how frigid my fingers were until I put them on.

"All right, I'm an idiot," said Kiggs after we'd ridden a few miles in silence. "I had fully intended to scoff at your fear of riding after dark, but if it keeps snowing like this, we're not going to be able to make out the road."

I had been thinking the opposite: the road now stood out, two parallel white lines where snow filled in the wagon tracks. It was nearly dark, however. This was the longest night of the year, and the heavy cloud cover was working toward making it even longer.

"There was an inn at Rightturn," I said. "The other villages were too small."

"Spoken like someone unaccustomed to traveling with a prince!" he laughed. "We can commandeer any manor house along the way. The question will be, which one? Not Remy, unless you want to spend the evening with Lady Corongi and her cousin the reclusive duchess. If we can make it all the way to Pondmere Park, that would minimize our travel time in the morning. I have duties to attend to tomorrow."

I nodded as if I did too. I'm sure I did, but I could not remember a single one.

"I've been meaning to tell you all day," said Kiggs, "that I had some additional thoughts on being a bastard, if you'd like to hear them."

I could not stop myself laughing. "You . . . really? All right then."

He reined his horse back even with mine. He had not put up his cloak hood, and there was snow in his hair. "You'll find me eccentric, perhaps, but I haven't been able to stop thinking about that. No one ever asks.

"My father was a Samsamese admiral. My mother, Princess Laurel, was the youngest daughter of Queen Lavonda and was, according to legend, a bit headstrong and spoiled. They ran off when she was fifteen years old; it was as dreadful a scandal in Samsam as here. He was demoted to freighter captain. I was born on dry land but was often at sea as a baby. They didn't take me on their final voyage: the day before they were to set sail from the Ninysh port of Asado they met Dame Okra Carmine, who persuaded them to let her take me to Goredd, to meet my grandmother."

I had considered her short-range prognostication talent a bit silly; I was wrong.

He stared up at the clouds. "They perished in a terrible storm. I was five years old, lucky to be alive, but feeling quite at sea myself. I didn't even speak Goreddi. My grandmother didn't take to me right away; Aunt Dionne hated me instantly."

"Her own sister's child?" I cried.

He shrugged; his cloak flapped in the wind. "My very existence was an embarrassment to everyone. What were they to do with this unexpected child, his low-class manners—even for a Samsamese—and his mortifying ethnic surname?"

"Kiggs is a Samsamese name?"

He smiled ruefully. "It's not even Kiggs; it's Kiggenstane. 'Cutting-stone.' Somebody up the family tree was a quarryman, apparently. But everything worked out. They got used to me. I showed them I was good for a thing or two. Uncle Rufus, who spent years at the court of Samsam, helped smooth my way."

"You looked so sad, praying for him this morning," I blurted out.

His eyes glittered in the twilight; his breath made mist in the cold. "He's left a tremendous hole in the world, yes. Only my mother's death compares. But you see, this is what I've been aim-

"ing toward, the thing I keep imagining myself telling you because I feel you'll understand it."

I held my breath. The silent snow came down all around us.

"I have such mixed feelings about her. I mean, I loved her, she was my mother, but . . . sometimes I'm angry with her."

"Why?" I asked, but I knew. I'd felt exactly that. I could barely believe he was about to utter it aloud.

"Angry with her for leaving me so young—you may have felt that too, about your mother—but also, to my mortification, angry with her for falling in love so recklessly."

"I know," I whispered into the icy air, hoping and fearing that he would hear me.

"What kind of villain begrudges his own mother the love of her life?" He gave a self-deprecating laugh, but his eyes were all sadness.

I could have reached right across and touched him. I wanted to. I gripped the reins tighter and stared at the track ahead.

"You're not a villain," I said. Or else we were two villains in a pod.

"Mm. I rather suspect I am," he said lightly. He went silent; for some moments there was only the crunch of hooves in snow and the squeaking of cold saddle leather. I looked over at him. The frosty air had reddened his cheeks; he blew into his hands to warm them. He gazed back at me, his eyes deep and sorrowful.

"I didn't understand," he said quietly. "I judged her, but I didn't understand."

He averted his eyes, tried to smile, broke the moment of

strangeness. "I won't fall prey to the same destructive impulsive-ness, of course. I'm on my guard against it."

"And you're engaged, anyway," I added, trying to sound flip-pant because I feared he might hear my heart beating, it was pounding so violently.

"Yes, that's a nice assurance against the unexpected," he said, his voice rough with some emotion. "That, and faith. St. Clare keeps me to my rightful course."

Of course she did. *Thanks for nothing, St. Clare.*

We rode on in silence. I closed my eyes; snow blew against my cheeks, stinging like sand. For a moment I let myself imagine that I had no dragon scales and he was unfettered by promises already made. There in the freezing darkness, under the endless open sky, it might well have been true. No one could see us; we might have been anyone.

It turned out someone did see us, however, someone with an ability to see warm objects in darkness.

I felt a hot blast against my skin, smelled sulfur, and opened my eyes to see my grandfather in all his hideous reptilian hugeness land on the snowy road ahead.

Twenty

My horse reared, and I was on the ground, flat on my back in the snow, not a whisper of breath left in me.

Kiggs was off his horse in an instant, sword drawn, making himself a wall between me and the brimstone blackness, the muscular furl of wing against sky. He reached back left-handed to help me to my feet, groping around in the air; I forced myself to sit up, put my hand in his, pull breath back into my lungs. He heaved me to my feet and we stood there, hand in hand, and faced the dread behemoth, my grandfather.

To my utter shock I recognized Imlann, even as darkness rapidly descended. It wasn't Orma's nonsensical description; it came from my mother, from the memory box, which had given a smoky belch inside my mind. I knew the contours of his spiny head; the arch of his snaky neck resembled Orma's. . . .

Orma. Neck. Right. I fumbled at my neck, left-handed

because Kiggs still had my right, seeking the cord to Orma's earring. Kiggs stepped forward a little, shielding me again, and said, "You are in violation of Comonot's Treaty—unless you have the documents to prove otherwise!"

I grimaced. It was easy to think of dragons as feral file clerks when there wasn't an enormous, choleric specimen snorting sulfur in your face. I found the earring, flipped its tiny switch, and tucked it back into my clothes.

Orma was going to kill me; I hoped he'd help me first.

The dragon screamed, "You smell of saar!"

He meant me. I cringed. Kiggs, who didn't understand Mootya, cried, "Stand down! Return to your saarantras immediately!"

Imlann ignored that, fixing his beady black eyes on me and screeching, "Who are you? Which side are you on? Have you been spying on me?"

I didn't answer; I didn't know what to do. Imlann thought I was a saarantras. Would Kiggs assume the same if he learned that I knew Mootya? I kept my eyes on the snow.

Kiggs waved his sword. A lot of good that was going to do.

"You feign deafness," cried my grandfather. "What can I do to make you hear? Shall I kill this irritating little princeling?"

I flinched, and the saar laughed, or what would have been a laugh from a human. It was more like crowing, a horrid hoot of victory. "I bit a nerve! Surely you can't be so attached to a mere human? Perhaps I will not kill you after all. I still have a friend on the Board of Censors; maybe I'll let him turn you inside out."

I had to do something; I could think of only one thing to try. I stepped forward and said, "It's you the Censors should be after."

Imlann recoiled, rippling his serpentine neck sideways and emitting a blast of acrid smoke from his nostrils. Kiggs pulled my arm and cried, "What are you doing?"

I couldn't reassure him. A saarantras wouldn't have, and that's what I had to appear to be if we were to bluff Imlann long enough for Orma to get here.

If Orma was even coming. How far was it? How fast could he fly?

"I've contacted the embassy," I cried. "Eskar is on her way, with a committee."

"Why don't you transform, and we'll have this out properly?"

It was a frighteningly reasonable question. "I obey the law, even if you do not."

"What's to stop me from killing you this instant?"

I shrugged. "You apparently don't know about the device implanted in my head."

The dragon cocked his head to one side, flaring his nostrils, appearing to consider; I hoped he reached a conclusion favorable to letting me live a bit longer. I added: "It's in my tooth. Flame me, or hit me with any percussive shock, and it will explode, destroying you too. If you bite off my head and swallow it, my tooth will continue to signal from inside your stomach. The embassy will track you down, General Imlann."

He looked mystified; he'd never heard of such devices—he

couldn't have; I was making this up—but then, he'd been away from the Tanamoot for sixteen years. I lifted my chin haughtily, though I was shaking, and said, "The game is up. Surrender now and tell us everything. Where have you been hiding?"

That broke the spell. Smugness crept over him. I only knew it for smugness from my maternal memories; all my human eyes saw were the spines at the base of his head shift their angle. He said: "If you don't know that, you know nothing worth knowing; I shall leave you to your disgusting infatuation. Plans are unfurling, all in their proper time; I shall let them. We shall meet again, and sooner than you expect."

He turned with a serpentine ripple, swiping at us with his spiky tail, ran forward, and launched himself into the air. He made a wide, low circle in the sky, presumably scanning for embassy dragons, then flew swiftly south, disappearing in the clouds.

My knees trembled and my head throbbed, but I was elated. I could barely believe that had worked. I turned toward Kiggs; I must have been wild-eyed with relief.

He backed away, his expression closed, saying, "What are you?"

St. Masha and St. Daan. I'd saved us, but now I had to pay for it. I raised my hands as if in surrender. "I am what I ever was."

"You're a dragon."

"I'm not. By Heaven's hearthstone, I'm not."

"You speak Mootya."

"I understand it."

"How is that possible?"

"I am very, very smart."

He didn't question that; I would have. He said, "You've got a draconian device. It is illegal for humans to be in possession of quigutl-built communication machinery——"

"No! I've got nothing! It was a bluff."

He was breathing heavily now, delayed-onset panic finally catching up with him. "You bluffed him? A Porphyrian double ton of fire and brimstone, fangs like swords, claws like . . . like swords! And you just . . . bluffed him?"

He was yelling. I tried not to take it personally. I folded my arms. "Yes. I did."

He ran his hands roughly through his hair. He bent double as if he might vomit, scooped up some snow, rubbed it over his face. "Sweet Heavenly Home, Seraphina! Did you think about what might have happened to us if that hadn't worked?"

"No better plan presented itself." Heavens, I sounded as cold as any dragon.

He had dropped his sword at some point; he picked it out of the snow, wiped it on his cloak, and resheathed it, his eyes still wide and shocked. "You can't just . . . I mean, brave is one thing. This was madness."

"He was going to kill you," I said, my chin quivering. "I had to do something."

Damn propriety. Forgive me, St. Clare.

I stepped forward and took him in my arms. He was exactly my height, which surprised me; my awe of him had made him seem taller. He emitted a whimper of protest, or maybe surprise, but wrapped his arms around me and buried his face in my hair, half weeping, half scolding me.

"Life is so short," I said, not sure why I was saying it, not even sure if that was really true for someone like me.

We were still standing there, clinging to each other, our feet ice-cold in the snow, when Orma landed on the next hilltop, followed closely by Basind. Kiggs lifted his head and stared at them, big-eyed. My heart fell.

I'd told him I had no devices. I'd lied right to the prince's face, and here was the proof: the dragon I'd called, and his dim-witted sidekick.

Twenty-One

Speculus, for us Goreddis, should be spent in contemplation of one's sins and shortcomings. It's the longest night of the year, representing the long darkness of death for the soul who rejects the light of Heaven.

It was certainly the longest night I have ever lived through.

Kiggs, of course, had drawn his sword again, but it hung from his hand in a desultory manner. It had been useless against one dragon; it was merely token resistance against two.

"We're not in danger," I said, trying to reassure him but fearing my good intention was as futile as his sword. "It's Orma, and behind him is Basind. I didn't call Basind."

"But you did call Orma? With that device you don't have?"

"I don't have the one I told Imlann about—I invented that on the spur of the moment—and I was trying to reassure you, and I . . . I forgot."

267

"I see. So Orma gave you this device and came instantly when called as if he were your lap dog, because he—how did you put it exactly?—he feels nothing for you?"

"We're not . . . no. It's not like that."

"Then what is it like?" he cried, furious with me. "Are you his agent? Is he your thrall? There is something between you, beyond this facade of mentorship, beyond what dragons and humans should ever engage in. It is not normal, and I can't work out what it is, and I am sick of guessing!"

"Kiggs . . ." I had no other words.

"Prince Lucian, if you would be so kind," he said. "Tell them to shrink down."

Orma approached, head lowered in a submissive stance. He had apparently told Basind to flatten himself into the snow, because Basind did a good impression of a lizard run over by a cart—a giant lizard, and an unthinkably enormous cart.

"You are all under arrest," said Kiggs, loudly and slowly. "You two, for unauthorized transformation; Maid Dombegh, because you are clearly in cahoots with two unauthorized dragons—"

"Association with dragons is not a crime," I said.

"Possession of a quigutl-made transmission device is not a crime," I said.

"Possession of a quigutl-made transmission device is. Aiding and abetting the delinquency of dragons is. I could go on." He turned to the dragons and said, "You will shrink yourselves down now."

Orma cried, "Seraphina, if I have transformed for nothing, I am going to be in an unquantifiable amount of trouble. Tell me why I shouldn't bite your head off. It couldn't make things any worse for me."

268

I translated that as: "We'll come along quietly, Prince, and will comply with your every reasonable demand, but we cannot shrink ourselves down because you don't have clothing for us, and we would freeze."

"Are you in love with Prince Lucian?" screamed my uncle.

"What were you up to when I arrived? You weren't going to mate right here in the snow, were you?"

I gave myself a moment to get my voice under control before saying, "The dragons suggest that they walk ahead. Their sharp eyes can make out the road more easily than ours. They won't flee."

"I told you not to go after Imlann," screeched my uncle. "I know he was here; I smell him. Why did you not keep him here so I could kill him?"

That was too much. I shouted back, "You can't have it both ways, Orma!"

"Get back on your horse," said Kiggs, who'd been able to round up the animals. They were still skittish in the continuing presence of full-sized dragons, so it took me some time to get on. Kiggs held my mare's bridle, but he would not look at me.

The dragons kept their heads down, docilely, as they followed the road; they left slushy footprints, huge and clawed, behind them. The prince and I followed in painful silence.

It gave me a lot of time to think. How had Imlann found us? Had he tracked us from the coppice, or had he been waiting for us to come back along the same road? How could he know we would return?

"Prince Lucian," I began, drawing my horse up alongside his.

"I would rather you not speak, Maid Dombegh," he said, his eyes upon the saar.

That hurt, but I plowed ahead. "I suspect Imlann knew where we were going and that we were coming back. Someone at the palace may have told him—or someone at the palace *is* him. Who knew where we were going today?"

"My grandmother," he said tersely. "Glisselda. Neither of them is a dragon."

I hardly dared suggest it, but I had to. "Might Glisselda have mentioned it in passing to the Earl of Apsig?"

He turned toward me sharply. "If she had—which I deem unlikely—what are you suggesting? That he's a traitor, or that he's a dragon?"

"He came out of nowhere two years ago—you said so yourself. He takes no wine. He's got fair hair and blue eyes." He'd discerned the scent of my scales, too, but obviously I could not include that detail. "He was part of your uncle's last hunting party," I hazarded. That wasn't evidence, though, so much as circumstance.

"You're omitting a substantial amount of counterevidence," said Prince Lucian, finally engaged, even if just to refute me. "I thought we'd concluded he was Lars's half brother."

"You said it was a rumor. It might be false," I dared not suggest what now occurred to me: if Josef was a dragon, he might be Lars's father.

"He plays viola like an angel. He professes to hate dragon-kind."

"Imlann might adopt such an attitude strategically, to deflect suspicion," I said. I couldn't address the accusation of angelic viola

270

playing without bringing up my own mother, who'd played flute with an eerily human cadence, according to Orma.

"All I ask is that you consider the possibility. Inquire whether anyone saw Josef at court today."

"Will that be all, Maid Dombegh?"

My teeth chattered with cold and nerves. "Not quite all. I want to explain Orma."

"I really don't care to hear it," he said, spurring his horse a little ahead.

"He saved my life!" I cried at his back, determined to make him hear it whether he wanted to or not. "Orma was my tutor when I was little. You recall that his family is flagged for scrutiny. Well, the Censors feared he might become too attached to his students, for he dearly loved teaching and was good at it. They sent a dragon called Zeyd to test him. She lured me up the bell tower of St. Gobnait's with the promise of a physics lesson, then dangled me out over the plaza, as if she might drop me. If Orma rescued me, you see, that would indicate that he was compromised. He should not have cared that much."

I swallowed. My mouth still went dry, recalling the terror of my shoes falling, the wind roaring in my ears, the tilting world.

The prince looked at me sarcastically, and I hastened to add, Kiggs was listening in spite of himself, my horse pulled up even with his. "Orma arrived," I said, "and my first thought was, *Hurrah, he's rescued me!* But he leaned against the balustrade, utterly unconcerned with my welfare, and began trying to convince Zeyd that it would be the end of her career—to say nothing of the peace—if she dropped me. She shook me around, let me slip a bit

271

in her grasp, but he never flinched. He didn't care about me at all; he was just helping out his fellow saar.

That part still hurt, frankly. "She finally set me down on the walkway. Orma took her arm and they walked away together, leaving me alone, weeping and barefoot. I crawled down the stairs, all four hundred twenty of them, and when I finally made it home, Orma scolded me for trusting a dragon and called me an idiot savant."

"But he's a dragon," said Kiggs sensibly, fiddling with his horse's reins.

Cack. I supposed it couldn't matter if I told him. "I didn't know back then."

He studied me now, but I couldn't meet his eye. "Why are you telling me this?"

Because I want to tell you something true, and this is as close as I can manage. Because I think, at some level, you will understand this story. Because I need you to understand it.

I said, "I want you to understand why I have to help him."

"Because he was so cold to you?" Kiggs said. "Because he left you to walk home alone and called you an idiot?"

"Because he—he saved my life," I stammered over my rising confusion.

"You'd think, as Captain of the Queen's Guard, I'd have heard this story before. A dragon almost killing someone is no small matter, and yet your father didn't jump right in to see her prosecuted?"

My stomach knotted. "No."

272

Kiggs's expression hardened. "I wish I knew how much of your story was true."

He spurred his horse forward, leaving me alone.

We approached the city at a crawl; dragons are not as fast as horses on foot, and these two seemed in no hurry. It was long after midnight by the time we reached the stable at the foot of the hill.

The dragons transformed in sight of the stable, cooling and condensing and folding themselves into a pair of naked men. They followed me in with the horses while Kiggs went to see what spare clothing John Ostler might have for them. Orma no longer had his false beard; I hoped he'd at least stowed his spectacles somewhere safe before transforming. "I'm astonished you're not hurt," he said through chattering teeth, a bit more sympathetic as a human. "How did you contrive not to get yourself killed?"

I pulled him aside, away from Basind, and told him how I'd bluffed Imlann. Orma's eyes narrowed as he listened. "It's lucky he believed you were a saar. I could not have predicted that your peculiarities could be so useful."

"I don't think the truth ever crossed his mind."

"The truth?" said Kiggs, who had stepped up right behind us, his arms heaped high with tunics and trousers. "Don't tell me I missed it," he said, passing clothing to the saarantrai.

I could not meet his gaze. He snorted in disgust.

Basind, bless his thick skull, was the only one among us who seemed to be enjoying himself. During the long haul home he had kept asking Orma what was going to happen next, and whether we were there yet. Now, back in his saarantras, he croaked, "Are they going to throw us in the dungeon?" He seemed almost gleeful at the prospect.

"I don't know," said Kiggs unhappily, his shoulders sloping. He'd had only four hours' sleep the night before; exhaustion was catching up with him. "I'm turning you over to the Queen and the Ardmagar. They'll sort out what to do with you."

We obtained new horses and set off again, this time toward the city gate. Kiggs did not wish to reveal the sally port to dragons. The guards gruffly blocked our way but fell back when they recognized their prince. We wound our way through the untouched snow of the sleeping city, back up the hill to the castle.

Neither the Queen nor the Ardmagar was awake, of course, but Kiggs would not let us out of his sight. He kept us cooped up in the anteroom to the Queen's study under the watchful eye of three guards. Basind, seated by my uncle on an elegant velvet settee, dozed off against Orma's shoulder. Kiggs paced endlessly. His chin was gritty with stubble; his eyes glinted with an edgy, feverish energy, the last dregs of exhaustion. He couldn't keep his gaze in one place; he looked everywhere but at me.

I couldn't stop looking at him, even though something terrible threatened to rise in me every time I did. My body was filled with restlessness; my left forearm began to itch. I needed to get away from here, and I could think of only one way to do it.

I rose; the three guards leaped to attention. Kiggs had to look at me then. I said, "Prince, I hate to be a nuisance, but I need the garderobe."

He stared at me as if he didn't understand. Was *garderobe* not what they called it in polite society? What would Lady Corongi say? The chamber of unfortunate necessity? Urgency to be gone made my voice unnaturally high: "I am not a dragon. I can't just duck down a ravine or piss brimstone into the snow." The latter referenced something Basind had done on the way home.

Kiggs blinked rapidly, as if to wake himself up, and made two hand gestures. Before I knew it, one of our guards was marching me down the hallway. He seemed determined I should be made as uncomfortable as possible: we bypassed all the relatively warm latrines of the inner keep and crossed Stone Court, through the snow, out toward a soldiers' jake-hole on the southern wall. We passed the night guard, clustered around charcoal braziers, cleaning their crossbows and laughing raucously; they fell silent and stared as their comrade herded me past.

I didn't care. He could have marched me all the way to Trowebridge. I just needed to be somewhere away from Kiggs.

I shut the door of the little room and scrupulously bolted it. The latrine smelled better than I had feared; it was a two-seater and dumped directly into the defensive ditch below. I could see the snowy ground through the holes. An icy wind gusted up, enough to freeze the staunchest soldier's nether end.

I opened the shutter of the paneless window to let in some light. I knelt upon the wood between the dragon's eyes (as some call such holes). I rested my elbows upon the windowsill, my head in my hands. I closed my eyes, repeating mantras Orma had taught me to quiet my mind, but one thought kept buzzing around me, stinging me like a hornet, over and over.

I loved Lucian Kiggs.

I emitted a single, sour laugh, because I couldn't have chosen a more ludicrous place to have this realization. Then I wept. How stupid was I, letting myself feel things I should not feel, imagining the world could be other than it was? I was a scaly fiend; I could have confirmed it with a hand up my sleeve. That could never change.

Thank Allsaints the prince had both principles and a fiancée to act as barriers between us; thank Heaven I'd alienated him by being a filthy liar. I should rejoice in these obstacles; they had saved me from abject humiliation.

And yet my mind, in its perversity, kept returning to what had happened after Imlann flew off. For one moment—a moment transfixed in my obstinate memory—he had loved me too. I knew it, beyond question. One moment, however fleeting, was far more than I had ever believed myself worthy to receive, and it was far short of enough. I should never have allowed even that much; knowing what I was missing only made everything worse.

I opened my eyes. The clouds had parted; the moon shone gloriously across the snowy rooftops of the city. It was beautiful, which only made me hurt the more. How dare the world be beautiful when I was so horrifying? I pulled up my outer sleeves and carefully untied the cloth band binding the sleeve of my chemise. I turned that last sleeve back, exposing my silver scales to the night.

The moon gave enough light that I could discern each scale in the narrow, curling band. The individual scales were tiny compared with a real dragon's scales, each the size of a fingernail, with hard, sharp edges.

Hatred tore at my insides. I was desperate to stop feeling it; like a fox in a snare, I'd have gnawed my own leg off to escape it. I drew my little dagger from the hem of my cloak and stabbed myself in the arm.

The dagger glanced off, but not without jabbing the tender human skin beside the scales. I clamped my lips together to muffle my cry of surprise, but my dull dagger hadn't broken the skin. I sliced at the scaly band with the side of the blade this time, which was hard to do quietly; the steel slipped and sparked. I could start a fire with those sparks; I wanted to burn the whole world.

No: I wanted to put the fire out. I could not live, hating myself this hard.

A terrible idea bloomed in me like frost upon glass. I flexed my wrist to bring the edges of the scales up; I edged the knife under the end of one. What if I pulled them off? Would they grow back? If it left my arm scarred, would that really be worse?

I pried. The scale didn't budge. I worked the knife under slowly, back and forth, as if I were peeling an onion. It hurt, and yet . . . I felt a glacial coldness wash over my heart, extinguishing the fire of shame. I gritted my teeth and pried harder. A corner came up; I doubled over in pain and inhaled frigid air sharply through my teeth. I felt the freeze again, all through me, and experienced it as relief. I could not hate when my arm hurt this much. I squeezed my eyes shut and gave one final pull.

My scream filled the tiny room. I cradled my arm, weeping. Dark blood welled up where the scale had been. The scale glittered on the end of my knife. I flicked it down the jake-hole; it twinkled as it fell.

I had almost two hundred scales on my arm alone. I couldn't do it. It was like yanking out my own fingernails.

Orma had once told me that when dragons first learned to take human form, centuries ago, some had been prone to harming themselves, rending their own flesh with their teeth because the intensity of human emotions had taken them unprepared. They had rather endure physical pain than mental anguish. This was one reason among many that they kept their human emotions so tightly under wraps.

If only I could have done that. It never worked; it just put the feeling off until later.

Soldiers were pounding on the door in response to my scream. How long had I been in here? The cold had caught up with me: I shivered as I sheathed my knife and wrapped up my bloody wrist with my chemise binding. I mustered what dignity I could and opened the door.

My guard glared at me from under his helmet visor. "Queen Lavonda and Ardmagar Comonot are awake and waiting on your presence," he snapped. "St. Masha and St. Daan, what were you doing in there?"

"Female things," I said, watching him balk at the mention of the unmentionable.

Even my human half could frighten people. I brushed past him, hating that. Somewhere in my heart, the flame still burned.

Twenty-Two

By the time I arrived, Kiggs had debriefed the Queen and Comonot and had taken himself off to bed. I felt his absence like a punch in the stomach.

The Queen's study reminded me of my father's, though it had fewer books and more antique statuary. The Queen sat behind a broad desk, precisely where my father would have sat. Ardmagar Comonot took a thronelike chair near the windows; behind him, the sky was beginning to glow pink. They'd each brought a little entourage, who stood along the walls as if guarding the books from our grubby hands. We three miscreants were not offered seats.

I was relieved that no one had thought to notify my father. He would have been furious with me, but maybe that wasn't obvious to others. Maybe they feared he'd turn his baleful lawyer's gaze on them.

Orma showed no concern for my long absence, although he did sniff rather loudly when I drew near. He would notice I was bleeding. I had no intention of discussing it.

"One request," said Orma, speaking first, way out of turn. "Excuse Basind from these proceedings. Allot his blame to me. He's a newskin, inexperienced and singularly stupid. I am supposed to be teaching him; he merely followed my lead."

"Granted," said Comonot, raising his jowly chin. "Newskin Basind, go."

Basind saluted his Ardmagar and left without so much as a nod to the Queen.

"Prince Lucian has given us his account of your encounter with the dragon Imlann," said the Queen, frowning as she followed the newskin with her eyes. "I would like to hear your version, Maid Dombegh."

I told all I could, underscoring our commitment to the peace and our desire to uncover the truth, the better to protect the Ardmagar.

The Queen listened impassively; Comonot seemed touched that we'd undertaken to measure this threat. One might almost have taken them for their opposites: Comonot the sympathetic human, Queen Lavonda the dispassionate saar. Perhaps those qualities were what had enabled them to reach an agreement after centuries of distrust and war. Each saw something familiar in the other.

"Maid Dombegh has committed no material violation of the treaty," said the Queen. "I see no justification for holding her. Possession of a transmitting device is against the law, but I am in-clined to overlook that, if she gives it back."

I plucked the earring from the cord around my neck and handed it to Orma.

Comonot addressed Orma. "By rights, I should revoke your scholarship and travel permissions for your unauthorized trans-formation. However, I'm impressed with your initiative and your drive to protect your Ardmagar."

Apparently I'd lent sufficient color to that part of the story. Orma saluted at the sky, saar fashion.

"I elect to waive your penalties," said Comonot, glancing side-long at the Queen as if to gauge her reaction to his magnanimity. She looked merely tired. "We shall discuss the best course of ac-tion at council. A lone malcontent poses little threat to me, thanks to the fine security of my hosts, but he is still in breach of treaty and must be apprehended."

Orma saluted again and said, "Ardmagar, may I take advan-tage of this unexpected audience to petition you privately?"

Comonot assented with a wave of his thick fingers. The Queen and her attendants left for breakfast, leaving Comonot with just a small retinue of saarantrai. I made to leave also, but Orma's hand on my elbow restrained me. "Would you dismiss your retainers as well, Ardmagar?" said Orma.

The Ardmagar complied, to my astonishment. Orma must have seemed particularly harmless, despite his notorious father.

"All in ard," said Orma. "This involves the Censors, and I did not wish—"

"I do not see that your family could sink much further," said the Ardmagar. "Quickly, if you please. I find this body gets irritable without its breakfast."

Orma squinted without his spectacles. "I have been hounded by the Censors for sixteen years: relentlessly tested, monitored, retested, my research sabotaged. How much is enough? When will they be satisfied that I am all I should be?"

Comonot shifted warily in his seat. "That is a question for the Censors, scholar. They fall outside my jurisdiction; indeed, I am as subject to them as you are. That is as must be. Their neutrality keeps checks on us when we descend into the monkey mind."

"There is nothing you can do?"

"There is something *you* could do, scholar: voluntary excision. I have one scheduled myself, almost as soon as I get back." He tapped his large head; his plastered-down hair gave it the appearance of a seaweed-covered rock. "I shall have all emotional detritus removed. It's unexpectedly refreshing."

Orma dared not look disturbed; I hoped the little muscle working near his jawline was noticeable only to me. "That would not do, Ardmagar. They inevitably remove memories as well, and that would spoil my research. But what if I hunted Imlann down?" Orma seemed not to know when to quit. "Would that not prove where my loyalty lies, or put the state in my debt—"

"The state does not repay debts in this fashion, as you well know," said Comonot.

The quickness of his interjection raised my hackles; he was lying. "Basind shouldn't be here, but he is," I snapped. "Eskar explicitly said it was a favor to his mother, for turning in her husband."

"I don't recall the case, but that is certainly not policy," said Comonot, his voice a warning.

"Seraphina," said my uncle, his hand hovering near my arm.

I ignored him; I wasn't finished. "Fine. Call it an exceptional circumstance, but could not an exception be made also for my uncle, who has done noth——"

"Scholar Orma, who is this person?" asked the Ardmagar, suddenly on his feet.

I turned toward my uncle, openmouthed. His eyes were closed, his fingers tented in front of his chin as if he were praying. He inhaled deeply through his nose, opened his eyes, and said, "Seraphina is my nameless sister's daughter, Ardmagar."

Comonot's eyes bugged alarmingly. "No . . . not with that . . ."

"With him, yes. The human, C——"

"Do not say his name," ordered the Ardmagar, suddenly the most dispassionate of saarantrai. He considered a moment. "You reported that she died childless."

"Yes, I reported that," said Orma. My heart broke a little along with his voice.

"The Censors know you lied," guessed the Ardmagar shrewdly.

"That's a mark against you; that's why they won't let you go. Odd that it was not reported to the Ker."

Orma shrugged. "As you say, Ardmagar, the Censors aren't accountable to you."

"No, but you are. Your scholar's visa is revoked, saar, as of this instant. You will return home; you will put yourself down for excision. Failure to report to the surgeons within one week's time will result in a declaration of *magna culpa*. Do you understand?"

"I do."

Comonot left us. I turned to Orma so full of rage and horror and sorrow that for a moment I could not speak. "I assumed he knew," I cried. "Eskar knew."

"Eskar used to be with the Censors," said Orma softly.

I threw up my hands in futile despair, pacing around him; Orma stood very, very still, staring at nothing. "I'm sorry," I said. "This is my fault. I ruin everything, I—"

"No," said Orma evenly. "I should have sent you out of the room."

"I assumed you intended to introduce me to him, like with Eskar!"

"No, I kept you here because I ... I wanted you here. I thought it would help." His eyes widened in horror at himself. "They're right. I am emotionally compromised beyond redemption."

I wanted so badly to touch his shoulder or take his hand so he would know he was not alone in the world, but I couldn't do it. He would swat me away like a mosquito.

Yet he'd taken my elbow and wanted me to stay. I struggled with tears. "So you'll be going home?"

He looked at me like my head had fallen off. "To the Tanamoot? Never. It's not just a matter of sweeping away 'emotional detritus,' not for me. The cancer runs too deep. They'd excise every memory of Linn. Every memory of you."

"But you'd be alive. *Magna culpa* means if they find you, they can kill you on sight." Papa would have been shocked at how many times I'd played the lawyer tonight.

He raised his eyebrows. "If Imlann can survive in the south for sixteen years, I imagine I can manage a few." He turned to go, then thought better of it. He removed his earring and handed it back to me. "You may still need this."

"Please, Orma, I've already gotten you in so much trouble—"

"That I can't possibly get into more. Take it." He wouldn't stop glaring at me until I'd put the earring back on its cord. "You are all that's left of Linn. Her own people won't even say her name. I—I value your continued existence."

I could not speak; he had pierced me to my very heart.

As was his wont, he bid me no farewell. The full weight of everything that had befallen me, on this longest night of the year, landed squarely upon me, and I stood a very long time, staring at nothing.

Twenty-Three

I'd been up all night; I staggered off to bed.

I can't usually sleep during the day, but in truth I did not wish to be awake. Awake was a distinctly unpleasant state to be in. I hurt all over, and when I wasn't fretting about my uncle, I could not stop thinking about Lucian Kiggs.

An indignant pounding woke me halfway through the afternoon. I had fallen asleep in my clothes, so I rolled out of bed and staggered to the door, barely opening my eyes. A shimmering being, pearly and opalescent, brushed past me imperiously: Princess Glisselda. A gentler presence, who led me to a chair, was Millie.

"What did you do to Lucian?" cried Glisselda, looming over me, hands on her hips.

I couldn't pull myself into full wakefulness. I stared at her, uncomprehending. And what was there to say? That I had saved his life and made him hate me, all in one go? That I had felt things I should not, and I was sorry?

"The council has just adjourned," she said, pacing toward the hearth and back. "Lucian told us all about encountering the rogue in the countryside, about your bravery in persuading the dragon not to kill you. You're quite the pair of investigative heroes."

"What did the council decide?" I croaked, rubbing an eye with the heel of my hand.

"We're sending a group of dragons—a petit ard, we're calling it—into the country, led by Eskar." She toyed with her long string of pearls, tying it in a large knot. "They're to stay in their saaran-trai except in an emergency; they'll start at the column of rooks as one place they know Imlann has recently been and attempt to sniff him out from there.

"But you see, here's what perplexes me." She scowled and shook the knotted necklace at me. "You were so helpful and knowledgeable, one would expect Lucian to be singing your praises unto Heaven's dome. He's not. I know he arrested you on little pretext. He's mad at you, evidently, but he won't say why; he's shut himself in his beastly tower. How do I mediate if I don't know what's going on? I can't have you two at odds!"

I must have reeled a bit, because Glisselda snapped, "Millie! Make this poor woman some tea!"

Tea helped, although it also seemed to moisten my eyes. "My eyes are watering," I said, just to clarify to everyone.

"It's all right," said Glisselda. "I'd weep too if Lucian were that angry with me."

I couldn't work out what to tell her. This had never happened to me before: I always knew which things were tellable and which were not, and while I had not liked lying, it had never felt like such a burden. I tried to remember my rules: simpler was always better. I said, my voice shaky, "He's angry because I lied to him."

"Lucian can be touchy about that," said Glisselda sagely. "Why did you lie?"

I gaped at her as if she'd asked why I drew breath. I couldn't tell her that lying wasn't so much something I did as something I was, or that I had wanted to reassure Kiggs that I was human, desperate that he not be frightened of me because I had known, there among the blowing snow and ash, that I . . .

I could not even think the word with his fiancée right here, and that was itself another lie. It never ended.

"We—we were so terrified after facing Imlann," I stammered. "I spoke without thinking, trying to reassure him. Honestly, in that moment, I forgot I even had the—"

"I see the open sincerity in your face. Say just that to him, and it will be well."

Of course, I had already said that to him, more or less, and it had made things worse. Princess Glisselda stepped toward the door, Millie like a shadow behind her. "There will be a meeting between you, and you will make up. I shall arrange it."

I rose and curtsied. She added, "You should know: Earl Josef was absent from the palace all day yesterday. Lucian mentioned your suspicions, and I made him ask around. Apsig claims he was in town visiting his mistress but has not been forthcoming with her name." She looked almost apologetic. "I did mention your expedition to him at the ball. He wanted to know why Lucian would speak with you. It was ill-advised, perhaps.

"But," she added, brightening again, "our eye is upon him now."

The girls took their leave, but Glisselda paused in the doorway, raising a finger as if to scold me. "I can't have you and Lucian feuding! I need you!"

I stumbled into the other room and flopped back onto my bed when she had gone, wishing I shared her optimism, wondering whether she'd be so keen to patch things up between us if she knew what I held unspoken in my heart.

I awoke at midnight in a panic because something was on fire.

I sat bolt upright, or tried to; the morass of my feather mattress pulled me back down as if the bed tick were trying to eat me. I was drenched in sweat. The bed curtains wafted gently, illuminated by the perfectly tame fire in the hearth. Had I been dreaming? I recalled no dream, and I knew the fire was . . . still burning. I could almost smell smoke; I could feel the heat of it inside my head. Was something happening to the garden of grotesques?

Saints' dogs. I'd have believed I was going mad if things like this didn't happen in my mind all the time.

I flopped back in the bed, closed my eyes, and entered my garden. There was smoke in the distance; I ran until I reached the edge of Pandowdy's swamp. Mercifully, Pandowdy itself was underwater, sleeping, and I was able to pick my way past it. It was

At the heart of the swamp crouched Fruit Bat, and he was on fire.

the least human of all my grotesques, a sluglike, wallowing creature. It filled me with pity and dread, but it was one of mine as surely as Lars was.

Or not exactly: the flames came from my memory box, which he clutched to him, his entire body curled around it. He whimpered again, which snapped me out of my shock. I rushed over, grabbed the thing—it seared my fingers—and hurled it into the black water. It hissed, throwing up a cloud of foul steam. I knelt before Fruit Bat—he was just a child!—and examined his bare stomach, the insides of his arms, his face. He had no visible blisters, but his skin was so dark that I wasn't sure I would recognize the look of burns. I cried, "Are you hurt?"

"No," he said, prodding himself with his fingertips.

St. Masha's stone, he was talking to me now. I struggled with fear as I said, "What were you doing? Prying open my box of secrets?"

He said, "The box caught fire."

"Because you tried to look in it?"

"Never, madamina." He crossed his thumbs, making his hands into a bird, the Porphyrian gesture for supplication. "I know what's yours and what's mine. It burst into flames last night. I threw myself upon it so it would not harm you. Have I done well?"

I turned sharply toward the water; the tin box bobbed, but the fire had not gone out. I was beginning to feel the pain of the flames myself, now that Fruit Bat wasn't smothering them with his body.

I knew, without knowing how, that it had caught fire when Imlann landed in the snowy field, just as it had flooded at the sight of Comonot. It was extremely fortunate that Fruit Bat had leaped upon it when he did; if I had been seized by a memory while Imlann bore down on us, it would have been more than just an imaginary box in flames.

I turned back to the boy. The whites of his eyes shone starkly against his dark face. "What's your name? Your real name," I said.

"Abdo," he said. The name hit a light chord of déjà vu, but I could not place it.

"And where are you, Abdo?"

"I am at an inn, with my family. Holding the box gave me a headache; I was in bed all day. My grandfather is very worried, but I can sleep now and ease his heart."

The burning box had been causing him pain, but he'd held on to it for more than a day. "How did you know to help?" I said.

"There are two sacred causes in this world," he said, holding up his pinkie and ring finger. "Chance and necessity. By chance, I was there to help when you had need."

He was a little philosopher. Maybe in his country they all were. I opened my mouth to question him further, but he put his hands upon my cheeks and gazed at me earnestly. "I heard you, sought you, and have found you. I have reached for you, across space and sense and the laws of nature. I do not know how."

"Do you speak to others this way? Do others speak to you?" My fear melted away. He was so innocent.

He shrugged. "I only know three other ityasaari, in Porphyry. But you know them too: they are here. You named them Newt and Miserere and Pelican Man. None of them speak to me with their minds, but then, none of them called me. Only you."

"When did I call you?"

"I heard your flute."

Just like Lars.

"Madamina," he said, "I must sleep. My grandfather has been worried."

He released me and bowed. I bowed back uncertainly, and then looked toward the flaming box. Pandowdy burbled underwater and gave an irritable flop of its tail, sending the box bobbing back toward me. I felt the headache intensely now. I could not put off dealing with the box; the memory would surely engulf me against my will if I suppressed it, just as the other one had. I glanced at Abdo, but he had curled on his side, asleep under a large skunk cabbage. I guided the box toward shore with a sturdy cattail.

The box exploded at my touch in a burst of pyrotechnic hysteria. I choked on the smoke, wondering how it was possible that I could taste anger and feel the smell of green against my skin.

I burst from the mountainside and fly into the sun. My tail lash buries the exit under an avalanche. The combined mass of twelve old generals will exceed this icefall; I have merely bought myself a delay. I must not waste it. I dive east, with the wind, careening through low lenticular clouds into a glacial cirque.

There is a cave beneath the glacier, if I can reach it. I skim the chalky meltwater too closely; the cold scalds my ventrum. I push off the moraine with a spray of stones, elevate quickly to avoid pinnacles of ice sharp enough to gut me.

I hear a roar and a rumble behind me, high up the mountain. The generals and my father are free, but I have flown just enough. Too fast: I slam into the edge of the cirque, send shale skittering down the cliff face, and worry that they will spot the crushed lichens. I writhe into the cave, blue ice melting at my touch, easing my passage.

I hear them cross the sky, screaming, even over the roar of the glacial streams. I move deeper in, lest I make too much vapor and give myself away.

The ice cools my thoughts and condenses my rationality. I saw and heard what I should not have: my father and eleven other generals speaking together upon his board. Words upon a board must be boarded, as the ancient saying goes. They could kill me for eavesdropping.

Worse: they spoke treason. I cannot board these words.

The cave makes me claustrophobic. How do quigutl stay squeezed into crevasses without going mad? Perhaps they don't. I distract myself by thinking: of my hatchling brother, who is studying in Ninys and safe if he will stay there; of the quickest route back to Goredd; and of Claude, whom I love. I do not feel love when I take my natural shape, but I remember it and want it back. The vast, empty space where the feeling once was makes me writhe in discomfort.

Oh, Orma. You are not going to understand what has happened to me.

Night comes; the gleaming blue ice dims to black. The cave is too tight to turn around in—I am not as lithe and serpentine as some—so I back out, step by step, up the slick passage. The tip of my tail emerges into the night air.

I smell him too late. My father bites my tail on the pretext of pulling me out, then bites me again, behind the head, in chastisement.

"General, put me back in ard," I say, submitting to three more bites.

"What did you hear?" he snarls.

There is no point pretending I heard nothing. He did not raise me to be an imperceptive fool, and my scent in the passageway would have told him how long I listened. "That General Akara infiltrated the Goreddi knights, and that his actions led to their banishment." That is the least of it; my own father is part of a treacherous cabal, plotting against our Ardmagar. I am loath to utter that aloud.

He spits fire at the glacier, bringing the cave entrance crashing down. "I might have buried you alive in there. I did not. Do you know why?"

It is hard to play submissive all the time, but my father accepts no other stance from his children, and he outweighs me by a factor of two. The day will come when the strength of our intellects counts for more than physical power. That is Comonot's dream and I believe in it, but for now I bow my head. Dragons are slow to change.

"I permit you to live because I know you will not tell the Ardmagar what you heard," he says. "You will tell no one."

"What is the foundation of this belief?" I flatten myself further, no threat to him.

"Your loyalty and your family honor should be basis enough," he cries. "But you admit that you have neither."

"And if my loyalty is to my Ardmagar?" Or to his ideas, anyway.

My father spits fire at my toes; I leap back but smell singed talons.

"Then heed this, Linn: my allies among the Censors tell me you're in trouble."

I have heard no official word, but I have expected this. I flare my nostrils and raise my head spines, however, as if I were startled. "Did they say why?"

"They board details, but it doesn't matter what you did. You're on the list. If you reveal what was said upon my board—or whom you saw, or how many—it will be your word against mine. I will number you a dangerous deviant."

In fact I am a dangerous deviant, but until this moment I had been a dangerous deviant who was torn about returning to Goredd. I am no longer torn.

My father climbs the glacier face so that he might launch himself more easily. The ice is weakened by summer's heavy melt; blocks as large as my head break off beneath his claws, tumble toward me, dash to pieces. His collapse of the tunnel has put the glacier under stress; I see a deep crack in the ice.

"Climb, hatchling," he cries. "I shall escort you back to your mother's. You won't go south again; I shall see to it that the Ker cancels your visas."

"General, you are wise," I say, raising the pitch of my voice, imitating the chirp of the newly hatched. I do not climb; I am completing a calculation. I must stall him. "Put me back in ard. If I am not to go south again, is it not time I was mated?"

He has reached the top of the ice cliff. He arches his neck, muscles rippling along it. The moon has risen behind him, giving him a formidable gleam. He is intimidating; my cover is almost in earnest. I have a few more vectors to account for, and friction. Will friction be friend or foe? I extend a wing inconspicuously, trying to more accurately gauge the temperature.

"You are the daughter of Imlann!" he shrieks. "You could have any one of those generals you saw today. You could have all of them, in whatever order you wish."

It is a challenge to keep him talking while my mouth is busy. I recoil in overstated awe, histrionic for a dragon, but my father accepts this unquestioningly as his due.

"I will arrange it," he says. "You are not the mightiest female, but you fly well, and your teeth are sound. They will be honored to join their lines with mine. Only promise to break any weak eggs before they hatch, as I ought to have broken Orma's."

Oh, Orma. You are the only one I will miss.

I expel a swift, surgical ball of flame, targeting a slim buttress beneath the ice wall. Its destruction tips the structural balance. A crevasse yawns behind my father; the ice screams as the face of the glacier shears off. I spring back, out of the path of flying ice, and scramble down the moraine, bounding over boulders until I can push off into the air. I tack into the winds of the glacial collapse, circling upward. I should fly as fast as I can toward anywhere else, away, but I cannot bring myself to leave. I must see what I have done: it is my pain, I have earned it, and I will carry it with me the rest of my days.

It is no less than either of us deserves.

As per my calculation, the ice beneath his calefactive bulk was too soft and slick for his claws to get good purchase. He could not push off in time; he has tumbled backward into the crevasse. A spire of ice from higher up—from an area not figuring in my algebra—has fallen on top of him, pinning his wing. Maybe piercing it. I circle, trying to determine whether I have killed him. I smell his blood, like sulfur and roses, but he snarls and thrashes, and I conclude he is not dead. I switch on

296

every quigutl device I have and shed them down upon his body; they twinkle in the moonlight, and I estimate someone might mistake him for treasure, from a distance. He will be found.

I circle the sky, bidding farewell to the Tanamoot—mountains, sky, water, all dragonkind. I have broken my family, my father, my promises, everything. I am the traitor now.

Oh, Orma. Keep yourself safe from him.

The bed curtains danced their ghostly sarabande in the warm air currents. I stared at them for some time, seeing nothing, feeling wrung out and boneless.

Each subsequent memory filled gaps in my understanding. That first memory, so long ago, had forcefully ripped the scales from my blind eyes and destroyed my peace, I thought perhaps for good. The next had left me resenting her thoughtless selfishness; I could admit that to myself now. I envied her after the third, but now . . . something was different. Not her—she was dead and unchangeable—but me. I was changed. I clasped my aching left wrist tightly to my chest, understanding the nature of it.

I felt her struggle this time, felt echoes of my own. She had chosen Papa over family, country, her own kind, everything she'd grown up with. She had cared about Orma, insofar as dragons could care; that went a long way toward earning my sympathy. As for the ringing emptiness at the very heart of her, that was only too familiar. "I thought I was the only one who'd ever felt that, Mother," I whispered to the bed curtains. "I thought I was all alone, and maybe a little bit mad."

The feather bed had stopped trying to devour me; it seemed a cloud, rather, lifting me toward some bright epiphany: she had uncovered the existence of a cabal hostile to the Ardmagar. However personally difficult it was, however much more Kiggs despised me or the Ardmagar condemned me, I could not hoard these words.

Twenty-Four

But whom could I tell? Kiggs was mad at me. Glisselda would wonder how I knew and why I had not come forward sooner. I supposed I could lie and say Orma had only just told me, but the very thought of Orma made me sick at heart.

I should tell Orma. It struck me that he would want to know.

I rose at first light and sat at the spinet, hugging myself against the morning chill. I played Orma's chord, having no idea whether he would answer or whether he had already departed for parts unknown.

The kitten buzzed to life. "I'm here."

"That's eighty-three percent of what I wanted to know."

"What's the other seventeen?"

"When do you leave? I need to talk to you."

There was a silence punctuated by thumps, as if he were

setting down heavy books. If he was packing up every book he owned, he'd be lucky to be gone within the week. "Do you remember that newskin I was burdened with? He's still here."

Saints' dogs. "Haven't you been deemed unfit to mentor him?"

"Either no one cares that I'm leading him toward deviancy—possible, given how useless he is—or they think he'll be a help packing, which he is not."

The kitten broadcast some disgruntled muttering, and then my uncle said clearly, "No, you're not." I smiled wan sympathy at the kitten eye. "In answer to your question," he said at last, "I will depart for *home* and the *surgeons* in three days, upon your New Year, after I've *packed* up everything here. I *will* do *exactly* what is required of me by *law*. I am *caught*, and I am *chastened*, and there is no other *alternative*."

"I need to talk to you alone. I want to say goodbye while you still know me."

There was a very long pause, and for a moment I thought he had gone. I tapped the kitten eye in concern, but at last his voice came through, weakly: "My apologies, this body's ridiculous larynx seized up, but it seems to be functioning again. Will you come into town tomorrow with the rest of the court, to watch the Golden Plays?"

"I can't. Tomorrow is dress rehearsal for the Treaty Eve concert."

"Then I don't see how it will be possible to speak with you. Here's where I emit a thunderous oath, I believe."

"Do it," I urged him, but this time he really was gone. I puzzled over all his odd emphases while I tended my scales and dressed and drank my tea. I may have witnessed the first known incidence of a dragon attempting sarcasm. It was a pity I didn't know how the spinet device worked because it surely could have recorded his utterance for future generations of dragons to learn from: *This, hatchlings, is a valiant effort, but not quite it.*

I tried to laugh at that, but it rang hollow. He was leaving; I did not know when or where or for how long. If he was fleeing the Censors, he couldn't risk staying near me. He would be gone for good. I might get no chance to say goodbye.

Something had changed during the day I'd spent abed. The halls were devoid of chatter; everyone went about their business looking grim and anxious. Dragons loose in the countryside didn't sit well with anyone, apparently. As I walked to breakfast, I noticed people scuttling into side rooms at my approach, refusing to meet my eye or bid me good morning if they found themselves forced to pass me in the corridor.

Surely no one was blaming me? I'd found Imlann, but I hadn't sent the petit ard after him; that had been up to the Queen and the council. I told myself I was imagining things until I entered the north tower dining hall and the entire room fell silent.

There was space on the bench between Guntard and the scrawny sackbutist, if either of them moved over an inch. "Your pardon," I said, but they pretended not to hear. "I would like to sit here," I said, but each had an extremely interesting bowl of groats in front of him and couldn't look up. I hoisted my skirts and stepped over the bench in unladylike fashion; they couldn't scoot fast enough then. In fact, the sackbutist decided his breakfast wasn't that fascinating after all and abandoned it entirely.

I couldn't catch the serving lad's eye; nobody at the table would acknowledge me. I couldn't take it: these fellows were, if not exactly friends, colleagues and the authors of my praise song. Surely that counted for something. "Out with it, then," I said. "What've I done to earn the silent treatment?"

They looked at each other, sidelong and shifty-eyed. Nobody wanted to be the one to talk. Finally Guntard said, "Where were you last evening?"

"In bed, asleep, making up for a sleepless night the night before."

"Ah, right, your heroic expedition to find the rogue dragon," said a crumhornist, picking his teeth with a kipper bone. "Well, now you've given the dragons an excuse for roaming Goredd freely, and Princess Glisselda an excuse for having us all jabbed!"

"Jabbed?" All around the table, musicians held up bandaged fingers. Some of the fingers were rude ones. I tried not to take that personally, but it wasn't easy.

"The princess's species-check initiative," grunted Guntard. There was only one foolproof way to tell a saarantras: the silver blood. Glisselda was trying to flush out Imlann, if he was concealed at court.

A lutist waved his fish fork dangerously. "Look at her; she has no intention of letting herself get poked!"

Dragons don't blush; they turn pale. My red cheeks might

have banished doubts, but of course they didn't. I said, "I'll gladly cooperate. This is the first I'm hearing of it, is all."

"I told you oafs," said Guntard, throwing an arm across my shoulders, suddenly my champion. "I don't care what the rumors say, our Phina's no dragon!"

The bottom fell out of my stomach. Blue St. Prue. There was a huge difference between "won't take a jab like the rest of us" and "is rumored to be a dragon in disguise." I tried to keep my voice light, but it came out squeaky: "What rumor is this?"

Nobody knew who'd started it, but it had run through court the day before like fire over summer fields. I was a dragon. I'd gone not to hunt down the rogue but to warn him. I could speak Mootya. I had devices. I had willfully endangered the prince.

I sat there, stunned, trying to work out who could have said all these things. Kiggs might have, but I was unwilling to believe him so spiteful. No, *unwilling* was too tepid: it was unthinkable. I had little faith in Heaven, but I had faith in his honor, even when he was angry. Perhaps especially while angry—he struck me as someone who would cleave harder to his principles under duress.

But then who?

"I'm not a dragon," I said feebly.

"Let's test that right now," said Guntard, slapping his palms on the table. "Put everybody's mind at ease and have a spot of fun, all in one go."

I recoiled, thinking he intended to stab me—with what, his porridge spoon?—but he rose and grabbed my left arm. I yanked it away ungently, my smile brittle as glass, but rose to follow, hoping he'd feel no need to grab me again if I came willingly. Eyes followed us from all quarters.

We crossed the eerily silent dining hall and stopped at the dragons' table. There were only two this morning, a pasty male and short-haired female, lowly amanuenses who had not gone hunting Imlann, but were left behind to run the embassy offices. They sat stiffly, rolls halfway to their mouths, staring at Guntard as though he were some talking turnip who had sneaked up on them.

"Your pardon, saarantrai," cried Guntard, addressing the whole room, tables, windows, serving lads, and all. "You can recognize your own kind by smell. True?"

The saarantrai exchanged a wary glance. "The word of a saarantras does not hold up in court on certain issues, and this is one," said the male, fastidiously wiping his fingers on the tablecloth. "If you're hoping to evade the species check, we can't help you."

"Not me. Our music mistress, Seraphina. She will submit to the bleed, as will all of us who must, but there have been vicious, hateful rumors circulating and I want them put to rest." Guntard put one hand to his chest and the other in the air, like a blowhard in a play. "She is my friend, not some vile, deceitful dragon! Smell her and affirm it."

I couldn't move; I had wrapped my arms around myself, as if that alone prevented me from spontaneously combusting. The saarantrai had to rise and approach me in order to get close enough to discern anything. The female sniffed behind my ear, holding my hair aside like a dark curtain. The male bent over my left hand theatrically, he'd get a noseful. I'd changed the bandage on my self-inflicted wound this morning, but he would unquestionably discern it. Maybe I smelled edible; my blood was red as any Goreddi's.

I clenched my teeth, bracing for the blow. The saarantrai stepped away and reseated themselves without a word.

"Well?" demanded Guntard. The entire room held its breath.

Here it came. I said a little prayer.

The female spoke: "Your music mistress is not a dragon."

Guntard started clapping, like a handful of gravel tossed down the mountainside, and little by little more hands joined in until I was buried under an avalanche of applause.

I gaped at the saarantrai. They could not have failed to smell dragon. Had they assumed I was a bell-exempt scholar and kept quiet out of respect for my supposed research? Perhaps.

"Shame on all of you, believing rumors!" said Guntard. "Seraphina has never been anything but honorable, fair, and kind, a fast friend and an excellent musician—"

The male saar blinked, slowly, like a frog swallowing its dinner; the female gestured toward the sky in a subtle but unmistakable way. My doubts dissolved: they'd smelled me. They'd lied. Maybe they hoped I *was* an unauthorized dragon, just to spite Guntard and everyone else nodding agreement at all the noble, moral, non-draconian qualities I possessed.

I had never seen the rift between our peoples laid out so starkly. These saarantrai wouldn't lift a finger for the humans in this room; they might not have turned in Imlann himself. How many dragons would take his side if their choice was between submitting to Goreddi bigotry and breaking the law?

Guntard was still clapping me on the back and extolling my human virtues. I turned and walked out of the hall without my breakfast. I imagined Guntard failing to notice I had gone, clapping at the empty air.

"I want you to take tomorrow off. See the Golden Plays, visit your family, go out drinking, anything; I'll handle dress rehearsal," said Viridius, in his suite after choir practice. He'd been dictating a composition; his comment surprised me so that I jammed the quill awkwardly against a rough patch of parchment, creating an enormous inkblot.

"Have I done something wrong, sir?" I asked, dabbing at the mess with a rag.

He leaned back on his velvet cushion and gazed out the window at the overcast sky and the snowy courtyard. "Quite the contrary. You improve upon everything you touch. I think you've earned a day of rest."

"I just had a day of rest. Two, if being beset by dragons counts as rest."

He chewed his lower lip. "The council passed a resolution last night—"

"The species-check initiative? Guntard told me."

He gazed at me keenly. "I thought you might prefer not to be here."

My hands went clammy; I wiped them on my skirts. "Sir, if

you are referring to a rumor circulated about me, by persons unknown, I can assure you—"

He put his gout-swollen, clawlike hand on my forearm and raised his rusty brows. "I'll put in a good word for you," he said. "I know I'm not the cuddliest old brick, not always easy to work with, but you've done well. If I don't say so often, it doesn't mean I don't notice. You're the most talented thing we've had round these parts since Tertius was taken from us, may he dine at Heaven's table."

"Put in a good word for me *why*?"

His thick lips quivered. "Seraphina, I knew your mother."

I gasped. "You are mistaken, sir." The room seemed not to contain enough air.

"I heard her perform at Château Rodolphi in Samsam, some twenty years ago, when I was traveling with Tertius—rest he on Heaven's hearthstone. She was utterly captivating. When Tertius told me she was a saar, I didn't believe him at first."

Viridius gestured toward the ewer; I poured him a cup of water, but when I brought it to him, he said, "No, no, for you. You've gone purple around the gills. Calm yourself, child. I've known all along, haven't I? And said nothing?"

I nodded shakily. The cup clattered against my teeth.

He idly tapped his cane on the floor until he thought I was ready to listen again. "I asked Linn to teach at St. Ida's, where I was headmaster at the time. She said she couldn't; she was a student herself, just finishing up her research. I sponsored her petition for bell exemption, that she might pursue her research here without terrifying the librarians—or her students, because I hoped she'd teach. It seemed ideal.

I found myself desperate to slap him, as if he were the author of all my troubles. "It wasn't ideal."

"In hindsight, perhaps that's not surprising. She could really pass, your mother, and she was something extraordinary. She wasn't bothered with daintiness or coyness or other flavors of silliness; she was strong and practical, and she took no nonsense from anyone. If I'd any interest in women, even I could have seen my way to loving her. It was academic, of course, like the idea that one might shift the entire world with a long-enough lever. One could, but one can't. Close your mouth, dear."

My heart palpated painfully. "You knew she was a saar and my father was human, and you never told anyone?"

He heaved himself to his feet and limped over to the window. "I'm a Daanite. I don't go around criticizing other people's love affairs."

"As her sponsor, weren't you supposed to report her to the embassy before it went too far?" I said, my voice full of tears. "Couldn't you have warned my father, at the very least?"

"It seems so obvious, in retrospect," he said quietly, examining a spot on the front of his loose linen shirt. "At the time, I was merely happy for her."

I took a shaky breath. "Why are you telling me now? You haven't decided to—"

"To give up my peerless assistant? Do I look mad to you, maidy? Why do you think I'm warning you about the bleed? We'll spirit you away somewhere, or we'll find one trustworthy person high up who can keep a secret. The prince——"

"No," I said, too quickly. "There's no need. My blood is as red as yours."

He sighed. "So I've gone and revealed how much I admire your work for nothing. Now you'll feel free to laze around self-importantly, I suppose."

"Viridius, no," I said, stepping toward him and impulsively kissing his balding head. "I'm well aware that that's your job."

"Damned right," he grumbled. "And I've earned it, too."

I helped him back to his gout couch, and he finished dictating the major theme and two subthemes of his composition, along with an idea for metamorphosing each into the other, involving an extraordinary transposition. I jotted everything down mechanically at first; it took some time for me to settle down after Viridius's revelation about my mother, but the music calmed and then awed me. I was gawping inside, like a country girl seeing the cathedral for the first time. Here were flying buttresses and rose windows of music; here columns and vaulting, more prosaic structural elements; and all of it in service to a unified purpose, to clarifying and perfecting the majestic space inside, a soaring expanse as awe-inspiring as the architecture that bounded it.

"I suspect you of not taking me seriously," grumped Viridius as I cleaned my pens and made ready to depart.

"Sir?" I said, stricken. I had spent the last hour in awe of his artistry. That qualified as taking someone seriously, to my mind.

"You are new enough to court that perhaps you don't

understand the damage rumors can do. Get gone, maidy. There is no shame in a strategic retreat while you wait for Scandal, that damned basilisk, to turn its withering gaze elsewhere—especially if you're someone who, in fact, has something to hide."

"I'll bear that in mind," I said, giving him half courtesy.

"No, you won't," he muttered as I turned to go. "You're too like your mother."

Daylight failed impossibly early, assisted by a glowering cloud cover; more snow was coming. After a full day of errands and tasks, I had only the princess's harpsichord lesson left. She'd had a hectic day herself, overrun with council-related duties; five messengers found me over the course of the day, each requesting a further delay of her lesson until it had been pushed back to almost suppertime. As I approached the south solar one last messenger intercepted me; I must've rolled my eyes, because the lad stuck out his tongue before scurrying up the hall.

The note had clearly been dictated. It read: *The princess requests that you meet her downstairs in the second laundry. It is urgent. Come immediately.*

I blinked at the parchment in confusion. Why would Gliselda want to meet in such an obscure place? Perhaps she was afraid of being overheard.

I ducked down a servants' stairway to the narrow, utilitarian passages below. I passed under the great hall and the chambers of state, past storerooms, servants' quarters, and the barred, gloomy entrance of the donjon. I passed a sweltering laundry, but it was the wrong one—or so I deduced by the distinct absence of Princess Glisselda. I questioned a laundress, who pointed me further down the corridor into darkness.

I reached the furnace belonging to the hypocaust for the Queen's bathroom. Three grimy men fed coal into its open mouth, which reminded me uncomfortably of Imlann's.

The men leered at me, too, leaning on their shovels and grinning toothlessly.

I paused, the stink of coal heavy in my nostrils. Had I understood the laundress properly? Surely no one would want to wear clothing washed in such close proximity to coal fumes?

I considered asking the hypocaust stokers for directions, but there was something ominous in their aspect. I watched them shoveling; I could not seem to turn away. The heat blasted against my exposed face, even from this distance. Their silhouettes were dark holes in the frantic firelight. Acrid smoke permeated the entire room, making my eyes and lungs sting.

It was like the Infernum, the torments that awaited souls who rejected the light of Heaven. Somehow, eternal pain was still considered preferable to having no soul at all. I wasn't sure I saw why.

I turned my back upon this hellish vision. A dark, horned figure stepped directly into my path.

Twenty-Five

To my dumbfoundment, it was Lady Corongi; I'd mistaken the two peaks of her old-fashioned butterfly hennin. "Is that you, Maid Dombegh?" she asked, peering as if her eyes were not adjusted. "You seem lost, dear girl."

I emitted a small laugh of relief and gave courtesy, but did not think I should confess that I was to meet the princess somewhere down here. "I was just on my way to Glisselda's music lesson."

"You've chosen an eccentric route." She glanced toward the grimy troglodytes behind me and wrinkled her powdered nose in distaste. "Come, I will show you the way back." She stood waiting, her left elbow jutting out like a chicken's wing; I deduced I was supposed to take it.

"So," she said as we walked back up the narrow corridor together. "It has been some time since we spoke."

"Er . . . I suppose it has," I said, uncertain as to her point.

312

She smirked under her veil. "I hear you've become quite the brave adventuress since then, dallying with knights, sassing dragons, kissing the second heir's fiancé."

I went cold. Was that story going around too? Was this what Viridius had meant, that rumors gained momentum as they careered along until they were utterly beyond our power to halt? "Milady," I said shakily, "someone has been telling you lies."

Her hand upon my arm had tightened into a claw. "You think you know so much," she said, her voice incongruously pleasant. "But you are outmaneuvered, my pet. Do you know what St. Ogdo says about arrogance? 'There is blindness in sight, and folly in cleverness. Be patient: even the brightest fire burns itself out.'"

"He was talking about dragons," I said. "And what have I done to make you think me arrogant? Is it because I criticized your teaching?"

"All shall become clear, to the righteous," she said lightly, dragging me along. We turned west; we entered a laundry.

The second laundry.

The cauldrons were all upturned and the laundresses gone up to supper, but the fires still roared. Bedsheets hung from the ceiling racks, their hemlines grazing the floor, wafting like gowns at a ghostly ball. Shadows flickered grotesquely against these pale screens, growing and shrinking with the fickle firelight.

One shadow moved with purpose. There was someone else here.

Lady Corongi led me through the labyrinth of drying linens to the far corner of the room, where Princess Dionne awaited us, pacing like a caged lioness. This felt wrong. I stopped short; Lady

Corongi hauled me forward. The princess sneered. "I suppose it would be fair to let you explain yourself, Maid Dombegh."

The room had no other door and only the tiniest window, high up the wall, completely steamed over. I began to sweat in the heat; I couldn't tell what she wanted explained. My dodging the bleed? My rumored dragonhood? Lady Corongi's other accusation? All of these? I dared not guess. "Explain what, exactly, Your Highness?"

She drew a dagger from her bodice. "Kindly note: I was fair. Clarissa, hold her."

Lady Corongi was shockingly strong for one so petite and genteel. She put me in a wrestling hold—"the belt buckle," it's called, though it's like a buckle for the shoulders and neck. Princess Dionne moved as if to grab my left arm; I quickly presented her with my right. She gave a small nod and sniffed, satisfied that I was cooperating. I expected her to jab one of my fingers, but she pushed up my sleeves, wrenched my hand back, and drew her knife swiftly across my pale wrist.

I cried out. My heart was galloping like a horse. I jerked my hand away and a spray of red splotches bloomed across the linens hung in front of us like a field of poppies or some hideous parody of a bridal sheet.

"Well. That's irritating," said the princess, disgusted.

"No!" cried Lady Corongi. "It's a trick! I have it on good authority that she reeks of saar!"

"Your good authority got it wrong," said Princess Dionne, wrinkling her nose. "I smell nothing, and you don't, either. Rumor changes with the telling; perhaps she wasn't the one originally implicated. They all look alike, these common brutes."

Lady Corongi let go of me; I collapsed to the floor. She lifted the hem of her gown fastidiously, pinkies raised, and kicked me with her pointy shoes. "How did you do it, monster? How do you disguise your blood?"

"She's not a saarantras," said a calm female voice from beyond the forest of sheets. Someone began crossing the room toward us, paying no attention to the maze, pushing linens aside and barging straight through. "Stop kicking her, you bony bitch," said Dame Okra Carmine, letting the bloodied sheet fall in place behind her.

Princess Dionne and Lady Corongi stared, as if Dame Okra's solid shape made a more convincing ghost than all the billowing sheets around her. "I heard a scream," said Dame Okra. "I considered calling the Guard, but I decided to see what had happened first. Maybe someone merely saw a rat." She sneered at Lady Corongi. "Close enough."

Lady Corongi kicked me one last time, as if to prove that Dame Okra couldn't stop her. Princess Dionne wiped her dagger on a handkerchief, which she tossed into a nearby hamper, and stepped genteelly around my prone form. She paused to glare down at me. "Do not imagine that being human is all it takes to regain my esteem, strumpet. My daughter may be a fool, but I am not."

She took Lady Corongi's arm, and the pair of them departed with the dignified air of noblewomen who have nothing to be ashamed of.

Dame Okra held her tongue until they were gone, then rushed to help me, clucking, "Why, yes, you are an idiot for following them into an empty laundry room. Did you imagine they had a fine pillowcase to show you?"

"I never imagined this!" I cradled my arm, which bled alarmingly.

Dame Okra recovered Princess Dionne's handkerchief and wrapped my wrist. "You do smell of saar," she said quietly. "A bit of perfume would cover that right up. That's how I do it. Can't let a little thing like parentage stand in our way, can we?"

She helped me to my feet. I told her I needed to get to the south solar; she pushed up her glasses with a fat finger and scowled at me like I was mad. "You need help, on multiple fronts," she said. "My stomach is pulling two directions at once, which is highly irritating. I'm not sure which way to go first."

We emerged upstairs in the vicinity of the Blue Salon. Dame Okra raised a hand in warning; I held back while she peered around the corner. I heard voices and footsteps, the sounds of Millie and Princess Glisselda heading away from the south solar, where they'd waited for a music lesson that never happened.

Dame Okra squeezed my elbow and whispered, "Whatever her mother may say, Glisselda's no fool."

"I know," I said, swallowing hard.

"Don't you be one either."

Dame Okra pulled me around the corner, into the path of the girls. Princess Glisselda emitted a little scream. "Seraphina! Saints in Heaven, what have you done to yourself?"

"Looks like she has a good excuse for being late," said Millie.

"You owe me——"

"Yes, yes, shut up. Where did you find her, Ambassadress?"

"No time to explain just now," said Dame Okra. "Take her someplace safe, Infanta. There may be people looking for her. And see to her arm. I have one more thing to attend to, and then I will find you."

The handkerchief had soaked through; there was a streak of blood all the way down the front of my gown. My sight grew dim, but then there was a young woman at each of my elbows, propping me up, moving me on, chatting away. They swept me upstairs into an apartment I deduced was Millie's. ". . . you're nearly the same size," Glisselda squealed excitedly. "We'll finally have you looking pretty as can be!"

"First things first, Princess," said Millie. "Let's see that arm."

I needed stitches; they called the Queen's own surgeon. He administered a glass of plum brandy, then another, until I had choked down three. I appeared immune to its dulling effects, so he finally gave up and stitched me up, tut-tutting at my tears and wishing aloud that I had been drunker. I'd expected the girls to look away, but they did not. They gasped, clutching each other, but watched every needle jab and tug of thread.

"Might one inquire how you did this to yourself, Music Mistress?" asked the surgeon, a phlegmatic old fellow without a hair on his head.

"She fell," Glisselda offered. "On a sharp . . . thing."

"In the basement," added Millie, which I'm sure bolstered the story's credibility immensely. The surgeon rolled his eyes but could not be bothered to inquire further.

"How did it happen?"

Once the girls had shooed him out, Glisselda grew grave.

The spirits seemed finally to have reached my head; between brandy and blood loss and a dearth of supper, the room began to swim before my eyes. As much as I wanted to lie—because how could I tell Glisselda that her own mother cut me?—I could come up with no plausible alternative story. I would omit Princess Dionne, at least. "You've heard the rumor that I am a . . . a saar?"

Heaven forfend that she had heard the other rumor.

"It was vicious," said the princess, "and evidently unfounded."

"I hadn't been bled yet. Some zealous, uh, vigilantes decided to do it for me."

Glisselda leaped to her feet, seething. "Isn't this exactly what we hoped to avoid?"

"It is, Princess," said Millie, shaking her head and putting the kettle on the hearth.

"Seraphina, I'm appalled it came to this," said the princess.

"My original idea—"

"And Lucian's," said Millie, apparently allowed to interrupt the second heir.

Glisselda flashed her an irritated look: "One of his Porphyrian philosophers helped too, if you're going to be that way about it. *The* idea was that we should all be jabbed, everyone, from Grandmamma herself to the lowliest scullion, noble with common, human with dragon. It would be fair.

"But several nobles and dignitaries argued vociferously against it. 'We should be exempt! We are people of quality!' In the end, only courtiers of less than two years' tenure and commoners must get tested—and you see the result, my Millie? Vigilantism, and that bastard Apsig gets off without a scratch."

Glisselda ranted on; I couldn't focus on it. The room swayed like the deck of a ship. I was thoroughly inebriated now; I suffered the illusion that my head might fall off, for it seemed too heavy to support. Someone spoke, but it took some minutes for the words to penetrate my consciousness: "We ought to at least change her out of that bloody gown before Dame Okra comes back."

"No, no," I said, or intended to. Intention and action were curiously blurred, and judgment seemed to have retired for the night entirely. Millie had a tall privacy screen, painted with weeping willows and water lilies, and I let myself be persuaded behind it. "All right, but just the top gown needs replacing," I said, my words floating over the screen like vapid, ineffective bubbles.

"You bled fearfully," called Millie. "Surely it soaked straight through?"

"No one can see what's beneath . . .," I began, fuzzily.

Glisselda popped her head around the edge of the lacquered screen; I gasped and nearly pitched over, even though I was still covered. "I shall know," she chirped. "Millie! Top and bottom layers!"

Millie produced a chemise of the softest, whitest linen I had ever touched. I wanted to wear it, which addled my judgment still further. I began to undress. Across the room, the girls bickered over colors for the gown; apparently accounting for my complexion and my hair required complicated algebra. I giggled, and began explaining how to solve a quadratic complexion equation, even though I couldn't quite remember.

I had removed all my clothing—and my good sense along with it—when Glisselda popped her head around the end of the screen behind me, saying, "Hold this scarlet up to your chin and let's see—oh!"

Her cry snapped the world back into hard focus for a moment. I whirled to face her, holding Millie's chemise up in front of me like a shield, but she'd gone. The room reeled. She'd seen the band of silver scales across my back. I clapped a hand to my mouth to stop myself screaming.

They whispered together urgently, Glisselda's voice squeaky with panic, Millie's calm and reasonable. I yanked Millie's chemise over my head, almost tearing a shoulder seam in my rush because I couldn't work out where all my limbs were or how to move them. I curled up on the floor, balling up my own gown, pressing it to my mouth because I was breathing too hard. I waited in agony for either of them to say something.

"Phina?" said Princess Glisselda at long last, rapping upon the screen as if it were a door. "Was that a . . . a Saint's burthen?"

My foggy brain couldn't parse her words. What was a Saint's burthen? My reflex was to answer no, but mercifully I managed to hold that in check. She was offering me a way out, if only I could make sense of it.

I had managed to stay silent. She couldn't hear the tears coursing down my cheeks. I took a deep breath and said shakily, "Is what a Saint's burthen?"

"That silver girdle you wear."

I thanked all the Saints in Heaven, and their dogs. She had not believed her own eyes. How crazy was that, to think you'd seen dragon scales sprouting out of human flesh? It must have been something, anything else. I coughed, to clear the tears out of my voice, and said as casually as I could, "Oh, that. Yes. Saint's burthen."

"For which Saint?"

Which Saint . . which Saint . . I could not think of a single Saint. Luckily, Millie piped up, "My aunt wore an iron anklet for St. Vitt. It worked: she never doubted again."

I closed my eyes; it was easier to produce coherent thoughts without vision distracting me. I injected some truth: "At my blessing day, my patron was St. Yirtrudis."

"The heretic?" They both gasped. No one ever seemed to know what Yirtrudis's heresy had consisted of, but it didn't seem to matter. The very idea of heresy was dreadful enough.

"The priest told us Heaven intended St. Capiti," I continued, "but from that day to this, I've had to wear a silver girdle to, uh, deflect heresy."

This impressed and apparently satisfied them. They handed me a gown; scarlet had won the argument. They did my hair and exclaimed at how lovely I was when I bothered to try. "Keep the gown," insisted Millie. "Wear it on Treaty Eve."

"You are all generosity, my Millie!" said Glisselda, pinching Millie's ear proudly, as if she'd invented her lady-in-waiting herself.

A rap at the door was Dame Okra, who stood on tiptoe to peer past Millie's shoulder. "She's all patched up? I've found just the person to whisk her away to safety—after which I require a word with you, Infanta."

Millie and the princess helped me to my feet. "I'm so sorry," Glisselda whispered warmly in my ear. I looked down at her. Everything seemed shinier viewed through three brandy glasses, but the glittering at the corners of her eyes was real enough.

Dame Okra ushered me out the door, toward my waiting father.

Twenty-Six

The chill wind in the open sledge did little to sober me up. My father drove, seated close, sharing the lap rug and foot box. My head bobbed unsteadily; he let me rest it on his shoulder. If I were to weep, surely the tears would freeze upon my cheeks.

"I'm sorry, Papa. I tried to keep to myself; I didn't mean it to go wrong," I muttered into his dark wool cloak. He said nothing, which I found inexplicably encouraging. I gestured grandly at the dark city, a suitable backdrop to my drunken sense of epic tragic destiny. "But they're sending Orma away, which is my fault, and I played my flute so beautifully that I fell in love with everyone, and now I want everything. And I can't have it. And I'm ashamed to be running away."

"You're not running away," said Papa, taking the reins in one gloved hand and hesitantly patting my knee with the other. "At least, you need not decide until morning."

"You're not going to lock me up for good?" I said, on the verge of blubbering. Some sober part of my brain seemed to observe everything I did, clucking disdainfully, informing me that I ought to be embarrassed, yet making no move to stop me.

Papa ignored that comment, which was probably wise. Snow spangled his gray lawyer's cap; little droplets stuck to his brows and lashes. He spoke in measured tones. "Did you fall in love with anyone specific, or simply with the things you cannot have?"

"Both," I said, "and Lucian Kiggs."

"Ah." For some time the only sounds were of harness bells, horses snorting in the cold, and packed snow creaking under the sledge runners. My head waxed heavy.

I jerked awake. My father was speaking: " . . . that she never trusted me. That cut more deeply than anything else. She believed I would stop loving her if I knew the truth. All the gambles she took, and she never took the one that mattered most. One in a thousand is better odds than zero, but zero is what she settled for. Because how could I love her if I couldn't see her? Whom did I love, exactly?"

I nodded, and jerked awake again. The air was alive, bright with snowflakes.

He said: " . . . time to mull it over, and I am no longer afraid. I am sickened that you inherited her collapsing house of deceit, and that instead of tearing it down, I shored it up with more deceit. What price must be paid is mine to pay. If you are afraid on your own behalf, fair enough, but do not fear for me—"

Then he was shaking my shoulder lightly. "Seraphina. We're home."

I threw my arms around him. He lifted me down and led me through the lighted doorway.

❧

The next morning, I lay a long time, staring at the ceiling of my old room, wondering whether I'd imagined most of what he'd said. That didn't sound like a conversation I could have had with my father, even if we'd both been drunk as lords.

The sun was obnoxiously bright and my mouth tasted like death, but I didn't feel bad otherwise. I peeked at my garden, which I'd neglected last night, but everyone was peaceful; even Fruit Bat was up a tree, not demanding my attention. I rose and dressed in an old gown I found in my wardrobe; the scarlet I'd arrived in was too fine for everyday. I descended to the kitchen. Laughter and the smell of morning bread drifted toward me up the corridor. I paused, my hand upon the kitchen door, discerning their voices one by one, dreading to step into that warm room and freeze it up.

I took a deep breath and opened the door. For the merest moment, before my presence was noticed, I drank in the cozy domestic scene: the roaring hearth, the three fine bluestone platters hung above the mantelpiece, little window altars to St Loola and St. Yane and a new one to St. Abaster, hanging herbs and strings of onions. My stepmother, up to her elbows in the kneading trough, looked up at the sound of the door and paled. At the heavy kitchen table, Tessie and Jeanne, the twins, had been peeling apples; they froze, silent and staring, Tessie with a length of peel dangling from her mouth like a green tongue. My little half brothers, Paul and Ned, looked to their mother uncertainly.

I was a stranger in this family. I always had been.

Anne-Marie wiped her hands on her apron and tried to smile. "Seraphina. Welcome. If you're looking for your father, he's already left for the palace." Her brow crumpled in confusion. "You came from there? You'd have passed him on the way."

I could not remember anyone meeting us at the door last night, now that I thought of it. Had my father sneaked me into the house and upstairs without telling her? That sounded more like Papa than a conversation about love, lies, and fear.

I tried to smile. It was an unspoken covenant with my stepmother: we both tried. "I—in fact, I'm home to retrieve something. From my, uh, room. That I forgot to take with me, and need."

Anne-Marie nodded eagerly. *Yes, yes, good.* The awkward stepdaughter was leaving soon. "Please, go on up. This is still your house."

I drifted back upstairs, lightly dazed, wishing I had told her the truth, because what was I going to do for breakfast now? Astonishingly, my coin purse had made the whole journey and wasn't languishing on the floor of Millie's room. I'd buy myself a bun somewhere, or ... my heart leaped. I could see Orma! He had hoped I'd come see him today. That was a plan, at least. I would surprise Orma before he disappeared for good.

I pushed that latter thought aside.

I packed the scarlet gown carefully into a satchel and made up the bed. I could never fluff the tick like Anne-Marie; she was going to figure out that I'd slept here. Ah, well, let her. It was Papa's to explain.

Anne Marie required no farewells. She knew what I was, and it seemed to put her at ease when I behaved like a thoughtless saar. I opened the front door ready to head into the snowy city when there came a pattering of slippered feet behind me. I turned to see my half sisters rushing up. "Did you find what you came for?" asked Jeanne, her pale brow wrinkled in concern. "Because Papa said to give you this."

Tessie brandished a long, slender box in one hand, a folded letter in the other.

"Thanks." I put both in my satchel, suspecting I should view them in privacy.

They bit their lips in exactly the same way, even though they weren't identical. Jeanne's hair was the color of clover honey; Tessie had Papa's dark locks, like me. I said, "You turn eleven in a few months, do you not? Would you—would you like to come see the palace for your birthday? If it's all right with your mother, I mean."

They nodded, shy of me.

"All right then. I'll arrange it. You could meet the princesses." They didn't answer, and I could think of nothing more to say. I'd tried. I waved a feeble farewell and fled through the snowy streets to my uncle's.

Orma's apartment was a single room above a mapmaker's, nearer to my father's house than St. Ida's, so I checked there first. Basind answered the door but had no idea where my uncle had gone. "If I knew, I'd be there with him," he explained, his voice like sand in my stockings. He gazed into space, tugging a hangnail with his teeth, while I left a message. I had no confidence it would be delivered.

Anxiety hastened my feet toward St. Ida's.

The streets were jammed full of people out for the Golden Plays. I considered walking down by the river, which was less crowded, but I hadn't dressed warmly enough. The crush in the streets stopped the wind, at least. There were large charcoal braziers set every block or so to keep playgoers from freezing; I took advantage of these when I could wedge myself close enough.

I had not intended to watch the plays, but it was hard not to pause at the sight of a giant, fire-belching head of St. Vitt outside the Guild of Glassblowers' warehouse. A blazing tongue ten yards long roared forth; everyone shrieked. St. Vitt caught his own eyebrows on fire—unintentionally, but Heavens, was he fierce with his brow aflame!

"St. Vitt, snort and spit!" chanted the crowd.

St. Vitt had not been possessed of such draconian talents in life, of course. It was a metaphor for his fiery temper or for his judgment upon unbelievers. Or, as likely as not, somebody at the Guild of Glassblowers had awakened in the middle of the night with the most fantastic idea ever, never mind that it was theologically questionable.

The Golden Plays stretched the hagiographies all round because the fact was, no one really knew. *The Lives of the Saints* contained many contradictions; the psalter's poems made things no clearer, and then there was the statuary. St. Polypous in the *Lives* had three legs, for example, but country shrines showed as many as twenty. At our cathedral, St. Gobnait had a hive of blessed bees; at South Forkey, she was famously depicted as a bee, big as a cow, with a stinger as long as your forearm. My substitute patroness, St. Capiti, usually carried her severed head on a plate, but in some tales her head had tiny legs of its own and skittered around independently, scolding people.

Delving deeper into the truth, of course, my psalter had originally coughed up St. Yirtrudis. I had never seen her without her face blacked out or her head smashed to plaster dust, so surely she had been the most terrible Saint of all.

I kept moving, past St. Loola's apple and St. Kathanda's colossal merganser, past St. Ogdo slaying dragons and St. Yane getting up to his usual shenanigans, which often involved impregnating entire villages. I passed vendors of chestnuts, pasties, and pie, which made my stomach rumble. I heard music ahead: syrinx, oud, and drum, a peculiarly Porphyrian combination. Above the heads of the crowd, I made out the upper stories of a pyramid of acrobats, Porphyrians, by the look of them, and . . .

No, not acrobats. Pygegyria dancers. The one at the top looked like Fruit Bat.

I meant Abdo. Sweet St. Siucre. It *was* Abdo, in loose trousers of green sateen, his bare arms snaking sinuously against the winter sky.

He'd been here all along, trying to find me, and I'd been putting him off.

I was still staring at the dancers, openmouthed, when someone grabbed my arm. I startled and cried out.

"Hush. Walk," muttered Orma's voice in my ear. "I haven't much time. I gave Basind the slip; I'm not confident I can do it again. I suspect the embassy is paying him to watch me."

He still held my arm; I covered his hand with my own. The crowd flowed around us like a river around an island. "I learned something new about Imlann from one of my maternal memories," I told him. "Can we find a quieter place to talk?"

He dropped my arm and ducked up an alley; I followed him through a brick-walled maze of barrels and stacked firewood and up the steps of a little shrine to St. Clare. I balked when I saw her—thinking of Kiggs, feeling her dyspeptic glare as criticism—but I kissed my knuckle respectfully and focused on my uncle.

His false beard had gone missing or he hadn't bothered with it. He had deep creases beside his mouth, which made him look unexpectedly old. "Quickly," he said. "If I hadn't spotted you, I'd have disappeared by now."

I took a shaky breath; I'd come so close to missing him. "Your sister once overheard Imlann consorting with a cabal of treasonous generals, about a dozen in all. One of them, General Akara, was instrumental in getting the Goreddi knights banished."

"Akara is a familiar name," said Orma. "He was caught, but the Ardmagar had his brain pruned too close to the stem; he lost most of his ability to function."

"Does the Queen know?" I asked, shocked. "The knights were banished under false pretenses, but nothing has been done to correct this!"

My uncle shrugged. "I doubt Comonot disapproved of that consequence."

Alas, I believed that; Comonot's rules were applied inconsistently. I said, "If the cabal could infiltrate the knights, they really could be anywhere."

Orma stared at St. Clare, pondering. "They couldn't be quite anywhere, not easily. There would be a danger of law-abiding dragons sniffing them out at court. They could count on there being no other dragons present among the knights."

It hit me then, what Imlann might have been doing. "What if your father has been observing the knights? He might have burned their barn and shown himself as a final assessment of their capabilities."

"A final assessment?" Orma sat down impiously on the altar, deep in thought. "Meaning Akara didn't just have the knights banished for vengeance? Meaning this cabal has been deliberately working toward the extinction of the dracomachia?"

There was one clear implication of this; we both knew what it was. My eyes asked the question, but Orma was already shaking his head in denial.

"The peace is not a ruse," he said. "It is not some ploy to lull Goredd into false complacency until such time as dragonkind regains a clear superiority of—"

"Of course not," I said quickly. "At least, Comonot did not intend it that way. I believe that, but is it possible that his generals only pretended to agree to it, all the while making St. Polypous's sign behind their backs—so to speak?"

Orma fingered the coins in the offering bowl on the altar, letting the copper pieces dribble through his fingers like water. "Then they have gravely miscalculated," he said. "While they sat around waiting for the knights to grow old, a younger generation has been raised on peaceful ideals, scholarship, and cooperation."

"What if the Ardmagar were dead? If whoever took his place wanted war? Would this cabal need you and your agemates? Couldn't they fight a war without you, especially if there were no dracomachia against them?"

Orma rattled coins in his hand and did not answer.

"Would the younger generation stand against the elder, if it came to it?" I pressed on, remembering the two saarantrai in the dining hall. I was being hard on him, but this was a crucial point. "Can the current batch of scholars and diplomats even fight?"

He recoiled as if he'd heard that accusation before. "Forgive me," I said, "but if war is brewing in the hearts of the old generals, your generation may have some painful decisions to make."

"Generation against generation? Dragon against dragon? Sounds treasonous to me," said a grating voice behind me. I turned to see Basind mounting the steps of the shrine. "What are you doing here, Orma? Not offering devotions to St. Clare, surely?"

"Waiting for you," said Orma lightly. "I only wonder that it took you so long."

"Your wench led me here," said Basind greasily. If he was hoping to get a reaction from Orma, he was disappointed. Orma's face remained completely empty. "I could report you," said the newskin. "You're having trysts in roadside shrines."

"Do," said Orma, waving a dismissive hand. "Be off. Scamper and report."

Basind looked uncertain how to respond to this bravado. He

pushed his limp hair out of his eyes and sniffed. "I'm charged with seeing you report to the surgeons in time."

"I gathered that," said Orma. "But you will recall that my niece—yes, my niece, daughter of my nameless sister—wished to bid me farewell, and wished to do so in private. She is half human, after all, and it pains her that I will not recognize her when I see her again. If you would but give us a few more minutes—"

"I do not intend to take my eyes off you again." Basind bugged his eyes to underscore the point.

Orma shrugged, looking resigned. "If you can endure human blubbering, you have a stronger stomach than most."

My uncle shot me a sharp look, and for once we were in perfect understanding. I began to wail noisily, giving it everything I had. I howled like a banshee, like a gale down the mountainside. I bawled like a colicky baby. I expected Basind to stubbornly stand his ground—this seemed a very silly way to drive him off—but he recoiled in revulsion, saying, "I will stand guard just outside."

"As you wish," said my uncle. He watched until Basind had turned his back to us, then closed in, speaking directly into my ear: "Continue to wail, as long as you can."

I looked at him, sorrowing in earnest, unable to say any words of parting because I had to expend all my breath on loud crying. Without a backward glance, Orma ducked behind the altar and out of sight. There must have been a crypt under the shrine, as sometimes happened; the crypt would surely connect with the great warren of tunnels under the city.

I wailed, for real and for true, staring down St. Clare, beating on the hem of her robe with my fist until I was hoarse and coughing. Basind glanced back, then looked again, startled. I could not let him work out where Orma had gone. I looked past Basind, over his shoulder, pretending to see my uncle's face in the shuttered alley windows behind him, and I cried, "Orma! Run!"

Basind whirled, perplexed at how Orma could have reached the alley without his seeing. I rushed him, shoving him into a pile of firewood, causing a little avalanche of logs. I took off running as fast as I could. He recovered far more quickly than anticipated, his flat-footed gait echoing behind me, his silver bell ringing out a warning.

I wasn't much of a runner; each step seemed to drive a spike into my knees, and the hem of my gown, sodden with dirty snow, clung to my ankles, nearly tripping me. I ducked left and jogged right, sliding on bloody ice behind a butcher's. I climbed a ladder onto someone's work shed, hoisted it up after myself, and used it to climb down the other side. That struck me as clever until I saw Basind's hands grip the far edge of the roof. He was strong enough to pull himself up; that was unexpected. I jumped off the ladder and crash-landed, causing a ruckus among the chickens in someone's little yard. I sprinted through the gate into yet another alley. I turned north, then north again, making for the crowded river road. Surely the crowd would stop Basind—not just slow him down, but restrain him. No Goreddi could stand idly by while a saarantras chased one of their own.

Basind's breath rasped close by my neck; his hand hit my swinging satchel but couldn't quite get a grip on it. I burst out of the alley into bright sunlight. People scattered before me, crying out in surprise. It took a moment for my eyes to adjust, but what I saw then stopped me short. I heard Basind stop running at almost the same moment, arrested by exactly the same sight—we'd emerged in the middle of a cluster of men in black-feathered caps: the Sons of St. Ogdo.

Twenty-Seven

I did the first thing that occurred to me. I pointed at Basind and cried: "He's trying to hurt me!"

It's possible he was; I'm certain he looked guilty, chasing me out of an alley like that; and I knew, in my heart, that I was maligning one dragon to save another. But I should never have said such a thing, not to the Sons of St. Ogdo, who needed little enough excuse to harm a saar.

They mobbed him, slamming him up against the side of a building, and I knew I had started something far larger than I had intended. There must have been forty Sons in this cluster alone; their numbers were growing daily, with the Ardmagar here.

My eyes met those of one of the Sons, and with a shock, I recognized the Earl of Apsig.

He was disguised—homespun clothes, a cobbler's apron, a squashed hat holding his black feather but nothing could alter those arrogant blue eyes. He'd surely seen me when I dashed from the alley; he tried to conceal himself now, ducking behind his fellows, averting his face while they chanted St. Ogdo's Malediction Against the Worm: *Eye of Heaven, seek out the saar. Let him not lurk among us, but reveal him in his unholiness. His soulless inhumanity flies like a banner before the discerning eyes of the righteous. We will cleanse the world of him!*

I looked around desperately for the Guard and spotted them approaching from the north, riding toward us in a unit.

They were escorting the royal coaches around to the Golden Plays. The Sons noticed them too, and called to each other. Leaving just two men to restrain Basind, who hung limply between them, the rest spread across the roadway, just the way they'd been standing when I came crashing out of the alley.

The Sons had been waiting here for the Ardmagar's coach.

Out of the corner of my eye I saw Josef duck up the alley. He had the right idea. I'd been in riots before; the novelty wore off quickly.

I shouldered my way through the crowd and reached the alley just as the Guard reached the front line of Sons. Shouts rang out behind me, but I didn't turn to look. I couldn't. I fled the fighting as fast as my cold feet would carry me.

The Sons had gangs all over town, I discovered. I had not, in fact, started the worst day of rioting our city had ever seen, but that was cold comfort. The Sons had seized the Wolfstoot Bridge; in the warehouse district, they were throwing bricks. I kept to the alleys but still had to cross the major arteries of the city without getting my skull cracked open. Orma was lucky to be underground.

I had hoped to reach my father's. I made it as far as the cathedral; from there, the action in the plaza and upon Cathedral Bridge looked grim. The Guard had subdued the plaza, but the Sons had erected a barricade upon the bridge and set it on fire, and they were holding their ground behind it.

Someone had vandalized the Countdown Clock, switching the heads of the Dragon and Queen and posing them suggestively together. A question was scrawled across the clock face: *But how long until the filthy quigs go home?* Another hand had written in answer: *Not until we drive the devils off!*

The cathedral could provide me with refuge until the Guard retook the bridge. I was not the only one who hoped so. There were about fifty people in the nave, mostly children and elders. The priests had corralled them all together and were treating injuries. I didn't care to huddle with everyone else. I skirted the eastern side of the Golden House without the priests noticing and crept quietly toward the south transept.

The megaharmonium hulked in its alcove under a tarp, defense against dust and greasy fingers. I wandered behind it for a closer look and because the chapel offered a space away from the questioning eyes of the priests. Behind the megaharmonium were bellows as tall as my shoulder. Did someone have to sit back here, pumping endlessly, going slowly deaf? That sounded like unpleasant work.

The chapel looked like it had stood empty a long time; the

walls were stripped of decoration, leaving only traces of gilt in the cracks of the wood paneling. I could discern dark shapes that had once been painted letters. It took some squinting, but I finally read the words *No Heaven but this.*

That was the motto of St. Yirtrudis. I shivered.

Above me, her outline was just visible beneath layers of white-wash. There was a rough patch where her face had been chiseled off, but around it her shadow lingered: her outstretched arms, her billowing gown, her . . . hair? I hoped that was her hair and not tentacles or spider legs or something worse. Nothing was clear but the silhouette.

I heard muttering out in the transept and poked my nose out of the chapel. There stood Josef, Earl of Apsig, minus his black-feathered cap. He talked quietly with a priest. The priest's back was to me, but he wore a string of amber prayer beads around his neck. I drew back quickly and crouched behind the instrument, watching their feet between the legs of the bench. They conferred, embraced, and then parted. By the time I felt safe to rise, Josef had departed through the southern doors.

I crept back to the great crossing, stood behind the Golden House, and looked for the priest he'd been speaking with among those tending injuries in the nave. None of them wore amber beads.

A peculiar movement in the north aisle of the nave caught my eye. I thought the figure, cowled and cassocked, was a monk at first, except for how strangely he was moving. He stood frozen in unnatural attitudes for long stretches, followed by almost imperceptible motion. It was like watching the hands of a clock or clouds on a still day, all of this punctuated by extremely brief bursts of motion. He obviously intended stealth but seemed unfamiliar with the usual means of achieving it.

I suspected a saar.

I lay low until the figure reached the north transept, where I had a better viewing angle. I looked full at him, recognized his profile, and froze.

It was the Ardmagar.

I followed him toward the shadowy apse, keeping my distance. The floor of the apse was marble, so finely polished it looked wet. Hundreds of tiny candles reflected off the gilded ceiling vaults, lending a shimmer to the incense-spiced air. Comonot walked more normally now, past grim St. Vitt and devious St. Polypous. He proceeded to the chapel at the very end, where St. Gobnait, round-cheeked and benevolent, sat enthroned, her blessed beehive in her lap, her head crowned with golden honeycomb. Her eyes shone a brilliant unearthly blue, the whites a glaring contrast to her burnished face.

Comonot paused, lowered his cowl, and turned to face me, smiling.

The smile took me aback, coming from a dragon, but it evaporated the instant he recognized me. He turned away from me, back toward the Holy Skep, which the monks took outside in springtime to be a dwelling for her blessed bees.

"What do you want?" said Comonot, addressing St. Gobnait.

I addressed his plastered-down hair: "You should not be out on your own."

"I crossed the city on foot without incident," he said, gesturing grandly. I was hit by a waft of incongruous perfume. "No one looks twice at a monk."

They'd look twice at a scented monk, but no good could come of arguing the point. I kept on doggedly. "There's something I must tell you, about my grandfather."

He kept his back to me, pretending to examine the Skep. "We know all about him. Eskar is probably biting his head off right now."

"I have maternal memories—" He scoffed at this, but I persisted. "Imlann revealed to my mother that he isn't alone in despising the peace. There's a cabal. They're waiting for Goredd to weaken sufficiently, at which point I can only guess—"

"I'm sure you don't have a single name."

"General Akara."

"Caught and modified, twenty years ago."

I gave up trying not to antagonize him. "You never informed our Queen."

"My generals are loyal," he sniffed over his shoulder. "If you wish to convince me of a plot, you'll have to do better than that."

I opened my mouth to argue, but an arm wrapped around my throat from behind, choking off my voice, and then someone stabbed me in the back.

Twenty-Eight

O r tried to, anyway.

My attacker released me with a cry of dismay. His dagger made no dent in my scaly midriff; he dropped the weapon on the marble floor with a ringing clang. Comonot whirled at the sound, drawing a sword concealed in his robes. I ducked; the Ardmagar struck faster than I'd believed possible in a man of his age and girth—but then, he wasn't an ordinary man. By the time I raised my head, there was a dead priest on the floor of the apse, his robes a tangled mass of black, his life a wash of crimson pooling before the bishop's throne. His blood steamed in the frigid air.

I glimpsed the string of amber prayer beads at his throat. This was surely the priest I'd seen speaking with Josef. I rolled him over and cried out in alarm.

It was the clothier who'd threatened me. Thomas Broadwick. Comonot's nostrils flared. This could not be good, a saarantras smelling fresh death. I heard voices and the scuffle of feet rushing up the apse toward us; the din of our brief battle had not gone unnoted. I froze in panic, not knowing whether to urge the Ardmagar to run or to turn him in myself.

He'd saved my life, or I'd saved his. Not even that was clear.

Three monks reached us, skidding to a stop at the sight of our gruesome tableau. I turned to Comonot, intending to follow his lead, but he was unexpectedly shocked and pale; he looked dumbly at me, shaking his head. I took a deep breath and said, "There's been an assassination attempt."

Comonot and I were not officially detained, but "voluntarily" confined to the bishop's study until the Queen's Guard arrived. The bishop had good food and wine sent up from the seminary kitchens, and welcomed us to peruse his library.

I would have been happy to make free with the books, but Comonot would not stop pacing, and anytime I moved at all he flinched, as if he feared I might come over and touch him. I probably could have cornered him behind the lectern if I'd had a mind to.

At last he burst out: "Explain this body to me!"

He was asking the right person. I had addressed similar questions from Orma twenty dozen times. "What specifically perturbs you, Ardmagar?"

He seated himself across from me, looking directly at me for the first time. His face was white; sweat plastered his hair to his forehead. "Why did I do that?" he said. "Why did I reflexively kill that man?"

"Self-preservation. He'd stabbed me; he was likely to go for you next."

"No," he said, shaking his jowls. "That is, perhaps he would have attacked me, but that's not what went through my mind. I was protecting you."

I almost thanked him, but he seemed so profoundly disturbed by the whole thing that I hesitated. "Why do you regret protecting me? Because of what I am?"

He regained some of his hauteur: his lip curled and his heavy lids lowered. "What you are is every bit as repulsive to me as it ever was. He poured himself a large glass of wine. "However, I am now in your debt. If I had been alone, I might be dead."

"You shouldn't have come here alone. How did you leave the entourage without being seen?"

He took several large gulps and considered the air in front of him. "I was never in my carriage. I had no intention of viewing the Golden Plays; I have no interest in your queer religion or the dramas it spawns."

"Then what were you doing in the cathedral? Not finding religion, one assumes."

"Not your concern." He sipped wine, his eyes narrowing in thought. "What do you call doing something on behalf of someone else for no apparent reason? Altruism?"

"Er, you mean what you did for me?"

"Of course that's what I mean."

"But you had reason: you were grateful I had saved your life."

"No!" he shouted. I jumped, startled. "That didn't occur to me until after the deed was done. I defended you without even thinking. For the merest moment I . . ." He paused, his breath labored, his eyes glazed with horror. "I had a strong feeling about what happened to you. I may have cared! The idea of you hurting made me . . . hurt!"

"I suppose I'd call that empathy," I said, not exactly feeling empathy myself for how much the idea disgusted him.

"But it wasn't me, you understand?" he cried, the wine already making him histrionic. "It was this infernal body. It fills with a great surge of feeling before one has a chance to think. It's a species-preservation instinct, maybe, to defend the young and helpless, but I care nothing for you. This body wants things I could never want."

It was, of course, at that very moment that Captain Kiggs opened the door.

He looked embarrassed. I don't imagine I looked much different. The last time we'd spoken I'd been under arrest. "Ardmagar Maid Dombegh," he said, nodding. "You've left a bit of a mess up by the Skep. Care to tell me what happened?"

Comonot did the talking; we'd gone up the apse to speak privately, in his version. I held my breath, but Comonot let nothing slip about my background or my maternal memory. He simply claimed I'd had confidential information for him.

"Pertaining to what?" asked Kiggs.

"Pertaining to none of your business," grumped the Ardmagar.

He'd had enough wine that he could no longer find the door to the mental room where he was supposed to stow his emotions. If he even had such a room.

Kiggs shrugged, and Comonot continued, detailing the swift and bloody fight. Kiggs pulled Thomas's dagger out of his belt, turning it in his fingers. The tip had crumpled grotesquely. "Any idea how this happened?"

Comonot frowned. "Could it have hit the floor in such a way as to—"

"Not likely, unless he threw it straight at the stones," said Kiggs, looking full at me for the first time. "Seraphina?"

That old, inconvenient feeling bubbled up in response to his using my first name. "He stabbed me," I said, staring at my hands.

"What? No one told me this! Where?" He sounded so alarmed that I looked up. I wished I hadn't; it hurt to see him concerned about me.

I felt around near my right kidney. The hole went through my cloak and through all my layers of gown, unsurprisingly. Could I refasten my belt to cover it? I glanced at Kiggs again; his mouth had fallen open. He had a point: I should be dead.

"Did Glisselda not tell you? I've got a . . . a Saint's burthen. A silver girdle that protects me from heresy. It saved me."

Kiggs shook his head in wonder. "It's always something unexpected with you, isn't it. A word to the wise: a blow hard enough to do this"—he held up the bent dagger—"is going to leave a painful bruise, or even a laceration. I'd let the palace physicians have a look at it."

"I'll bear that in mind," I said. My back was sore; I wondered what bruised scales looked like.

"Ardmagar, the city is secured," said Kiggs. "A contingent of Guardsmen is here to escort you back to Castle Orison. I expect you to stay there for the rest of your visit."

Comonot nodded hastily; if he had once doubted the sense of remaining under guard, he did no longer.

"What were you doing here alone?" asked Kiggs. Comonot gave him almost the same answer he'd given me, his voice now soggy with melodrama. Kiggs's brow creased. "I'm going to let you reconsider that answer. Someone knew you'd be here. You are withholding information material to this case. We have laws about that; I'm sure my grandmother would be happy to summarize them for you at dinner this evening."

The Ardmagar puffed up like an angry hedgehog, but Kiggs opened the door, signaled his men, and had the old saar packed off in a matter of minutes. He closed the door again and looked at me.

I stared down at the bishop's ornate Porphyrian rug, agitated and anxious.

"You didn't help the Ardmagar escape his guard, I suppose?" he said.

"No," I said.

"Why were you up at the Skep with him?"

I shook my head, not daring to look at him.

Kiggs put his hands on his hips and wandered across the room, pretending to examine the framed calligraphic rendering of

St. Gobnait's benedictio hung between the bookcases. "Well," he said, "at least we know who the would-be assassin was."

"Yes," I said.

He slowly turned to face me, and I realized "we" hadn't meant him and me. It meant him and the Guard. "So you knew him," he said lightly. "That rather changes the color of things. Do you know why he might have tried to kill you?"

With shaking hands, I rifled through my satchel, underneath the crimson gown and the gift from my father, until I found my coin purse. I emptied it onto the seat of the bishop's lectern, the nearest horizontal surface; a shadow across my hands was Kiggs stepping into the window light, drawing near to see. I picked the lizard out of the heap of coins and handed it to the prince without a word.

"That's a little grotesque," he said, turning it right side up in his hand and studying its face. He smiled, though, so at least he hadn't instantly assumed it was another illegal device. "There's a story here, I presume?"

"I gave coin to a quigutl panhandler, and it gave me this in exchange."

The prince nodded sagely. "Now the quig will think it's found a particularly fruitful street corner, the neighbors will get upset, and we'll be called in twice a week to escort him back to Quig-hole. But what's the connection to the dead clothier?"

Ah, now the lying had to start: there was a collapse and vision in the middle of this story, tangling it up with shame and fear. I said, "He saw the transaction. He was very upset, and he called me all kinds of terrible things."

"And yet he brought you back to the palace," said Kiggs quietly.

I looked up, shocked that he knew, but of course the barbican guard would keep records and report to him. His eyes were tranquil, but it was the calm of a cloudy summer sky: it could change to stormy with little warning. I had to tread carefully. "His brother Silas insisted that they offer me a ride to make up for Thomas's rudeness."

"He must have been exceedingly rude."

I turned away from him, tucking my purse back into my bag. "He called me a worm-riding quig lover, and told me women like me get thrown into the river in sacks."

Kiggs was silent long enough that I looked up and met his gaze. His expression was a tangle of shock, concern, and annoyance. He turned away first, shaking his head and saying, "It's a pity the Ardmagar killed him; I'd have liked to discuss these women in sacks. You should have brought this to my attention, or your father's."

"You're right. I should have," I murmured. My need to conceal myself was a hindrance to doing right, I was beginning to notice. He returned his attention to the figurine in his hand. "So what does it do?"

"Do?" I hadn't bothered to check.

He mistook the question for a deeper ignorance. "We confiscate demonic devices every week. They all do something, even the legal ones."

He turned it over in his hands, prodding it here and there with curious fingers. We were both leaning over the thing now, like two

349

small children who've captured a cicada. Like friends, I pointed out a seam at the base of its neck; Kiggs grasped my meaning at once. He pulled its head. Nothing. He twisted it.

"Thluuu-thluuu-thluuuuu!"

The voice rang out so brightly that Kiggs dropped the figurine. It did not break, but bounced under the lectern, where it continued to jabber while Kiggs groped around for it. "That's quigutl Mootya, isn't it? Can you understand it?" he asked, turning his head toward me as he searched for it by feel.

I listened carefully. "It seems to be a rant about dragons transforming into saarantrai. 'I see you there, impostor! You think you've fooled them, that you pass invisibly in a crowd, but your elbows stick out funny and you stink. You are a fraud. At least we quigutl are honest. . . .' It goes on in that vein."

Kiggs half smiled. "I had no idea quigs held their cousins in such contempt."

"I doubt they all do," I said, but realized I didn't know. I was less frightened of quigs than most people, but even I had never bothered to learn what they think.

He twisted the figurine's head back, and the grating, lisping speech ceased. "What horrible tricks one could play with a device like this," mused the prince. "Can you imagine setting it off in the Blue Salon?"

"Half the people would leap up on the furniture, shrieking, and the other half would draw their daggers," I said, laughing. "For additional amusement, you could bet on who would do which."

"Which would *you* do?" he said, and there was suddenly a

sharpness in his tone. "My guess is neither. You'd understand what it was saying, and you'd be standing stock-still, listening hard. You wouldn't want anyone to hurt a quig, not if you could stop that from happening."

He stepped toward me; every inch of me quivered at his proximity. "However practiced you are at deception, you cannot anticipate every eventuality," he said quietly. "Sooner or later, something takes you by surprise, you react honestly as yourself, and you are caught out."

I reeled a bit, in shock. How had he turned interrogator so fast? "Are you referring to something specific?" I said.

"I'm just trying to understand what you were doing here with Ardmagar Comonot, and why you were stabbed. This does not explain it." He wagged my figurine, pinched tightly between his thumb and forefinger. "It was no spur-of-the-moment crime; the man was disguised as a priest. Who told him Comonot would be here? Did he expect Comonot to meet someone else—someone he also intended to kill—or were you just in the wrong place at the wrong time?"

I stared, openmouthed.

"Fine," said Kiggs, his expression closed. "Better silence than a lie."

"I have never wanted to lie to you!" I cried.

"Hm. That must be a wretched existence, forced to lie when you don't want to."

"Yes!" I could hold back no longer; I wept, hiding my face in my hands.

Kiggs stood apart from me, watching me weep. "That all came

"out harsher than I intended, Phina," he said, sounding miserable. "I'm sorry. But this is two days in a row that someone has stabbed you." I looked up sharply; he answered my unasked question. "Aunt Dionne confessed, or rather lamented Lady Corongi's faulty intelligence to anyone who would listen. Selda was heartsick to learn it was her own mother who cut you."

He stepped closer; I kept my eyes on the gold buttons of his doublet. "Seraphina, if you are in some sort of trouble, if you need protection from someone, I want to help. And I can't help if you give me no indication of what's going on."

"I can't tell you." My chin trembled. "I don't want to lie to you, but if I don't, then there's nothing I can say. My hands are tied."

He handed me his handkerchief. I stole a glance at his face; he looked so worried that I couldn't bear it. I wanted to take him in my arms as if he were the one in need of reassurance.

My father's words from the night before came back to me. What if he was right? What if there was a chance, any chance, that Kiggs wouldn't despise me if he knew the truth? One chance in a million was still better than zero. I felt dizzy at the thought of it; it was too like hanging over the parapet of the bell tower, watching your slipper spinning through space, falling to the plaza below.

It wasn't just my scales between us. He had duties and obligations and an overweening need to do the right thing. The Kiggs I loved could not love me the way things stood; if he could have, he would not have been my Kiggs. I had reached for him once, and he had been terrified enough that he hadn't protested, but I couldn't imagine him tolerating it again.

Kiggs cleared his throat. "Selda was beside herself with worry this morning. I told her you'd be back, no question, that Aunt Dionne hadn't frightened you off for good. I sincerely hope that's true."

I nodded shakily. He opened the door for me and held it, but caught my arm as I passed. "Aunt Dionne is not above the law, first heir or not. If you wish to pursue justice for your arm, Selda and I would support you."

I took a deep breath. "I'll consider it. Thank you."

He looked pained; something important still had not been said. "I've been angry with you, Phina, but also worried."

"Forgive me, Prince——"

"Kiggs. Please," he said. "I've been angry with myself as well. I behaved rather foolishly after our encounter with Imlann, as if I could blithely disregard my obligations and——"

"No," I said, shaking my head a bit too vehemently. "Not at all. People do strange things when they're terrified. I hadn't given it a second thought."

"Ah. It is a great relief to hear you say that." He didn't look relieved. "Please know I consider myself your friend, what bumps we have encountered upon that road notwithstanding. The heart of you is good. You're an intelligent and fearless investigator, and a good teacher too, I hear. Glisselda swears she couldn't do without you. We want you to stay."

He still had hold of my arm. I extricated myself gently and let him take me home.

Twenty-Nine

The sky was just growing dark when our carriage rolled into Stone Court. Princess Glisselda waited to meet us; she fussed over me and fussed at Kiggs for letting me get hurt once again, as if protecting me ought to have been his priority when the entire city was up in arms. Kiggs smiled at what a little mother hen she was. Glisselda placed herself firmly between us, giving an arm to each, chattering away as was her wont. I pleaded abject tiredness and broke up our little trio at the earliest opportunity.

I was exhausted, though it was not yet five o'clock. I trudged up to my room and threw myself into a chair, letting my satchel drop to the floor between my feet.

I could not continue living in such close proximity to Kiggs if it was always going to hurt this much. I would stay through Treaty Eve, tomorrow night, and then I would give Viridius my notice. Maybe not, even. I would simply disappear, run off to Blystane or

Porphyry or Segosh, one of the big cities, where I could disappear into the crowds and never be seen again.

My left wrist itched under its bandage. I just wanted to look at the scale scab, I told myself. See how it was getting on. I began unfastening the bandage, pulling at it with my teeth when it was difficult to undo.

There was, indeed, a crusted scab where the scale had been; it squatted malevolently among smooth silver scales to either side. I ran a finger over it; it felt rough and sore. Compared with that fat black scab, the scales were not so ugly. Trust me to turn my native hideousness into something even more hideous. I hated that scab. I pried up an edge, then had to look away, gritting my teeth and cringing with revulsion.

Still, I did not intend to stop until I had torn a hole in myself again.

The satchel at my feet fell open. I must have kicked it. Out of the bag fell the long, slender box and the letter, which just this morning—it seemed longer ago than that—my sisters had handed me on my father's behalf. I backed off my wrist for the moment and took up the box. My heart pounded painfully; the box was the right size and shape to contain a specific musical instrument. I wasn't sure I could stand the heartbreak if it didn't.

I fetched the letter and opened it first.

My daughter,

I suspect you will remember little of our conversation last night, which is just as well. I fear I babbled on foolishly.

However: I owe you this, at least. Your mother had more than one flute, or I could never have borne breaking the other. I still regret that, not least for your look of betrayal. I was the monster in our household, not you.

What comes, comes. I have made my peace with the past and with the future. Do what you feel you must, and do not be afraid.

All my love, for good or ill,

Papa

With shaking hands I opened the wooden case. Inside, wrapped in a long strip of saffron fabric, was a flute of polished ebony, inlaid with silver and mother-of-pearl. It took my breath away; I knew it at once for hers.

I put it to my lips and played a scale, smooth as water. Both my wrists twinged painfully as my fingers moved. I took the saffron strip and wound it around my scabby left wrist. It came from both my parents. Let it remind me I was not alone, and protect me from myself.

I rose renewed, and headed for the door. There was work yet to be done, and I was the only one who could do it.

Comonot was important enough that he had been given a room in the royal family's private wing, the most luxurious and heavily guarded part of the palace. As I approached the guard station, my stomach fluttered anxiously. I had no clear plan for how to bluff this time, no lie I could tell them. I would ask to be allowed through to see the Ardmagar, and see what happened.

I nearly balked when I recognized Mikey the Fish, one of the guards from before, but I gripped my saffron-bound wrist, lifted my chin, and stepped up to him anyway. "I need to speak with the Ardmagar," I said. "How do I go about doing that?"

Mikey the Fish actually smiled at me. "You follow me, Music Mistress," he said, opening the heavy double doors for me and nodding to his fellows.

He escorted me into the forbidden residential area. Bright tapestries lined the corridor walls, punctuated by marble statues, portraits, and pedestals supporting fine porcelain and fragile spun glass. The Queen was known for loving art; apparently this was where she kept it. I scarcely dared breathe lest I knock something over.

"Here's his suite," said Mikey, turning to go. "Watch yourself—Princess Dionne claims the old saar made a pass at her."

I found that distressingly easy to believe. I watched the guard retreat down the hall and noted that he did not turn back toward his post but went deeper into the residence. He'd been told to let me in, and was off to report that I'd arrived. Well, I would not question my good fortune. I knocked on Comonot's door.

The Ardmagar's servant—a human lad, assigned to him from among the castle page boys—answered the door at once, making a very peculiar face at the sight of me. Someone else had been expected, evidently.

"Is that my dinner? Bring it through," said the Ardmagar from the other room.

"It's some woman, Your Excellence!" cried the boy as I stepped past him into what was evidently the study. The boy yapped at my heels like a terrier: "You're not to enter unless the Ardmagar says you may!"

Comonot had been writing at a wide desk; he rose at the sight of me and stared, speechless. I gave him full courtesy. "Forgive me, sir, but I was not finished talking to you earlier, when we were so rudely interrupted by your would-be assassin."

He narrowed his eyes shrewdly. "Is this about that cabal theory of yours?"

"You disregarded the message out of disgust for the messenger."

"Sit down, Seraphina," he said, gesturing toward an upholstered chair carved with curlicues and embroidered with elegant, improbable foliage. His room was all velvet brocade and rich dark oak; the very ceiling had large carved pinecones protruding from the center of every coffer, like some giant's scaly fingertips. This wing of the palace maintained a more elaborate standard of decor than my own.

He'd had time to sober up since our talk in the bishop's library, and he now held me in a gaze as piercing as Orma's. He seated himself across from me, thoughtfully running his tongue over his teeth.

"You must think me a superstitious fool," he said, tucking his hands into the voluminous sleeves of his embroidered houppelande.

I needed more information before I could reply; it was possible I did.

"I admit," he said, "I have been. You are something that should not be. Dragons have difficulty with counterfactuals."

I almost laughed. "How can I be counterfactual? I'm right here."

"If you were a ghost claiming the same, should I believe you? Should I not rather consider you a symptom of my own madness? You showed me, at the cathedral, that you have some substance. I wish to understand the nature of that substance."

"All right," I said, with some apprehension.

"You have a foot in both worlds: if you have maternal memories, you've seen what it is to be a dragon, contrasted with what it's like to be a saärantras, contrasted yet again with what it's like to be human—or nearly so."

This I was prepared to handle. "I have experienced those states, yes."

He leaned forward. "And what do you think of being a dragon?"

"I—I find it unpleasant, frankly. And confusing."

"Do you? Maybe that's not unexpected. It's very different."

"I tire of the incessant wind-vector calculations, and the stench of the entire world."

He tented his fat fingers and studied my face. "But you have some understanding, perhaps, of how alien this shape is to us. The world around looks different; we easily get lost, both inside our-selves and out. If I as saärantras react differently than I as dragon would react, then who am I now, really?

"Do I love you?" he asked. "It occurs to me that one possible motive for defending you would be love. Only I'm not sure what that one's like. I have no way to measure it."

"You don't love me," I said flatly.

"But maybe I did for just a moment? No?"

"No."

He had withdrawn his arm from his sleeve entirely; his hand emerged from the neck hole of his houppelande and scratched his jowly chin. I stared, astonished by this maneuver. He said, "Love requires extreme correction. It's the emotional state we teach our students to guard against most carefully. It presents an actual danger to a saar because, you see, our scholars who fall in love don't want to come back. They don't want to be dragons anymore."

"Like my mother," I said, crossing my arms tightly.

"Exactly!" he cried, insensible of the fact that I might take offense at his tone. "My government has clamped down on all hyperemotionality, but especially love, and it is right that we have done so. But being here, being *this*, I find myself curious to feel everything, once. They'll mop up my mind when I get home—I won't lose myself to it—but I want to measure this danger, stare right into the fearsome jaws of love, survive its deadly blast, and find better ways to treat others who suffer this malady."

I almost laughed. As much heartache as I'd already endured over Kiggs, I could not disagree with the words *fearsome* or *malady*, but I couldn't let him think I approved of his plan, either. "If you ever do experience love, I hope it generates some sympathy for the heartbreaking, impossible choices my mother had to make alone, between her people and the man she loved, between her child and her very life!"

Comonot bugged his eyes at me. "She chose wrongly on both counts,"

He was making me angry. Unfortunately, I had come here for a specific purpose I had not yet achieved. "General, about the cabal—"

"Your obsession?" He replaced his arm in his sleeve and drummed his fingers on the arm of his chair. "Yes, while we're contemplating counterfactuals, let us consider this. If you learned of some cabal from a maternal memory, then the information is nearly twenty years old. How do you know they haven't been caught and disbanded?"

I folded my hands tightly, trying to contain my irritation. "You could tell me easily enough."

He tugged an earring. "How do you know they didn't disband themselves when Imlann was banished?"

"Imlann still appears to be pursuing their purpose, as if he believes they still exist," I said. "They had the knights banished; he's checking up on whether the dracomachia is sufficiently dead. If it is, they find a way to gain power. Having you assassinated would do, or perhaps they're leading a coup in the Tanamoot right now."

Comonot waved me off; the rings on his thick fingers glinted. "I'd have heard word of a coup. Imlann could be working alone; he is delusional enough to believe others are with him. And if a cabal wished me dead, could they not kill me more easily while I was in the Tanamoot?"

"That would only gain them a civil war; they want Goredd dragged into it," I said.

"This is far too speculative," he said. "Even if a few disgruntled generals were plotting against me, my loyal generals—to say nothing of the younger generation, who have benefited most directly from the peace—would quickly subdue any uprising."

"There was just an attempt on your life!" I cried.

"Which we foiled. It's over." He removed one of his rings and replaced it absently, thinking. "Prince Lucian said the man was one of the Sons of St. Ogdo. I cannot imagine the Sons collaborating with a dragon cabal, can you? What kind of dragon would think it a viable option to make use of them?"

A fiendishly clever dragon, I suddenly realized. If the Sons started assassinating people, the Queen would be forced to crack down on them. Imlann would have his dirty work done for him by anti-dragon zealots, and then have his anti-dragon zealot problem quashed by the Crown—all while he watched and waited like the reptile he was.

"Ardmagar," I said, rising, "I must bid you good evening." He narrowed his eyes. "I haven't convinced you you're wrong, and you're too stubborn to give this up. What do you intend?"

"To talk to someone who will listen," I said, "and who, when faced with something previously thought to be counterfactual, adapts his philosophies to reality and not the other way around."

I walked out. He made no attempt to stop me.

Kiggs waited in the corridor, leaning against the opposite wall, a little book in his hand. He snapped it shut at the sight of me and tucked it away in his scarlet doublet.

"Am I that predictable?" I said.

"Only when you do exactly what I would have done."

"Thank you for telling the guards to let me pass. It saved a lot of embarrassment on both sides."

He bowed, a more exaggerated courtesy than I deserved. "Selda thinks I ought to ask you, one more time, what the pair of you could possibly have to discuss. I promised I would, though I expect—"

"I was just coming to find you both. There are things I should have told you that I . . . I haven't," I said. "I'm sorry for it. But let's find your cousin first; she needs to hear this too."

He looked as if he weren't certain whether to trust my sudden willingness to talk. I'd earned this skepticism; even now, I had no intention of telling the truth about myself. I sighed, but tried to smile at him. He escorted me toward the Blue Salon.

Thirty

Gisselda spotted us at once across the sparkly crush of courtiers; she smiled, but something in our expressions rapidly changed hers to quizzical. "Excuse us," she said to the bevy of gentlemen surrounding her. "Important affairs of state, you know."

She rose imperiously and led us into a little side room furnished with a lone Porphyrian couch; she closed the door and gestured for us to be seated. "What's the latest from the city?" she asked.

"Curfew. Lockdown," said Kiggs, seating himself gingerly, as if he had an old man's aches and pains. "I'm not looking forward to tomorrow if news spreads that Comonot killed a citizen in the cathedral—never mind that it was self-defense."

"You can't suppress that information?" I asked, lingering near the door, not wanting to sit beside him, not knowing what to do with myself if I didn't sit down.

"We're trying," he snapped, "but the citizenry found out about Imlann and the petition and awfully fast. The palace is full of leaks, apparently."

I had an idea who one leak might be. I said, "I have a lot to tell you both."

Glisselda grabbed my arm and wedged me onto the couch between her and Kiggs, smiling as if we were the happiest, coziest grouping ever conceived. "Speak, Phina."

I took a deep breath. "Before Comonot was attacked, I saw the Earl of Apsig at the cathedral speaking with a hooded priest who I believe was Thomas Broadwick," I began.

"You believe," said Kiggs, shifting in his seat, his very posture skeptical. "Meaning you're not completely certain. I don't suppose you heard what was said?"

"I also saw Josef in town earlier, reciting St. Ogdo's Malediction with a group of the Sons," I continued stubbornly.

"If he's joined the Sons, that's serious," said Kiggs, "but here's the hole in your reasoning: either he's a Son of St. Ogdo or he's a dragon. You can't have it both ways."

Thanks to my conversation with Comonot, I was ready for this argument. I explained how fiendishly clever it was to get the Sons involved, adding, "Orma said Imlann would be where we least expect. Where less than with the Sons?"

"I still don't see how it would be possible for a dragon to live here at court—for more than two years—and not be sniffed out by other dragons," said Kiggs.

"Obviously he pretends to despise them so that he can quit the room whenever they enter," said Glisselda.

365

"He could mask his scent with perfume easily enough," I said, feeling miserable. Here I was, monstrous and wedged in between the pair of them, and they had no idea. I squeezed my hands between my knees to keep myself from fingering my wrist. "But listen," I said. "There's more."

I explained what I suspected about Imlann and the cabal, simply omitting my maternal memory: that Imlann was here to determine how dysfunctional the dracomachia had become, and that the cabal surely had an interest in seeing Comonot dead. "Maybe it's over, maybe that one attempt was their best, but I don't think we can chance it. I think they'll try again."

"'They' being whom?" asked Kiggs. "This cabal you've suddenly pulled out of thin air? The Sons? Imlann, in a mysterious new plurality?"

"Lucian, stop being a pedant," said Glisselda, putting an arm around me.

I continued. "Much of this is extrapolation, but it would be unwise to ignore the possibility—"

"Extrapolation from what?" said Kiggs. Glisselda reached around behind me and smacked the side of his head. "What? It's an important question! What's the source of this information, and how reliable is it?"

The princess lifted her chin defiantly. "Phina is the source, and Phina is reliable."

He didn't argue, although he squirmed, clearly wanting to.

"I would tell you if I could," I said. "But I have obligations of my own, and—"

"My first obligation is the truth," he said bitterly. "Always."

Glisselda straightened, shifting a little away from me, and I realized the mention of my "obligations" had brought my own loyalties into question beyond the point where she could still defend me. She spoke evenly: "Whether this cabal really exists or not, the fact is that someone tried to kill the Ardmagar and failed. There isn't much time left for another attempt."

Kiggs exhaled noisily through his lips in frustration and ran a hand down his face. "You're right, Selda. We can't afford to do nothing. Better too cautious than not cautious enough."

We set aside our quibbles and put our heads together, formulating a plan, circumventing the Queen and Comonot, taking all the weight of the peace upon ourselves. We just had to keep the Ardmagar safe for one more night, to make it through Treaty Eve without anyone dying, and then Comonot would return home. If this cabal really existed and killed him in the Tanamoot, well, that would be out of our hands.

✺

Kiggs would tighten palace security, although it was already nearly as strong as he could make it, unless we intended foreign dignitaries to dance with members of the Guard at the ball. He would also inform Ambassador Fulda that he believed real danger to Comonot lurked here at home, and would request that Eskar and the petit ard be recalled so they could help. They'd been many miles away at last report; it was unclear whether they would make it back in time. Glisselda was to stick to the Ardmagar as best she could; she complained that she'd have no chance to practice the

Tertius before the concert, but I could tell by the gleam in her eye that intrigue interested her more than music.

I had duties, of course, assisting Viridius and preparing the entertainments. That would be my focus until the ball itself, when I'd take turns babysitting the Ardmagar.

Privately, I set a few additional tasks for myself. I wanted all three of my fellow half-breeds present. We were going to need all the help we could get.

I looked for Abdo in the garden of grotesques as soon as I returned to my rooms. He was hanging upside down in his fig tree, but he leaped down at my approach and offered me gola nuts.

"I glimpsed your troupe today from afar," I said, seating myself cross-legged on the ground beside him. "I wished I could have introduced myself because I feel awkward asking for your help when I haven't even met you."

"Do not say so, madamina! Of course I will help if I can." I told him what was afoot. "Bring your whole troupe. I will make space for you on the performance docket. Dress . . . er . . ."

"We know what is appropriate for the Goreddi court."

"Of course you do. Forgive me. There will be others of our kind there, other . . . what was the Porphyrian word you used?"

"Ityasaari?"

"Yes. Do you know Loud Lad and Miss Fusspots, from the garden?"

"Of course," he said. "I see everything you permit me to see." I suppressed a shudder, wondering whether he could taste my emotions in the wind as Jannoula had. "I will want you all to help each other and work together, just as you help me."

"Yours are the orders, madamina. Yours the right. I will be there and ready."

I smiled at him and rose to go, dusting off my skirts. "Is *madamina* Porphyrian for 'maidy,' like *grausleine* in Samsamese?"

His eyes widened. "No, indeed! It means 'general.'"

"Wh–why would you call me that?"

"Why did you call me Fruit Bat? I had to call you something, and every day you come here as if reviewing your legions." He smiled sheepishly and added: "Once, long ago, you told someone here—that girl with beautiful green eyes, the one you sent away. You said your name aloud, but I misheard it."

All around us, an astonished wind blew.

　　　　　　　　　　　　　　　✕

I did not know where Lars slept at night, but there had been enough broad hints from various quarters that I feared I might end up seeing more of Viridius than I cared to.

I waited until morning, made myself a fortifying cup of tea, and went straight to the garden. I took Loud Lad's hands, whirl-ing out into a vision. To my astonishment, the whole world seemed spread below me: the city, glowing pink in the light of dawn; the shining ribbon of river; the distant rolling farmland. Lars stood upon the crenellations of the barbican, each foot on a separate merlon, playing his pipes for the dawn and for the city at his feet. My ethereal presence didn't stop him; I let him finish, secretly rel-ishing the feeling that I was flying above the city, buoyed by his music. It was exhilarating to be so high up and not fear falling.

"Is thet you, Seraphina?" he said at last.

It is. I need your help.

I told him I feared for the Ardmagar, that I might need him at a moment's notice, that others of our kind—Abdo and Dame Okra—would be there to help, and how to recognize them. If he was astonished to hear there were other half-dragons, Lars's Samsamese stoicism didn't let it show. He said, "But how will this danger come, Seraphina? An attack on the castle? A traitor within the walls?"

I did not know how to tell him whom we suspected. I began cautiously: *I know you don't like discussing Josef, but—*

He cut me off. "No. I hev nothink to say about him."

He may be involved. He may be the one behind everything.

His face fell, but his resolve did not. "If so, I will standt with you against him. But I am sworn not to speak of what he is." He fingered the chanter of his war pipes absently. "Perheps," he said at last, "I come armedt."

I don't think Kiggs will allow anyone but the palace guard to arrive armed.

"Always I hev my fists and my war pipes!"

Er . . . yes. That's the spirit, Lars.

It would be a memorable evening, if nothing else.

I knew better than to contact Dame Okra with my mind. I didn't need my nose all black and blue for Treaty Eve.

I worked fast and crabby all morning, directing the hanging of garlands, the placing of chandeliers and sideboards, the moving of the harpsichord—which looked like a coffin as four men carried it through the door without its legs—and countless other last-minute details. All the while I conscientiously attempted to get Dame Okra's attention without contacting her. My attempts to will her into appearing, to project fake need—my sighing and fretting and muttering, "I sure could use Dame Okra's help!"—met with universal failure.

I barely had time to rush to my rooms and dress for dinner; I had already set out the scarlet gown Millie had given me, so I didn't have do any thinking and only had to switch my outer garment. No risky nakedness for me: a maid might show up any minute to arrange my hair. Glisselda had insisted upon this point, going so far as to threaten me with Millie if I didn't swear not to do my own hair.

The maid arrived; my hair was beaten into submission. My first reaction, upon seeing myself in the mirror, was shock at how long my neck was. My hair usually obscured that fact, but when it was all piled up on my head, I looked positively camelopardine. The décolletage of Millie's gown wasn't helping matters. Feh.

I hung Orma's earring from a golden chain around my neck, more to settle my nerves with something treasured than because I thought it could be useful; who knew where he was or whether he could even receive its signal. It made an intriguing pendant. I no longer feared the Ardmagar recognizing it. Let him say two words to me about Orma; let him try. He would get more than he bargained for.

Surely no one would try to do him in while I was there, exco-riating him.

I'd never attended a feast of such magnitude. I was seated as far as possible from the high table, of course, but I had an unimpeded view of it. The Ardmagar sat between the Queen and Princess Dionne; Kiggs and Glisselda sat on the Queen's other side, both of them scanning the room anxiously. I took this as simple vigilance at first, until Glisselda spotted me, waved eagerly, and pointed me out to her cousin. It took him a moment to see me, even so, because I didn't look quite like myself.

He did smile eventually, once he stopped looking astonished.

I can barely recall the kind and number of dishes; I should have taken notes. We had boar and venison and fowl of all kinds, a peacock pie with its great tail fanned out, sallats, soft white bread, almond custard, fish, figs, Zibou dates. My tablemates, distant relations of the dukes and earls at the other end of the room, laughed gently at my impulse to try everything. "Can't be done," said an elderly fellow with a goat's beard. "Not if you hope to walk away from the table under your own power!"

The feast ended with a towering, flaming, six-tiered torte representing the Lighthouse of Ziziba, of all things. Alas, I was truly too full—and by this point, too anxious—to have any.

Thank Heaven I could rely absolutely upon my musicians, because I got caught in the crush of people heading for the great hall and never could have gotten there fast enough to get everyone in place. By the time I entered, the symphonia was already scraping out the overture, one of those infinite-cycle pieces that could be played over and over until the royal family arrived and the first dance could begin.

Someone grabbed my upper right arm and whispered in my ear, "Ready?"

"As ready as we can be for the unknown," I replied, not daring to look at him. He smelled almondy, like the marchpane torte.

I discerned his nod in my peripheral vision. "Selda's stowed a flask of Zibou coffee for you somewhere onstage in case you start getting drowsy." Kiggs clapped me on the shoulder and said, "Save me a pavano."

He disappeared into the crowd.

Thirty-One

No sooner had he left than Dame Okra was upon me. "What do you need now?" she asked crabbily.

I drew her toward the wall of the great hall, away from the mass of people; we stood by a tall candelabra, like a sheltering tree. "We have some concern for the Ardmagar's safety tonight. Can I count on your help if I need it?"

She lifted her chin, scanning the crowd for Comonot. "What shall I do? Tail him?"

"Observe him discreetly, yes. And keep your stomach, er, focused."

Her thick glasses reflected candlelight up at me. "Fair enough." I caught her satin sleeve as she turned to plunge into the party. "May I contact you with my mind?"

"Absolutely not!" She headed off my objections: "If you need me, I'll be there."

I sighed. "Fine. But it's not just me; one of the others might need you."

The creases beside her mouth deepened. "What others?"

I opened and shut my mouth, astonished that I could have forgotten that she did not live inside my head. Only Abdo could see the garden. "The others . . . like us," I whispered urgently.

Her face underwent a full spectrum of emotion in mere seconds—astonishment, sorrow, wonderment, joy—ending on one she was particularly good at: annoyance. She smacked me with her fan. "You couldn't tell me this? Do you have any idea how old I am?"

"Er, no."

"One hundred twenty-eight!" she snarled. "I spent that many years thinking I was alone. Then you prance into my life, nearly giving me a paroxysm, and now you deign to tell me there are more. How many are there?"

"Eighteen, counting you and me," I said, not daring to keep anything back from her anymore. "But only two others here: the bagpiper"—she guffawed, apparently remembering him—"and one of the pygegyria dancers. A little Porphyrian boy."

Her brows shot up. "You invited pygegyria dancers? Tonight?" She threw back her head and laughed. "Whatever else may be true of you, you do things your own way, with a refreshingly self-assured pigheadedness. I like that!"

She took off into the colorful crowd, leaving me to puzzle out that compliment.

Speaking of pygegyria, I hadn't seen the troupe. I reached out:

Where are you?

The small reception hall. We are too many for your tiny dressing rooms.

Stay there. I am coming to meet you.

I slipped into the corridor and found the double doors of the small hall easily enough. I hesitated, my hands upon the brass door handles. Abdo was so different from the others I had met—his mind worked more like mine, or Jannoula's—that I had some anxiety about meeting him. Once I'd met him, he was in my life inextricably, for good or ill.

I took a deep breath and opened the doors.

Ululations and an explosive burst of drumming greeted me.

The troupe were all in motion, a circle within a circle, each turning a different direction. For a moment I could focus on nothing; it was a blur of colored scarves and shimmering veils, brown hands and jingling strings of coins.

The circles opened, dancers spinning off tangentially, revealing Abdo in the center, in a bright green tunic and trousers, his feet bare, his arms undulating. The others shimmered at a distance, chains and coin scarves jingling. He whirled, his arms spread wide, the fringe upon his belt making a halo at his center.

For the first time, I understood the point of dancing. I was so used to music being the vehicle for expression, but here he was speaking to me not with his mind but with his body: *I feel this music in my very blood. This is what it means to be me, right here, right now, solid flesh, ethereal air, eternal motion. I feel this, and it is true beyond truth.*

376

The heavens seemed to turn with him, the sun and moon, time itself. He whirled so fast he seemed to stand still. I could have sworn I smelled roses.

With a crash of drums he froze, still as a statue. I wasn't certain whether Porphyrians applauded, but I went ahead and clapped. That broke the spell; the dancers smiled and broke formation, chattering among themselves. I approached Abdo, who awaited me with shining eyes.

"That was beautiful," I said. "I think your audience will love you, whether they want to or not."

He smiled.

"I've put you on the program late, when people will need something to wake them up. There's food and drink for performers in the little room off the——"

"Madamina!" cried an old man. It took me a moment to recognize him as the one who'd wanted to meet me after Prince Rufus's funeral; he was draped with silks now. I assumed he was the grandfather Abdo had mentioned. "Your pardon!" he said. "You are come to here, try to speak at Abdo, but he cannot speaking at you without help. Your pardon."

"He—what?" I wasn't convinced I had understood.

I looked to Abdo, who looked annoyed. He made a number of hand gestures at the old man, who gesticulated back urgently. Was he . . . deaf? If so, how did he speak such fluent Goreddi in the garden? He finally convinced the old man to go, which I found astonishing. He was ten, maybe eleven years old, but the old man was deferential.

All the dancers were. He was the leader of this troupe.

He smiled at me apologetically, and I heard his voice in my mind: *Loud Lad and Miss Fusspots. I know what I'm to do. I will not fail you.*

You can't talk? I thought back, not wanting to blurt out the obvious.

He gave a pained, small smile, threw back his head, and opened his mouth as wide as he could. His long tongue, his gums, his palate, everything, as far into his throat as I could see, gleamed with silver dragon scales.

That night simultaneously dragged on forever and passed in a whirlwind blur. Kiggs had stationed the Guard everywhere there was space; there were a few out of uniform casually assaulting the buffet table, and one onstage spooking my musicians. The royal cousins and I spotted each other watching the Ardmagar; Glisselda danced with him three times, or danced near him with Kiggs. Dame Okra engaged him in chitchat near the refreshments table; I stood onstage behind the curtain, scanning the crowd through the gap. Nobody did anything suspicious—well, Princess Dionne smiled a lot, which was unusual, and gossiped with Lady Corongi, which was not. The Earl of Apsig danced with every lady in the room; he seemed never to grow tired.

Viridius was there in a wheeled chair, several young men keeping him supplied with wine and cheese. That much rich food would leave him foul-tempered and incapacitated for a week; I did not understand how he calculated that it was worth it.

The symphonia cleared the stage while Lars and Guntard brought out the harpsichord for Princess Glisselda's performance. She was suddenly beside me in the wings, giggling and clutching at my arm. "I can't do this, Phina!"

"Breathe," I said, taking her hands to still them. "Don't speed up during the arpeggios. Keep the pavano stately. You're going to be wonderful."

She kissed my cheek and stepped into the light, where she abruptly transformed from a nervous, squealing little girl into a dignified young woman. Her gown was the blue of Heaven; her golden hair, the sun. She held herself poised, raised a hand to the audience, kept her chin high and proud. I blinked, amazed, but I should not have been surprised by this calm, commanding presence. She was still growing into it, but the foundation was something she seemed naturally to possess.

Musical ability, on the other hand . . . well. She was breathtakingly mediocre, but it didn't matter. She made up some ground on the performance end with sheer poise and presence, and she absolutely put Viridius in his place. I watched him from behind the curtain. His mouth hung open. That was satisfying on several levels.

I watched Comonot, too, since no one else seemed to be doing it. Dame Okra had been distracted by her least favorite person, Lady Corongi, and was eyeballing her suspiciously. Kiggs, off to the left, smiled warmly at his cousin's performance. I felt a pang; I looked elsewhere. The Ardmagar—whom I was ostensibly watching—stood at the back with Princess Dionne, not speaking, watching the performance, a glass in one hand, the other arm around the princess's waist.

She didn't seem to mind, but . . . ugh.

I was shocked at the revulsion I felt. I, of all people, had no business being disgusted by the idea of a human with a saarantras. No, surely my squirm had its origin in the noxious personalities involved, and the fact that I'd just pictured the Ardmagar in a state of undress. I needed to scrub my mind clean.

Glisselda finished, to thunderous applause. I expected her to skip straight off the stage, but she did not. She stepped to the front, raised a hand for silence, and then said, "Thank you for your generous applause. I hope you've saved some, however, for the person most deserving of it, my music teacher, Seraphina Dombegh!"

The applause began again. She gestured for me to join her onstage, but I balked. She strode over, grabbed my arm, and pulled me out. I curtsied to the sea of faces, deeply embarrassed. I looked up and saw Kiggs; he gave me a little wave. I tried to smile back but rather suspect I missed.

Glisselda gestured the crowd into silence. "I hope Maid Dombegh will forgive me for interrupting her careful scheduling, but you all deserve some excellent music as a reward for sitting through my paltry offering: a performance from Seraphina herself. And please, help me petition the Queen to make Phina a court composer, the equal of Viridius. She's too good to be merely his assistant!"

I expected Viridius to scowl, but he threw back his head and laughed. The audience clapped some more, and I took the opportunity to say to Glisselda, "I didn't bring any of my instruments down."

"Well, there's a harpsichord right behind us, silly," she whispered. "And I confess: I took the liberty of fetching your flute and your oud. You choose."

She'd brought my mother's flute. I felt a pang when I saw it: I wanted to play it, but it was somehow too personal. The oud, a long-ago gift from Orma, would be easiest on my right wrist; that decided me. Guntard brought me the instrument and plectrum; Lars brought me a chair. I cradled the melon-shaped instrument in my lap while I checked harmonics on all eleven strings, but it had kept good tune. I cast my gaze out into the audience while I did so. Kiggs watched me; Glisselda joined him, and he put an arm around her. Nobody was watching the Ardmagar. I reached for Lars with my mind and sent him in that direction; once I was satisfied that he had traversed the crowd, I closed my eyes and began to play.

I did not set out to play anything in particular; I take the Zibou approach to oud, improvising, looking for a shape in the sound, like finding pictures in the clouds, and then solidifying it. My mind kept returning to Kiggs standing with Glisselda, an ocean of people between us, and this gave my music-cloud a shape I did not like, sad and self-absorbed. As I played, however, another shape emerged. The ocean was still there, but my music was a bridge, a ship, a beacon. It bound me to everyone here, held us all in its hands, carried us together to a better place. It modulated (ripples on the sea) and modulated again (a flight of gulls) and landed squarely upon a mode I loved (a chalky cliff, a windswept lighthouse). I could make out a different tune, one of my mother's, just below the surface; I played a coy melody, an enigmatic variation, referencing her tune without bringing it up explicitly. I made a pass at her song, circled, touched it lightly before swooping past once more. It would draw me back into its orbit again and again until I gave it its due. I played her melody out in full, and I sang my father's lyrics, and for a shining moment we were all three together:

A thousand regrets I've had in love,
A thousand times I've longed to change the past.
I know, my love, there is no going back,
No undoing of our thousand burdens.
We must go on despite our heavy hearts.
A thousand regrets I've had in love,
But I shall never regret you.

The song released me then, and I was free to improvise again, my circles growing ever wider, until I once again encircled the world with music.

I opened my eyes to an audience of open mouths, as if they hoped to retain the taste of that last ringing note. Nobody clapped until I stood up all the way, and then it was so loud it drove me back a step. I curtsied, exhausted and exhilarated.

When I lifted my eyes, I saw my father. I hadn't even realized he was here. He was as pale as he had been after the funeral, but I understood his expression differently now. He wasn't furious with me; his was an expression of pain and of steely determination not to let it get the best of him. I blew him a kiss.

Kiggs and Selda stood together on the left, bringing me a little pain of my own. They smiled and waved; they were my friends, both of them, however bittersweet I might find that. At the back, Dame Okra Carmine stood together with Lars and Abdo, who jumped up and down with glee. They'd found each other; we all had.

Playing at the funeral had exhausted me, but this time was different. Friends surrounded me, and the court gave me something back with their applause. For a lingering moment I felt like I belonged here. I curtsied again, and quit the stage.

The relentless millstone of night ground our vigilance to dust; by the third hour after midnight, I found myself hoping someone would knife Comonot just so we could get it over with and go to bed. It was hard keeping an eye on him when he seemed not to get tired himself. He danced, ate, drank, chatted up Princess Dionne, laughed in wonder at the pygegyria dancers, and still had the energy of three ordinary men.

I heard the bell chime the fourth hour and had about decided to ask my comrades whether I couldn't slip out for a catnap, when Kiggs himself stepped into the open space beside me and took my hand. "Pavano!" was all he said, smilingly pulling me into a promenade.

My weary brain had ceased to process the dances, but the music snapped into focus, as did the candles, the stately dancers, the entire room. Kiggs was better than coffee.

"I'm beginning to think we've been all wrought up for nothing," I said, stepping with far more energy than I'd had a moment ago.

"I will merrily consider us mistaken once Comonot is safely

home," said Kiggs, his eyes tired. "Don't pay Pau-Henoa until he gets you to the other side."

I looked for the Ardmagar among the dancers, but he was not there for once. I finally spotted him leaning against a wall, watching, speaking to no one, a cup of wine in his hand and a glazed look in his eye. Was he getting tired? That was good news.

"Where's Princess Glisselda?" I asked, not seeing her.

He handed me around. "Either napping or discussing something with Grandmother. She intended to do both but was unclear on the order."

Maybe I could get a nap after all. Right now I didn't want one. I didn't want this dance to end, or Kiggs to let go of my hand. I didn't want him to turn his eyes away, or live any other moment but this one.

A feeling rose in me, and I just let it, because what harm could it do? It only had another thirty-two adagio bars of life in this world. *Twenty-four. Sixteen. Eight more bars in which I love you. Three. Two. One.*

The music ended and I let him go, but he did not let go of me.

"One minute, Phina. I have something for you."

He led me toward the stage, up the steps, and into the wing where I had already spent much of the evening. In the corner sat Glisselda's coffee flask, long empty; beside it was a small bundle wrapped in cloth that I had not disturbed, not knowing who it belonged to. He picked it up and handed it to me.

"What is it?"

"Obviously, you won't know until you open it," he said, his eyes glittering in the half light. "Happy New Year!"

It was a slim volume, calf-bound. I opened it and laughed. "Pontheus?"

"The one and only." He was standing right next to me, as if to read over my shoulder, not quite touching my arm. "It's his final book, *Love and Work*, the one I mentioned before. It is, as you might expect, about work, but also about thought and self-knowledge and what is good in life, and . . ."

He trailed off. There was, of course, one other word in the title. It sat between us like a lump.

"And truth?" I said, thinking it a neutral subject and realizing too late that it absolutely wasn't.

"Well, yes, but I was going to say, er, friendship." He smiled apologetically; I looked back at the book. He added: "And happiness. That's why he's considered mad. Porphyrian philosophers all sign a pact to be miserable."

I couldn't help laughing, and Kiggs laughed too, and Guntard, who was in the middle of a shawm solo just then, glared at us backstage gigglers.

"Now I'm embarrassed," I said, "because I have nothing for you."

"Don't be ridiculous!" he said vehemently. "You gave us all a gift tonight."

I turned away, my heart pounding painfully, and saw, through the gap in the curtains, Dame Okra Carmine standing in a doorway across the hall, urgently waving her long green sleeve. "Something's happening," I said.

Kiggs did not ask what, but followed me down the steps, through the whirl of dancers, and out into the corridor. There

Dame Okra Carmine pulled on Comonot's arm, preventing him from going anywhere, while bemused guards hesitated nearby, unsure whose side to take.

"He claims he's going for a nap, but I don't believe him!" she cried.

"Thank you, Ambassadress," said Kiggs, unsure why Dame Okra should be involved in this at all. I'd have to invent some reason. All the weight of this night came crashing down on me again.

Comonot, arms crossed and jaw set, watched as Dame Okra gave sarcastic courtesy and returned to the party. "Now that we're free of that madwoman," he said, "might I be permitted to go about my business?"

Kiggs bowed. "Sir, I'm afraid I must insist that you take a guard or two with you. We have some concerns for your safety this evening, and . . ."

Comonot shook his head. "Still convinced there's a plot against me, Seraphina? I wish I could look at that memory of yours. Your paranoia in this matter is almost enough to have me looking over my shoulder. That's another human-body response, isn't it? Fear of the dark and the unknown? Fear of dragons?"

"Ardmagar," I said, deeply disturbed that he had mentioned my maternal memory so cavalierly, "please just humor us in this matter."

"You have precious little to go on."

"The peace depends upon your continued leadership," I pleaded. "We have a lot to lose if anything happens to you." His eyes sharpened shrewdly. "Do you know who else it depends upon? The Royal House of Goredd—one of whose princes, if I recall correctly, was recently murdered. Are you watching your own as hawkishly as you're watching me?"

"Of course," said Kiggs, but the question clearly took him aback. I could see him trying to account for the whereabouts of his grandmother, aunt, and cousin, and coming to the disturbing conclusion that he didn't know where any of them were.

"I know you don't know where your auntie is," said Comonot with a disconcerting leer.

Kiggs and I stared at him in horror. "What are you implying, Ardmagar?" said Kiggs, a tremor in his voice.

"Merely that you aren't as observant as you think," said Comonot, "and that—" He broke off abruptly; his face paled. "By all that glitters, I'm as stupid as you are."

He took off at a run. Kiggs and I were on his heels, Kiggs crying, "Where is she?"

The Ardmagar turned up the grand marble stair. He took the steps two at a time. "Who did the assassin intend to stab," cried Comonot, "before he settled for Seraphina?"

"Where is Aunt Dionne, Ardmagar?" Kiggs shouted.

"In my rooms!" said the saar, who was panting now.

Kiggs sprinted past him up the stairs, toward the royal family's wing of the palace.

Thirty-Two

Comonot and I reached his quarters at the same time; Kiggs had arrived well before us with a few guards he'd picked up along the way. We entered just as a guard rushed back out, and we soon saw why: Kiggs had sent him running for the physician.

Kiggs and the other guard helped Princess Dionne off the floor, trying to get her into a semi-upright position on the couch. Kiggs reached a couple of fingers into her mouth, trying to make her vomit. She obliged, a sticky purple mess right into the guard's waiting helmet, but she didn't look any better afterward.

She'd gone green; her eyes showed a disturbing amount of white, and she couldn't seem to focus them. "Apsig! Wine!" she croaked. The guard, taking that as a request, began to pour her a glass from the bottle on the table, but Kiggs slapped the glass out of his hand. It shattered across the floor.

"The wine has made her ill, obviously," said Kiggs through

gritted teeth, trying to keep his aunt from falling off the couch as she convulsed. Comonot rushed in to help restrain her. "How long have you had that bottle, Ardmagar?"

"That's not mine. She must have brought it with her." His eyes grew wide. "Did she intend to poison me?"

"Don't be an idiot!" said Kiggs, letting his anger run roughshod over his manners. "Why would she have drunk it herself?"

"Remorse at what she was about to do?"

"That's not how it works, you stupid dragon!" cried Kiggs, his voice choked with tears, wiping foam from her lips. "Why was she meeting you here? Why was she bringing you wine? Why do you think you can come to Goredd and playact being human when you know nothing about it?"

"Kiggs," I said, tentatively placing a hand on his arm. He jerked away from me.

Comonot leaned against the back of the couch, stunned. "I—I don't know *nothing*, exactly. That is, I'm feeling something. I don't know what it is." He turned pleading eyes toward me, but I did not know what to tell him.

The physician arrived with three female assistants. I helped them carry Dionne to the bed, where they stripped her, sponged her, bled her, fed her charcoal powder, and examined the wine and vomit closely for clues to which antidote they should use. Comonot, who had no business seeing her unclothed, wandered in unchallenged and stood gaping at her. Kiggs paced the outer room.

A terrible notion struck me. I turned to rush out, but Comonot grabbed my sleeve. "Help me," he said. "I feel something—"

"Guilt," I snapped, trying to free myself.

389

"Make it go away!" He looked nakedly terrified.

"I can't." I glanced over at the commotion on the bed; Dionne was convulsing again. I felt a pang of pity for the foolish old saar. We were all at a loss, dragon and human both, in the face of death. I put a hand to his fleshy cheek and spoke as to a child: "Stay. Help as you can; she may yet be saved. I have to make sure no one else dies tonight."

I hurried out to Kiggs. He sat on the couch, elbows on knees, hands covering his mouth, eyes wide. "Kiggs!" He did not look at me. I knelt before him. "Get up. This isn't over." He looked at me blankly. I let myself touch his disheveled hair. "Where's Selda? Where's your grandmother? We need to make sure they're safe."

That did it. He leaped to his feet. We rushed to their respective suites, but neither Queen nor princess was napping in her own bed. "Glisselda intended to talk to her," Kiggs said. "They're probably together. In the Queen's study, or . . ." He shrugged. I turned that direction, but he grabbed a lantern, caught my arm, and took me through a concealed door in the wall of the Queen's bedroom into a maze of passages.

The way was narrow; I walked behind him. When I could stand the silence no longer, I asked, "You heard your aunt say 'Apsig'?"

He nodded. "The implication seems clear enough."

"That Josef gave her the wine? Was it intended merely for the Ardmagar, or—"

"Both, without question." He looked back at me, his face in

shadow: "Aunt Dionne was supposed to have met Comonot at the cathedral."

"Thomas could not have mistaken me for her."

"I imagine he recognized you and decided on the spur of the moment that he may as well kill you instead. But recall: you saw Josef near the scene."

"You thought that was too circumstantial."

"I did until his name popped up just now!" he cried, the stress of the evening overriding his usual circumspection.

We reached the Queen's study only to find it empty. Kiggs swore.

"We should split up," I said. "I'll check back at the great hall."

He nodded grimly. "I'll mobilize the Guard. We'll find them."

I was already reaching for Abdo with my mind as I scurried toward the hall. *Abdo, find Lars. Wait for me near the stage. Can you see Dame Okra?*

Abdo spotted the ambassadress near the desserts, then told me he was off to the dressing rooms to find Lars. I reached for Lars to let him know Abdo was coming.

I considered breaking my word and reaching for Dame Okra, but she had been cranky enough earlier and I needed her help now. I needed her power, odd as it was, to live up to its peculiar promise. When I reached the great hall, she was right where Abdo had indicated, having a lively conversation with Fulda, the reclusive dragon ambassador. I skirted the dancing couples, marveling that anyone still had the energy for a volta when it must be nearly dawn. I drew up beside Dame Okra and said, "Pardon me, Ambassador Fulda, but I need to steal Dame Okra for one moment. I fear it's urgent."

The good manners were more for her benefit than his. She drew herself up importantly—it didn't make her any taller—and said, "You heard her, Fulda. Shoo."

Ambassador Fulda's eyes shone as he stared at me. "So you're Maid Dombegh. I am intrigued to make your acquaintance at last."

I stared back at him, wondering what he'd heard.

"Oh, fie!" cried Dame Okra, swatting him. "She's no more special than I am, and you've known me for years. Come, Seraphina!" She took my arm and hauled me away. "All right, what do you want?" she said when we were off in a corner by ourselves.

I took a deep breath. "We need to find the Queen and Glisselda."

"They're not in the study, I suppose?"

I goggled at her. "What does your stomach tell you?"

"My stomach does not take requests, little maidy!" she said haughtily. "It directs me, not the other way around."

I leaned down into her froggy face, demonstrating beyond all doubt that I was not merely her equal in snarling but would surpass her one day. "You told me your stomach enables you to be in the right place at the right time. The Queen and Glisselda may be in mortal danger this very moment, so I'd say the right place is wherever they are, and the right time is before they come to harm!"

"Well, thank you for the additional information," she sniffed.

"I do need something to go on. It's not magic, you know. It's more like indigestion."

"Is it pointing you anywhere, or not?"

She considered a moment, tapping a finger against her lips. "Yes. Through here."

She led me toward one door of the hall just as Kiggs came through another. I called and waved; he darted straight across the dance floor toward us, scattering and confounding the dancers. Dame Okra didn't wait for him but plunged into the corridor, toward the east wing. I followed her at a distance until Kiggs caught up.

"Where are we going?" he asked breathlessly.

"We've worked out the location of Glisselda and the Queen," I said, dreading his next question.

"Where are they?"

"St. Vitt, how should I know?" growled Dame Okra, increasing her speed.

Kiggs turned incredulous eyes on me. "What is this?"

"She has a hunch. I trust it. Let's give her a chance."

Kiggs grunted skeptically but followed. We arrived at the door to his beastly tower. Dame Okra rattled the handle, but it was locked. "Where does this go, and do you have a key, Prince?" asked Dame Okra.

"They wouldn't be up there," he grumbled, but he fished for his key.

"How would they have gotten in?" I asked as the lock clicked.

"Glisselda has a key. It's not impossible, but it's not plausible either—" He stopped short. Hollow voices echoed down the spiral stair. "Saints' bones!"

Dame Okra made as if to stomp straight up the stairs, but Kiggs stopped her, staring upward intently. He put a finger to his lips and moved silently, a hand on the hilt of his sword; we followed his lead. The door at the top was slightly ajar, letting light and sound drift down toward us. We heard laughter and three ... no, four different voices. Kiggs motioned us to stay still.

"That's plenty. Lovely," said a voice I took to be the Queen's.

"Thank you!" chirped a voice that was clearly Glisselda's. "Shouldn't we wait for my mother and Cousin Lucian?"

A third voice made a muffled reply, followed by the clink of glass upon glass as another wine goblet was filled.

Kiggs turned to us and counted down with his fingers: three, two, one ...

He threw the door open just as the Queen, Glisselda, and Lady Corongi toasted the new year with a glass of wine. Josef, Earl of Apsig, stood a little apart, the wine bottle in his hand.

Thirty-Three

"Oh, there you are, Lucian!" chirped Glisselda, who stood facing the door.

"Don't!" cried Kiggs, lunging across the room toward his grandmother, who was the only person who'd put her glass all the way to her lips.

"I thought there might be a lovely view of the sunrise from up here," continued his cousin, registering his actions but slowly. Her face fell as Kiggs grabbed the glass from her hand. "What's going on?"

"Someone poisoned your mother. Something in the wine. We shouldn't trust this wine either: I suspect it's from the same source. Your glass, please, Lady Corongi," said Kiggs. Lady Corongi handed over her glass, looking scandalized.

"I hope you're wrong," said the Queen, sitting down shakily on a stool. She leaned her elbow against a nearby table covered with books and charts. "I fear I had a swallow of mine before you burst through that door."

"We need to get you to the physicians," said Dame Okra, a certainty in her voice that no one dared question. She helped the Queen to her feet and led her to the stair.

"Dr. Ficus is at the Ardmagar's suite," Kiggs called after her, "but Dr. Johns should be—"

"I know where we're going!" cried a cranky voice already halfway down.

"Selda, you didn't drink a drop, I hope?" said Kiggs, turning to his cousin.

Selda leaned against the side of a bookcase as if she were dizzy, but said, "No. You burst in just in time. But what about you, Lady Corongi?"

The old woman shook her head curtly. Whatever poison may have been in the drink, it could not have compared with the poison she glared at the Earl of Apsig.

Josef had gone completely white. He handed the bottle to Kiggs and raised his hands as if in surrender. "Please," he said, "I know this looks bad—"

"I notice you haven't poured yourself a glass, Earl Josef," said Kiggs lightly, setting the bottle on the worktable. "You're not a saar, are you?"

"I am Samsamese!" sputtered Josef. "We do not partake of the devil's . . ." He trailed off, and then turned wide-eyed to Lady Corongi. "You were counting on that. What was your plan, witch? The Queen and princess drink, you pretend to drink, you all collapse, and when I run for the physicians, what? You steal away in secret? You leave me to take the fall for your crimes?"

"Are you accusing this noble lady of something, you monster?" cried Glisselda, putting a protective arm around the petite woman's shoulders. "She has been my teacher for almost my entire life!"

The whites of Josef's eyes shone; he looked unbalanced. His lips moved as if he were performing some dread calculus in his head; he ran both hands through his blond hair. "Prince," he croaked, "I can come up with nothing to persuade you. It is my word against hers."

"You gave my aunt a bottle of poisoned wine," said Kiggs. His earlier ire had turned to ice.

"I swear to you, I never suspected. Why would I question a gift her dear friend Lady Corongi told me to deliver?" He was flailing now, grasping for any argument he could. "You don't know this wine here is poisoned—you assume so. What if it's not?"

"I know you were in the cathedral the day Seraphina was stabbed," said Kiggs, absently rearranging objects on his worktable.

"I saw you talking to Thomas Broadwick," I said, folding my arms.

Josef shook his head vehemently. "I was delivering a message for the Sons of St. Ogdo. It was coded; I had no idea what it meant," he pleaded.

"Liar!" I cried.

"Ask her!" he shouted back, pointing toward Lady Corongi. "She's the one who put me in touch with the Sons. She's the one who supplies them with intelligence from the palace. She is the mother of all my troubles!"

"Nonsense," sniffed Lady Corongi, looking at his pointer finger as if it offended her more than anything he'd said. "Prince, I fail to see why you have not bound this miserable creature hand and foot already."

Josef opened his mouth to retort, but at that very moment a horrifying sound—"Thluu-thluu-thluuu!"—arose from somewhere near Kiggs. Princess Glisselda leaped onto a stool, crying, "St. Polypous's legs, where is it?" Josef drew his dagger and looked around wildly.

Only Lady Corongi stood frozen, eyes wide with astonishment, as the voice lisped, "I see you there, impostor!"

I looked to Kiggs. He nodded at me and opened his hand behind his back, revealing my lizard-man figurine.

He said, "Who is it calling an impostor, Lady?"

Lady Corongi snapped out of her shock with a shudder. I faced her. Her fierce blue eyes met mine only for a second, but in that fragile eternity I glimpsed the mind behind the manners; in that endless instant, I knew.

Lady Corongi charged into Glisselda, who still stood on the stool. Glisselda screamed and folded in half over Corongi's shoulder. The venerable lady whirled and bolted down the stairs.

Shock froze us in place for a heartbeat too long; Kiggs recovered first, grabbed my arm, and dragged me down into darkness after her. Josef shouted something after us, but whether he called to us or to Corongi, I could not discern. At the bottom of the stairs, Kiggs looked right and I looked left. I saw the edge of Lady

Corongi's skirt disappearing around a corner. We dashed after, following the faintest of trails—an open door, the ghost of her perfume, a curtain ruffled by a nonexistent breeze—until we reached a cabinet that had been pulled out from the wall, revealing an entrance to the passageways.

Kiggs broke off pursuit. "That was a mistake, Lady," he said. He dashed back into the corridor; three doors along was a guardroom. He threw open the door, shouted for attention, and made five hand signals in quick succession. Guards poured out and scattered in all directions. Kiggs dashed back to the shifted cabinet; there was already a guard beside it, who saluted and handed us a lantern as we passed.

"What have you asked them to do?" I said.

He demonstrated the signs as he spoke: "Spread the word; all hands; seal the lower tunnels; notify the city garrison; and . . ." His eyes met mine. "Dragon."

It was an impressive array of signals. "Will they be following us down?"

"Soon. It will take time to get everyone in position. There are seven entrances."

"Counting the sally port?"

He made no reply but plunged onward into darkness. Of course the palace guard would not be able to reach the sally port in time; that was why he was sending word to the city, but they would be too late. My heart sank in despair. Glisselda might be dead before any of us could reach her.

I had troops of my own that I could rally. I activated Orma's earring on its chain, praying that he would hear it, that he had not already traveled some ridiculous distance, and that he could reach us in time. Then I reached for Abdo.

Where are you? he said. *We were getting worried!*

Bad things are happening. I need you and Lars to run, as fast as you can, to the northwest face of Castle Hill. The sally port in the side of the hill might have a hostile dragon emerging from it shortly.

Or it might have a very strong, wickedly fast old woman. There was still some uncertainty on that point.

How do we get down the castle wall on that side?

St. Masha's stone. *You will find a way.* I hoped that was true.

And what are the two of us to do against a hostile dragon?

I don't know. All I know is I am in the tunnels right now, behind it, and if you and Lars show up there will be twice as many people as there would be otherwise. We don't have to kill it; we just have to delay it until my uncle gets here.

I let him go because I could tell he was going to protest again and because I kept tripping over the uneven floor when my concentration was elsewhere.

We passed the three doors, now unlocked and ajar, and knew that Lady Corongi had come this way as well. When we reached the natural cavern area, Kiggs drew his sword. He looked me up and down. "We should have armed you before coming down here!" His eyes looked haunted in the lantern light. "I want you to turn back."

"Don't be ridiculous."

"Phina, I don't know what I'd do if you were hurt! Please go back!" He squared himself as if he intended to block my way.

"Stop it!" I cried. "You're wasting time."

A veil of grief fell across his face, but he nodded and turned back toward the job at hand. We set off at a run.

We reached the mouth of the cave, but there was no one visible, just women's clothing scattered all over the floor like a shed skin. Kiggs and I glanced at each other, remembering the folded gown we'd found here before. It had been right in front of us, and we hadn't had the wit to see it.

Glisselda had clearly put up a struggle while "Lady Corongi" undressed, so there was some hope the creature was not yet able to fly. We dashed out of the cave into the slick, snowy grass, looking around for the pair of them. Glisselda screamed; we turned toward the sound of her voice. Above the cave entrance, silhouetted against the growing pink of the sky, stood a wiry, naked man, Glisselda thrown over his shoulder.

He'd been at court disguised as an old woman for almost Glisselda's whole lifetime. Doused in perfume, avoiding other saar, worming his way close to Princess Dionne, he had bided his time with a patience only reptiles possess.

For all my exposure to saarantraí I had never before seen one change from human to dragon. He unfolded himself, stretched, telescoped, unfurled some more. It seemed logical as it happened, all his human parts plausibly dragon: his shoulders separating into wings, his spine extending back to tail, his face lengthening, his skin bursting out in scales. He managed the entire thing without letting go of Glisselda; he finished with her clasped firmly in his front talons.

If we had been smart, we would have charged him while he was transforming, but we'd stood rooted to the spot, too dumbfounded to think.

All doubt was finally removed: it was Imlann.

He would not be able to fly for several minutes; a newly transformed saar is soft and weak, like a butterfly fresh from the chrysalis. His jaw worked; he could still spit fire. I pulled Kiggs back inside the cave before the fireball hit the dirt at the entrance, sending up a spray of scorched stones in a burst of brimstone. Imlann couldn't work up a very big gobbet yet, but if he craned his neck down into the cave, he wasn't going to need full flame, especially if Kiggs refused to retreat.

How long would it take Lars and Abdo to get here? And Orma, if he was even coming? I saw only one course of action, and turned to head back out of the cave.

"Are you mad?" cried Kiggs, grabbing my arm.

I was mad, as it happened. I turned back and kissed him squarely on the mouth, because this really could be the last thing I ever did, and I loved him, and it made me desperately sad that he would never know. The kiss startled him into releasing my arm, and I dashed out of his reach, out onto the snowy hillside.

"Imlann!" I cried, jumping and waving my arms like a fool. "Take me with you!"

The monster cocked his head and screamed, "You're not a dragon; we resolved that in the laundry. What in blazes are you?"

This was it. I had to be interesting enough that he wouldn't kill me out of hand, and there was only one piece of information that could work: "I'm your granddaughter!"

"Not possible."

"Yes, possible! Linn married the human, Clau—"

"Do not speak his name. I want to die never having heard it uttered. He is a nameless thing, antithetical to ard."

"Well, your nameless daughter bore a child to her nameless thing husband."

"Orma told us—"

"Orma lied."

"I should kill you."

"You'd do better to take me with you. I could be of use in the coming conflict." I spread my arms, posing dramatically, my crimson gown like a gaping wound in the snowy hillside. "Being a half-breed has given me formidable abilities that neither dragons nor humans possess. I can contact other half-breeds with my mind; I can direct them at a distance with a thought. I have visions and maternal memories. How do you imagine I knew who you were?"

Imlann's nostrils flared, though I could not discern whether he was skeptical or intrigued. Down in the cave, Kiggs stirred, moving himself slowly and silently into position to attack.

"I know all about your cabal," I said, feeling the urgency of keeping my mouth moving. "I know the coup back home is going forward as we speak."

Imlann raised his spines as if alarmed that I could know that. Had I guessed right? Despair washed over me, but I kept going: "You've killed the Ardmagar and half the royal family; war is coming. But Goredd is not sufficiently weak that you will be able to walk right in. You're going to need my help."

403

Imlann snorted, smoke curling from his nostrils. "Liar. I know you bluffed me before. You should not have been so quick to brag. Even if I believed in your powers, your loyalty lies with the prince-ling in the cave. Which of your 'formidable abilities' will you use when I lean down and roast him? I've worked up quite a good flame now."

I opened my mouth, and there was a sound like the world ending.

It wasn't me, although I was ridiculously slow to comprehend that. Lars, who'd sneaked up on the left, had started up his great war pipes, brawling and caterwauling and screaming musical ob-scenities at the dawn. Imlann jerked his head toward the sound and a shadowy figure leaped at him from the other side, vaulted up the dragon's neck, and clamped arms and legs around his still-soft throat. Imlann thrashed his neck around, but Abdo held tight—tight enough to prevent Imlann from spitting fire.

"Kiggs! Now!" I cried, but he was already there, stabbing at the foot that held Glisselda. Imlann uttered a gurgle and withdrew his foot reflexively. I reached Kiggs at just that moment; together we rolled Glisselda to one side. I helped the sobbing princess down the rocks toward the cave entrance while Kiggs, unwilling to leave well enough alone, took a stab at the dragon's other foot. Imlann lashed at Kiggs, knocking the prince down to our level. He landed on his back, all the air slammed out of him. Glisselda ran to his side.

There was a hot, sulfuric wind, and I looked up to see Imlann launching himself off the hillside, Abdo still clinging to his neck. I cried out, but there was nothing I could do. Abdo couldn't let go while he was in the air; the fall would kill him. Imlann circled lazily back toward us. If he was hardened enough to fly, he was too hard for Abdo to keep squeezing him flameless. He was coming back to torch us into cinders.

"Get back!" I cried to Glisselda and Kiggs, shoving them toward the cave. "As far as you can!"

"Y-your lying saved us!" gasped Kiggs, still dazed from his fall.

My lying. Yes. "Hurry! Run!" I urged him.

Something huge screamed through the sky just above us. I looked up to see Orma hurtling toward Imlann, and I wept with relief.

Thirty-Four

Imlann turned tail and fled, or appeared to. He let Orma nearly catch him before reeling around in the sky and grappling him. They pinned each other's wings and plummeted toward the earth but managed to escape each other's grasp before they hit the trees. They spiraled upward again, each looking for an opening. Imlann flamed; Orma, noticeably, did not.

He'd spotted Abdo and did not wish to harm him. The humanity of it took my breath away; the colossal stupidity of it filled me with despair.

Abdo, clamped onto Imlann's neck, would deprive Orma not only of the use of fire but also of the ability to bite Imlann's head off easily. Orma's only hope would be to successfully drop his father out of the sky, but his father was longer by a quarter. It was not going to be easy, and Abdo might still die.

From the city, something else huge and dark rose into the sky and approached the fighting pair at speed. It was another dragon, but I couldn't tell who. He circled the snarling pair at a safe distance, not engaging either of them, but watching and waiting.

Behind me, Kiggs spoke quietly to Glisselda. "Are you hurt?"

"I believe I may have a cracked rib, Lucian. But—is the Ardmagar really dead?"

"It was all a bluff. I've seen her do it before. It's her particular talent."

"Well, go fetch her, would you? She's standing in the snow in her ball slippers, and she's going to freeze."

I had not realized until that moment how cold I was. I didn't even have a cloak. Kiggs approached me, but I would not tear my eyes away from the sky battle. Imlann flew a little further east with each pass; soon they were going to be fighting above the city. If Orma was unwilling to risk the life of one little boy, was he really going to drop Imlann onto buildings full of people? My heart sank still lower.

The cathedral bells began to toll, a pattern not heard in forty years: the ard-call. *Dragons! Take cover!*

"Phina," said Kiggs. "Come inside."

I wouldn't be able to see the dragons from the cave mouth, the way they were positioned now. I stepped away from him, into even deeper snow. Kiggs came after me and put a hand on my arm, as if he'd drag me back, but his eyes were on the lightening sky as well. "Who is that third dragon?"

I suspected I knew, but I did not have the energy to explain.

"It's hovering uselessly," said Kiggs. "If it were an embassy dragon, I'd expect it to side with your teacher."

That last word jarred me. I'd expected him to say "uncle," truly. I had told the truth right in front of him, and he could not, or would not, believe it. He was offering me an easy way back to normal, and I was sorely tempted. It would have been so simple not to correct him, to let it go. It would have been effortless.

But I had kissed him, and I had told the truth, and I was changed.

"He's my uncle," I said, loudly enough to ensure Glisselda heard it also.

Kiggs did not let go of my arm, although his hand seemed to turn to wood. He looked to Glisselda; I did not see what expression she wore. He said, "Phina, don't joke. You saved us. It's over."

I stared at him until he met my eye. "If you're going to demand the truth from me, you could at least have the courtesy to believe it."

"It can't be true. That doesn't happen." His voice caught; he'd gone pink to his ears. "That is, what Aunt Dionne might have been planning . . . I'll allow that *that* happens. Maybe, sometimes."

It had been about to happen at Lady Corongi's suggestion, too, I suddenly realized.

"But interbreeding is surely impossible," Kiggs continued stubbornly. "Cats and dogs, as they say."

"Horses and donkeys," I said. The cold wind made my eyes water. "It happens."

"What did you say about my mother, Lucian?" asked Glisselda, her voice tremulous.

Kiggs didn't answer. He released my arm but didn't walk away. His eyes widened. I followed his gaze in time to see Orma pull out of a drop barely in time, shearing off a chimney and a tavern roof with its tail. The sound of the crash reached our ears a moment later along with the screaming of panicked citizens.

"Saints in Heaven!" cried Glisselda, who had come closer behind us without my hearing, clutching her side. "Why won't that one help him?"

In fact, "that one" was gliding lazily back toward us. He grew larger and larger, finally landing just downhill from us; a gust of brimstone wind forced us back a step. He stretched his snaky neck, and then proceeded to do the opposite of what Imlann had done, collapsing in upon himself, cooling and condensing into a man. Basind stood stark naked in the snow, rubbing his hands together.

"Saar Basind!" I cried, even though I knew how futile it was to be furious with him. "You're leaving Orma to be killed. Change back at once!"

Basind's eyes swiveled toward me, and I stopped short. His gaze was sharp; his motions were smooth and coordinated as he picked his way toward me through the snow. He flicked his lank hair out of his eyes and said, "This fight has nothing to do with me, Seraphina. I've gathered the pertinent data on your uncle, and now I get to go home."

I gaped at him. "You're—you're from the—"

"The Board of Censors, yes. We test your uncle regularly, but he's been tough to catch. He usually notices and spoils the test. This time he was experiencing excessive emotionality on several fronts at once; he could not keep up his vigilance. The Ardmagar has already ordered Orma's excision, of course, saving me the trouble of having to argue the case."

"What has Orma done?" asked Glisselda, behind me. I turned; she stood on a stony outcrop, looking surprisingly regal as the sky turned pink and gold behind her.

"He put his half-human niece before his own people multiple times," said Basind, sounding bored. "He showed several emotions in quantities exceeding permissible limits, including love, hatred, and grief. He is, even now, losing a battle he could easily win, out of concern for a human boy he doesn't even know."

Orma was thrown against the bell tower of the cathedral while Basind spoke, crushing the belfry roof with his back. Slate and wood hit the bells, adding cacophony to the ard-call, which still pealed forth from churches all over the city.

"I offer him asylum," said Glisselda, crossing her arms over her chest.

Basind lifted an eyebrow. "He's ruining your city."

"He's fighting a traitor to his own kind. Imlann tried to kill the Ardmagar!"

Basind shrugged his bony shoulders. "Truly, that concerns me not a bit."

"You don't care whether the peace fails?"

"We Censors predate the peace; we will be here long after it has crumbled." He looked down at himself, seeming to notice for the first time that he was naked. He made for the mouth of the cave. Kiggs attempted to block his way; Basind rolled his eyes. "This silly body is cold. There is clothing on the floor. Hand it to me."

Kiggs did as he was told without complaint. I was astonished by his alacrity until I saw with my own eyes what he had remembered: it was Lady Corongi's gown. Basind put it on, grumbling that it was too tight but noticing nothing else wrong with it. He turned and sauntered away up the sally port, unchallenged.

"Lucian!" cried Glisselda. "Don't let him go. I'm not convinced he's friendly."

"The tunnels are all blocked. He'll be apprehended before he can do any harm."

If only that were true. The harm was done. I turned back to the sky, where my uncle was still getting the worst of it. Even if he survived, he'd be sent back to the Tanamoot to have his brain pruned. I couldn't bear it.

Imlann got the drop on him again, and this time Orma could not recover soon enough. He was on fire; he streaked through the sky and landed hard in the river, taking out the Wolfstoot Bridge. A cloud of steam billowed up where he had fallen.

I clamped a hand over my mouth. Imlann swirled the sky, screaming and flaming triumphantly, the newly risen sun glimmering upon his skin.

Treaty Eve was over. Usually we Goreddis toasted the new light and cried, "The dragon wars are done for good!" This year, however, everyone had run out into the streets to watch the dragons warring each other overhead.

I could still hear screams, but it was not the townspeople; it was the wrong pitch. Suddenly I realized the dark dots in the southern sky, which I had taken for a flock of birds, were flying too swiftly and growing far too large to be birds.

Eskar and the petit ard were returning.

The dragon Imlann, my maternal grandfather, did not attempt

to flee and did not bite his own tail and surrender. He flew head-long at the approaching dragons, flaming and bellowing and utterly doomed.

As Lady Corongi, he had been devious, ruthless, and calculating. He had tried to kill the entire royal family and his Ardmagar; he might have succeeded in killing his own son. His final charge was nothing short of suicide. And yet, as I watched him in full battle fury, slashing and snapping as if he would rip the sky itself apart, I felt a terrible sorrow rising in me. He was my mother's father. She had ruined his life as surely as her own by marrying my father, but had her stubbornness been so different from his doomed charge, in the end? Hadn't she too gone up against unbeatable odds?

Eskar alone could not drop him. Three dragons together finally set him on fire, and even then he stayed airborne longer than I could have imagined possible. When Eskar finally decapitated him, it was more mercy killing than victory. I watched my grandfather's body spiral down, bright as a comet, and I wept.

The church bells changed their pattern to the fire alarm as smoke began to billow up in the south part of town. Even dead, Imlann did a lot of damage.

I turned back toward the cave entrance, my eyes stinging, my hands and face bitterly cold, a dread emptiness in my chest. Kiggs and Glisselda stood together, both of them studying me anxiously but pretending not to. In the shadows behind them stood Lars, whom I'd all but forgotten. He clutched his pipes, white-knuckled.

"Phina," he said when I met his eye, "what hes happendt to Abdo?"

The dragon Abdo clung to had been set aflame and decapitated. I saw little hope. "I can't look for him, Lars," I said. The idea of reaching for Abdo's hand in my mind and coming up empty terrified me.

"Candt, or wondt?"

"I won't!"

Lars glowered ferociously. "You will! You owe him thet! He gave everythink for you, gladtly! He foundt the way down the wall, he threw himself at thet dragon, he didt all you esked and more. Findt him."

"What if he's not there?"

"Then you will findt him in Heaven, but you will findt him."

I nodded, picking my way through the snow toward Lars. Kiggs and Glisselda parted to let me pass, their eyes wide. "Keep me upright, will you?" I said to Lars, who silently put his bagpipe-free arm around me and let me lean my head against his chest. I closed my eyes and reached.

I found Abdo at once. Conscious, alert, almost unhurt, he was seated upon what at first appeared to be an island in the middle of the river. I swooped in with my vision-eye for a closer look. Abdo waved at me, smiling through tears, and only then did I realize what he was sitting on.

It was Orma.

Abdo, is that dragon alive or dead? I cried, but Abdo didn't answer. Maybe he didn't know. I circled. Orma's chest rose—was that a breath? Crowds of people lined the riverbanks, shouting and waving torches but too frightened to go any closer to him. A shadow crossed them, and they scattered, screaming. It was Eskar:

she landed on the strand and arched her neck down to my uncle in the river.

With a tremendous effort, he lifted his head and touched her nose with his.

"Abdo lives," I croaked, bringing myself back. "He's in the river with Uncle Orma. He must have switched dragons in mid-flight."

Lars squeezed me and kissed the top of my head, then checked his exuberance. "Your uncle?"

"Moving. Not well. Eskar's there; she'll see to his care." I hoped she would. Was she really no longer with the Censors? She was the one who'd made my uncle look after Basind. Had she known who he was? I wept into Lars's jerkin.

There was another hand on my shoulder. Princess Glisselda was giving me her handkerchief. "Are these your formidable mental powers?" she asked softly. "You can see your comrades in your mind? Is that how you found me?"

"She can see only other half-dragons," said Lars, glaring unnecessarily.

"There are more half-dragons?" whispered Glisselda, her blue eyes wide.

"*Mise*," said Lars. "I, myself."

The princess nodded slowly, her brow furrowed in thought. "And that little Porphyrian boy. That's who you're talking about, isn't it?"

Kiggs was shaking his head, pacing in a futile circle. "I might believe there was one in the world, but three?"

"Four, counting Dame Okra Carmine," I said wearily. "May as

well out the whole bunch, although I had a feeling Dame Okra would be irked that I had done so. "There could be seventeen of us together, if I located the rest." Eighteen, if I found Jannoula, or she found me.

Glisselda looked awed, but Kiggs set his jaw as if he wasn't buying it.

"You heard Basind call Orma my uncle," I told him. "Remember how you thought I loved him, how you were sick of guessing? Here's your explanation at last."

Kiggs was shaking his head stubbornly. "I just can't . . . Your blood runs red. You laugh and cry the same as anyone—"

Lars seemed to grow taller, looming protectively over me. I put a reassuring hand on his arm and told him in my mind: *It's time. I can do this.*

The prince and princess stared, mesmerized by how many sleeves and ties I had to undo. I held my bared arm toward them; sunlight flashed off the spiraling silver scales.

The icy wind blew. No one spoke.

Kiggs and Glisselda did not move. I did not look at their faces; I did not wish to read how many different words for disgust must be written there. I tugged my garments back into place, cleared the considerable lump out of my throat, and croaked, "We should get inside and see who else still lives."

The royal cousins started, as if waking from some terrible dream, and hastened into the cave, ahead of and away from me. Lars put his arm around my shoulders. I leaned on him all the way into the castle, weeping half my tears for Orma and half for myself.

Thirty-Five

All the palace was in an uproar when we got back, searching for Glisselda; no one but us had known where she'd gone. She stepped out of the tunnels a tired, cold, frightened girl, but within moments, before she'd even heard the fates of her mother and grandmother, she had put her queenliness on and was reassuring panicked courtiers and terrified heads of state.

Princess Dionne had not survived the night. The Queen held on, but barely. Glisselda hurried upstairs to be at her grandmother's side.

Kiggs went straight to his guards, demanding reports and making sure they had shifted smoothly to daytime duties. They had detained Basind; Kiggs decided he could use a good questioning and hastened off.

Lars and I were left to fend for ourselves. Without a word, he took my arm and led me through twists and turns of the corridors until we reached a door. Viridius's manservant, Marius, answered. Viridius was shouting in the background: "What kind of whore–son dog knocks before the sun is up?"

"The sun is up, Master," said Marius wearily, rolling his eyes and waving us through. "It's only Lars and—"

Viridius darkened the doorway of the bedchamber, hauling himself forward with two canes. His expression softened at the sight of us. "Pardon me, my dears. You've awakened an old man on the wrong side of the bed."

Lars, who was propping me up, intoned, "She needts a place to sleep."

"She hasn't a suite of her own anymore?" asked Viridius, clear-ing cushions and a robe off his couch for me. "Sit, Seraphina, you look terrible."

"Her true nature is revealedt to the princess and prince," said Lars, laying a hand on the old man's shoulder. "She shouldt not hev to face the worldt until she rests, quiet, away from peoples."

Marius went to the solarium to arrange a makeshift bed for me, but I fell asleep right there on the couch.

I dozed on and off all day. Viridius and Lars kept everyone away and asked no questions.

The next morning I awoke to Lars sitting at the end of my impromptu bed. "The princess was here," he said. "She wants thet we come to the Queen's studty when you are dressedt. A lot is heppenedt."

I nodded blearily. He gave me his arm and we went together.

Princess Glisselda had commandeered her grandmother's massive desk; eight high-backed chairs, most of them already occupied, had been placed in a semicircle before her. Kiggs sat behind her to the left perusing a folded letter; he flicked his eyes toward the door when Lars and I entered but did not raise his head. To the princess's right, like a gray shadow near the windows, stood my father. He smiled wanly. I nodded at him and followed Lars toward the two empty seats beside Dame Okra Carmine.

Abdo peeked out from behind her ample form and waved at me.

The Regent of Samsam, Count Pesavolta of Ninys, Ambassador Fulda, and the Ardmagar occupied the other seats. The Regent was clad all in severe black, his silver hair brushing his shoulders, while Count Pesavolta was wide, apple-cheeked, and bald; they wore similar sour expressions, however. Lars slumped beside me as if to make himself smaller, casting wary glances at the Regent.

Princess Glisselda folded her small hands on the desk before her and cleared her throat. She wore a white houppelande and the circlet of the first heir; golden netting restrained the exuberance of her curls. Small though she was, she seemed to fill the room with light. She said, "My mother is dead and my grandmother extremely ill. I am first heir by rightful succession. The incapacity of the Queen—St. Eustace leave her lie long as he may—necessitates my speaking, deciding, and taking action on her behalf." The Regent and Count Pesavolta shifted in their seats, grumbling. Glisselda snapped: "Counselor Dombegh! Precedent!"

My father cleared his throat. "When Queen Lavonia II was

incapacitated by stroke, Princess Annette served as acting Queen until she recovered. No Goreddi would question your right, Your Highness."

"You are but fifteen years old," said Count Pesavolta, his round face smiling but his eyes hard. "No disrespect intended."

"Queen Lavonda was but seventeen when she treated with me," said Comonot unexpectedly. He rested his hands on his knees, several quig-made rings on each finger; they gleamed like a miniature hoard against the dark blue of his houppelande.

"Her youth did not excuse her foolishness," said the Regent, glaring down his narrow nose.

Comonot did not acknowledge the comment; he was speaking only to Glisselda. "She was already Queen in her own right. Already a mother. She climbed Halfheart Pass through a raging snowstorm with only two goat-girls from Dewcomb's Outpost to guide her. I had assumed no rational being would brave that kind of weather, so I was not even in my saarantras to greet her. My scouts brought her into our cavern, this tiny, half-frozen girl, snow whirling around her. We all stared at her, not sure what to think, until she threw back her fur-lined hood and unwrapped the woolen shawl from over her face. She looked me in the eye, and I knew."

There was a long pause until Glisselda said, "Knew what, Ardmagar?"

"That I had met my match," said Comonot, his face sharp, remembering.

Glisselda nodded at the Ardmagar, a small smile on her lips. She held a hand out to Kiggs, who passed her the folded parchment.

"We received a letter this morning. Ambassador Fulda, would you please read it aloud?"

The ambassador fished a pair of spectacles out of his vest and read:

We the undersigned have seized the Kerama as of yesterday. We proclaim ourselves rightful rulers of the Tanamoot, all its lands and armies, until we are in turn removed by force.

The traitor Comonot yet lives. He is wanted for crimes against dragonkind, including but not limited to: making treaties and alliances against the will of the Ker; detrimental to our values and way of life; indulging in excessive emotionality;

fraternizing with humans; indulging deviants; seeking to alter our fundamental dragon nature and make us more human-like.

We demand his immediate return to the Tanamoot. Failure to comply will be tantamount to an act of war. Recognize, Goreddis, that you are in no position to fight. We expect you to act in accordance with your interests. You have three days.

"It's signed by ten generals," said Ambassador Fulda, refolding the parchment.

Comonot opened his mouth, but Glisselda silenced him with a gesture. "The dragon Imlann, as my governess, taught me that Goredd is mighty and the dragons are weak and demoralized. I believed it until I saw for myself how dragons fight. Orma destroyed the Wolfstoot Bridge and sheared off the top of St. Gobnait's; where Imlann fell, an entire city block burned. How much worse if they'd been fighting us and not each other? The dracomachia is a shambles. I fear the cabal is right: we would not last alone against dragons. As much as I admire you, Ardmagar, you're going to have to persuade me not to give you back."

She turned to Fulda. "Ambassador, will dragonkind stand with their Ardmagar?"

Fulda pursed his lips, thinking. "It's not a legal succession while Comonot lives. There may be those who reject the cabal for that reason alone, but I suspect the older generation will largely be in sympathy with their goals."

"I dispute that," said the Ardmagar.

"The younger generation," Fulda said, pressing on, "will likely stand firm in favor of the peace. This could turn into an inter-generational war."

"Infanta!" said the Regent of Samsam, shaking a bony finger as if to scold her. "Surely you have no intention of giving this creature political asylum? It was degrading enough that your noble grandmother—St. Eustace blindly pass her by—should have negotiated with it. Do not show it mercy when its own kind wants it dead."

"You would be inserting your country—and the unwilling Southlands with you—into a dragon civil war," drawled Count Pesavolta, drumming his fingers on his ample gut.

"If I may," interjected my father. "The treaty contains a clause forbidding Goredd from interfering in internal dragon affairs. We could not meddle in a civil war."

"You've tied our hands, Ardmagar," said Glisselda, her pretty little mouth curling sardonically. "We would have to break your own treaty to save you."

"We may have to break the treaty to save you," said the Ardmagar.

Glisselda turned to Ninys and Samsam. "You wish Comonot returned. I may decide I cannot do that. If it comes to war between Goredd and the dragons, can I rely on you? If not for help, then at least not to take arms against us opportunistically?"

The Regent of Samsam looked pale and peevish; Count Pesavolta hemmed and hawed. Each finally muttered something close to, if not exactly, yes.

"Goredd's treaty with Ninys and Samsam banished knights across the Southlands," continued Glisselda, her blue eyes cold and sternly fixed upon them. "I will not risk war unless we are free to revive the dracomachia. It would mean renegotiating that agreement."

"Your Highness," said my father, "many of the Samsamese and Ninysh knights were rumored to have fled to Fort Oversea, on the isle of Paola. Their dracomachia may be in healthier condition than ours. Altering the treaty could allow the knights of all three nations to work together."

The princess nodded thoughtfully. "I'd want your help drafting this document."

"It would be my honor," said my father, bowing.

The Regent of Samsam sat up straighter, his skinny neck extending like a vulture's. "If it means we might reinstate our valiant exiles, perhaps Samsam would be willing to negotiate some sort of nonaggression pact."

"Ninys would never side with dragons against Goredd," Count Pesavolta announced. "We stand behind you, of course!"

Glisselda gave an arch nod. Kiggs, behind her, had narrowed his eyes suspiciously. Ninys and Samsam would have squirmed in their seats had they realized what intense scrutiny would be upon them.

"This brings me finally to you," said the princess, indicating us half-dragons with an elegant gesture. "We have here a fearless boy who grappled a dragon in his own version of dracomachia, a man who can design sophisticated engines of war—"

"And musical instruments," mumbled Lars.

"—a woman who can tell the near future with her stomach, and another who may be able to find me more people of extraordinary talent." Glisselda smiled warmly at me. "At least, you mentioned there are more. Are they all so talented?"

I almost said I didn't know, but it occurred to me suddenly that I might. If I'd thought about it, I'd have known what to expect from these first three: Abdo was always climbing and balancing; Lars built gazebos and bridges; Dame Okra pulled up weeds before they had a chance to sprout. Every one of my grotesques engaged in idiosyncratic behaviors. Pelican Man stared at the stars. Pandowdy was a monster in his own right. Jannoula—if I ever dared to look for her again—could climb right into my mind, but maybe not just mine.

"I think we would be something formidable, all together," I said. "And I think I could find the rest, if I went looking. I've wanted to find them."

"Do it," said Glisselda. "Whatever you need—horses, guards,

money—speak to Lucian, and Lucian will make it so." She nodded to her cousin; he nodded back, although he avoided looking in my direction.

The Regent could stand it no longer. "Your pardon, Highness, but who are these people? I know Count Pesavolta's ambassadress, but the rest? A highland lout, a Porphyrian child, and this . . . this woman—"

"My daughter Seraphina," said Papa, his face hard.

"Oh, that explains everything!" cried the Regent. "Princess? What's going on?"

Princess Glisselda opened her mouth, but no words came out.

In that moment of hesitation, I realized she was embarrassed—for me, for all of us. We were the punch line of a hundred dirty jokes. How could she speak of such disgusting things to the leader of a foreign land?

I rose, ready to spare her the mortification. My father had the same idea and found his voice first: "I married a dragon. My daughter, whom I love, is half dragon."

"Papa!" I cried, terrified for him, grateful, sad, and proud.

"Infanta!" sputtered the Regent, leaping to his feet. "By St. Vitt, these are unnatural abominations. Soulless beasts!"

Count Pesavolta snorted. "I can't believe you were worried about our loyalty but are ready to trust these things. How can you ever be sure which side they will take, dragon or human? My ambassadress already seems determined to choose Goredd over Ninys. Surely this is only the first wave of her treachery?"

"I choose what's right," snarled Dame Okra, "as I expect you will too, sir."

Comonot turned to Ninys and Samsam, his eyes bright but his voice filled with calm authority: "Can you not see that it's no longer a question of dragon versus human? The division now is between those who think this peace is worth preserving and those who would keep us at war until one side or the other is destroyed.

"There are dragons who see the good of the treaty. They will join us. The young have been raised with peaceful ideals; they won't sympathize with these grizzled generals who want their hoards and their hunting grounds back."

He turned toward Glisselda and gestured toward the sky. "Something we dragons have learned from you is that we are stronger together. We need not take on the entire world alone. Let us stand together now for the peace."

Princess Glisselda rose, stepped around the great oaken desk, and embraced Comonot, removing all doubt. She would not turn him over to his generals. We would be going to war for peace.

Thirty-Six

The meeting adjourned; the Regent and Count Pesavolta couldn't quit the room fast enough. Glisselda and Kiggs already had their heads together, planning how best to address the council at noon. The princess smiled sheepishly at her cousin. "You were right: Ninys and Samsam took it poorly. I hoped to be efficient, but I should have met with everyone separately. Gloat, if you must."

"Not at all," said Kiggs gently. "Instinct did not fail you. They'd have learned of the half-dragons eventually and accused us of duplicity. They'll get over it."

I stared at the back of the prince's neck as if it could reveal whether he himself was used to the idea yet. If his refusal to look at me was any indication, the answer was no. I tore myself away and left them to their planning.

My father waited for me in the corridor, his arms crossed and his eyes anxious. He held out a hand when he saw me. I took it, and we stood in silence.

"I'm sorry," he said at last. "I have lived in this prison so long, I . . . I suddenly found I couldn't do it anymore."

I squeezed his hand and let go. "You only did what I was about to. What now? There must be repercussions within the lawyers' guild for lawyers who break the law." He had a wife and four other children to support; I could not bring myself to point that out.

He smiled mirthlessly. "I've been preparing my case for sixteen years."

"Excuse me," said a voice to my left, and we turned to see Comonot standing there. He cleared his throat and ran a jeweled hand over his jowls. "You are—were—the human involved with the nameless . . . that is, with Linn, daughter of Imlann?"

Papa bowed stiffly.

Comonot stepped closer, cautious as a cat. "She left her home, her people, her studies, everything. For you." He touched my father's face with his thick fingers: the left cheek, the right, the nose and chin. My father endured it stonily.

"What are you?" said the Ardmagar, an unexpected roughness in his voice. "Not a depraved maniac. You are known in the north as a dispassionate interpreter of the treaty—you realize that? You've defended dragons in court when no one else would do it; don't imagine we haven't noticed. And yet it was you who lured our daughter away."

"I did not know," said my father hoarsely.

"No, but she knew." Comonot laid a hand atop my father's balding head, mystified. "What did she see? And why can't I see it?"

Papa extricated himself, bowed, and set off down the hall. For a fleeting instant, in the sad curve of his shoulders, I saw what Comonot could not: the core of decency; the weight he had carried so long; the endless struggle to do right in the wake of this irreversible wrong; the grieving husband and frightened father; the author of all those love songs. For the first time, I understood.

Comonot seemed unfazed by my father's hasty retreat. He took my arm and whispered in my ear breathily, like a small child: "Your uncle is at the seminary infirmary."

I goggled at him. "He transformed?"

The Ardmagar shrugged. "He was adamant that no saar physician come near him; he seems to believe they'd excise him on the spot. He'll be gone tomorrow in any case."

I pulled away from him. "Because Basind will take him away to have his brain pruned?"

Comonot licked his thick lips, as if he needed to taste my bitterness to understand it. "Not at all. I'm pardoning Orma—not that the Censors will obey the edicts of an exiled Ardmagar. At midnight Eskar squirrels him away, and even I don't know where. It may be a very long time before you see him again."

"Don't tell me you're indulging emotional deviants!"

His pointed gaze held an intelligence I had not appreciated before. He said, "Indulging, no, but perhaps comprehending the hidden complexities better. I thought I knew which things we dragons should learn and which were unnecessary, but I see now that my opinions had calcified. I was as set in my thinking as the crusty old generals who've stolen my country."

He reached for my hand, lifted it, and clapped it to the side of his neck. I tried to pull away, but he held firm and said: "Let this signify my submission to your tutelage, since I doubt you would agree to bite the back of my neck. You are my teacher. I will listen, and I will try to learn."

"I will try to be worthy of your reverence," I said, my mother's words coming to me from the depths of the memory box. I felt compelled to add my own: "And I will try to sympathize with your efforts, even when you fail."

"Well put," he said, releasing me. "Now go. Tell your uncle you love him. You do love him, don't you?"

"Yes," I said, suddenly hoarse.

"Go. And Seraphina," he called after me, "I'm sorry about your mother. I believe I am." He gestured toward his stomach. "There, yes? That's where one feels it?"

I gave him full courtesy and hurried away.

⸙

An aged monk led me to the infirmary. "He's got the place to himself. Once the other invalids learned there was a dragon coming, they miraculously got well! The lame could walk and the blind decided they didn't really need to see. He's a panacea."

I thanked the man and entered quietly in case my uncle was sleeping. At the far end of the ward, beside the only window, he lay propped up by pillows, talking to Eskar. I drew closer and realized they weren't talking, exactly. Each raised a hand toward the other, touching just the fingertips together; they took turns running their fingertips down the other's palm.

I cleared my throat. Eskar rose, stone-faced and dignified. "Sorry!" I said, unsure why I was apologizing. It wasn't as though I'd caught them doing something naughty.

Except maybe I had, from a dragon's viewpoint. I clamped my mouth shut to prevent giggling. Eskar did not look like she would forgive giggling.

I said, "I wish to speak to my uncle before you take him away. Thank you for helping him."

She stood aside but showed no inclination to leave until Orma said: "Eskar, go. Come back later." She nodded curtly, drawing her cloak around her, and left.

I looked askance at him. "What were you two—"

"Stimulating cortical nerve responses," said my uncle, smiling eerily. The monks evidently had him on something for the pain. He seemed loose in the middle and soft around the edges. His right arm was wrapped and splinted; his jawline was mottled with white, what passes for bruising when you've got silver blood. I could not see where he'd been burned. His head lolled against the pillows. "She is rather majestic in her rightful shape. I'd forgotten. It's been years. She was Linn's agemate, you know. Used to come over to my mother's nest to gut aurochs."

"Do we trust her?" I said, hating to bring it up when he seemed so unconcerned. "She was responsible for Zeyd and Basind. Are you sure—"

"Not for Basind."

I frowned but did not pursue it. I tried to lighten my own mood by teasing him: "So you're off the hook, you devious old deviant."

His brows drew together, and I wondered whether I'd joked a bit too far. It turned out something else bothered him: "I don't know when I'll see you again."

I patted his arm, trying to smile. "At least you'll know me when you do see me."

"It could be a very long time, Seraphina. You could be middle-aged and married and have six children by then."

He was really out of it if he was talking this kind of nonsense. "I may be middle-aged, but no one would marry me, and surely I can't have children. A mule can't. Half-breeds are the end of the line."

He gazed beatifically into space. "I wonder if that's really true."

"I'm not wondering. I've come to say goodbye and wish you good journey, not speculate about my reproductive capabilities."

"You talk like a dragon," he said dreamily. He was getting drowsier.

I wiped my eyes. "I'm going to miss you so much!"

He rolled his head toward me. "I saved the little boy. He leaped from Imlann's neck to mine, and then I fell into the river, and he danced. He danced right on my belly, and I could feel it."

"He was dancing on you. Of course you could feel it."

"No, not that way. The other way. I wasn't in my saarantras, but I was . . . happy, for all that my legs were broken and the river icy. I was happy. And then Eskar landed, and I was grateful. And the sun shone, and I felt sad for my father. And for you."

"Why for me?"

"Because the Censors had finally fooled me, and I was going to be excised, and you would weep."

I was weeping now. "You'll be safe with Eskar."

"I know." He took my hand, squeezed it. "I can't bear that you'll be alone."

"Not alone. There are others of my kind. I'm going to find them."

"Who will kiss you? Who will rock you to sleep?" His voice was slow, drowsy.

"You never did," I said, trying to tease him. "You were more father to me than my father, but you never did that."

"Someone should. Someone should love you. I will bite him if he will not."

"Hush. You're talking nonsense now."

"Not nonsense. This is important!" He struggled to sit up straighter and failed. "Your mother once told me something, and I need to tell you . . . because you need . . . to understand it . . ."

His eyes fluttered shut, and he was quiet so long I thought he had fallen asleep, but then he said, in a voice so soft I could barely hear: "Love is not a disease."

I leaned my forehead on his shoulder, all the words I'd never spoken to him rushing my throat at once, forming a terrible lump there. Hesitantly he stroked my hair.

"I'm not completely certain she was right," he murmured, "But

I cannot let them cut you out of me, nor her either. I will cling to my sickness . . . if it is a sickness . . . I will hold it close to me like the . . . the sun, and the . . . "

He faded away again, this time for good. I sat with my arms around him until Eskar returned. I smoothed his hair off his forehead and kissed him lightly. Eskar stared. "Take good care of him, or I'll . . . I'll bite you!" I told her. She looked unconcerned.

The sky outside was blue, cold, and very far away; the sun was too bright to look at, let alone hold close to me. "But I will try, uncle," I murmured, "though it burns me. I will keep it close."

I hurried homeward through the slushy streets. I had a prince to find.

Thirty-Seven

When I reached the palace, there was a great crush of carriages at the gates. The city magistrates, the bishop, the Chapter, the guild leaders, the Queen's Guard—every important person in the city had arrived at once. Indoors, I was carried toward the great hall by a crowd of people, more than would comfortably fit inside, it turned out. Half of us were diverted back out to Stone Court.

Apparently the council had been short. We were about to hear the official results.

A balcony halfway up the wall was opened up to both the hall and the courtyard, such that someone with a loud voice could be heard in both places. Glisselda appeared there, waving to the roaring throng. She acted on her grandmother's behalf, but everyone who saw her that day, clad in white for her mother, her golden hair shining like any crown, knew they were in the presence of the next Queen. She awed us into silence.

She handed a folded letter to a herald, a particularly vociferous fellow, whose voice rang out clearly over the hushed crowd.

Generals of the Tanamoot:

Goredd rejects the legitimacy of your claim to sovereignty over the Dragon Lands. Ardmagar Comonot yet lives; petty threats will not induce us to turn him over, nor do we recognize the validity of these trumped-up charges against him. He is our proven friend and ally, author and champion of the peace, and the legitimate ruler of the Tanamoot.

If you push this toward war, do not foolishly imagine we are helpless, or that your own people will choose to fight for you rather than for continued cooperation between our species. This peace has been a true blessing upon the world, which is changed for the better; you cannot drag it back into the past.

Devoutly hoping we may settle this with words, I am,
Her Highness Princess Glisselda, First Heir of Goredd,
On behalf of Her Majesty Queen Lavonda the Magnificent

We applauded with heavy hearts, knowing that this was all the pretext the generals would need for war. Another conflict was coming, whether we willed it or not. I saw smirks on faces in the crowd and feared that some among us willed it in fact.

It took forever for the crowd to disperse; everyone wanted a

435

chance to petition the princess or the Ardmagar, swear loyalty, argue. The palace guard managed the crowds as best they could, but I did not see Kiggs anywhere. It wasn't like him not to be right in the thick of things.

Princess Glisselda had also contrived to disappear. I suspected Kiggs might be with her. There were two places outside the royal wing where someone like me could look. I had just set foot upon the grand stair, however, when a voice behind me stopped me short: "Tell me it isn't true, Seraphina. Tell me they're lying about you."

I looked back. The Earl of Apsig crossed the atrium toward me, his boots echoing upon the marble floor. I didn't ask what he meant. Ninys and Samsam had spread the news to every corner of the court. I gripped the balustrade tightly, bracing myself. "It's no lie," I said. "I am half dragon—like Lars."

He neither flinched nor rushed up to hit me—as I'd half feared he would. His face went slack with despair; he flopped himself onto the broad stone steps and sat with his head in his hands. For a moment I considered sitting beside him—he looked so sad!—but he was too unpredictable.

"What are we to do?" he said at last, throwing up his hands and looking up with red-rimmed eyes. "They've won. Nowhere is exclusively human; no side in this conflict is ours alone. They infiltrate everything, control everything! I joined the Sons of St. Ogdo because they seemed to be the only people willing to take action, the only ones looking the treaty in the eye and calling it what it was: our ruin."

He ran his hands through his hair, as if he might pull it out by the roots. "But who connected me with the Sons and urged me to get involved? That dragon, Lady Corongi."

"They're not all out to get us," I said softly.

"No? How about the one that tricked your father, or the one that deceived my mother and made her bear a bastard?"

I drew a sharp breath, and he glowered at me. "My mother raised Lars as if he were my equal. One day he began sprouting scales out of his very flesh. He was only seven; he showed us all, innocently rolled up his sleeve—" His voice broke; he coughed. "My father stabbed her right through the neck. It was his right, his injured honor. He might have killed Lars, too."

He stared at the air as if disinclined to speak further. "You didn't let him," I prompted. "You persuaded him otherwise."

He looked at me as if I were speaking Mootya. "Persuaded? No. I killed the old man. Pushed him off the round tower." He smiled mirthlessly at my shock. "We live in the remotest high-lands. This sort of thing happens all the time. I took my great-grandmother's family name to avoid awkward questions if I went to court in Blystane. Highland genealogies are complex; none of the coastal Samsamese keep track of them."

So that's what he was: not a dragon, but a parricide who'd changed his name. "What about Lars?"

"I told him I would kill him if I saw him again, and then I set him loose in the hills. I had no idea where he went until he popped up here, an avenging ghost sent to haunt me."

He glared at me sullenly, hating me for knowing too much, never mind that he himself had told me. I cleared my throat. "What will you do now?"

437

He rose, straightened the hem of his black doublet, and gave mocking courtesy. "I am returning to Samsam. I will make the Regent see sense."

His tone chilled me. "What kind of sense?"

"The only kind there is. The kind that puts humans first over animals."

With those words he stalked away across the atrium. He seemed to take all the air with him when he left.

I found Glisselda in Millie's room, weeping, her head in her hands. Millie, who was rubbing the princess's shoulders, looked alarmed that I had entered without knocking. "The princess is tired," said Millie, stepping toward me anxiously.

"It's all right," said Glisselda, wiping her eyes. Her hair was loose around her shoulders, and her blotchy pink cheeks made her look very young. She tried to smile. "I am always pleased to see you, Phina."

My heart constricted at the sight of her sorrow. She'd just lost her mother and had the weight of an entire realm thrust onto her shoulders, and I was a bad friend. I couldn't ask after Kiggs; I didn't know why it had ever seemed like a good idea.

"How are you holding up?" I said, taking a seat across from her. She looked at her hands. "Well enough in public. I was just taking a little time to . . . to let myself be a daughter. We have to sit vigil with St. Eustace tonight, the eyes of the world upon us," and we thought a quiet, dignified sorrow would be most fitting. That means taking some time to bawl like a baby now."

I thought she was referring to herself in the plural, as was her royal right, but she continued, "You should have seen us drafting that letter after council. I would weep, and Lucian would try to console me, which started him weeping and made me sob the more. I sent him to his beastly tower, told him to get it all out."

"He's lucky to have you looking out for him," I said, and meant it, however torn up I felt.

"The reverse is true," she said, her voice breaking. "But it is nearly sunset, and he has not yet come down." Her face crumpled; Millie hastened to her side and put an arm around her. "Would you go fetch him, Phina? I would take it as a great kindness."

It was a rotten time for my lying skills to fail me, but too many contradictory feelings crowded in on me at once. If I was kind to her for selfish reasons, was that worse than being virtuously unhelpful? Was there no course I could take that would not leave me wracked with guilt?

Glisselda noticed my hesitation. "I know he's been a bit cantankerous since learning you were half dragon," she said, leaning in toward me. "You understand, surely, that he might find it difficult to adjust to the idea."

"I think no less of him for it," I said.

"And I . . . I think no less of you," said Glisselda firmly. She rose; I rose with her, thinking she intended to dismiss me. She raised her arms a little and then dropped them—a false start—but then she steeled herself to it and embraced me. I hugged her back, unable to stop my own tears or to identify their source as relief or regret.

She let me go and stood with her chin raised. "It wasn't so difficult to accept," she said stoutly. "It was simply a matter of will."

Her protest was too vehement, but I recognized her good intention and believed utterly in her steely will. She said, "I shall scold Lucian if he is ever less than courteous to you, Seraphina. You let me know!"

I nodded, my heart breaking a little, and departed for the East Tower.

❧

At first I wasn't sure he was there. The tower door was unlocked, so I rushed up the stairs with my heart in my throat only to find the top room empty. Well, not entirely—it was full of books, pens, palimpsests, geodes and lenses, antique caskets, drawings. The Queen had her study; this was Prince Lucian's, charmingly untidy, everything in use. I hadn't appreciated the surroundings when we'd been up here with Lady Corongi. Now, all I saw were more things to love about him, and it made me sad.

The wind ran an icy finger up my neck; the door to the outer walkway was open a crack. I took a deep breath, willed down my vertigo, and opened the door.

He leaned upon the parapet, staring out over the sunset city. The wind tousled his hair; the edge of his cloak danced. I gingerly stepped out to him, picking my way around patches of ice, pulling my cloak tight around me for courage and for warmth.

He looked back at me, his dark eyes distant though not exactly unwelcoming. I stammered out my message: "Glisselda sent me to remind you, um, that everyone will be sitting with St. Eustace for her mother as soon as the sun goes down, and she, uh . . ."

"I haven't forgotten." He looked away. "The sun is not yet set, Seraphina. Would you stand with me awhile?"

I stepped to the parapet and watched the shadows lengthen in the mountains. Whatever resolve I might have had was setting with that sun. Maybe it was just as well. Kiggs would go down to his cousin; I would go traveling in search of the rest of my kind. Everything would be as it should be, on the surface at least, every untidy and inconvenient part of myself tucked away where no one would see it.

Saints' bones. I was done living like that.

"The truth of me is out," I said, my words crystallizing into cloud upon the icy air.

"All of it?" he said. He spoke less sharply than when he was truly interrogating me, but I could tell a lot was hinging on my answer.

"All the important parts, yes," I said firmly. "Maybe not all the eccentric details. Ask, and I will answer. What do you want to know?"

"Everything." He had been leaning on his elbows, but he pushed back now and gripped the balustrade with both hands. "It's always this way with me: if it can be known, I want to know it."

I did not know where to begin, so I just started talking. I told him about collapsing under visions, about building the garden, and about my mother's memories falling all around me like snow. I told him how I'd recognized Orma as a dragon, how the scales had erupted forth out of my skin, how it felt to believe myself utterly disgusting, and how lying became an unbearable burden.

It felt good to talk. The words rushed out of me so forcefully that I fancied myself a jug being poured out. I felt lighter when I had finished, and for once emptiness was a sweet relief and a condition to be treasured.

I glanced at Kiggs; his eyes had not glazed over yet, but I grew suddenly self-conscious about how long I'd been talking. "I'm sure I'm forgetting things, but there are things about myself I can't even fathom yet."

"'The world inside myself is vaster and richer than this paltry plane, peopled with mere galaxies and gods,'" he quoted. "I'm beginning to understand why you like Necans."

I met his gaze, and there was warmth and sympathy in his eyes. I was forgiven. No, better: understood. The wind rushed between us, blowing his hair about. Finally I managed to stammer, "There is one more . . . one true thing I want you to know, and I . . . I love you."

He looked at me intently but did not speak.

"I'm so sorry," I said, despairing. "Everything I do is wrong. You're in mourning; Glisselda needs you; you only just learned I'm half monster—"

"No part of you is monster," he said vehemently.

It took me a moment to find my voice again. "I wanted you to know. I wanted to go on from here with a clean conscience, knowing that I told you the truth at the last. I hope that may be worth something in your eyes."

He looked up at the reddening sky and said with a self-deprecating laugh, "You put me to shame, Seraphina. Your bravery always has."

"It's not bravery; it's bullheaded bumbling."

He shook his head, staring off into the middle distance. "I know courage when I see it, and when I lack it."

"You're too hard on yourself."

"I'm a bastard; it's what we do," he said, smiling bitterly. "You, of all people, understand the burden of having to prove that you are good enough to exist, that you are worth all the grief your mother caused everyone. Bastard equals monster in our hearts' respective lexicons; that's why you always had such insight into it."

He rubbed his hands together against the cold. "Are you willing to hear another self-pitying 'I was a sad, sad bastard child' story?"

"I'm happy to hear it; I've probably lived it."

"Not this story," he said, picking at a patch of lichen on the balustrade. "When my parents drowned and I first came here, I was angry. I did play the bastard, behaving as badly as such a young boy could contrive to behave. I lied, stole, picked fights with the page boys, embarrassed my grandmother every chance I got. I kept this up for years until she sent for Uncle Rufus—"

"Rest he on Heaven's hearthstone," we said together, and Kiggs smiled ruefully.

"She brought him all the way back from Samsam, thinking he'd have a firm enough hand to keep me in line. He did, although it was months before I would submit. There was an emptiness in me I did not understand. He saw it, and he named it for me. 'You're like your uncle, lad,' he said. 'The world is not enough for us without real work to do. The Saints mean to put you to some purpose. Pray, walk with an open heart, and you will hear the call. You will see your task shining before you, like a star.'

"So I prayed to St. Clare, but I took it a step further: I made her a promise. If she showed me the way, I would speak nothing but the truth from that day forward."

"St. Masha and St. Daan!" I blurted out. "I mean, that explains a lot."

He smiled, almost imperceptibly. "St. Clare saved me, and she bound my hands. But I'm skipping ahead. Uncle Rufus attended a wedding when I was nine years old, to provide a royal presence. I went with him. It was the first time they'd trusted me out of the castle walls in years, and I was anxious to show I could handle it."

"My father's wedding, where I sang," I said, my voice unexpectedly hoarse. "You told me. I do vaguely remember seeing the pair of you."

"It was a beautiful song," he said. "I've never forgotten. It still gives me chills to hear it."

I stared at his silhouette against the rusty sky, dumbfounded that this song of my mother's should be a favorite of his. It glorified romantic recklessness; it was everything he scorned to be or do. I could not stop myself. I began to sing, and he joined in:

Blessed is he who passes, love,

Beneath your window's eye

And does not sigh.

Gone my heart and gone my soul,

Look on me love, look down

Before I die.

One glimpse, my royal pearl, one smile

Sufficient to sustain me,

Grant me this,

Or take my life and make it yours:

I'd fight a hundred thousand wars

For just one kiss.

"Y-you're not a bad singer. You could join the castle choir," I said, casting about for something neutral to say so I wouldn't cry. My mother was as reckless as his, but she'd believed in this; she'd given everything she had. What if our mothers were not the fools we had taken them for? What was love really worth? A hundred thousand wars?

He smiled at his hands upon the parapet, and continued: "You sang, and then it hit me like a lightning strike, like the clarion of Heaven: the voice of St. Clare, saying, *The truth will out!* You yourself embodied the truth that could not be concealed or contained—not by a hundred fathers, or a hundred nursemaids— that would burst forth unbidden and fill the world with beauty. I knew I was to investigate the truth of things; I had been called to do this. I fell to my knees, thanked St. Clare, and swore I would not forget my vow to her."

I was staring at him, thunderstruck. "I was the truth, and beautiful? Heaven has a terrible sense of humor."

"I mistook you for a metaphor. But you're right about Heaven because otherwise how is it that I am in this position now? I made a promise and have kept it to the best of my ability—though I have lied to myself, may St. Clare forgive me. But I hoped to avoid this very trap where I am caught between my own feeling and the knowledge that uttering the truth aloud will hurt someone very important to me."

I barely dared think which truth he meant; I both hoped and dreaded that he would tell me.

His voice grew dense with sorrow. "I have been so preoccupied with you, Phina. I keep second-guessing myself. Could I have kept Aunt Dionne from Comonot's suite if I hadn't been dancing with you? I was so intent upon giving you that book. We might never have noticed Comonot leaving the ball but for Dame Okra."

"Or you might have stopped them both, and then gone up and toasted the New Year with Lady Corongi," I said, trying to reassure him. "You might be dead in that other scenario."

He threw up his hands, despairing. "I have struggled all my life to put thought before feeling, not to be as rash and irresponsible as my mother?"

"Ah, right, your mother, and her terrible crimes against her family!" I cried, angry with him now. "If I saw your mother in Heaven, you know what I would do? I would kiss her right on the mouth! And then I would drag her to the bottom of the Heavenly Stair and point at you down here, and say, 'Look what you did, you archfiend!'"

He looked scandalized, or startled anyway. I could not stop myself. "What could St. Clare have been thinking, choosing me as her unworthy instrument? She would have known I couldn't speak the truth to you."

"Phina, no," said Kiggs, and at first I thought he was scolding me for maligning St. Clare. He raised a hand, let it hover a moment, and then placed it over mine. It was warm, and it stole my breath away. "St. Clare did not choose wrongly," he said softly. "I always saw the truth in you, however much you prevaricated, even as you lied right to my face. I glimpsed the very heart of you, clear as sunlight, and it was something extraordinary."

He took up my hand between both of his. "Your lies didn't stop me loving you; your truth hasn't stopped me either."

I looked down reflexively; he was holding my left hand. He noticed my discomfiture and with a deft and delicate touch folded back my sleeve—all four of my sleeves—exposing my forearm to the frigid air, the fading sunset, and the emerging stars. He ran his thumb along the silver line of scales, his brow puckering in concern at the scab, and then, with a sly glance at me, he bowed his head and kissed my scaly wrist.

I couldn't breathe; I was overcome. I didn't usually feel much through my scales, but I felt that to the soles of my feet.

He replaced my sleeves, respectfully, as if draping a Saint's altar. He kept my hand between his, warming it. "I was thinking about you, before you came up. Thinking, praying, and reaching no conclusion. I was inclined to leave love unspoken. Let us get through this war; let Glisselda grow into her crown. The day will come, please Heaven, when I can tell her this without throwing us

447

all into chaos. Maybe she would release me from my promise, but maybe not. I may have to marry her in any case, because she must marry, and I remain her best option. Can you live with that?"

"I don't know," I said. "But you're right: she needs you."

"She needs us both," he said, "and she needs us not to be so distracted by each other that we are unable to do our parts in this war."

I nodded. "Crisis first, love later. The day will come, Kiggs. I believe that."

His brow creased fretfully. "I hate keeping this from her; it's deceit. Small lies are no better than big ones, but if we could please keep everything to a minimum until—"

"Everything?" I said. "Porphyrian philosophy? Amusing tales of bastardy?"

He smiled. Ah, I could last a long time on those smiles. I would sow and reap them like wheat.

"You know what I mean," he said.

"You mean you're not going to kiss my wrist again," I said. "But that's all right, because I am going to kiss you."

And I did.

If I could keep a single moment for all time, that would be the one.

I became the very air; I was full of stars. I was the soaring spaces between the spires of the cathedral, the solemn breath of chimneys, a whispered prayer upon the winter wind. I was silence, and I was music, one clear transcendent chord rising toward Heaven. I believed, then, that I would have risen bodily into the sky but for the anchor of his hand in my hair and his round soft perfect mouth.

No Heaven but this! I thought, and I knew that it was true to a standard even St. Clare could not have argued.

Then it was done, and he was holding both my hands between his and saying, "In some ballad or Porphyrian romance, we would run off together."

I looked quickly at his face, trying to discern whether he was proposing we do just that. The resolve written in his eyes said no, but I could see exactly where I would have to push, and how hard, to break that resolve. It would be shockingly easy, but I found I did not wish it. My Kiggs could not behave so shabbily and still remain my Kiggs. Some other part of him would break, along with his resolve, and I did not see a way to make it whole again. The jagged edge of it would stab at him all his life.

If we were to go forward from here, we would proceed not rashly, not thoughtlessly, but Kiggs-and-Phina fashion. That was the only way it could work.

"I think I've heard that ballad," I said. "It's beautiful but it ends sadly."

He closed his eyes and leaned his forehead against mine. "Is it less sad that I'm going to ask you not to kiss me again?"

"Yes. Because it's just for now. The day will come."

"I want to believe that."

"Believe it."

He took a shaky breath. "I've got to go."

"I know."

I let him go inside first; my presence was not appropriate for tonight's ritual. I leaned against the parapet, watching my breath puff gray against the blackening sky as if I were a dragon whispering smoke into the wind. The conceit made me smile, and then an idea caught me. Cautiously, avoiding ice, I hauled myself up onto the parapet. It had a wide balustrade, adequate for sitting, but I did not intend merely to sit. With comical slowness, like Como- not attempting stealth, I drew my feet up onto the railing. I re- moved my shoes, wanting to feel the stone beneath my feet. I wanted to feel everything.

I rose to standing, like Lars upon the barbican, the dark city spread at my feet. Lights twinkled in tavern windows, bobbed at the Wolfstoot Bridge construction. Once I had been suspended over this vast space, hanging and helpless, at a dragon's mercy. Once I had feared that telling the truth would be like falling, that love would be like hitting the ground, but here I was, my feet firmly planted, standing on my own.

We were all monsters and bastards, and we were all beautiful. I'd had more than my share of beautiful today. Tomorrow I'd give some back, restore and replenish the world. I'd play at Prin- cess Dionne's funeral; I'd put myself on the program this time, on purpose, since there was no longer any need for me to stay out of the public eye. I might as well stand up and give what I had to give. The wind whipped my skirts around, and I laughed. I stretched my arm up toward the sky, spreading my fingers, imagining my hand a nest of stars. On impulse, I threw my shoes as hard as I could at the night, crying, "Scatter darkness! Scatter silence!" They accelerated at thirty-two feet per second squared, landing some- where in Stone Court, but Zeyd was wrong about the inevitability of hurtling toward our doom. The future would come, full of war and uncertainty, but I would not be facing it alone. I had love and work, friends and a people. I had a place to stand.

Cast of Characters

At Dombegh House

Seraphina Dombegh—our charming heroine, often called Phina

Claude Dombegh—her father, a lawyer with a secret

Amaline Ducanahan—Phina's counterfeit mother

Linn—Phina's real mother, alas

Orma—Phina's mysterious mentor

Zeyd—Phina's former tutor, a dragon

Anne-Marie—Phina's not-so-wicked stepmother

Tessie, Jeanne, Paul, and Nedward—the moderately wicked stepsiblings

THE GOREDDI ROYAL FAMILY

Queen Lavonda—a monarch who faces down dragons

Prince Rufus—the Queen's only son, inexplicably murdered

Princess Dionne—the Queen's surly daughter, first heir to the throne

Princess Glisselda—Princess Dionne's cheerful daughter, second heir to the throne

Princess Laurel—the Queen's other daughter, dead of elopement

Prince Lucian Kiggs—Princess Laurel's embarrassing bastard, fiancé of Princess Glisselda, Captain of the Queen's Guard, possessor of too many descriptors

AT COURT

Viridius—the irascible court composer

Guntard—a professional musician

scrawny sackbut player—exactly as you imagine

Lady Miliphrene—Princess Glisselda's favorite lady-in-waiting, called Millie

Lady Corongi—Princess Glisselda's governess, an antique despot

Dame Okra Carmine—the Ninysh ambassador, an antique darling

Josef, Earl of Apsig—a Samsamese lordling

Regent of Samsam—the regent of Samsam

Count Pesavolta—the ruler of Ninys

Our Draconic Friends

Ardmagar Comonot—the leader of the dragon world

Ambassador Fulda—the dragon with the best manners

Undersecretary Eskar—Fulda's laconic second-in-command

Basind—a walleyed newskin

Noble Banished Knights

Sir Karal Halfholder—obeys the law, even if the infernal fiends do not

Sir Cuthberte Pettybone—his somewhat less humor-impaired comrade

Sir James Peascod—once knew General Gann from General Gonn

Squire Maurizio Foughfaugh—one of the last practitioners of dracomachia

Squire Pender—the other one

IN TOWN

Sons of St. Ogdo—unhappy with the treaty

Lars—the genius behind the clock

Thomas Broadwick—a cloth merchant

Silas Broadwick—the reason they call them Broadwick Bros. Clothiers

Abdo—a dancer in a pygegyria troupe

A pygegyria troupe—and there's the rest of them now

IN PHINA'S HEAD

Fruit Bat—the climber

Pelican Man—putting the grotesque in "grotesque"

Miserere—the feathery one

Newt—the wallowing one

Loud Lad—the noisy one

Jannoula—too curious for her own good

Miss Fusspots—the finicky one

Pandowdy—the swamp thing

Nag and Nagini—the speedy twins

Gargoyella and Finch—mentioned in passing

Five more—to be named in a future publication

In Legend and in Faith

Queen Belondweg—the first Queen of united Goredd, subject of the national epic

Pau-Henoa—her trickster rabbit companion, also called the Mad Bun and Hen-Wee

St. Capiti—representing the life of the mind, Phina's patroness

St. Yirtrudis—the spooky heretic, Phina's other patroness, alas

St. Clare—lady of perspicacity, Prince Lucian Kiggs's patroness

Glossary

Allsaints—all the Saints in Heaven, invoked as a unit. Not a deity, exactly; more like a collective

apse—part of a cathedral behind the quire and altar (and Golden House, in Goreddi cathedrals), often with radiating chapels

ard—Mootya for "order, correctness"; may also denote a battalion of dragons

Ardmagar—title held by the leader of dragonkind; translates roughly to "supreme general"

aurochs—large, wild cattlebeast; extinct in our world, but existed in Europe until the Renaissance

binou—type of bagpipe, used in traditional Breton music in our world

cloister—peaceful garden surrounded by a colonnade, where monks may engage in peripatetic meditation

Comonot's Treaty—agreement that established peace between Goredd and dragonkind

Daanite—homosexual; named for St. Daan, who was martyred for that particular quality, along with his lover, St. Masha

dagged—deep scalloping, as of houppelande sleeves

dracomachia—martial art developed specifically for fighting dragons; according to legend, it was invented by St. Ogdo

Golden House—model of Heaven found in the center of Goreddi cathedrals and larger churches

Golden Plays—dramas depicting the lives of the Saints, put on by the guilds of Lavondaville during Golden Week

Golden Week—cluster of Saints' days at midwinter, bookended by Speculus and Treaty Eve. It is traditional to see the Golden Plays, walk circuits around the Golden House, hang Speculus lanterns, throw parties, give gifts to friends and charities, and make grandiose pronouncements for the coming year.

Goredd—Seraphina's homeland (adjective form: Goreddi)

Heaven—Goreddis don't believe in a singular deity, but they believe in an afterlife, the dwelling of Allsaints

houppelande—robe of rich material with voluminous sleeves, usually worn belted; women's are floor-length; a man's might be cut at the knee

ityasaari—Porphyrian for "half-dragon"

Ker—council of dragon generals that advises the Ardmagar

Lavondaville—Seraphina's hometown and the largest city in Goredd, named for Queen Lavonda

Mootya—language of dragons, rendered in sounds a human voice can make

nave—main body of a cathedral, where the congregation gathers for services

newskin—dragon who is inexperienced at taking human form and living among humans

Ninys—country southeast of Goredd (adjective form: Ninysh)

oud—lutelike instrument, common in Middle Eastern music in our world, often played with a pick, or plectrum

Porphyry—small country, almost a city-state, northwest of the Southlands; originally a colony of dark-skinned people from even further north

psalter—book of devotional poetry, usually illustrated; in Goreddi psalters, there's a poem for each of the major Saints

pygegyria—Porphyrian for "bum-waggling"; an acrobatic variation of belly dancing

pyria—sticky, flammable substance used in dracomachia for setting dragons on fire; also called St. Ogdo's fire

Quighole—dragon and quigutl ghetto in Lavondaville

quigutl—subspecies of dragon, which can't transform. They are flightless; they have an extra set of arms and terrible breath. Often shortened to "quig."

quire—enclosed area behind the altar of a cathedral (or behind the Golden House in a Goreddi cathedral), where the choir and clergy sit facing each other on benches

saar—Porphyrian for "dragon"; often used by Goreddis as a short form of "saarantras"

saarantras—Porphyrian for "dragon in human form" (plural form: saarantrai)

462

sackbut—medieval ancestor of the trombone

St. Bert's Collegium—once St. Jobertus's Church, now a school in Quighole where saarantrai scholars teach mathematics, science, and medicine to those brave enough to attend

St. Capiti—patroness of scholars; carries her head on a plate

St. Clare—patroness of the perceptive

St. Gobnait's—cathedral in Lavondaville; St. Gobnait is patroness to the diligent and persistent. Her symbol is the bee, hence the skep in her cathedral.

St. Ida's—music conservatory in Lavondaville; St. Ida is the patroness of musicians and performers

St. Masha and St. Daan—the lovers; often invoked in anger, perhaps because it's safe—it's hard to imagine paragons of romantic love actually smiting anyone

St. Ogdo—founder of dracomachia; patron of knights and of all Goredd

St. Vitt—champion of the faith; this one will smite people, particularly unbelievers

St. Willibald's—covered market in Lavondaville; St. Willibald is the patron of marketplaces and news

St. Yirtrudis—the heretic; it's an open question how there can be a heretical Saint

Samsam—country south of Goredd (adjective form: Samsamese)

shawm—medieval instrument similar to an oboe

skep—old-fashioned beehive made of woven straw

Southlands—three nations clustered together at the southern end of the world: Goredd, Ninys, and Samsam

Speculus—Goreddi holiday on the winter solstice, intended to be a long night of reflection

Tanamoot—dragons' country

transept—wings of a cathedral built perpendicular to the nave

Treaty Eve—celebration commemorating the signing of Comonot's Treaty, concurrent with New Year's Eve

Ziziba—very distant land indeed, far to the north; home to many strange beasts such as crocodiles and camelopards (adjective form: Zibou)

Acknowledgments

My heartfelt thanks to: my sisters (including Josh); my parents, stepparents, and in-laws; Dr. George Pepe; Mac and the Children's Book World gang; my intrepid Beta Readers; the Sparkly Capes and Oolicans; Epicurus; George Eliot; Lois McMaster Bujold; and Arwen, Els, and Liz.

Thanks to Dan Lazar, my agent, who has the singular ability to see things that aren't there yet. Thanks to Jim Thomas, my editor, who understands the correlation between laughing at my jokes and getting me to work hard.

To Scott and Byron, who made me laugh when I was grumpy and gave me reasons to keep working. And thanks to Una, whose tiny whippet bladder ensured that I went for several walks each day.

SERAPHINA

Bonus Material

A Q&A with Rachel Hartman

Rachel Hartman's Favorite Authors

"The Audition,"
a Prequel Short Story

A Q&A with Rachel Hartman

Seraphina is full of remarkable characters and concepts. Where do you get your ideas?

A better question might be where *don't* I get my ideas; they can be so plentiful. At times, I have even imagined my mind as a fishing net. As I go about my day, ideas collect in the net, seemingly unbidden. As you might imagine, most of these ideas don't turn out to be productive. But the trick is to entertain all comers—you can never be sure which idea will turn into something more.

For example, many years ago, when I was dealing with my parents' divorce, I had an idea: What if you married someone with a secret, and you didn't learn about it until it was too late? Despite how difficult a time that was for me, I held on to the idea. It turned out to be the very first inkling of what would eventually grow into *Seraphina*.

Is there something that inspires you to turn such ideas into stories?

In the novel, Seraphina's mother leaves Seraphina a mind pearl, a moment from her life so vividly recorded that Seraphina can experience what her mother was thinking and feeling. Part of what motivates me as a writer is to do the same for readers. It might be as simple as the feeling I get walking down the street under wet trees, the drizzle on my face, my dog tugging the leash, clarinet music drifting down from a window above. For me, art is the desire to preserve the intangible feeling of such a moment, hidden in all the littlest details, and then to communicate that to others.

I'm also excited by the fantasy genre in general. It can be a terrific laboratory for thought experiments. For example, what if dragons could transform into humans? You can entertain the strangest ideas and then follow them through to their logical conclusions. What could be more fun?

The world of *Seraphina* is incredibly well realized. When did you first conceive it?

Believe it or not, it was way back in the seventh grade. I had to write a narrative poem for English class and ended up writing a long (and silly) one called "The First Adventure of Sir Amy," about a girl knight. She lived in a land called Goredd (because it rhymed with Fred, which was the name of her horse).

I wrote some myths set in Goredd when I was a teenager, and then in my twenties I wrote and illustrated a comic book about the girl from the poem, which really solidified Goredd in my imagination.

Once you decided to write a novel based on Goredd and its characters, how long did it take? What was that process like?

The creation of *Seraphina* took many twists and turns. Originally I wrote the story as a family drama, consisting largely of Phina and her father keeping secrets from each other.

It wasn't long, however, before I realized that the story I'd written wasn't taking advantage of this huge world I'd created. Draft after draft, the story expanded to better fill it. It took several iterations for me to get to the point where the plot was on a scale comparable to the larger canvas. The entire process, from inception to publication, took about nine years. That includes four distinct versions of the book, two different publishers, and a few years of only being able to write during my son's naptimes!

The choice to set the world in a medieval time period is interesting, especially with all the saints. Are you a student of the real Middle Ages?

When I was sixteen I had an opportunity to live in England for a year. The medieval art, architecture, and literature that I was exposed to exerted a grip on my imagination that has never let go. I'm also fascinated by the fact that, even though we tend to think we know what the Middle Ages was all about, there's plenty that would be alien to us.

For example, religion pervaded all aspects of medieval life to a degree we moderns would never understand. Even in a fictional Middle Ages, I couldn't imagine that religion wouldn't have its fingers in absolutely everything. I got the idea for the saint-based religion of Goredd when traveling in Ireland. There are lots of obscure Irish saints, and scholars believe that some of them used to be minor pagan deities who were converted when the Irish became Christian. In Goredd, St. Gobnait, the patroness of the cathedral in Lavondaville, is named for one of these Irish saints—possibly a pagan smith-god—whose sacred well I visited.

The story features several strong, intelligent, and independent women. Not only Seraphina but also Princess Glisselda, Dame Okra Carmine, and even Undersecretary Eskar (though she's a dragon, of course!). Is that a realistic reflection of our history's medieval past?

I've read a lot about the real lives of medieval women. One book I found particularly inspiring was *Women in the Medieval Town*, by Erika Uitz. Using historical records, Uitz shows how medieval women were actually far more involved in business than is generally supposed. They weren't allowed to own businesses, but there were exceptions. A widow, for example, could inherit her husband's business or his place in a guild. Wherever the law presented a loophole, women took advantage of it; wherever obstacles could be circumvented, disregarded, or knocked down, women found the way to do it.

Talk about the dragons in the story. Where did the idea come from for them to be able to take human form? What about their struggle with human emotions and sensations?

When I wrote that comic book about Goredd, I planned on having dragon characters. I quickly discovered, however, that I was bad at drawing dragons; they came out looking like fanged kangaroos. I decided that if dragons could take human form, I could just draw humans, which would be a lot easier. What I didn't realize until much later was that this lazy solution was a gold mine of interesting questions and ideas.

For example, if dragons could take human shape, just how far would the transformation go? Would their internal organs be human as well? They would have a different set of senses, surely. As apex predators, dragons in their natural state would have excellent eyesight and a keen sense of smell. Would they find those senses frustratingly muted while in human form? Conversely, would human skin seem extra sensitive compared to their usual scaly hides? Would their clothes itch? As fire-breathers, dragons wouldn't have much sense of taste; they'd burn their taste buds right off. So what would it be like, then, to taste something sweet for the first time?

From tactile feeling, it was a short hop to emotional feeling.

Reptiles and apex predators tend not to be very social, and dragons are both. In their natural state they might not have emotions beyond the relatively straightforward fight-or-flight response, which in humans might manifest as anger or fear. The softer emotions—love, empathy, sorrow—are surely a messy mammalian characteristic that evolved to help us bond with our young and to facilitate social groups. When these reptilian apex predators assumed human form and their brains started to process such emotions, what sort of shock would they experience?

I decided that most of them would find it overwhelming, and that dragons would be likely to react with strict rules and repression. That's the seed from which all of dragon society grew.

Seraphina's garden of grotesques is another fascinating element of the story. Where did that idea come from?

The garden of grotesques was inspired by an ancient mnemonic device known as the memory palace. The idea behind a memory palace is that you memorize the layout of an enormous building with lots of connected rooms. If you want to remember items on a list, you visualize walking through the palace, leaving one item in each room. I was struck by how much the concept resembled my writer's mind, which is so full of places and people. And I was deeply intrigued by the idea that the mind might have its own geography. Phina takes it a bit further and makes it more literal, but it's the same idea.

Seraphina is a compelling character. How much of yourself

do you see in her, or in any of the characters? Are any of them modeled after real people?

I put a lot of myself into Seraphina but also into all the characters. Being a writer is something akin to being an actor: you have to dig deep and find the part of yourself that's a dragon, a musician, or a queen. It's an exercise in radical empathy.

That said, I also draw from my observations of others. If you put my friends and family into a big bag and shook them up, you might be able to piece together a character or two, but there is no one-to-one correspondence.

Several of the characters are named after real people who share traits with them. Lucian Kiggs is named after Lucian of Samosata, an ancient Greek satirist. Lars is named after the drummer of the (very loud) rock band Metallica. Abdo is named for George Abdo, a popularizer of the classical Egyptian style of belly dancing known as raqs sharqi. Orma is named after a guy I once met named Norman. I suspected he was a dragon (don't ask why), but "Norman the Dragon" just didn't have the right ring to it. The obvious solution was to remove the consonants from each end of his name.

Seraphina and Kiggs talk a lot about philosophy and philosophers. It's an important part of their relationship. Is philosophy important to you in your life?

It is, to a certain extent. I am drawn to the philosophy of Epicurus, who felt that happiness was the greatest good, and that the only things we need to be happy are autonomy, friendship, and time to contemplate our problems. While I'm an artist and not a philosopher, I'm fascinated by the degree to which the two disciplines intersect. Both ask the big questions: What is goodness? What is truth? Is there a point to it all?

Philosophy and art can sometimes be two sides of the same coin, like theoretical and experimental physics. (My husband is a physicist, so forgive me this comparison!) The theorists (like philosophers) reason themselves into a particular position; the experimentalists (like artists) run those theories through mazes and hit them with rubber chickens to see how they hold up.

Art doesn't offer definitive answers. It offers possibilities, more questions, and—at its best—a different lens through which to view the world. If you find philosophers or anyone else who's smug about having found answers, bring them to art. Art, like a rambunctious toddler, will play with those answers until they break.

What about music? Does it play as large a role in your life as it does in Seraphina's?

I love music, but I'm no court composer! When I was about ten, I started to study the cello. My sisters both played string instruments, and we had great fun playing and singing together. Our particular favorite was early music, meaning music that dates from the Renaissance and before. I modeled the music of Goredd after early baroque and wrote all the songs in the book, though only "Peaches and Cheese" has a tune that goes with it.

I almost always listen to music while I write. I tend to put a song on endless repeat as a way of sustaining a specific mood for a scene. Italian polyphony, for example, is evocative of majestic cathedrals, whereas something a touch surreal—a band like Yes or an artist like Frank Zappa—is better suited to writing about the garden of grotesques. I find that a really strong song can handle many listens and still be my friend afterward.

Are there any books so influential that they changed your life? Which ones?

Oh my, yes. I'll have to limit myself to two, or I could go on all day. First is Tove Jansson's *Finn Family Moomintroll*, which my mother read to me when I was five. She wouldn't read it again because she thought it was creepy; I solved that problem by learning to read. Second is Mark Alan Stamaty's *Who Needs Donuts?* I loved that book intensely as a child, and it continues to be the most surreal picture book I have ever read. It taught me that anything, no matter how grotesque or bizarre, is possible in art.

When did you start writing, and why?

It didn't cross my mind that writing was something one could do—for a career or for fun—until I was in the sixth grade. My teacher introduced the concept of creative writing, and I was instantly in love with it. I would pursue my creative writing assignments above and beyond what was required, sometimes to the detriment of my other homework. One day she returned one of my poems

with a note at the bottom that said, *Rachel, you are a real writer!*
I believed her, because she was my favorite teacher, and writing
has been a part of my identity ever since.

It took me a long time to decide to make a career of it, though.
Maybe already believing that I was a writer set me back; I didn't
have to publish anything to prove it to myself. Then I had a baby
and moved to Canada. In a way, I was starting my life over; it was
the perfect opportunity to get serious about writing.

I'm really glad I did.

Rachel Hartman's Favorite Authors

To me, art—whether it's books or painting or theater—is a conversation that's been going on since the beginning of history, with voices chiming in from every side, saying, "Here's what I felt, thought, and saw. Here's what it meant to be me."

Sometimes those voices are able to bridge time and place to speak directly to our experiences. At such moments, it's almost as if the mind *behind* the art can be perceived. It's like meeting a new friend, one who has the power to change our lives. Sadly, in many cases, we aren't able to thank this new and valuable friend.

That's one of the reasons why I write. It's my thanks, and my casting forward to some young reader of the future who needs to hear me say, "Others have walked this way. You are not alone."

Here are some of the authors who are in conversation with *Seraphina*:

Terry Pratchett. He asks a lot of the same questions I do, and comes up with hilarious answers. I love his Discworld books, particularly *Going Postal*, *Thud!*, and his Tiffany Aching series.

Lois McMaster Bujold. Her Miles Vorkosigan books are like Jane Austen in space, but it was *The Curse of Chalion* that showed me it was possible to write a story that was both large and personal.

George Eliot. *Middlemarch* is my single favorite book of all time. It's a model of compelling world-building, exquisite characterization, and delicately rendered variations on themes.

Diana Wynne Jones. She unabashedly positions her personal preoccupations at center stage; I aspire to be that transparent and humane. *Howl's Moving Castle* and *Fire and Hemlock* showcase her unique magic in all its complexity.

John Green. I had always thought that we wrote the same genre, "Books Where the Author Is Preoccupied with Philosophy," but I've since been told that that's not a genre. My favorite book of his is *An Abundance of Katherines*, the most nakedly epistemological of his treatises.

Anne McCaffrey. Her Harper Hall trilogy was a great favorite of mine when I was twelve. Like *Seraphina*, it deals with dragons and music. I owe it a debt of inspiration, even if we worked the subject from different angles.

Epicurus. None of his books survive. Most of what we know of his philosophy, we know from other writers. He's worth looking for, but you really have to look. There is joy in the search.

Before Seraphina was assistant to the court composer, she had to try out for the job!

Meet Orma, Glisselda, Viridius, and Seraphina for the first time in—

THE AUDITION

I t is perfectly normal—human, even—to want moral support during a difficult audition. I couldn't have taken my father. If he'd had any inkling that I wished to become the assistant to the court composer, he'd have tried to stop me, and auditions are arduous enough without climbing out my bedroom window first. My half siblings would have told Papa, and I had no friends to ask. So if I wanted a sympathetic face in the crowd, my only choice was my music teacher, the dragon Orma.

He's better than nothing, I told myself, but that was debatable. He'd spent years in human shape, but inside he was still a dragon: an unemotional, hyperrational being who, hard as he tried, could not quite master manners or understand why blurting out criticisms during my flute performance was utterly unhelpful. By the final day of auditions, I regretted having brought him.

As we climbed Castle Hill that balmy autumn afternoon, I decided to send him back. It was impossible to hurt a dragon's feelings, but I still felt guilty. He'd dressed up for our palace visit in a dark doublet and hose, and had even slicked down his shrubby hair, though it was slowly puffing back up as it dried. He sauntered along beneath the golden linden trees, oblivious to my anxiety, probably solving equations in his head.

When we reached the stern shadow of the barbican gate, I stopped him and said, "Thank you for accompanying me to these difficult auditions, Orma. Today I have merely to give Princess Glisselda her music lesson. That won't interest you. If you've been neglecting work at the conservatory, I shouldn't keep you from it."

"You're one of three finalists," he said, pushing his spectacles up his beaky nose. "You were the most inexperienced and the only female in a field of twenty-seven. I initially put your odds at one in fifteen hundred. The lute master and the troubadour are still in it, though—"

"Get to the point," I said, glancing over my shoulder at the helmeted guards in the gatehouse. They watched us with detached interest. Orma was exempt from the bell most dragons were required to wear; he looked like nothing more than a tall, gangly scholar. Still, I always worried that men with swords would use them in preemptive self-defense if they worked out the truth.

Orma said loudly, "You have a twelve percent chance of becoming Master Viridius's assistant."

My shoulders sagged. "Twelve whole percent? Thanks."

"You're welcome."

His incomprehension of my tone nettled me. "And you still want to come?"

"Of course." He scratched his beard. "These are the best odds you've faced yet."

We walked on. The smile I gave the barbican guards was entirely fake, but I'd worn my best gown, the dark blue merino, and Orma managed to keep quiet. We looked respectable enough. The guards didn't question us, though their eyes followed Orma. They probably thought he was bothering me; they weren't wrong.

I was the last finalist to arrive at Master Viridius's office. The aged composer sat not at his desk but upon a gout couch, with his legs propped up to keep them comfortable. His clawlike hands were wrapped in bandages; his knees and feet were grossly swollen. The sight of him had filled me with horror on the first day of auditions and pity on the second, but had not diminished my determination to be his assistant. I had long admired the old composer's music. His *Fantasias* were the first keyboard pieces Orma had taught me, and I'd instantly loved their liveliness and strength.

Master Viridius frowned as I came in. "Maid Dombegh! You deign to join us," he drawled. "You will go third, as our designated laggard."

I curtsied, abashed.

He waved a hand irritably. "Wait your turns in the antechamber. I have a fearsome headache and can't bear the sound of nervous squirming."

The lute master, whose trial was first, followed a page boy out to wherever Princess Glisselda awaited her lesson. The rest of us filed into the narrow antechamber. It had a bench along each wall; Orma and I sat opposite the troubadour. Orma put his feet up on the troubadour's bench, rudely blocking the walkway until I swatted his knees. I kept myself occupied by composing motets in my head and watching the troubadour. He wore silk hose he probably couldn't afford, held his plumed cap in his lap, and looked anxious. Beside me, Orma jotted notes in a little book. I glanced over. He'd written *Books to Look for in the Queen's Private Library*.

"You can't go to the Queen's private library," I whispered harshly at him.

"Then this list is for you," he said, not bothering to whisper. "You'll have access, surely, when you get the job. I'll list the books in the order I'd like to read them."

"*When* I get the job? Twelve percent, Orma!"

He shrugged. "Twelve percent if you don't do anything unpredictable. There's a sixty-eight percent chance that you will surprise me. I can show you my work."

He turned a page and began calculating. I closed my eyes, exasperated.

An hour and six pages of algebra later, the lute master returned, raging, flailing, and blackened from head to toe. He brushed against the troubadour's knee in passing, leaving a dark smudge, marched into Master Viridius's office, and slammed the door. Even so, we heard him plainly: "I will not be humiliated in this manner! I withdraw my name from your consideration, sir!"

He burst open the door and stalked out, shedding a cloud of

486

coal dust behind him. The troubadour, dabbing at his dirtied silk with a handkerchief, met my eye and smiled weakly. It was down to the two of us now.

The page boy returned with the next summons. The troubadour straightened his doublet, made St. Ida's sign, and left. The door of Master Viridius's office opened; I turned to see the old man standing there, propped with two canes, staring after the troubadour. He noticed me watching him and scowled from under his bushy eyebrows. "The lute master is an idiot," said the old composer gruffly. "Never even gave the brat her lesson, because he got lost down a coal chute. I'm sure you need not worry about a thing."

I hadn't been worried until he said that, of course. He pulled his head back into his office like some cranky, liver-spotted turtle and closed the door.

I turned to my moral support, suddenly needing some—but Orma was gone.

Anyone might receive a call of nature, even a dragon; I didn't require an elaborate narration of where he was going every time he left the room. Anyone *else*, however, might be relied upon to come straight back. Minutes crawled by, and I grew more convinced that he'd wandered somewhere he shouldn't.

The page boy skipped back into the room. I thought he was summoning me to the princess's lesson, but he said impudently, "Are you here with that beardy villain? The one with the nose?"

"Yes," I said, already on my feet.

"He's met with a bit of awkwardness; he said you'd help him."

"Where is he?" I said.

The lad gave me directions—up the stairs, to the right—but showed no inclination to accompany me. I rushed up the corridor as fast as I dared; the Queen's council had just been dismissed, and the hallway was full of my betters. When I reached the grand marble staircase, I hoisted my skirts and took the steps by twos, earning disapproving looks from descending ladies-in-waiting. My face grew warm with embarrassment and exertion, but I didn't slow down. At the top, I ducked up the right-hand corridor and ran headlong into a girl standing on a chair.

She screamed, but did not fall or drop the bucket she held, which sloshed alarmingly. "St. Daan in a pan! Are you blind?" she cried.

It took me a second to catch my breath. "Excuse me," I said.

"You are evidently some species of oaf," she said, sneering at me from her perch. "I suppose you can't help it."

She was petite but not much younger than me. I guessed fifteen. Golden curls framed her face like the sun risen above her gown of sky-blue silk. She'd planted her chair before a set of double doors. She tapped her foot on the wooden seat, swirling the chunky liquid in her pail. Whatever it was, it smelled foul.

"Take this." She thrust the reeking bucket at me. "You may as well help. You're tall; I can't quite reach, even with the chair."

"I'm sorry, I can't stay," I said, recoiling from the stench. "My music teacher—"

"That beanpole of a scholar?" she said. "He's fine. He tripped over me, too, but we made it up and I sent him on his way."

I looked past her up the corridor. "Where is he?"

She scowled and shoved the pail in my face. "He's *fine*. Your assistance, oaf."

My hands accepted the bucket over the protestations of my nose, which had caught an overpowering whiff of fish. I gazed into the brown ooze. Silver scales winked merrily in the murk; the dark buttons lurking in the depths were surely eyes. I swallowed my revulsion. "What do I do with it?"

"What do I do with it, *Your Highness*," she corrected, folding her hands in front of her stomach. Beaded birds frolicked among golden clouds on her bodice.

I fell into my deepest curtsy, awkwardly executed thanks to the bucket in my hands. *Your Highness* plus her age could only equal the Queen's granddaughter, Princess Glisselda, although I did not see how it was possible. To my knowledge, she ought to have been at a music lesson with the troubadour at this very moment.

"Rise," she said. "I did not catch your name."

"Seraphina Dombegh, Your Highness." I straightened, holding the fishy ferment away from my body. The smell persisted, undiminished by distance.

The princess hopped down, light as a finch. She barely came up to my shoulder. "Well, Maid Dombegh," she said, "we are setting a trap for my last prospective music tutor."

My mouth fell open. This bucket of goo was meant for me!

Clearly, the princess didn't realize who I was. My voice quavered a little as I said, "Is there some particular problem with this tutor, that you feel the need to—"

"Oh no," she said breezily. "I've not met any of Viridius's finalists. I despise them all equally, on principle. I sent the first one—that weedy lute master—on a wild-goose chase through the cellars, ending with a special trip down the coal chute."

I dreaded to ask but had to know: "What did you do to the troubadour?"

Her eyes lit up; she hopped on her toes. "I'll show you!"

She pushed open the double doors and led me through a small study, or perhaps a schoolroom, furnished with two tables and a bookcase. A map spread on one table had been heavily annotated; pens, books, and wooden markers were scattered across it. She picked her way across to the windows, which overlooked a walled garden with a hedge maze at the far end. The princess plopped herself down on the embrasure seat and opened the casement. She patted the embroidered cushion beside her. I balanced on its edge, the bucket on my knees.

"Observe: the plume of his silly hat," she said, pointing. A bracelet of river pearls dangled from her little wrist.

Indeed, I could tell where my comrade-at-musical-arms stood among the box hedges. His feather bobbed dubiously in the autumn sunshine as if he were trying to decide between two directions.

He chose the left-hand path. "Not much further now!" cried Princess Glisselda, pounding the casement with her fist.

"Princess," I said, my mouth almost too dry to speak, "he sings like an angel. You should have heard his auditions. He'd make a superb assistant to Master Viridius, and an excellent tutor for you, if you would but—"

"Give him a chance?" she said, looking at me sidelong. "I am. The music master and I are at war; I am giving this fellow fair warning of our vendetta, a chance to learn what a morass he's walking into before he commits to it. In fact, I've had a real morass prepared just for him. I thought a literal approach would make things clearest. There he goes."

The feather abruptly disappeared. Shouts rose from the center of the maze. I gaped at her, appalled. "He didn't deserve that," I said.

"All wars have casualties," she said, her eyes fixed on the scene below.

I stared into the brown ooze meant for me. "What do you intend to do with this, uh, substance?" I said, tipping it, watching how it clung to the side of the pail.

"Isn't it gloriously vile?" she squealed, turning away from the window and clapping her hands. "It's fermented fish heads. It symbolizes how unpalatable I find the idea of music instruction. We shall spill it upon this final villain and be rid of two noxious things at once.

"We must hurry, though," she fretted, "or it won't be ready when he walks in."

He. I stared into the mesmerizing ferment and had an inkling of an idea. Maybe I could still salvage this, giving the princess a lesson by stealth and revealing my identity only when the thing was done.

I rose and smiled at her. "If you want to set this up so it falls on his head when he opens the doors, you've been going at it from the wrong side."

She fetched the chair from the hallway; I climbed upon it and showed her how one might balance the pail on top of the double doors, slightly ajar. The princess laughed and capered, delighted with me, and even I could not help taking a sober satisfaction. I felt safer with the bucket where she couldn't reach it.

"Of course, anyone might spot the trap through the crack," I said, stepping down and studying the setup from another angle. "You'll want to draw your victim's attention toward something else. What if you sat in his line of sight, playing your instrument?"

She made a rude face. "I think not."

"You don't have it with you?" Had I trapped us in here without it?

She scorned to answer, but turned toward a hanging tapestry and pulled it aside, revealing a door. She quit the schoolroom; I hesitated, and then followed her into a much larger salon with tall windows and chairs grouped into conversational clusters.

In front of the windows stood a harpsichord, covered against dust.

"Is that your instrument?" I asked.

She snorted, an unexpected sound from such a highborn girl. "It's Viridius's. He doesn't let me touch it. He has not forgiven me for filling it with frogs." When I blinked at her uncomprehendingly, she said, "It has been *war*, Seraphina."

She turned and flounced off toward the windows. I stared after her.

I was beginning to dread the possibility of getting this job, but it shamed me to think I might be defeated by fear in this final trial, which had nothing to do with my musical abilities. I took a deep breath and whipped the sheet off the harpsichord.

Princess Glisselda turned at the sound and raised an eyebrow at me. I sat at the keyboard and let my fingers say hello, thrilling at the texture of the notes.

"What instrument does Viridius have you playing?" I said. "Dulcimer?"

"How did you know?" she asked.

"That's the usual first instrument for fashionable young ladies," I said, indulging in a few arpeggios. "But there's a reason it's called the dull-cimer."

"That's what I said! I made that exact joke!" she cried. "And the old tyrant barked at me that it was the easiest instrument to learn and I was tone-deaf as a boiled beet."

Ouch. Clearly, both sides fired volleys in this war.

Glisselda crossed the room, her arms folded and a scowl crumpling her elfin face. "I know what you're up to, and it isn't going to work," she said.

I looked up from the keys. "I'm sorry, I don't—"

"You're just like the rest of them," she cried. "Grandmamma, and my mother, and everyone. Music is supposed to teach me discipline, they say! The dullness of the dulcimer will make me mild and discreet and dispassionate!"

I put my hands on my knees, facing her. "You're not interested in music even a little."

"Absolutely not," she said fiercely.

I tried to smile, but my heart was sinking. "So what are you interested in?"

I had her answer narrowed down to three before she even opened her rosy mouth. She would say *gowns* or *balls* or *boys*. I was already thinking of ways to relate any of these three to music—gowns was hardest—and so I didn't hear her answer at all.

"I'm sorry, what?" I said stupidly.

She glared poison at me but repeated her answer: "Statecraft."

We stared at each other a long moment, Princess Glisselda's mouth a tense line, her fingers worrying a bead on her bodice. I sensed I had been handed a bright pebble of truth and that she was waiting to see what I would do with it.

Statecraft. *Statecraft.*

"You know," I said, speaking slowly so my thoughts could get a sufficient head start on my speech, "music is not as irrelevant to statecraft as you might suppose."

She rolled her eyes theatrically.

I pushed on. "No, really. Music teaches you about harmony, about resolving tension and finding balance—and that's just the notes. The kind of negotiation one must undertake with one's instrument, well. A diplomat could only hope to listen so closely and respond with such sensitivity."

I turned from her and played a few experimental chords. "If you're too timid with your instrument, it takes advantage. The notes will sound incompetent even if you play them right. If you are too harsh"—this seemed a likelier problem for our princess; I slammed out a few samples—"it exacts a subtle revenge in timbre. Sometimes an unsubtle revenge, depending on the instrument."

I looked at her sidelong; she was staring at the harpsichord lid, her gaze unfocused.

"Any instrument would wish to be spoken to respectfully," she said quietly.

I nodded. "And authoritatively. It's a balance. Luckily for the beginner, the harpsichord is a forgiving, easygoing partner. You may hit the wrong key, but it won't be out of tune, and the timbre is fairly constant no matter how much you bang on it."

The princess seated herself beside me on the bench, watching my hands work, her brows drawn in thought. "*Forgiving* and *easygoing* are qualities one misses in Viridius," she said at last. "And—and quite possibly myself."

The chords were transposing themselves toward a piece I knew, though I wasn't sure of it yet. Princess Glisselda kept watching my hands as the song revealed itself to be Viridius's *Suite Infanta*, which he'd written in her honor when she was just a toddler. I'd always thought it a strange piece, all merriment on the surface with a hidden sharpness underneath, like a knife wrapped in ribbons, but as I played it now I began to understand. Princess Glisselda recognized it, of course, and sat up a little straighter.

At last she interrupted me: "Show me what you're doing."

"Of course," I said, and began to show her the basic melody with the right hand. She didn't catch on right away, but she worked at it, brow furrowed and tongue protruding in concentration. I'm not even sure how long we sat there, going over that line, but when she got it, she looked up at me in triumph.

And then said, incongruously, "Here he comes."

There was a crash and a shout from the next room. The

princess leaped to her feet and bolted through the tapestry into the little schoolroom; I followed right on her heels. I'd been so engrossed in teaching that I'd forgotten all about Orma.

Of course, it wasn't Orma. It was Master Viridius, red-faced and shouting. The fermented fish had spattered his bald head, doused his ample stomach thoroughly, and drenched the bandages on his hands. In his confusion at being attacked from above, he had landed hard on the floor. Princess Glisselda was extending her slender hand to him, trying to help him up, her lips pressed tightly together in a vain attempt to disguise her amusement. He lashed out with his canes whenever she got near him. I darted around behind him and propped him up to sitting.

"Well?" he sputtered, brushing me off. "How was she?"

I stammered, "Sh-she——"

"Superior to you, you old walrus," Princess Glisselda cut in, as if the question had been directed at her.

From the way they were glaring at each other, I suddenly realized it had.

"Your exacting standards were met, one hopes?" he sneered at her, accepting my silently proffered handkerchief and dabbing at his doublet with it.

"She let me play your harpsichord," she said sweetly, batting her eyes at him. He paused in his dabbing and glowered at me. The little princess hopped around the puddle of fish ooze on the floor, making her way toward the door.

"You knew," I called after her before she disappeared completely. "You knew I was the candidate all along."

She paused in the doorway and smiled. "Well, of course I did. Diplomacy is only part of statecraft, Seraphina. There's also spying. Besides," she said, drawing a curlicue in the fish sauce with the toe of her slipper, "did I ever explicitly state otherwise?" She flashed me an impish smile and took off down the hall, skipping by the sound of it.

I helped Master Viridius to a chair, my mind racing. He met my eye, looking unexpectedly sheepish. "She told me this morning," he said. "You were the only one who would be given a chance, and even then she made no promises. I had no idea what idiocy she had in store for the others, or what games she would play with you, and I am sorry. Unfortunately"—he sighed heavily—"she's part of the job. I can't teach her anymore; it raises my pulse and gives me palpitations."

"She is a spirited individual," I said, measuring my words in case she had tiptoed back and was listening to us. I would have put nothing past her at that point.

Master Viridius was trying to stand; I helped haul him to his feet. He propped himself upon his canes and said, "Congratulations, Maid Dombegh. Report to me in three days. I shall arrange your quarters by this evening; move in when you like. We'll see to it that your door locks." He smiled mirthlessly. "That brat once filled my harpsichord with frogs. You never know what she's capable ot."

Capable was an apt description of this princess. I wouldn't forget.

I tried to help him to the stairs, but he waved me off. As I watched him hobble away, I heard steps behind me and turned to see a page boy—the same impudent rascal who'd directed me upstairs—leading Orma toward me.

"Here you go, Scholar," said the lad, holding out an arm as if formally presenting me. "Your student, whole and unharmed."

"I wasn't worried," said Orma.

The boy laughed. "More fool you," he said, turning on his heel and scampering off.

I met Orma's eye. "Princess Glisselda sent that page boy to call you away, didn't she. And then she lured me up here after you."

He raised his eyebrows. "I don't know what you're talking about. I received a personal invitation to the Queen's private library. It was quite a fortuitous coincidence."

Quite. The princess must have been listening to our conversation in the antechamber.

Orma's nostrils flared; he had a keen nose. "Did your audition involve fermented fish sauce? That's quite an expensive delicacy in—"

"Yes," I said, laughing at him. "The princess learned so much from me that she required a light snack."

"You got the job, then?"

I met his eyes. He wasn't happy—dragons don't work that way—but there was something there, something I wasn't imagining. Some satisfaction, maybe, that he had taught me well.

"I got the job," I said, my voice breaking a little.

If he was surprised by the emotion, he gave no indication. He said, "I'm perplexed that my calculations were so far off. I'm missing something obvious. If I can predict that you'll surprise me with such consistency, then surely—"

I felt an unaccountable surge of affection for the old dragon then, and I threw my arms around him, even though I knew he hated being touched. He couldn't quite get used to having non-scaly skin. He tensed and held very still, waiting for me to release him.

"Speaking of surprises," I said, smacking him on the chest, where I'd felt an odd flatness under his doublet, "you're unexpectedly rectangular just now."

A human might have been sheepish about it, but Orma simply shrugged. "I didn't have a chance to finish the book I started. But it's not a problem—you got the job. You can bring it back for me when I'm done."

I laughed, disinclined to be cross with him, and together we left the castle. Golden leaves drifted around us down the long hill into town, and our shadows stretched before us across the surface of the world.

As a child, RACHEL HARTMAN played cello, lip-synched Mozart operas with her sisters, and fostered the deep love of music that inspired much of *Seraphina*. Rachel earned a degree in comparative literature but eschewed graduate school in favor of bookselling and drawing comics. Born in Kentucky, she has lived in Philadelphia, Chicago, St. Louis, England, and Japan. She now lives with her family in Vancouver, Canada.

Visit SeraphinaBooks.com and RachelHartmanBooks.com to learn more.